Copyright © 2024 Sean Hall
Published by Cosmic Quill Publishing
Printed in the USA

ISBN 979-8-9919914-0-7 (paperback)
ISBN 979-8-9919914-2-1 (ebook)

Editor: Oren Eades
Cover Design: Sean Hall
Book Design: Jason Arias

COSMIC QUILL
— PUBLISHING —

RELIC

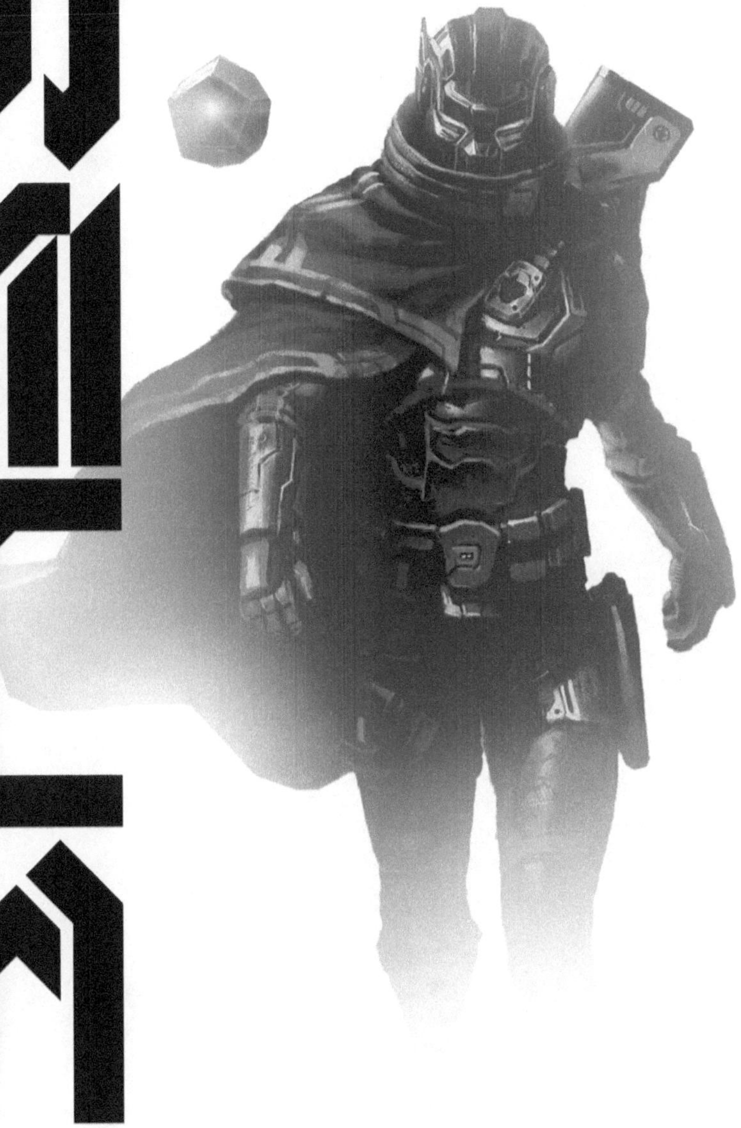

SHADOW IN THE WIND

A LOUD BOOM echoes through the stratosphere as my ship, the *Astra*, shadows and disperses the clouds in front of me. A metallic aurora billows through the skies, a magnetic dance shimmering translucent shades of chartreuse and jade. The arid dunes lie restless below, a dry beige desert stretching for miles in every direction.

There isn't much to this planet anymore. Not for a long time.

This desolate wasteland, a remnant of a civilization lost by those controlled by greed and wealth, has been my forced refuge for several lunar cycles. This world, among many others, has fallen victim to years of detrimental terraforming by different galactic unions and corporations, hoarding natural resources and mining planets to their cores. Forsaking this planet nearly a century ago, they soon realized they'd achieved all they desired; the scattered memories of the thriving life that once flourished here have now fled.

Distorted rays of light reflect off my front window as I peer out the cockpit. I tilt the controls to the right, which banks the vessel twenty percent sideways, allowing my holoscreen display to scan quickly over the environment and map out a yellow grid model of the silhouetted debris below. My attention shifts as the radar system chimes, telling me arrival is rapidly growing closer. So, with a quick push downward on the controls, I pierce through the thick vapors of the clouds. The g-force of the acceleration pins my helmet back against the headrest as it plunges the *Astra* towards the soil below.

Clearing the clouds above, I begin skimming steadily along the auburn dunes at a low altitude, and the station comes into focus. At this altitude and speed, I tend to lower my artificial gravity to feel the balance and force of the craft. As I ease up on the throttle, the *Astra* transitions smoothly into its landing sequence. The ship's thrusters pivot downward, gradually bringing the vessel to a steady hover, sending plumes of sand spiraling into the sky.

I've made it back.

With the sun nearly down, I enter the safeguard shutdown protocol into my ship's command console with an eight-button sequence, like so many times before. It's a mundane pattern that has nearly worn out the buttons. I can hear hisses and pressure bursts in the background through the cabin's hull as the ship's gases release into the atmosphere, dissipating one after the other. As the vessel slowly descends to the cracked, dehydrated crust, it releases a final surge of energy from the thrusters that sends a cloud of debris briefly into the air. Amid the sounds of metal clanking from the landing struts adjusting as they shift into position, I settle with a slump on the surface as the mechanisms finalize their alignment.

I disengage my x-crossed safety harness from the center of my chest, and the belts retract into the seat. I stand and make my way towards the loading dock. I place my hand on the cockpit's console, and a low-volume chime chirps as the door slides open to the left. Grabbing my pack from the floor, I throw it over one shoulder and head down the stairs and through the common room corridor.

The ship is a Darkstar-DS9 model stealth fighter, a discontinued, specialized covert armored vessel built for the Elite-Operation Specialists, or EOS Division, a military force known far and wide as the Galactic Command Alliance, better known as Galacom. It's capable of sub-light acceleration, near-impossible combat maneuvers, and radar and targeting system cloaking, and has an arsenal that could take out a dozen ships. Most importantly, the hull is retrofitted in advanced armor for traveling through the larger interstellar wormhole jump points to opposite sides of the galaxy. Other vessels this size can't withstand the pressure and need to travel to more secure jump points.

Nowadays, we are the same. We are known only as *Astra and the unknown pilot*.

When I located the vessel, it was just a hunk of scrap getting ready to be dismantled for parts in the northern section of the Zeo-5 system, a place ravaged by planetary battles, system wars, and mining, and absent of most life—just one massive white star circling a few habitable planets that the galaxy had nearly forgotten. A group of starship scrappers must have acquired it through scavenging faction wars and battles, seemingly gathering old parts for profit.

Being out there looking for usable parts and components myself, I'd unforgettably used the last of my credits obtaining it from the junker who ran the salvage yard where I had discovered it. I had about thirty thousand credits saved up at the time from doing odd jobs around the galaxy that I could spend on the ship, and they would let it go for about twenty-eight thousand. Digital Credits are used far and wide, being the most common galactic currency.

I knew a Darkstar in any condition was an insanely rare find. It's what I used to fly when I was in the EOS Division. I thought I'd never see one again, but to my surprise, there it sat, undisturbed. Galacom had only made a handful of them throughout the galactic sectors, as they'd never made it past the earliest prototype stage for a handful of selected operatives. I was fortunate enough to fly one for a short time during my duty. The modified direct fusion drive for sub-light travel and plating the hull in the galaxy's strongest most expensive metal, Endonium, must have been too expensive for Galacom to keep funding their manufacture. The scrappers hadn't known what they had, and I used that to my advantage. I got them down to twenty thousand, and I paid to have it hauled to the nearest spaceport the same night.

I spent nearly an entire cycle rummaging for parts to rebuild it from the ground up with the additional ten thousand credits I had left in my account. It was a gamble using all of my credits to get it up and running, but with some trial and error, I ended up with the fastest ship in the galaxy—although that may just be my biased opinion.

Reaching the back bay door, I put my hand to the ship's hull, thinking about how much time I've put into this fighter and the nostalgia and memories connected to it, as if it were me in that junkyard, left for dead, broken-down, useless, aged, and left to be forgotten.

To be honest, it had given me hope. For nearly a year, it had kept my hands occupied and my thoughts anchored. Throughout my journeys across countless solar systems, it has remained one of the few constants that keeps me grounded and steady.

As these reveries flicker in my mind, I approach the controls for the loading dock. As I turn the green switch to the left, the cabin's pressure drops, and the hydraulics release with a measured slowness. The bay door begins to part, gradually unveiling a magnificent sunset. Its vibrant yellow-orange radiance floods the ship's cabin, almost blinding in its intensity.

I grasp my advanced-warfare Odyssey XR-7 Rifle with multi-variable zoom scope and holographic sight from the weapons station located by the door. Residual grease and grime cover the upper receiver and extended suppressor; it is in need of a deep cleaning.

Despite its present condition, the XR-7 is renowned as one of the best rifles available. Built for resilience, it has never failed me, even in the thick of battle. I've subjected it to mud, dust, rain, and grime, yet it has performed flawlessly every single time. Constructed from ultra-light alloy materials, it boasts temperature-resistant parts and is fully sealed, rendering it resistant to corrosion and perfectly operable even in the vacuum of space.

The XR-7's innovative design includes an advanced terrain modifier. This feature enables the rifle to gauge the gravitational pull of any celestial body and accordingly adjust the energy expended with each shot, accounting for varying atmospheric pressures and resistances.

I secure the two-point sling around my chest and heave the rifle to my back, and it magnetizes into place with a firm attracting clank. I fasten my CXR-9 pistol to my hip with a single elegant motion. It clicks into place beside the three separate cartridges attached to my belt.

The compact pistol is the sidearm model of the Odyssey XR-7. It has parallel capabilities, but minimized options. The CXR-9 has a lower magazine capacity and smaller-caliber ammunition, and its multi-tracking holographic tracing sight range can be used at short to midrange at best. It is a worthy sidearm to have at your side; it gets the job done when all else fails.

With my sidearm snugly holstered, I pause for a moment, acknowledging the need to test another critical piece of equipment. Nestled within my armor's wrist is a kinetic barrier shield. A tap activates the mechanism, and in seconds, a luminous translucent blue forcefield emerges. Shaped like an oval, this shimmering barrier protrudes just beyond my forearm, poised to fend off both physical and energy attacks. As the undulating waves of light fluctuate across its surface, I deactivate it and brace myself for the outside.

Descending the ramp, I press the controls, sealing the bay door firmly behind me. With each measured step, the base's entrance grows ever closer. In the background, the muted whirs and clicks of the *Astra* signal the initiation of its defense protocols—a deterrent for any ambitious thieves or scavengers that might lurk nearby. As I push forward, the dense, moisture-laden atmosphere of the planet clings to my armor, an unwanted reminder of this awful place.

Turkken emerges as a bleak canvas of desolation. Across its long sprawl of cracked rocky terrain and ghost towns stand in haunting solitude, the foreboding region of the Deathly Flats stretches endlessly, punctuated only by the harsh lines of deep canyons. Mountains rise as relics of a world long changed. Where once there may have been a flourish of life, now only silence prevails, and the planet drifts, a lone wanderer in the cosmic abyss.

I despise the air here. It's thin and dry, as if you have one hand pressing on your chest while trying to take a breath. My face winces as the slight smell of it trickles through my purifier unit into my nasal cavity. After decades of mining and excavating for natural resources, the stench of the ruptured core still fills the air. It has a tinge to it, like hot metal and sulfur.

I hate it. No matter where you go on this planet, the odor stays with you.

When I arrived here, the Turkken atmosphere had increasingly high traces of poisonous gases, and its oxygen levels were falling. Fortunately, my ship, division pilot's helmet, and the back module that regulates my division-grade space combat undersuit have zero difficulties filtering the toxins. Although they probably wouldn't be deadly in small doses, I'd just as soon not find out what prolonged exposure would do to me. A slow death as my vital organs fail and I suffocate? No, thank you; I'll keep the suit on.

My division combat gear, once a symbol of cutting-edge military technology, now carries the weight of years gone by. More than half a decade has elapsed since its prime, and there's no doubt advancements have been made. The once-pristine breastplate now bears a web of scars—ricochet marks and deep gashes from countless close encounters. My advanced exo-helmet, designed to protect against the harshest of adversities, showcases scorch marks marring its left side. The once-reliable forearm comm unit and the wrist display modules, integrated seamlessly into my gear, now show signs of age and are in dire need of resoldering and a software update. My battle worn kinetic forearm shield needs a charge. The sturdy combat boots, which have taken me through countless terrains, now show signs of wear, their soles growing thin. Draped at my side, my dark grey cloak, once a sign of distinction, is stained with soot and dirt and yearns for a thorough cleanse.

The sun, casting its golden rays, throws my shadow forward, a grim silhouette against the alien terrain. It seems like a haunting reflection of the man I once was, reduced now to a mere echo—a hollow, armored shell standing against the winds of time.

So, who have I become? A specter drifting aimlessly through the stars? Or just another interstellar wanderer, constantly on the move?

Once, I had an identity: a proud pilot of the Elite-Ops Specialist Division under the umbrella of Galacom. This massive galactic military force has its tendrils spread throughout numerous sectors, laying claim to most habitable zones, and the core planets. The moniker Elite-Ops Specialist Division for Galacom is quite a mouthful; thus, we often simply referred to ourselves as The Division. Though if you searched any official records, the EOS Division would be notably absent. We operated in the shadows, a covert tradition of functioning under the radar. When Galacom wanted discreet actions without the threat of sparking a galactic conflict, they dispatched us. We were the unseen hand that ensured peace, even if it meant working in the grey zones of morality.

Vast swathes of the galaxy remain untamed and uncharted, treacherous areas marked by electromagnetic anomalies that most pilots dare not venture into. These regions, swirling with the chaos of massive black holes, raging solar storms, insurmountable gravity wells, and densely packed asteroid belts, have swallowed countless brave souls trying to navigate their perilous paths. In these wild spaces, even the most seasoned pilots fear to tread, knowing that a single misstep could mean oblivion.

Under the auspices of the Unified Galactic Alliance Accord, Galacom maintains vigilance over the core systems, ensuring peace and security for all factions that have endorsed this universal accord. Yet, this vision of a united galaxy is not universally shared. Numerous planets and territories have spurned Galactic Command's offer of alliance, choosing instead to rule by their own unique codes and edicts. This divergence from a united vision has given birth to myriad criminal factions and lawless zones—places I've come to know all too well in my occupation. Each planet, each territory, possesses its own set of rules, and navigating these multifarious laws can become a complex task without access to a comprehensive databank.

Once, I stood at the helm of my team, leading as captain and commander for over a decade. I've borne witness to the vastness of the universe, traversing countless solar systems and undergoing secret operations that will never see the light of day. In the mottled silhouettes of the galaxy, dictated by the sporadic brilliance of alien suns, under the unyielding aegis of Galacom, my missions sculpted a clandestine panorama of order, wielding an invisible, yet omnipotent, authority throughout the celestial void.

My time as an operative saw me delving into the profundities of astral espionage and sublight skirmishes on the fringes of known systems. In the glistening azure orbits of Veseus-1, humanity found its cradle, and among the interstellar routes stretching across the singular, expansive galaxy, my team and I became the silent arbiters of its safety and expansion. I once orchestrated the extraction of a key scientific team from the militarized research facilities on Darnak's Edge, skirting through the anomalous peripheries of the Rekhan Wormhole, where temporal fluctuations threatened to hurl us into the unknown. During the Veil Uprising, we performed a tactical insertion onto the insurgent-controlled planetoid of Zethra, disabling an anti-wormhole weapon that could sever crucial star system links and plunge countless colonies into isolation and despair.

My body tells another story—one of bullet wounds and scars, of survival against all odds. A lingering pain in my shoulder serves as a poignant reminder of battles past, and the memories, once so vivid, now feel like fragments of a dream, slipping away with the sands of time.

Having fulfilled my military obligations, I turned my back on that life, seeing it for what it was: a phase, a chapter that had closed. The skills and instincts I'd honed there had saved my skin more times than I could count, but by the end, there was one beacon that shone brighter than any other: Avery Beck.

Avery wasn't just a woman; she was my anchor, my compass. With her, the world's chaos dimmed, and our shared dreams took shape. Together, we envisioned a life far removed from the relentless grind and shadows of my military past. But fate can be cruel, and in its capricious twist, it took her from me. Every waking moment since has been haunted by her absence. Her laughter, her touch, the comfort of her presence—all are echoes that grow fainter with each passing day.

Who does that make me now? A shadow, a specter adrift in a world that's lost its color. I yearn for a glimpse of the life I once knew—one untouched by the weight of sorrow and the thirst for revenge. But this world's cruelty didn't begin with Avery's departure. I've been its victim since long before— an orphan of fate, unfamiliar with the embrace of parents, shuffled between foster homes, only to find solace in the harsh streets. My teenage years were a blur of missteps and close calls until a chance encounter led me to the imposing doors of Galacom Flight School. It was an escape, a promise of a new beginning. But every new beginning has its end.

The Flight Academy was meant to be a new chapter. It's where I met my comrade in arms. Ezrek Valleion, the man who would become my most trusted ally, my brother in every sense but blood. The irony? He also became the very person who would plunge my world into darkness, robbing me of my heart's very beat—Avery.

I remember that night with piercing clarity. A tempest raged, lightning splintered the skies, and the rain was relentless in its fury. I watched helplessly as life faded from Avery's eyes. There I was, sprawled beside her, my cold fingers reaching for hers, her hazel gaze growing distant as rain mixed with the crimson tide flowing from my gunshot wounds.

She was taken, and, by some twisted joke of fate, I was left behind. A stranger would later say I was clinically dead for two minutes, that I shouldn't have lived given the bullets that tore through my body, or the devastating fall that ended in a rain-choked alley. But I did. Every agonizing breath after was a haunting reminder of the space she left behind.

For years, I grappled with the guilt and torment of surviving, constantly questioning my undeserved second chance. But the mists of despair have since cleared, revealing a singular purpose: to avenge Avery's death at the hands of the very man I once considered family—Ezrek Valleion.

Five years have passed since that life-shattering night, and with every second, the weight of my guilt and my need for retribution grows. I've dedicated my life to setting right the wrongs, to ensuring that justice is meted out.

As for me? Those who've crossed paths with my ship know it as *Astra*. But I never disclose my identity, never give a name. If they did know, it'd be Owen Beck. But to most, I remain a faceless pilot, my identity shrouded, only a passerby.

While my journey takes me across the galaxy, I've become a prime target for Z's elite cybernetically augmented soldiers: the Novas Guard, the soulless soldiers of Ezrek's ship, the *Novascar*. The faceless legionnaires are distinguished only by alphanumeric codes like NG-1506, and they're relentless in their chase. Yet they've never been able to pin me down.

For years, I've pursued Ezrek, always one step behind, chasing a ghost that slips through my grasp every time. But this isn't just about justice anymore—it's about Avery. Her unwavering passion for the lost civilizations she once studied has become my beacon in the dark. That ancient tale, a forgotten world said to hold immeasurable power, feels like my last chance at finding meaning. Maybe it's futile. Maybe I'm chasing shadows. But every step I take is for her—a relentless pursuit of closure in the void her loss left behind. It's the only thing that keeps me moving forward.

My hand raises in the beams of sunlight, feeling for the silver metallic ring strung around my neck. It's one of the last pieces of her I have left, besides her research.

During my countless voyages across the far reaches of space, I've brushed shoulders with a diverse array of interstellar hunters. Some remained veiled in secrecy, while others, their defenses lowered by the intoxicating brews, have freely shared their tales and treasures. On one such random encounter, destiny interfaced with my journey in the form of a mysterious relic.

The merchant, a heavyset man teetering on the edge of consciousness, held a digital star map aloft. Its holographic constellations shimmered and trembled in the air, a chaotic display born of both technology and his drunken hands. To most, it might have seemed like just another scrap of space junk. But I recognized the distinct patterns etched within the light— ancient symbols that whispered of something far more significant.

Taking it from him wasn't my proudest moment, but desperation and opportunity often go hand in hand. Over shared drinks and feigned camaraderie, I lulled him into a stupor, his laughter giving way to the heavy breathing of drunken slumber. With a swift and practiced motion, I transferred the data module to my own device.

This wasn't just another star map. Decryption revealed its age to predate all known galactic annals. Armed with this mysterious guide, I was driven by the hope of uncovering the long-lost secrets of the Khu'Val. That, with the help of Avery's journal, deciphering constellations, and the digital map, helped get me where I am today.

Dr. Henrik Novikoff, a leading figure in multi-world archaeology, first uncovered and translated the Khu'Val symbol, known as the *Val'Ara*. An authority in his domain, Novikoff pioneered the discovery of artifacts and insights into the elusive Khu'Val—an advanced utopia lost to the archives of time. He successfully unraveled much of their cryptic language, dubbing it *Khu'Vala*, a script originating from intricate ancient glyphs.

Dr. Novikoff was convinced that the Khu'Val weren't just legends. He believed they hailed from a distant corner of the galaxy and might still be out there.

Over time, as fewer artifacts were found, their tale became a children's bedtime story. Many argued with Novikoff, believing the Khu'Val originated from planet HN4-1, where the first artifacts were discovered. But Novikoff had his research and exploration sites to back his theories. Sadly, when he passed away, his beliefs faded with him.

Unraveling the history of the Khu'Val is no straightforward task. Between ancient artifacts and fragmented translations, discerning myth from reality becomes a puzzle. The Khu'Val stand as a profound mystery, the sole advanced civilization we've documented beyond our origins on Veseus-1. Whispers of their tech, leagues ahead of its time, have persisted, with tales of their control over time itself being the most alluring.

From our birthplace on Veseus-1, we've journeyed to only a percentage of the galaxy, but it's revealed a universe abundant with life. Our home's dwindling resources nudged us to explore, leading to new colonies among an array of life forms ranging from dainty desert creatures to immense ice beasts. Yet, when it comes to sentient beings, it's just us and faint memories of the Khu'Val.

Adapting to diverse planetary habitats, our species has evolved in fascinating ways. On Ba'hala, for instance, generations wear gills as badges of their oceanic heritage. The dusky jungles of Rombaka have given birth to a human species with enhanced night vision and acute senses. And on planets bursting with advanced tech, we've pushed our genetic potential, redefining our human essence. While the universe shapes us, our innovations, especially in space, have preserved many in their original form.

Throughout my odyssey, I've sifted through planet after planet, chasing the elusive shadow of the Khu'Val and seeking answers about the one who betrayed me. My journey has been marked by elusive clues, countless challenges, and lingering memories. Yet my resolve never falters. Each clue, every rumor about their mysterious power, fans the flames of hope that I might find a way back to Avery, back to my wife. It remains my guiding star, my singular mission. After all, it's all I can hold onto, and I'll cling to it till the end.

My forearm display unit chimes, and I glance down. I can see my drone's battery indicator blinking orange on my screen, stating that its power cell is running on a low charge. I can tell from that alone that it has been a long few days of imaging miles and miles of empty desert terrain.

Shifting focus as I near the station door, I raise my hand to enter the codes into the keypad. I press a specific sequence of numbers I'd programmed when I arrived, and the airlock's door unlocks with a loud clang and depressurizes while sliding open. I enter through the first door, and it shuts behind me.

When the door has locked, the system's scanner activates an array of blue-toned lights that move over my entire body, scanning head-to-toe for contaminants and radiation. Once the scan is complete, a high-pressure mist comes from all angles, covering every inch of me. Then, a circular green light flashes above my head, indicating it has finished, and a low-volume synthesized female A.I. voice speaks through the station's comms. "Decontamination complete."

I mutter a sigh of relief as the second door closes. I release the latch of my exo-helmet, take it off immediately, and hang it to the left of the old researchers' spacesuits. With another deep breath in, my eyes close, and I let the air out of my lungs slowly.

I think to myself, *Was this another day wasted? What did I miss? It's been weeks on this planet with nothing to show for it. The coordinate on the map shows it should be within the fifty-mile radius we've searched.*

I need to transfer the imaging files recorded from the ship, so I detach a wire from my forearm module and insert it into the computer's mainframe. With a single swipe of a finger, the computer turns on. The system starts syncing immediately and transfers the information logged from this cycle's search. A large icon appears in the middle of the screen, initiating the files' upload. The status bar rises slowly, indicating scrubbing through the data may take a while, so I might as well call it a night. I'm exhausted.

I turn to see my old, tattered makeshift home—a barely surviving research base with white cylindrical shapes covering the ceilings, electrical wires dangling down, components hanging from the walls, flickering lights due to the power fluctuations, and unusable leftover items from the researchers strewn about. The few windows adjacent to the researchers' lab are covered with dust most of the time. The once-bright white of the airlock has now dulled to the neglected color of rust. It has lacked care for the better part of a decade.

It's empty and lonely, but I don't need much nowadays. The cold nights tend to be the cruelest part; if you're out at night, the scavengers aren't the only thing that could kill you. The temperature can get well below freezing, and you can only last a few hours past dark without the proper attire.

The mass of Turkken inhabitants have already fled this planet; I am one of only a few who call this place home anymore. It's just me and a few hundred strewn salvagers, traders, and natives either looking for a way out or too stubborn to leave.

Usually, I can't hear much at night but low rumbles as the hydrogen-cooled turbo generator hums, maintaining power and heat for the station. I've grown quite accustomed to the monotonous sounds. Lately, I can't sleep without them.

Luckily, no one has tried to break in or ransack the place since I've been here. I set up as far as I could from any signs of life, the double doors triple-lock seal, and I altered the security passcodes when I first arrived, so it's about as safe as you can get around these parts.

I only had to fix the purifier and heater when I first came, as the station is still, for the most part, in working order. With just a few hours of labor, I was able to take a hot shower and have drinkable water.

I head towards the bathroom, lean my hands on the sink, and look into the mirror. I take off each glove one by one and reach under the faucet. The automatic sensors pour cold water all over my hands, and I splash it onto my face. It spills onto the floor as I clean the sweat and oil from my face and unkempt beard.

Looking up, I hardly recognize the man staring back at me. Greys are starting to come in, and that line wasn't there last year. My blue eyes have seemed to change hue to a dark grey.

I slowly place my hand to the mirror, and a digital reading system engages on the lower right-hand side. A small, barely operational lens appears, activating a full retinal scan, and a holographical readout of my vitals appears on the top-left of the mirror, showing my blood pressure, heart rate, body temperature, respiratory rate, and blood-oxygen levels.

[>: VITAL SIGNS // BRAIN SIGNAL NORMAL // [STATUS: STABLE]
[>: AGE: 38—MALE—5'7—WEIGHT: 165—BUILD: ATHLETIC]
[>: HR: 60 BPM—BP: 130/90—TEMP: NORMAL—BOL: NORMAL]

One-thirty over ninety for my blood pressure. Could be better. *Shit,* I think as I turn the water off with a wave of my hand. The airlocks system's AI voice chimes in. "Blood pressure high. Please implement proper precautions in daily dietary intake. I can create a nutritional routine if you wish."

"No thanks, computer."

"Are you sure?" says the AI.

"I'm good, computer," I reply.

"Very well, I will create your nutritional daily routine."

"No, comp–" I pause as I notice the command is already in motion. "Ugh. These voice command modules are so out of date."

Nearly over the hill. Where did the years go? I wonder as I wipe my face with an old towel and head to the lounge. I have a seat in a white chair in front of me, which isn't quite a perfect circle, but comes to a curved point at the top, sort of like an egg.

I toss my pack onto the table before me, and as I drop the bag, I hear a muffled voice from the bottom of the pack blurt out some loud profanities. "Hey, watch it, dick. I'm still in here."

The voice is stifled at first, but rustles upward, becoming more apparent. "So, another failure today? Huh, that makes, what, nine weeks? Do you want to talk about it?" he asks, as his upside-down triangular blue digital eye flickers with curiosity. *Nine weeks. Fuck, has it been that long?* I think, looking at him with my exhausted eyes. "Sorry, I must have disturbed your low-power conservation cycle with the impact, but please, not now, Tex. I set you to low-power mode for a reason. I am exhausted." I rest my head on my hand.

"Well, maybe we'd have better luck next time if you didn't suck. You giant headdick."

"It's dickhead," I reply.

"Oh, excuse me, Mr. Captain Dickhead." His eye twitches before he emits a sarcastic whir.

"Just go to your sleeping station, Tex. We try again at sunrise. We need to wait to see what the computer found; maybe we got lucky." My voice is barely audible, muffled through my fingers.

"Okay, okay, yeeeeesh. No need to be rude..." he says, his voice trailing out as he heads to the back of the airlock.

That bright ray of sunshine is my TX-49 model scouting drone, or, as I like to call him, Tex—a military drone that aids soldiers and researchers by mapping out terrain, breaking into heavy cyber defense systems of enemy factions, acting as a helpful A.I. tool for recording and translating, and serving as a complete knowledge databank filled with valuable tools.

The TX models are standard for all EOS Division teams; each team has a TX model stationed as their eye in the sky. Unfortunately, I couldn't secure one during my departure, but one stormy night back on a planet called Vola Prime, I managed to buy Tex from an underground merchant at a grungy local hub called the Wired Abyss.

He swore up and down that he was in complete working condition, but after I left, I found him to be corrupted beyond repair. Buying anything from the Wired Abyss was shifty. I soon realized his encoding and linguistics module was faulty and the circuitry that processes his thoughts and converts them to speech was corrupted. Shit, most of his systems were corrupted. I assume it's because some hacker tried to break through his military coding firewall and delete his programming for resale, but they deleted some of his primary encoding. He works as expected; however, he now tends to have a bit of a relentless mouth and a sassiness one could compare to a teenage adolescent going through puberty. I don't know if I could properly fix him, and don't know if I would. I've enjoyed the verbal sparring.

Through it all, thick and thin, Tex has always been there the last five years—through everything, every boring flight, every heavy fight, and everything in between. He has saved my life more times than I can count. He's one of the few things that remain from my past.

I watch as he hovers across the room—his palm-sized decahedron body shines in the light as the dark grey metal paneling that symmetrically covers him changes from a dark to light grey and his dim glow of blue light radiates from his digital eye. His middle eye is capable of 360-degree mapping capabilities, sonar, and partial x-rayed vision, and a highly advanced defensive system is lurking in there as well in case an enemy gets too close.

Though the little shit does tend to get on my nerves for the most part, his coding for his directives and obedience is trustworthy. I've come to relish having him around, lousy mouth or not.

I watch Tex hover over the table and attach to his station to sleep—well, since TX-49 models don't sleep, it's more of a recharge station. Their power cores can last decades if not centuries if they enter this mode every few months.

Most of our technology is powered by fusion energy—miniature versions of what powers my starfighter. It's also the same tech that powers my division combat suit, keeping my undersuit's proper pressure, oxygen levels, and electronics working. We've been far underground for days at a time, and it's been weeks since Tex and I have been back here, so I know he'll be there for the rest of the evening.

"Smell you later," he says as his voice slowly powers down, perfectly aligning with his station.

"Goodnight, Tex."

Tex was much more talkative today; maybe he has a bug in his system software as well, or perhaps he is just annoying me for the joy of it.

Either way, I could use a much-needed break. I place my gloves next to me and set my hands down flat. *Yeesh*—the table is freezing, and I notice my hands are trembling. *When was the last time I ate something?*

And when was the last time I got a good night's sleep, for that matter? I won-der. I know I need to get better about calorie intake, as I'm most likely dehydrated as well. I can practically hear Tex giving me some fresh shit about keeping up with my well-being, but he usually just likes to give me a hard time.

I unfasten my protection latch-by-latch—first, I take off the forearm bracer modules that control my suit, shield, weapons, ship, and Tex, then my torso armor, then my division combat outersuit with built-in armor, and then my boots, setting them on a withered off-white end table next to an aged, torn calendar from when the researchers were here. I guess that they were an excavation team, taking samples and doing experiments in the mines close to here. They must have been using this station as a base for years. The days until their contracts finally seemed to be done were crossed out in a thick red marker decades ago, one after another. They couldn't wait to get out of here.

What person in their right mind would choose to live here willingly? I think to myself. *Maybe this place had a charm to it before the dryness and dust consumed everything.*

After doing all the remaining nightly checks, shutdowns, and security protocols before showering off today's failures and calling it an evening, I walk towards the bed and rest on the edge, staring at Tex's station light as it intermittently glows teal against the rear wall. As it dims and glows to replicate the look of breathing virtually, it can almost be hypnotic.

I unzip my combat undersuit and lean back on the bed, resting my head and listening as the mainframe analyzes all the information from this week's trek. The sound of the drives trilling and whirling is entrancing as I relax my eyes and body on the bed, a thin old mattress made of four cargo crates, a thick, faded forest-green blanket, and a comfortable makeshift pil-low I made from extra covers.

Shifting to my left, my eyes rest on a small device sitting on the table next to the bed. I sit up and take it from the table. The brisk eight by four-inch rectangular box cools my hand, and as I flip it over, I see an engraving from

Avery etched into the back.

To the unknown,

Love,

Ave.

It is called an *Ornacron*, the only gift I still have from her besides my ring. It's quite the challenging musical instrument, but it travels light, and the sound can be soothing when my mind isn't right. She gifted it in hopes it would help me when I'm stressed out, or anxious, but lately, it's only doing the opposite. I can't get the damn thing to play properly.

I pull both sides outward, and the device engages. The center projects a holographic pinkish sphere above the middle. I place it in my lap and slowly begin to shift my hands around the orb. An angelic ethereal note begins to swell louder as I press my pointer finger into the sphere. Adding my other hand to the left side, an overwhelmingly bad-sounding dissonant three-octave chord plays. "Fuck," I say as I shut the device and toss it back onto the table.

I slump down into bed and close my eyes. I haven't played the same since she died. It takes a level of concentration and finesse I don't think I have anymore.

"Would you like me to switch the airlock to night mode?" the computer says in a low volume.

"Yes, computer," I say with my eyes still closed, still fiddling with the ring around my neck with my pointer finger and thumb.

The uninteresting sounds of the workstations analyzing the data weigh my eyes down like an anchor, closing them, opening them, closing, opening, and closing.

"Rest now," the smooth voice of the computer says.

I'm so tired. I can't match the dark any longer. Her voice is like a lullaby.

As soon as my eyes shut, I drift off to sleep, and an alert reads on the computer's mainframe display.

"One anomaly found."

AN ANOMALY

ALONE IN MY dreams, I toss and turn. The whispering voice calls out to me.

With my eyes still closed, I can nearly make out what she's saying. A ghostly form reaches out from above me.

It's the same dream again.

A womanly form emerges from the darkness, black cloth draping her shape, her faint specter hand reaching for mine, but I can't grasp it. I can't move at all. My muscles seem glued to the bed. It's like she's falling away into a vapor of obscurity, drowning in an infinite black sea of nothingness, but something's holding her.

And it feels like the more and more I try to move, the more she slips away.

Her face vanishes into a swirling black obscurity, and I awaken to a soft voice whispering like the wind as it crescendos into a near-scream. "Owen!"

As I suddenly jolt awake, I spring up in the bed and cry out, "Avery!?"

I'm covered in a warm, thick sweat and trying to catch my breath. Panting heavily, I try to remember where I am, and with my eyes fully open, I can see it was just another dream as the dust storms beat the outside hull and leftover cargo.

I look over to Tex, and he's still recharging on his station. I try to match my breathing to his lights to calm myself.

It's the same reoccurring nightmare.

"Avery," I whisper.

It's been five years. For five years, I have been haunted by these dreams, but they've become more frequent in the past few months, and I am not sure why. I feel like someone is replaying the night over and over in my head, making me watch, fueling my journey.

I look at the clock, and it's four in the morning. It will be sunrise soon. I should try to get some more rest before we leave.

After falling asleep for a few more hours, I'm awakened by the sounds of the system's check routine—widgets spinning and whirling and power modules adjusting as it alters from night mode to morning.

Her soft voice greets me. "Good morning, Owen. All system checks are normal. Did you sleep well?"

"Well enough." Still in bed, with my eyes half-open, I'm surprised I have the energy to produce any sound at all.

"Calculating your regular sleep patterns, I noticed you received two hours less than what your body normally needs to function at maximum capacity. Would you like me to set up a sleep schedule for you along with your nutritional dietary restrictions?"

"That won't be necessary, computer."

"Very well, Owen. I've added it to the list."

"Whatever." I say begrudgingly. "Was the data successfully processed?" I ask mid-yawn.

"That is correct, Owen. There is one anomaly to report from the material you provided."

"An anomaly?" I speculate to myself. I gradually roll to my side and muster the force required to get up and out of bed. My joints creak and my muscles groan as I shift myself. "Can you please pull it up on the center command mainframe?"

"Of course, Owen. Pulling up the files now," she says as the computer sifts through folders of data, pulling them up on the main display.

As I edge towards the brink of the bed, my shoulder unexpectedly dislocates, triggering a sharp pain from an old gunshot injury I received on Vola Prime. A low grunt escapes me as I swiftly tug at my arm, causing it to snap back into place with a jarring pop.

"Ow..." I mutter under my breath.

With one long stretch, I reach upward, stretching out all the aches and pains of the previous weeks. The discomfort is seemingly never-ending; it's part of me, and it's the fuel that drives me—a simple-but-effective reminder.

As I arrive at the computer, the holographic display illuminates on the center workstation's middle screen. I sit in the center chair and run a check on what the system has found. As the computer scrubs through the files, the screen zooms in on six seconds of footage.

"It looks to be from when Tex and I were soaring by the crest of Mount Noragöth."

The sector is a location northeast that's mainly controlled by a native colony known as the Dök Hundri, an elder settlement of scavengers, thieves, and desert nomads born on this planet. The Hundri are a resourceful settlement of people. However, if you were a traveler roaming the desert or an exploration team with no weapons and you crossed them, it would be the last thing you ever did. They are mediocre riflemen at best—sloppy, but they have the numbers.

The Dök Hundri like to set traps for traders and scavengers on roads, and the sky isn't any safer. The Hundri would fire electromagnetic pulse rockets, disabling your ship right out of the sky to steal any loose supplies, food, or weapons aboard the vessels. They murder innocent town folk whenever they can, taking anything of value, including their women. The northeast can be a treacherous region if you are unaware of its threats. It's harsh living out here sometimes, and I can hardly blame them for surviving, but at what cost?

I find the folder of what I'm looking for, raise my hands over the HUD, and press two fingers in the air to pause over twenty different frames my thermal imaging acquired.

"What is this, computer?" I ask.

"The data seems to have a slight corruption. I'm picking up readings of some massive electromagnetic disturbance underground in that area," says the computer.

It's pixelated, but I can see something is there. It's indistinct, but I can nearly make it out. I spin my hand to the left and right and the motion rewinds or fasts forwards the still images depending on which way I spin, clockwise being forward, and counterclockwise for the rewind feature.

"Computer, enhance frames ten through eighteen," I say eagerly, waving my hand back and forth on the images, trying to make out what it is.

The enhancing finishes and a message lights up the screen. "Image enhancement complete."

With a few more flips, I abruptly stop on frame thirteen. Leaning my head closer to the screen, I enlarge the top-left section of the picture by pressing my index finger and thumb together, then releasing them in opposite directions. Once the image comes into focus, my body goes stiff. I'm at a loss for words for a moment.

"Holy shit."

I can't believe what I'm seeing.

It's them—the symbol Novikoff termed the Val'Ara, the insignia of the Khu'Val.

It's engraved on a rock formation on the mountain closest to the Noragöth mountain. It's nearly illegible, but I'd know that symbol anywhere. It's written all over Avery's journal.

She had hundreds of sleepless nights reading through every book, every article, everything she could find regarding ancient history. Her knowledge was hard to surpass, as she was one of the brightest people I had ever met. She'd loved everything historical, and she'd always thought the past was the key to the present. I, however, was always looking to the future. We'd balanced each other out that way.

I think back to when we were airborne yesterday. *I don't remember seeing anything out of the ordinary other than a few encampments close to that region. The image is hard to read, but this must be what we have been looking for all this time. I know it—all the endless cycles of searching, these days that never end.*

Leaning back in my chair, I turn my head and shout, "*Tex!*"

The shout-out must have startled him, because he shoots up so quickly, he crashes into the lights above him, making a bang so loud I nearly think he'll be in pieces when I turn to him.

"Sorry, buddy. Didn't mean to startle you."

Tex shakes it off like an animal covered in water would. Regaining his poise, he hurries over to me, looking at the screen. Stopping mid-hover, he says sarcastically, "I'm sure you didn't, dick cheese. Give me a second while I make sure my ball bearings are still there."

He pauses a moment to count. "One...two... and... three. Perfect. I'm golden. So, what's up, Gigantor?" he says as he moves my head out of the way to see the computer, squinting his digital eye toward the screen.

"It's the symbol, Tex."

"It looks like the Val'Ara," he says. "Running an analysis on it. Give me a second."

His center eye changes from blue to green as he processes the data. "Holy shit Beck, we found it. It's a near perfect match." Tex says excitedly.

"Pack your shit. We leave in ten."

"I thought I gave the orders," I say.

"Not today, meat dick! Let's go!" Tex says, seemingly ready to get off this planet.

"Cool your jets, little buddy. This may turn out to be another dead end. Don't get too excited."

"Don't tell me what to do." He snickers.

As I shake my head, I stand up from the mainframe and instantly start programming the station to rest mode as Tex is in the background loudly grabbing our things. With my luck, we'll be back here in an hour or two with nothing to show for it. I start thinking about the journey up to this point. In our relentless pursuit of the Khu'Val, Tex and I have ventured far beyond the familiar boundaries of our galaxy. Each new planet we've encountered has been an eye-opening endeavor to the astonishing diversity of the cosmos.

One such world was Azura Prime, a planet covered in a perpetually shimmering blue mist. The atmosphere there is thick and heavy, concealing the surface beneath. As we descended through the thick clouds, the world revealed itself—an immense, interconnected network of crystalline formations, each gleaming with an otherworldly luminescence. These crystals emitted a hauntingly beautiful melody when touched, as if they held the memories of a thousand generations.

On Lumara, we encountered a planet bathed in perpetual twilight. Lumara is home to towering fungal forests, their bioluminescent flora providing a strange but captivating illumination. It was in these forests that we uncovered an ancient tome, written in the Khu'val language. Its pages spoke of celestial alignments and hinted at the existence of a hidden key to a secret path.

Our journey also took us to the desolate, rocky expanse of Jotarion IV. There, fierce electromagnetic storms rage across the barren landscape, creating breathtaking displays of lightning that danced across the horizon. We discovered unfathomable monoliths that seemed to harness the power of the storms. These monoliths held clues to other locations etched into their weathered surfaces. It took me months to decipher what I could of that data.

These planets, each with its own unique wonders and challenges, have been steppingstones in our relentless pursuit of the Khu'Val.

"Owen?" the computer's voice chimes breaking my thoughts.

"Yes, computer?"

"What should I do if you don't return?"

I hesitate. "I haven't decided yet."

A glitch interrupts her voice. "Would you like me to accompany you on your sh-ship?"

I recall that her AI system is too antiquated for the *Astra*. "Not now. We'll come back for you if needed," I reply, though I wonder why I feel the need to reassure a machine.

"Understood," she replies, her tone unchanged.

I pack the remaining provisions, including some precious Kuaviberries. They're a godsend—one serving provides a day's nutrition. I also pack water, weapons, and an old holographic photo of Avery and me, its delicate wiring nearly worn out.

I take a moment and stare around the airlock that has sheltered us for so long. "Computer, transfer all data to my command unit."

"All done, Owen. Need anything else?"

"One last request." I pause. "If I don't return by the next cycle, initiate total shutdown."

Her voice softens. "Understood. Will there be anything else?"

"That's it."

"Farewell, Owen." Her voice fades as the doors open to the desert.

"Thank you," I say, listening to the computer engage its sleep cycle section by section.

As Tex and I leave, the station's lights fade, casting us in darkness.

The winds whistle against my armor as the pebbles of sand beat my helmet.

Tex's voice breaks through comms. "You have a thing for broken things, huh?"

"What do you mean?"

"I don't know, you just have a hard time leaving things behind."

"Well, I do keep *you* around, don't I?"

"Exactly my point, I'm the worsssssst," Tex says, reaching the ship about ten paces ahead of me.

I press the start command button on my digital bracer, and the bay doors lower. Tex is the first aboard and starts the take-off sequence immediately. I drop my bag on the seat behind the pilot's chair with a loud clunk as he links the coordinates from the computer's discovered location to *Astra*'s guidance system.

Not knowing what we will encounter once we touch down, Tex and I must be prepared for anything. Flipping the toggles and sequences for the pre-flight check, I squint at the ship's mapping display one last time and hesitate for a moment when I see a distant shadow forming from a dark sandstorm on the horizon. Its mass covers over the entire surface, blacking-out the area, and I reminisce.

It's been five years. Five years since Ezrek took everything from me and left me for dead.

These scars on my chest and shoulder are a reminder every single day. I've dreamt of a million things that I would do when I find him. I know whenever I get my hands on him, it won't be enough to make him suffer the way I have. Not even to make him experience what Avery must have thought and suffered through that dreadful night, not knowing why her life was taken—the things that must have been racing through her mind before he murdered her while having to watch me bleed out on that rooftop.

Ezrek and his Novas Guard's interests in the Khu'Val has been both curious and alarming. Ezrek, a figure of malevolent influence, with resources and intelligence networks that span far and wide, has always been one step ahead of most. But his obsession with the Khu'Val seems personal, more profound than a mere quest for power. It's clear he believes in the legends and, more importantly, he believes the Khu'Val hold the key to unlocking that power.

Many have questioned why Ezrek, with all his might and knowledge, would be so entangled in these stories. Rumors swirl—some say he's after eternal life, while others think he seeks to reshape the universe to his vision. But no one knows for sure or how he knows so much. What's undeniable is his determination, as he's employed every resource to track down the civilization, even turning former allies into enemies in his relentless pursuit.

I know killing him would be the easiest thing I've ever had to do. He was my best friend, my brother, a dear friend to Avery—and the emptiness in his eyes when he pulled the trigger, I will never forget. Finding the Khu'val and killing Z in the process will be a resolution to my journey even if the power isn't real. Then I can rest.

The final checks complete, and the ship thrusts upward into the sky. Clouds start to disperse over the mountains, billowing slowly down their faces. At this altitude, I can see the endless miles of desert that wait ahead. Ave would have loved it.

Looking over to Tex, who's hovering casually in the seat next to mine, I say, "This will be the last time, I know it. I have a feeling it my gut I've never had before. The Crest of Mount Noragöth must be the place we were looking for. I know it is."

Tex replies, "Is it too late to go to the bathroom?"

"You don't pee, Tex."

"Right, right. Go back to the serious and brooding thoughts you were having."

Looking back, I let out a long, drawn-out sigh. Then, with a quick push downward on the side acceleration lever, the cells kick into overdrive, and in the blink of an eye, we vanish into the velvet horizon.

THE GIRL IN THE REFLECTION

FIVE YEARS AGO...

On a cold, wet world just at the edge of the core planets, I sit inert at the corner of the bed, and as I look at the apartment's floor-to-ceiling windows, I can subtly make out Avery's reflection as it paints the partially fogged glass in front of her. She somberly looks out at the lonely city lights from our eighty-seventh-story loft. The tall windows that frame the entire wall shield us from the dense, heavy rainfall. Her eyes are fixed upon the backdrop of the lively capital of Vola Prime, the dangerous metal jungle known as Akereon City.

Vola Prime isn't just a planet; it's a haven, a refuge for the lost, the stranded, and the impoverished. A significant portion of its inhabitants remain bound to its surface, their dreams of star-hopping adventures hindered by economic realities. Sure, hitching a ride to another planet isn't that expensive, but the real challenge is staying off Vola Prime indefinitely. That demands owning a ship armored enough to withstand interstellar travels. The associated costs are astronomical, both for the ship itself and for the necessary upgrades: achieving sub-light speeds and reinforcing it to navigate the immense, treacherous jump points that dotted the universe. Simply venturing out in a half-baked craft risks everything—from being relegated to the same struggles on a different planet to the worst-case scenario of getting stranded in deep space and running out of power.

Vola Prime stands out as one of the most densely populated planets in this solar system, a haven of endless oceans and perpetual rain. Although it's roughly four times larger than any other planet in our system, its population seems to burst at the seams. Its landscape is dominated by seven coastal cities, with Akereon City, the sprawling capital, sitting at the heart. This mega-continent covers nearly two-thirds of the planet, with the rest being tumultuous oceans sending rogue waves crashing against city barriers.

Towering buildings stretch skyward, overshadowing a society riddled with governmental corruption and economic disparities. Pockets of opulence blotch the city, but for most, including us, a life of luxury is just a distant dream. The elites of Akereon City hold the reins of power. Thanks to my military pension and Avery's steady job, we've carved out a modest life for ourselves, complete with a stunning view. It's all she wants—a view.

The continent is a mosaic of cities and settlements. Akereon City stands tall, matched in its vibrancy by its bustling counterpart, Lunaris. To the west lies the technological hub, Vespera, while the serene coastal city of Solacc rests to the east. Meanwhile, smaller communities like the villages in the Osaka District, as well as the traditional town of Celestia, settle quietly in the outskirts.

Tsunami waves crash continuously against the city's walls. These are consequences of Vola Prime's restless tectonic activities and unique moon–tide interactions. Most of humanity has moved away from the perilous coasts due to the relentless thunderstorm surges and the threat these tsunamis pose. Akereon City's infrastructure is built to endure both the severe weather and the occasional earthquakes.

The frequent rains are a product of our unique climate patterns, influenced heavily by our moons. For some, like me, the rain is comforting. Yet many in Akereon live in anticipation of the next devastating storm surge. Memories of the Great Flood, when countless lives were lost, remain fresh.

In the aftermath of such tragedies, the government pledged better protection. The community rallied, rebuilding with the planet's most prized material: Endonium. This metal, abundant in our planet's core, resists centuries of wear from saltwater, rain, and waves without corroding. Its atomic properties are unlike anything on our known Periodic Table. Once refined and stabilized, Endonium's dense structure makes it almost invulnerable.

It's no surprise that almost every metal artifact here is made of Endonium. The Galacom Central Command Center most notably serves as the pivotal operational hub and nerve center of the military and Endonium extraction on Vola Prime. Strategically located in downtown Akereon, it orchestrates and coordinates all military activities across the galaxy. Its significance lies not only in its role as the main administrative and command post, but also as the primary facility for extracting Endonium.

The wealthy and military thrive by refining and mass-producing this invaluable resource for various sectors. In Vola Prime, Endonium is in abundance, and everyone wants a piece.

Neon lights from nearby city structures irradiate the ceilings. The dance of pink and purple shades flows through the entire apartment like dawn swelling in the sky. The lights cascade over Avery's sun-bleached brunette hair, which is bundled into an untidy bun held together by a worn-down wooden pencil with bite marks all over it. She sits in the same chair she always does, in the same position as always, as if a sedentary life doesn't bother her one bit. She relaxes her body and sinks even more into the chair, letting all her day's worries subside.

She's savoring her favorite evening black tea, cupping both hands over her second-favorite oblong white mug to warm them. The thunder rumbles in the background while the lightning shows its face through the clouds. I can hear the repetitive pinging and panging of the echoing rain as it spills from our metal balcony. Cold wet drops are making their way onto the loft floor from the cracked-open window in front of Avery.

I look down at her bare feet as she begins to rub one of them against the back of her leg. She shivers as she feels the cold storm air moving gradually down her spine. She's practically always barefoot; it's like she doesn't believe in wearing shoes. Her feet are callused and dirty; I guess she feels it's a noble way to connect to the planet.

She's wearing a vintage off-white linen robe she bought from a small shop down the street, paired with her favorite comfy white underwear; she has a simple elegance, a subtle beauty about her inside and out. She never spends too much time in front of the mirror or worrying about what she's wearing. I honestly don't think she owns any makeup; she's just that type of person. She's never caught up in what others think of her, a freedom that not many of us have. I'm jealous of her carefree attitude at times.

She's just a good person, and I'm fortunate to say she loves me just as much as I love her.

Avery slightly shifts her weight backward as she turns her head over her left shoulder, causing her robe to fall gently. She smiles, and her hazel eyes reflect the ceiling's neon lights. In a mere whisper, she says, "Fuck."

She pauses with a soft, peaceful smirk on her face as she takes a deep breath in and then out. "I'm so excited to move on from this place. Don't get me wrong; there are things I'd always miss here. This view, for one. I don't think anything could ever replace this view. We've built a life together here, and this is our view."

She turns to look at me and says, "I'll miss it, but all I need is you." She takes another deep breath and returns her ardent gaze to the rainy night. "You have to promise me a view like this wherever it is we go. Whenever that is, of course."

I look to her with an immovable gaze. "We're not going to need much where we're going, but I promise, you'll have your view. On the first night, we'll watch the sunrise together. Just us, no one else for thousands of miles."

"We can start a new life," she says softly.

"One that you deserve, Ave."

"No, Owen—one that *we* deserve!" she exclaims. "Your past doesn't define you; tomorrow, you could change the course of your future with a simple thought. Be the man you want to be, honey. Be the man I know you are."

"You're too good for me," I say.

"I know." She smirks.

"I wish we could just tear all this shit down and start fresh—a world with no cities, no pollution, no people. Green as far as the eye can see, with just the two of us."

"That's what I want for us," she says before finishing her tea and setting it aside.

"Only a matter of time," I say, trying to reassure her.

A second passes. I can see Ave's mind working overtime. She seems nervous but, per usual, inquisitive about our new adventure. "It doesn't matter where we are, Owen," she says with a devoted tone. "The only thing that matters is that we are together, and yes, of course, that we also watch the sunrise."

"I love you, Ave," I say just as she turns back to the window after perking her lips together for a mimed kiss.

With nearly enough credits in our account, after tonight's job, we should have enough to leave tomorrow, I think. I can't look away from her.

So far, we've saved two hundred thousand credits. The Starliner-X2, a top-tier exploration starship fitted with an Advanced Direct Fusion Drive, comes with a price tag of one hundred twenty thousand credits. After tonight, I anticipate an additional two million credits after the job—clean and untraceable—added to our account. That sum would comfortably fund a lifetime of interstellar travel, letting us chase the perfect view across the galaxy. It's all for her, the promise I made.

I've already committed to a down payment on the Starliner, a tidy sum of forty thousand. I've arranged for the dealer to reserve the last available expedition model for me, assuring them the balance would be cleared by tomorrow. I've kept Ave in the dark about all of this, but by tomorrow's sunrise, after I tell her and we pack, thanks to Ichiyo, we'll be charting a course through the stars.

Ichiyo Mori isn't just another name in history; she's redefined our trajectory. A brilliant young engineer, she presented us with the Advanced Direct Fusion Drive, an invention that shifted the course of time itself. Without her foresight and aptitude, our species might've been but a footnote in the chronicles of the universe.

School wasn't a constant for me, but the lessons about Ichiyo were unforgettable. Hailing from Veseus-1, the homeworld of civilization, she charted a course for the stars, ensuring we didn't remain bound to just one planet. The inception of wormhole jump points, especially those mammoth ones safeguarded by Gravity Rings, reshaped interstellar travel. These Gravity Rings, a feat of engineering, encapsulate the unpredictable nature of larger wormholes with artificial gravity, granting us a safer passage through the cosmos.

Post-formation of Galacom, they began integrating visuals from the earliest days of wormhole exploration into their training regimens. I vividly recall watching those initial test flights, with ships hesitating on the brink of wormholes, then taking the plunge, disappearing and re-emerging light years away. Those recordings were not just educational; they were a demonstration of the daring spirit of our ancestors and the groundbreaking work of Ichiyo Mori.

Thanks to Ichiyo's innovations, we've explored and settled on countless new worlds. We've grown in numbers and spread far and wide. Yet Veseus-1 is now lost, its sun long extinguished.

Ironically, within our enormous galactic presence, I've found myself on Vola Prime. It's a challenging environment—wet, metallic, and often unforgiving. Yet it's also where I met Avery, making it priceless to me. My time here, serving with Galacom, has become more than just a stint on a cold planet; it's a chapter of my life I'll never forget.

I slowly lift myself out of bed to get some water from the kitchen. From our high-rise, the city usually stretches out like an illuminated starfield, a sight unobscured on clearer nights. Ave adores this panorama. Sure, we're not in the city's poshest district, but even through the rain's curtain, the view takes my breath away.

The ambient hum of airborne vehicles filters in, punctuated by the engine flutters characteristic of night traffic. These sounds are almost omnipresent. Yet, in those brief moments of stillness, the distant roaring of waves crashing against Akereon City's barriers becomes audible.

As I pull out a cup from the overhead cabinet, I set it on an automated hexagonal dock on the counter. It fits with a satisfying click. The water begins rising from the bottom to the top of the cup, and I look through the windows being battered by the rain down to the city's substructures, making out the dark, blurred, fragmented speckles of society below, walking through their augmented realities. They're like sheep blinded by the digital veils that consume their vision—the holographic billboards on every corner illuminating droning advertisements for the most popular items of the week, the endless merchants flooding the boulevards from corner to corner, the trash and grime filling the alleys.

There is little human interaction here, as many jobs have transferred to the android workforce. It's less expensive for the corporations to build androids once rather than hire the unreliable dying-out workforce for long-term employment—no injuries, no tiredness, just obedience. It's a goliath middle finger to us from the giant corporations that rule the world.

Takashi Cybernetics has eclipsed every competitor. As a well-known automaton manufacturer, they've harnessed the abundant resource of Endonium. For decision-makers like Takashi Sato, the choice is clear. As the unseen lord of cybernetics in Akereon, much of today's tech bears his imprint.

Yet, as automation has replaced jobs, the streets have burgeoned with the deprived. Protests have erupted. Many seek the underground's relative shelter against the planet's unpredictable weather. The elites, hidden in their ivory towers, barely lift a finger. Inadequate food, scant medicine, and a shortage of basic amenities paint a bleak picture. Corporate greed runs deep.

Shaking my head and setting my glass down, I murmur, "Just another reason to escape this place."

Avery's voice floats over. "Talking to yourself again?"

"Just lost in thought," I reply, heading to the bedroom, narrowly avoiding the pile of books she's scattered across the loft.

Her teasing retort follows me. "So, business as usual?"

"Yep, you know me and my mumbling." I pause, admiring her engrossment in her work.

She's knee-deep in a proposal, likely pitching for more funds for her research. Her fervor for ancient civilizations is infectious.

"New proposal with James?"

"Hopefully actually get some decent funds this time," Avery says.

Avery's mentor, Professor James Williams, is a renowned archaeologist, esteemed across various worlds for his knowledge of ancient languages and galactic history. His pioneering work has set the gold standard in studying ancient cultures. With similar enthusiasm, Avery, as an associate professor, toils alongside him, striving to unravel history's enigmas. Williams has been a steadfast guardian to Avery since her childhood. After the devastating Great Flood of Akereon City claimed the lives of her parents, Henry and Olivia Greyson, many years ago, James, who had been Henry's closest friend and trusted colleague, stepped in without hesitation. Bonded by their shared history, James felt an inherent responsibility to provide solace and care for Avery, considering his longstanding presence in her life. His unwavering commitment to her well-being has remained a constant pillar of support throughout the years, forging an unbreakable father–daughter-like bond.

Henry and Williams had worked together for decades, intending to understand our past, thinking of how it could lead to our future, and it seems like the apple didn't fall far from the tree; Avery is the spitting image of both her fathers.

Williams took Avery in and gave her a spectacular childhood filled with wonder and attention. He cared for her as if she was his own daughter, never faltering in the responsibility tragically bestowed upon him. He's a good man and a good father.

Avery's journey to her current position has been one of perseverance and determination, deserving of far-greater recognition. Growing up on Vola Prime, it was evident that her true aspirations were being suffocated behind a monotonous desk, immersed in endless paperwork day and night. With each passing year, she inches closer to the possibility of assuming the role of lead professor, succeeding Williams upon his retirement and settling on Prime for decades to come. While it may not be an undesirable life to some, deep-down, I am aware that it does not align with her deepest desires. Even Williams, who adores her with every ounce of his being, yearns for nothing more than to witness her breaking free from these confines, embarking on a galactic adventure, absorbing firsthand knowledge from the enormity of the universe. He cherishes her with all his heart, but understands that she is a free spirit destined for so much more.

I've told him my plans to leave in the morning, and he's beyond excited for her. He's promised to meet us at the launch bay before we depart. I think it's going to be one heavy goodbye, but I've promised him we'll visit.

Recognizing she was getting depressed; even with the cheerful smiles, the sadness that grew inside her was too vast to conceal. I think it was her demeanor at nights, looking out to the where the sea meets the sky, only to see haze and clouds. She was seeking a warm sunny life beyond this one. Being in the field, studying uncharted worlds, lost adrift in the cosmos exploring the galaxy that's unmapped by historical literature—that is her dream; that is where she belongs, and both Williams and I know it.

Avery and Williams spend most of their time reading paper after paper, recluses in their dark research lab at the Archaeology Center in Akereon City University. Their office is spilling over with history books from all sectors of the galaxy that are not cataloged in the historical data centers. One subject that consistently captivates Avery and James is the study of the cryptic ancient civilization known as the Khu'Val. Throughout history, countless civilizations have risen, conquered, and ultimately crumbled into the past. Yet the Khu'Val stand apart, intriguing the minds of scholars like Henry and James early on in their careers. The perplexing nature of why seemingly insignificant planets have uncovered fragments of their culture adds to the myriad of questions that intrigue Avery, her father, and the rest of the galaxy.

Williams often jokes about how Ave needs more of a life outside of work. If she isn't sleeping, you can always find her scribbling away in her dark-brown leather journal. She never leaves home without it; it's either in her bag or hidden in one of her favorite hollowed-out books on our bookshelf over the fireplace, *The Water's Edge* by Clive Ivory. I think the book resonates with her as an adventure tale about a nomad who travels from city to city, earning his way with no address and no responsibilities. Why did she hide it in another book? Never thought to ask. She can be paranoid at times.

We have all the technology in the world, but she doesn't trust it. She just loves the written word, hand to paper, away from the digital screens. The notebook itself does look like the writings of a babbling crazy person from a mental institution, but that's what I love about her—her drive never to give up, no matter the odds.

I pick my phone up from the nightstand and note the clock unit display as a small holographic digital readout of the time appears above the phone's screen. I see it's nearly time to go.

As I clumsily place the phone back on the nightstand, I manage to knock off my dust-covered service medals, which usually lay dormant on the corner.

"Hey, fumbles, don't hurt yourself," Ave says.

"Hah, hah," I reply.

Grabbing them from the floor, I set them back in their proper place. They haven't moved an inch since I departed from Galacom. They're just old reminders of the life I want no part of anymore, old memories trapped in a cocoon of dirt, leftovers of a forgotten life.

The Division had ripped every part of me away until nearly nothing was left, crafting me into the perfect soldier, flushing out who I was and fashioning me into one of the most highly decorated division pilots and soldiers Galacom had ever seen. I was trained to get the job done, specializing in hand-to-hand combat, weapons expertise, tactical strategies, and extraordinary piloting abilities of advanced aircrafts. I earned myself the Star of Valor, the Stellar Cross, Ace's Sun, and Wings of Honor.

Too many times, I questioned the morality of what I was doing, and too many times I felt myself slowly disappearing into a faceless soldier. I began to question who I was fighting for and why; they were just one side of the coin. I'd known for a while I had to get out before nothing of me was left. I'd sensed a shadow returned with me after every parting, growing darker and darker with each mission as the Galacom stole just a little more of me each assignment. They built me up to be someone I'm not.

Well, to them, I was just a tool.

One mission under Galacom still bothers me. It was a run-and-gun, based on sketchy intel, targeting a planet that supposedly housed enemy factions. But what I saw were families—innocent lives that Galacom was ready to sacrifice for a dubious outcome. I couldn't pull the trigger, so I aborted the mission, incurring a colossal loss in credits and time for the organization.

For a while, I grappled with my choices, wondering if my time would end in a blaze of glory or the slow decay of age. That changed the day Avery quite literally stumbled into my life at a café in Akereon City. The moment I helped her up and caught her radiant smile, I knew my life had shifted. She became my anchor, my reason to rethink the life I led with Galacom.

As my contract neared its end, I chose not to renew. The prospect of a simple, peaceful life beckoned, far from the chaos and orders of the past. With Avery, I discovered a life rich in ordinary moments, and that was all I needed.

Seeking employment, I landed a role as a cargo driver for Takashi Cybernetics, transporting goods between their main base and various distributors. They dangled a managerial position in their security division, but that wasn't what I sought. All I wanted was a predictable, mundane routine: work, home, eat, sleep, and repeat. That yearning for normalcy, and the love I found with Avery, now shapes my every day.

Placing my hands on the counter, I let out a long sigh. Avery looks over to me and asks, "You okay, babe?"

"Yeah, I'm just tired," I say, even though I know it isn't true. I'm thinking about the upcoming job with Z, but obviously, I don't want to say that.

"Well, let me know if there's anything I can do to help," she says, sending a quick smirk my way before returning to her papers.

I'm usually not one to express my genuine emotions, and I don't know how to tell her what I've been doing on these overnighters. I hate not telling her the truth, but the less she knows, the safer she stays. This way, after this one last job, we can get the hell out of here in the morning, leave everything behind, and never look back. Otherwise, it will probably be another grueling five to ten cycles to accumulate enough savings through conventional means.

This will be the last one, I think, hopefully convincing myself.

As my stomach begins to make a sound comparable to a garbage truck driving by, I turn to the freezer to grab a protein pod from inside before I leave for the night. I pause for a moment as I open the silver door, looking at an old photograph on the outside, a picture of just the three of us—Avery, myself, and my old best friend Ezrek—with our arms wrapped around one another. It's a cherished moment I'll never forget, a memory from when all of us went to an event at Avery's university before things started going sour.

The man in the picture is Ezrek Valleion, my former brother-in-arms, a brown-bearded curly-haired scruff of a man I would have taken a bullet for, no question. The picture is from a different time, a moment when honor and integrity still meant something to him.

From our earliest days at the Galacom Academy, Ezrek and I were two peas in a pod. Those rigorous training days bound us, forging an unbreakable bond. Side by side in countless operations, our symbiosis was undeniable. He'd pull me out of the jaws of death, and I'd do the same for him, time and again.

But when I stepped away, he plunged deeper. Tales of his new exploits trickled down through old Division comrades. Our paths had already begun to deviate by the end of my contract, and while the details of his dishonorable discharge remain murky, whispers of his new reputation have begun to stem from the shadows.

Perhaps my departure wounded him more than I'd realized. He had always seen us as a package deal—as soldiers, leaders, and brothers-in-arms. In his mind, our bond was meant to be unyielding. Only death should have parted us. Maybe, in his heart, my departure felt like a betrayal.

As the days rolled on, the gulf between us widened. I could sense a dark ambition festering within him, a relentless hunger for power and riches. It consumed him, making him unrecognizable.

Ave, curious about our estrangement, often probes for answers. But the truth about the man Ezrek had become is a burden too heavy to lay upon her. They'd never been particularly close, but they shared a bond of friendship. Deep down, I always felt Ezrek harbored some resentment, perhaps even jealousy, though its roots remained a mystery to me.

Our bond has been relegated to a mere professional courtesy. Without the allure of credits, I often wonder if there'd even be a thread left between us.

Ezrek has now entangled himself in a world of covert operations. He throws me these side jobs—nocturnal transports of concealed cargo, illicit arms smuggling, and coordinating missions for his newly minted mercenary team. They operated as highly skilled soldiers, their allegiance only to the highest bidder.

Ave believes I'm out doing some honest night's work, and while I can't say it's entirely upright, the credits make it tempting. As long as I'm not spilling blood, I rationalize it as our ticket out of here. The life of violence is behind me, and I yearn for a brighter horizon.

The upcoming job Ezrek's been meticulously crafting for months promises that escape—the final piece to the puzzle, setting both Ave and me free from this world.

"Avery." I whisper her name, feeling the weight of the world lifting momentarily. I lay on our bed, listening to the escalating rhythm of the rain and the cadence of her steps drawing closer. She slips in beside me, her hand tenderly tracing the contours of my face. I keep my eyes closed, etching every sensation into my mind. I turn to her, and her ethereal beauty reminds me that she is a treasure far more precious than anything I've ever deserved. And deep down, I think she realizes it too.

She's never judged me for my past, the things I've done. Even if she knows what I'm doing on these late jobs, I don't think she would say it. She's always been there for me through thick and thin, still showing me the way forward. I feel I'm deceiving her, but I figure if something goes wrong, the less she knows about my nightly runs, the better. I would never want to put her in harm's way.

Staring into her eyes, I can see that she is barely able to stay awake. After a yawn, she says, "Will you be out till morning again? I always hate waking up to an empty bed."

"Most likely, honey. I wouldn't worry."

"Can't you just stay for tonight?" she says with a hint of curiousness, moving her hair from her face.

"You know I can't, Ave. We need the money. I'll be back before you know it."

After a long, droning sigh, she stretches her arms and says, "Okay, just be safe and give me a kiss."

"I will. I love you. Now get some rest," I say, kissing her on the forehead and turning around.

"Hey, space cowboy, did you forget something?" she says, looking at me with those eyes, waiting for me to say it.

She's waiting for those familiar words, and as always, I find them hard to utter. Sensing my hesitation, Avery, with a touch of impatience, begins the familiar refrain. "Beyond the moons and stars," she says, her eyes expectantly fixed on mine from the bed.

Swallowing the lump in my throat, I manage to reply, "Home is wherever our love takes us."

A radiant smile illuminates her face. She gifts me a gentle kiss before turning away, taking her ring off and placing it in the small bowl on the nightstand, she can't stand sleeping with it on her finger. She then envelops herself within the blanket. Like an insect finding solace in its cocoon, she snuggles in, preparing to drift into sleep. I stand a moment, watching her fall asleep. She always looks like she's sleeping with such disdain, her face cantankerous and unsatisfied even on the most incredible day, but I know she loves it, she fiends for it.

I remove the pencil from her bun, and her hair falls to her cheeks. Gently moving it as I hesitate for a moment, I memorize the lines of her face— every curve, freckle, and imperfection, down to the small scar above her nose in between her eyebrows, which she got when she was a kid.

Tonight will change everything. She deserves the world, and I will do anything I can to give it to her.

As I quietly walk over to the closet, I glance over to Avery to make sure she's still sleeping with one last look. I reluctantly grab my black leather Endonium-lined ballistic jacket from where it's folded on a shelf, and as I slide it out, something metallic falls to the beige carpet rug.

The dull thud is quiet, but I look to Avery to see if it woke her, then pick it up and quickly realize it is, of course, the Ornacron.

I turn the device around and see she's engraved words on the bottom.

To the unknown,

Love,

Ave.

Looking up to where it had been under the jacket, I see that there's a small handwritten note from Avery sitting in its place. Unfolding the letter, I read, *"No matter where we end up, my heart is always with you."* A crude drawn heart sits pressed into the bottom of the page.

Grasping the Ornacron tightly in my hand, puzzled as to why she wants me to have it right now, I lay the note back down on the shelf, place the instrument inside my jacket pocket in front of my heart, and zip up the jacket with a fast pull. I reach for my locked sidearm, and with a biometric confirmation, it releases the lock. I tuck it into my back waistband and lift my coat over it.

Ensuring stability, I fasten my boots with steadfast hands and direct my attention toward the bookshelf. A surreptitious glance backward confirms Avery's peaceful slumber. With a resolute yet tender pull, my ring slips free from my finger. I tenderly open *The Water's Edge*, revealing a secret chamber where a few credit chips, Avery's intimate work journal—its pages a canvas to her life's musings—and a cluster of photographs reside. Now, my ring joins this cache of memories and tokens. I never take it with me on missions, especially not those tinted with the threat of capture or arrest.

I head for the door, unlocking the entrance with a quick swipe of my hand on the terminal. The door mechanism opens, and I take one last look at Avery, sound asleep, and think, *I should stay...*

I pause for a moment, then quietly close the door behind me.

0 0 0 4

FOR OLD TIMES' SAKE

THE LONG GREY metal corridors of the complex pull my focus as I walk away from the door. My awake neighbors scurry about as their nightly energy reverberates through the thick walls. The perfectly spaced doors funnel my eyes towards the elevator at the end of the hall. As I pass each apartment, the painted numerical figures centered on each of the entries glow in a warm orange-yellow. The fluorescent ceiling lights pulsate gently as I stand at the elevator, thinking about the events to come. A rush of anxiety and unsureness comes over me.

Get your mind right, I think as I push the worn, dimly lit ground-floor elevator button. *Everything I've ever done was at someone else's orders. My memories aren't my memories. Just a sheath of lies they told me to justify my actions. Those memories won't define me. This will set us free.*

I'm living for me now. I'm living for Ave.

The grey elevator doors open slowly with a ding as gears, weathered from years of use, clank together. Stepping inside, I can smell aged oil and grease lingering from years of neglect. The digital screen illuminates, and the greeter welcomes me. "Hello, valued consumer. Thank you for choosing The Ocean Place Apartments. Have a pleasant day."

The doors stick for a moment as they try to open and begin to screech and bang together loudly. Peering out the narrow crack between the doors, I look for the front desk receptionist and call out, "Hello?"

"Good evening," says the night receptionist from her desk. "I do apologize for that. Stay there and let me see if I can fix that for you."

"Sure thing," I say as I peer through the crack to see the large reception area. "Not like I'm going anywhere."

With a few clicks of her keyboard, the doors unhinge and skid open, and she turns to me and says, "Sorry about that. It seems every time we fix one thing, something else breaks. My name is Eliza. If you ever need anything, Mr. Beck, just let me know."

"Thank you, Eliza," I say, walking towards the front door and the scent of a floral spiced perfume hits my senses as she places her files into the drawer beneath her. "Don't worry about it."

I haven't seen her around here much. Her perfume is overwhelming, and she doesn't have the usual look of a receptionist; her hair is vibrant pink, tattoos trail from her chest to her neck, and to be honest, she's too beautiful to be working the graveyard shift at some loft complex. She looks like she should work at a cybercafé or the Wired Abyss —and come to think of it, I'd never told her my name.

"How did you know—" I begin, but she cuts me off.

"Mrs. Beck has been coming and going to the University. We've chatted a few times. She described you, and may I say, she is just delightful. She said you come and go at night sometimes, so I assumed."

"Oh, right. Thank you. Um, have a good night," I say, turning back towards the door.

"Another late work night?" she says with a glint of curiosity, fixing her pink undercut hair away from her face.

Turning back one last time, I sigh. "Yeah, something like that. Take care."

"You too, Mr. Beck." She returns to her nightly work, giving me a real dubious look as I reach the door.

Was she flirting with me? I can't tell. She had been overly friendly, but maybe that's just the job.

Opening the first security door of the complex, I can see through the lobby's windows that he's already there, waiting for me. The second door clicks open and swings outward as I say with a questioning tone, "Aden, you good, man?"

Looking up quickly, he throws me an over-the-top mischievous grin. "Beeeeecky boy! Who? Me? Ah, you know I'm good to go." He sniffles, wiping the snot from his nose onto his left sleeve. "I'm sharp as a knife." He gestures with his mechanical hand to show he's on the level.

His voice always sounds like it has been thrown into a garbage disposal too many times or had one too many nights drowning in the sauce. You can always tell a frost inhaler by their voice; it gives them a very unnatural rough frog-in-the-throat sound.

What the fuck happened to Aden Graves? I wonder as I look into his red-glowing cybernetic eyes, which seem barely able to focus on one thing at a time.

Aden appears more on edge than I've ever seen him. His constant twitching and the way sweat beads on his brow are telltale signs of nasal inhaler usage. At a glance, one could mistake him for a homeless person or someone who's lost their way mentally. His once-presentable appearance has degraded noticeably.

However, I'm not deceived by his disheveled appearance; Aden is largely harmless. Having spent most of his life behind a computer screen, he's never quite developed the knack for smooth interpersonal exchanges. He often comes off as unintentionally aggressive. The red gleam in his cybernetic eyes lends him a somewhat menacing aura, but he's genuinely one of the gentlest souls I've encountered.

Rain has darkened his white tank top, which looks as though it hasn't been changed in a week. His boots are laced haphazardly, and as raindrops hit the unique black hexagonal inlay inside his brown coat, they ricochet off.

A few years back, Aden found himself indebted to some dangerous individuals. Their retaliation was brutal. They cornered him in a desolate alley, not far from here, and left him battered and broken in the rain. His injuries were both physical and psychological, including the loss of his eyes and the crippling of his primary hand. His recovery was extensive, and the emotional scars drove him deeper into drug dependency. I've tried intervening, but it's a heart-wrenching truth that you can't save someone who doesn't wish to be saved.

To regain some semblance of his former self, Aden turned to the underground tech market, the Wired Abyss. There, he underwent procedures to replace his lost eyes and hand with advanced Endonium cybernetic enhancements. Among these, a distinctive polygonal device known as The3rdEye was implanted in his forehead. This modification offers unparalleled data access and system infiltration capabilities. Few possess the skill to harness its full potential, but in the world of underground tech, Aden is virtually unparalleled, a revered figure of legend. Once at the pinnacle of his profession, one can't help but wonder what the future holds for him now.

The figure standing before me is a ghostly echo of the Aden I once knew—the renowned intelligence operative who held unrivaled value in our division. He commanded our team's intelligence efforts for years. Technology seemed to flow through his veins and out his fingertips—a natural affinity nurtured since childhood, where he spent countless hours secluded, constructing motherboards out of household items, tinkering and fixing things that weren't broken, and driving his parents mad. Straight out of college at a younger age than most, his academic achievements placing him at the pinnacle of his class he was handpicked to join the prestigious Galactic Command Intel Division, GCID. His steady drive persisted throughout his contract until the debilitating grip of addiction, pressure, and anxiety, consumed him whole.

Perhaps it was the weight of the job, the relentless stress of safeguarding the lives of those under his watch, but Aden's discharge from the service came promptly after leading a separate team into a meticulously planned ambush, resulting in the tragic loss of every operative under his command. Years of dedicated service culminated in a single stormy night where faulty intelligence proved fatal. Whether he was deceived, fed misinformation, or simply too impaired to grasp the unfolding events, it mattered not. The outcome was devastation—no one survived.

Luckily for him, he wasn't sentenced to fifty years at Grievous Grey, the maximum-security holding facility on one of Vola Prime's moons, Grandis. Instead, they'd dismissed him to a rehab facility under military court order to help him get clean.

Yet years later, he's still the same old fucking Aden Graves.

The rain starts to pick up as cars and taxis hover by us through the dark, crowded streets. Looking to Aden again, I say, "You look like a ghost."

"I'm just pale, man. No need to be a dick," he says with a miffed tone.

"That's not what I meant, and you know it."

"I'm just pulling your dick. Thanks again for helping me out the other night at the Abyss. Those garlic noodles are the best in the system, aren't they?" he says as one eyebrow raises with question.

"No problem—that's what friends are for, right? And yeah, they are pretty much a mouth orgasm."

He pauses, glancing over his shoulder and then back at me. "You good?" I ask.

"What? Oh, yeah, absolutely," he responds hastily. "The ship is just around the corner, down the side alley. It's been given a false registration, so the scanners won't even bat an eye. Piece of cake." He chuckles, reaching into his pocket. He retrieves his Cryo-Frost inhaler and places it against his nose.

"What the fuck, man?" I shout, my grip tightening around his collar as I forcefully slam him against the building. The impact dislodges the inhaler, sending it clattering to the ground. With one arm firmly holding him against the wall, I say, "You need to pull yourself together right now. Don't you dare jeopardize this for me and Avery. I need you at your absolute best, Aden. I need you focused, and I won't let a damn junkie—no matter how close a friend—endanger both of us. You're capable of so much more, Graves."

"Alright, alright," he concedes, raising his other hand in surrender. "I was just trying to take the edge off before the mission," he says nervously, his trembling hands betraying his words. "You know how it is." He shrugs nonchalantly, his voice uncommitted.

"I need you clear-headed, Graves. I need Division-level skills tonight. Do not fuck this up."

"I'm straight as an arrow—don't worry about me!" Trying to explain, he says, "I've just had a lot on my mind recently. That's all."

I release his collar, and we turn back towards the alley as he fixes his jacket.

"Fuck, man, be careful. This is my favorite coat. I don't know what's gotten into you tonight," Aden remarks. "You're much edgier than normal."

"This is my last job, Aden, and you know that I need you with me, not somewhere else. This job is vital for Ave and me."

"I know, I know. I'm sorry, Beck." He gestures in a surrendering motion with his cybernetic hand.

"It's fine, brother. Just stay focused," I say.

My attention shifts as we start to walk around to the building's side, and I notice two A.C.P.D. officers across the street, staring in our general direction. *Police in this district?* I wonder. It can't be. They rarely make their presence known around these parts. Most of them are dirty, and would easily take bribes to look the other way.

Something about them just seems off—the way they look, the way they're standing next to each other. I can't put my finger on it.

Then Aden catches my attention. "I have all your equipment on board, and the whole team is ready," he states.

Glancing back over my shoulder, I see that the two men are gone. I look to the left and then to the right, but they're gone—I see just sewage condensation and crowded streets.

"What? Did I just imagine that? Where did—" I pause. "What did you say?" I ask, realizing Aden had just spoken.

"I said, 'How's Avery?'"

"Good. Sorry, man—my mind is in a million places right now."

"10-4, and all good, buddy. Just trying to lighten the mood."

My mind starts to grow blurry. All I can think about is the last few moments of Ave's face shining dimly in the nightly city lights. It's like time slows to a crawl, so I have a few more moments left of clarity, wishing I had stayed in bed with her just a few more minutes—just a few more.

Aden is still chattering away about some lotion he's considering buying for his dry elbows as we approach the dark-grey transport vessel. It's a simple two-engine vehicle, nothing fancy, but the point is to blend in, not to be noticed by authorities. The back bay doors open to reveal our third team member waiting at the bay's entrance—none other than Naomi Sato.

Droplets cascade from her hood, contrasting against the shades of grey and black. An air of mystery surrounds her as her mechanical bifocal device springs to life, casting a delicate green glow over her face, scanning from left to right. This device, known as the VS-X, is a cutting-edge military tool that adapts to lighting conditions, effortlessly adjusting brightness, targeting multiple enemies with partial x-ray and thermal vision. With this innovative contraption resting horizontally across her face like a pair of virtual-reality goggles, her eyes and part of her nose remain shielded. She is an icy-hearted assassin, a formidable force. Renowned for her proficiency in firearms, blades, hand-to-hand combat, stealth, and infiltration, she is undoubtedly a merciless executioner and, unfortunately, a troubling remnant of a somewhat regrettable romantic entanglement.

We found ourselves immersed in a stakeout mission, surveilling a local tech manufacturer during one of those late nights under Galacom. Avery was still far from entering my life and before my contract was done. After nineteen grueling hours confined together in that ship, boredom beginning to gnaw at Naomi's sanity.

To be honest, it had been far too long since I had experienced the warmth of another's touch. It's hard to blame anyone, especially when faced with Naomi's captivating beauty. But it came at a steep cost. She was undeniably alluring, yet wrapped in an aura of sheer fucking madness, a trail of bodies left in her wake.

During those endless hours, we delved into deep conversations. I shared the painful truth of my orphaned childhood bouncing between foster homes and surviving on the unforgiving streets. Slowly but surely, I clawed my way up, eventually finding solace in service.

She, on the other hand, confided in me about the tragic circumstances surrounding her birth. Her mother had tragically passed away while giving life to her, leaving her as the sole child of a father who always longed for a son. In her heart, she carries the burden of feeling perpetually inadequate in her father's eyes—a heavy weight she would never openly acknowledge.

Naomi's father is Takashi Sato, the towering figure of cybernetics in Akereon City—an esteemed position that has propelled him to the zenith of fame and influence. Renowned as a brilliant entrepreneur and inventor, he holds dominion over the creation and distribution of the city's infrastructure. His firm drive for wealth, power, and the advancement of humanity shackles him to his laboratory within the cybernetics company, rendering him a workaholic consumed by his ambitions.

Within the opulent walls of their estate, Naomi, a young and neglected child, experienced the anguish of growing up in the shadow of her illustrious father. As his anger morphed into insatiable greed, she often found herself fatherless, forgotten within the walls of luxury.

Behind the façade of his public persona, the higher-ups covertly shield the sordid underbelly of Takashi Sato's operations from prying eyes. Illegal dealings permeate his empire, with backroom trades involving illicit technologies, highly advanced weaponry that flouts the law, and scanners capable of jamming implants, as well as a device capable of digitally altering one's face called the *HALOFIELD*.

Whispers reached Naomi's ears—tales of her father's organization conducting heinous experiments on the homeless and drifters, their lives deemed expendable in the pursuit of cutting-edge technology. The grim truth emerged. A disconcerting surge in missing-person cases plagues our city, a sinister consequence of her father's actions.

Of course, there is no way to prove this, as his accountants' ledgers are all scrubbed through small shell companies and corrupt banks to launder his credits.

Naomi has long since given up trying to be his daughter. She sought out her way from under his rule. She could not care less about what her father thinks of her now; she has nothing to prove to him anymore. She hates the man who had tried to control her life, and she knows there isn't even a shred of honor left in his soul.

Growing up, she was constantly being berated for not being good enough, being the cause of her mother's death, and never succeeding to his expectations, and I think it ended up eventually making her snap one day. She became her own woman—a woman who earned the respect of the underground for her ferocious reputation.

Naomi, determined to forge her own path, has consistently refused to tread in her father's footsteps or inherit the burdens of the Sato family business. From an early age, she strove for excellence, an unwavering pursuit of perfection. By the tender age of twelve, she had already become a national champion in fencing. Upon reaching adulthood, Naomi wasted no time, diving headfirst into Galacom. Surpassing expectations, she quickly ascended the ranks, ranking among the elite in all her classes and training. Her unparalleled drive propelled her to achieve the unthinkable, a feat unmatched in the history of the service—becoming the youngest individual to complete the Galacom Division training camp—which undoubtedly only inflated her sense of self-worth.

Alas, her fierce determination and ambition proved to be a double-edged sword, much like the one she carries, ultimately leading to her dismissal from the service. It was a fiery incident where she left her commanding officer with a broken jaw and shattered forearm. In Naomi's account of events, her firm resolve to defend herself was unbending. Apparently, the commanding officer had crossed the line, intruding upon her personal space—or in her words, he'd touched her ass. In response, the CO spent four months in the medical bay.

Naomi's story remained unaltered, and she'd pleaded her case, but the forces at hand had felt wiping it under the rug was the best thing for everybody, leading to her discharge from service. After all those years of following their rules, just to receive a handshake and dismissal, she hated Galacom, probably even more than most of us.

As Aden and I finally arrive at the ship, Naomi greets me with a nod, her expression carrying a touch of wry amusement. "Hey, Beck. Looks like you've seen better days."

"Hey, Naomi. Good to see you too," I reply, unable to suppress a slight smirk. "Still murdering people for money?"

A mischievous grin dances across her pink lips as she smacks them together playfully. "You know a girl like me can never resist a good time," she says, her voice laced with a hint of dark humor, while Aden brushes past us, entering the ship.

Naomi strides into the vessel, and I trail closely behind, my gaze fixated on her sleek, all-black skintight armor, tailored impeccably to her form, accentuating all the curves of her body. It's evident that no expense was spared in its creation—a custom-made ensemble design specifically for her. Crisscrossed swords adorn her back, positioned above sheathed pistols neatly clipped around her waistband.

Naomi is a woman who seamlessly intertwines grace and danger, a breathtaking embodiment of deadly elegance.

"You ready for this?" I say to her.

"Why wouldn't I be? Aren't you?" she answers sharply.

"Well, I mean, this is your father we're about to rob. I just want to make sure there aren't any emotional attachments. I want everyone to be clear-headed for this; that's all. Just making sure you're good."

"Ask me that again, and we'll be one man short for this job," she replies abruptly, turning towards the bay door's controls. She angrily swipes downward on the console, and the hydraulic door begins to close.

"Noted," I say, trying to find my seat.

Naomi can be intimidating for most. Do I trust her? Not really. She's a good soldier, but I feel she wouldn't hesitate to stab me in the back if it suited her that day. Naomi isn't like Aden; yeah, we have a slight history, but she wasn't part of our team from the beginning like Aden, Ezrek and Kruger. She possesses knowledge, critical intel about Takashi's building, that Ezrek couldn't ignore. Alongside her already-formidable reputation, it became a compelling argument to have her join our ranks. The decision was Ezrek's. I had no hand in it.

I head through the ship's back, passing Aden, who's getting his tech cargo ready. He stops fiddling away on his laptop and reaches over, handing me my equipment. "Here, Beck. You might be needing these," he says with a trembling tone.

"Thanks. Everything okay?" I ask.

"I think—I think it's just the pre-mission jitters. I'll be fine."

"You got this. You're the best at what you do. I got you, Graves. I always do."

He pauses a moment, glancing at Naomi, then back to me before returning to the screen of his laptop.

Like I've said, he's not the best at holding a conversation.

Taking a seat on the cushioned surface behind me, I meticulously inspect my weapon and supplies, ensuring that everything is in perfect condition. My hands glide over the smooth metal of my rifle, conducting a thorough examination to detect any potential malfunctions. Sliding the rail back twice, I feel the satisfying click as it securely locks into place.

A low, resonant melody breaks my concentration as it reaches my ears from above. I recognize that voice instantly, and its volume steadily amplifies as the man descends the ladder with a clumsy clunk, dropping the last few steps and causing the grated metal floor to tremble under his weight. The cabin reverberates with each heavy footfall as he approaches me.

Kruger Briggs stands before me, a mountain in a land of hills. This colossal figure, easily towers over six feet, and though his frame carries excess weight, it's evident that much of it is muscle, honed from years in the field. He's a bulldozer of a man, not sculpted like some elite athletes, but sturdy, grounded, and tremendously powerful. His short, coarse hair, reminiscent of our division days, contrasts his pallid, scarred face. That face, with features that seem chiseled from stone, has a prominent squared jaw. And then there's that inescapable rank odor that clings to him, challenging anyone who gets too close.

"Kruger, how you been?" I nod, recognizing him as EOS Division's second-best when it comes to big guns and bigger explosions. His reputation for forging paths through chaos with explosives is legendary. Yet, when the smoke clears and his munitions are spent, those enormous, roughened hands become instruments of force themselves.

Along with being one unstoppable soldier, he's also great aboard as a mastership mechanic. Sharp as a tack with engines and mechanics alike, he can fix something better than new. His fingers breathe life into machinery, coaxing optimal performance from the most complex systems.

His voice, deep with a distinctive drawl, holds a hint of an accent from a region galaxies away from here, a long-lost ancestral touch. "Been through worse, seen more," he rumbles like an old-world warrior spirit in a new-age galaxy.

Before another word can escape my lips, he unleashes a belch of epic proportions, a raucous eruption that sounds through the air, lasting a seemingly eternal seven seconds.

"Damn," I say, wafting away the repugnant odor that assaults my senses. "I can practically smell your stomach."

Kruger grumbles lowly, a rich, thick accent rolling with every syllable. He turns towards me, brushing away the remnants of a salivating sneer with the back of his hand. "Beck," he growls, the corners of his mouth hinting at a begrudging grin, "you hard-to-kill roach, how many cycles since we last met?"

"Never long enough," I reply. "Still as pumped-up as ever, I see."

A smug laugh belts out as he flexes his chest and arm muscles, attempting to assert his dominance. Though he has maintained a decent level of physical fitness, his appearance leans more towards that of a circus strongman than a lean body builder. "Never allow myself to become weak," Kruger says.

Casting a sly glance at his robust midsection, I tease him. "Is that so?"

Ignoring my playful jab, Kruger snorts. "Watch yourself, Beck. Just ensure you steer clear when things get fire. It would be a shame to mark that handsome face."

Feeling the familiar weight of my gear, I efficiently load my sidearm. "Wouldn't dream of getting in your way." The final straps of my equipment secure in place, I insert the comms unit into my ear.

Kruger grumbles, "Just like old times, da?" He shifts his bulk, making his way to sit beside Aden.

Turning to Naomi, I ask, "And our new blood, Cillian? How's he holding up?"

She raises an eyebrow, her tone dry. "Considering the company? Probably more nervous than he'd like to admit."

Interested, I push a bit more. "How many missions with you?"

She nods, confidence in her eyes. "This is his second. But trust me, he's got potential."

Cillian Drake is one of the team's newest members, an early twenty-something kid known in the underground for his quick flying and getaway techniques—a solid wheelman to have for a job like this. Ezrek has spoken very highly of him, but I've never trusted new blood.

"Comms check," I say, touching the switch at my neck. "Cillian, you read? Over."

"Copy. You guys ready?" Cillian chimes in. "Ten minutes to drop point. Gear up, everyone. It may get a bit bumpy up ahead. The storm's picking up." His adolescent voice cuts to static as I hear the thunder start to boom through the hull.

I think now, the calm before the storm, is an excellent time to get my mind right. Just a few moments of silence are all I need. Closing my eyes, I take a few breaths in and out, slowing my heartrate to a steady beat. A few seconds of peace usually clears my mind before any mission.

The ship ascends into the dreary fog that billows between the colossal buildings. Nightly taxis and delivery trucks mostly inhabit the night routes through the sky. It's peaceful here, perfectly calm—right up until the moment is utterly obliterated as something slams down with a loud bang across from where I'm sitting.

"Owen!" Naomi says.

Slowly opening my eyes, I find her sitting directly across from my seat, staring dead at me. Uncrossing her long legs, she leans forward with a devilish, flirty look and says, "So, how's the wife? What's her name again? Anna?"

"It's Avery. You know it's Avery."

"My apologies to Mrs. Owen. What does she think about you being out and about all night with the likes of us?" she asks as she crosses her legs again. She grins. "Is she worth it?"

"What do you mean?"

"I mean, is she worth it? Leaving all of us and this fun behind."

"Avery showed me what a real life could be."

Kruger chimes in to the conversation. "Just leaving us all behind."

"'A real life?' This *is* your real life. This is who you are. You can try and hide it all you want, but you're the one in here with us, buddy. We are the same, Beck, and don't forget that," Naomi says. "We're killers cut from the same cloth." She slowly removes one of her swords from the sheath to set it in her lap. "And that's all we'll ever be. You are a killer, Beck. You should own that shit."

"You know, they have these modern energy swords these days. Far less... dangerous," Aden says, leaning in close to Naomi. He's probably trying to change the subject, but he ends up just irritating her more.

Naomi releases her blade in the dim cabin lighting. Its reflective sheen reflects the bright city lights. "This blade ties me to my past. It's a bridge from my ancestors to me. Every scratch, every nick tells a tale. An energy blade's glow can fade, but this?" She raises the sword, letting it glint menacingly. "It remains."

Aden grins, hands raised defensively. "Alright, alright, point taken." His red stare then shifts to me. "Did Ezrek mention the payout? Ten million credits waiting for us in those Takashi servers? Imagine what you could do with that type of score. Two million each."

Naomi's reply is dry. "I imagine yours will be short-lived, knowing your habits."

He looks offended for a moment, then falls silent, visibly ruminating on her words.

Turning to Naomi, I seek confirmation of our strategy. "Everything set?"

She nods. "The androids are predictable. Only a few guards to watch out for. And with most of the Takashi team off at that tech exhibition, it's the perfect time. Aden and Cillian will be our lookouts, coordinating from above."

"Copy."

Aden lifts his augmented right hand and it sections open in the center of his wrist. A metal cable emerges. He retrieves the wire and connects it with his computer. I hear a gentle click, and a bright red begins to shine from the center of his forehead as he gets The3rdEye engaged. His eyes change to a bright auburn hue as he begins to override the security of Takashi Cybernetics via orbiting satellites.

The ship shudders amid the wrath of the storm, its vibrations resonating with the uncertainty I feel. "So, Ezrek's set up at the rendezvous?" I shoot the question towards Naomi and Aden, looking for clarity.

"He's ensuring our escape routes and handling the fund transfers. It's all mapped out. He'll be waiting for us," Naomi responds.

"One last ride, for all we've been through," Kruger says.

As the storm's fury lessens, Cillian shifts the ship into its approach sequence for Takashi Cybernetics. The cabin's lights shift to a warning amber, signaling our proximity.

"Brace for the drop," Cillian announces through the comms.

Naomi and I stand and head to the bay door, and Briggs proceeds right behind us. Clutching the rappelling wires, we magnetically attach them to the backs of our tactical belts. With one click of a turn, they lock into position. The bay door opens, and the sound of the raging wind fills the cabin.

"Check," says Naomi.

"Check," says Kruger.

"Check," says Cillian.

"Check," says Aden.

"In position. Go," Cillian says as the ship halts high above the building.

Taking a few steps to look over the edge, I can see Takashi Cybernetics below in the distance through the clouds, since our altitude is about ten thousand feet.

"Looks like a long way down," Naomi yells over the sound of the wind and rain.

"We could just walk in the front door," I say loudly as I turn to face her, but even before I've finished the last word, she's already jumped from the ship and is plummeting towards the building.

I look back to Aden, not thinking he'll break his concentration, but he stops, his eyes meet mine, and he says, "Hey, Beck... watch your back."

"Always do," I say before running towards the star-filled night sky and taking one giant leap out the back of the ship, vanishing from his view.

THE DÖK HUNDRI

AS REALITY SUDDENLY becomes apparent, my blurry eyes clear from the foggy recollections that latch onto my thoughts. The syncopated golden light from the autopilot blinks endlessly on the control panel in front of me.

These lasting reveries have become more frequent as the days pass. I hardly even notice I drift off from time to time; I'm afraid I have succumbed to the lethargy of these monotonous flights over Turkken.

I switch off the autopilot and wrap my fingers around the stick to take control of the *Astra*. I ease the throttle with my left-handed lever, and the ship brakes into a low cruise over the sand with a rapid rumble.

Tex and I have reached the outskirts of the Great Flats of Turkken near the base of Mount Noragöth.

"The harsh winds are picking up from the East," says Tex. "We don't have much time to get to the coordinates of the anomaly. Maybe a few hours or so before that monstrous sandstorm reaches us."

The dusters here can be devastating, and their immense raw power can bog down your engines in no time. I look to the Navcom display in front of me in a hurry, my screen syncs with the coordinates, and an illuminated path inside my visor is laid in front of my eyes. The digital trail leads right through the encampment off in the distance. "Just a short walk through the camp up ahead," I say.

Tex hovers upward out of his chair, squinting his center eye toward the camp, and says, "Let me guess—we're going through the murder camp of death, aren't we?"

"I'm sure it'll be fine," I say, as I enter the landing sequence.

"Will you not look off dramatically into the distance when you say that? Just look at me. Always so melodramatic." Tex emits a series of clicks, akin to an annoyed tongue-click, followed by another dry remark.

"I don't know what you're talking about."

"There! You just did it again, you big nutbar. Haven't you ever seen a horror movie? That's how it starts. 'Oh, look at us, casually walking through this wasteland of terror—'Don't mind us!' Then *bam!* Dead."

His blue eye just stares at me waiting for a response.

"What the shit are you talking about?" I reply.

He pauses for a moment. "Nothing. You never listen to me anyway."

"Just pipe down and keep that eye peeled, tin can."

"Fine, but if you die, I'm taking the ship," he mumbles loudly, heading towards the back of the *Astra*.

"Sure thing, Tex."

We touch down near the lowest southern dune, about a klick away from the camp, and head out the back bay. Making sure I have the safety switch on, I toss my rifle over my shoulder, it magnetically locks with a *vwomp* connection sound, and we begin our hike up to the ridge.

Small trailing rocks and sand fall down the bank behind us as we make our way up to the peak of the dune. Small five-legged reptile-type creatures emerge from the rocks around us, making their way to any shade they can find, searching for a cold respite from the relentless sun. The shifting sands ever-changing, the hills of this scorched landscape seem alive.

I clutch the Trinocs scanner. As my helmet visor can only scan so far, these come in handy for long range scouting. I set them to tracer mode with a flip of the toggle on the top. I relax my body into the sand and lay in a prone position on top of the point. I start to survey the land ahead, and Tex lowers himself next to me to replicate my body language, marginally burying so his body is half-in-half-out of the sand.

With my eyes to the camp, the heat mirage clears, and my display begins marking each structure, tagging it to my surveying HUD. The base is enormous; many triangular-shaped sand-proof tents lay dormant and spread around the mobile village. Some shelters are carefully constructed from old ship parts and excavation drill towers, and cloth is draped from long cabling connecting several tents. A mammoth industrial machine lies broken-down in the middle of the camp; they've used it for shelter. Random stolen cargo and ship parts lay strewn over the land surrounding them. The mauve colored tents range in size, with the most oversized fitting probably a dozen or more people.

Scouting up the long canyon, I pass the encampment in the general direction of the coordinates. Despite increasing the zoom towards the peak, the far-off visual is hazy at best. "We'll have to move in closer to get a better look at the peak since we couldn't see anything from the air."

"Do you see anybody down below?" Tex asks, his voice slightly muffled.

"Maybe if you weren't buried in the sand, you could take a look for yourself, but no, I don't see any people yet. Someone's there, though; the fires are still burning."

"Awesome," Tex mumbles from the hot sand. He emerges and hovers next to me to get a better look at the camp. He shakes off the remaining sand and chimes in, "I can see a marking on the outside of one of the tents."

"What is it?" I ask.

"It's the Dök Hundri," he says as his display connects to mine, and I see the blood-red symbol.

"They are the ones I've heard stories about. I don't know much about them other than they are cut-throat scavengers," I say.

"Yeah, information seems very minimal. They appeared to try and keep their existence shrouded from the databases—they most likely wanted to ravage this land with no opposition for the resources. It looks like in a few of the debriefings, workers said many Hundri were forced from their villages if they were not willing to go; many died on the flats, but sooner or later, they evolved into drifting nomads of the flatlands. Let's tread carefully," Tex says.

"We have some movement," I say, my Trinocs still fixed on the tents.

Two figures clothed in tones of beige and sun-dried black emerge from the largest tent structure in the center. I flip the top toggle of the Trinocs, and a HUD appears over the individuals, giving me an x-rayed orange outline of their figures.

The two men head down a dusty path. They wear tattered scarfs shielding their faces and necks from the sun and sands. Their armor is mismatching and set in odd configurations, undoubtedly scavenged from the dead surrounding this area. Their mostly hidden faces are shadowed from the cloaks that drape over their heads. It is near-impossible to see distinct features from here. The taller of the two is dragging some sort of sizable brown knapsack behind him.

Breaking away from the line of sight, I look to the firmament; the sandstorm is approaching from the eastern sector. It's giant, one of the bigger ones I've seen here. "Shit, the storm's closing in," I say, lifting myself from the sand.

With caution, we make our way down the sandy slopes, approaching the scarce presence of the Hundri. The air hangs heavy with the lingering stench of death. Lifeless creatures dangle haphazardly, their skin torn away, releasing droplets of blood to the soil below. Animal skulls and entrails hang from stakes and dead branches protruding from the ground. The odor permeates the area, as the rotting corpses are undoubtedly in an advanced state of decay. Their weathered hides and repugnant skins have desiccated under the scorching heat.

I slow my pace to a crouching silent walk as I notice the bigger of the two Hundri raise his knapsack to the air. He releases the knotted rope tied to the end of the bag, then quickly flips the bag to the opposite end, and something big falls to the ground with a quick *thud* and a dust cloud.

"What was that?" Tex asks.

"I think—I think it was a person."

As we get a little closer, hiding behind some machinery, I can finally tell what had fallen from the bag. "It's a child," I say to Tex.

Her skin is scorched with sunburns that plague her entire body; they range in severity from her head to her feet. She's shivering, scared, and malnourished, and she can't be much older than fourteen, if I had to guess.

One of the Hundri grabs the innocent child from the ground and throws her into a small cage-like contraption. The child shrieks, "Let me go! Help, anybody!"

"She doesn't look like one of their own—a hostage, maybe. The data logs never said anything about them taking any prisoners before, especially a child. It seems their method was to just slaughter, steal, and run," Tex says as we silently move closer and closer towards the two Hundri members.

The child is alone, trapped in the cage like some wild animal. The smaller of the two starts to clear sand and loose debris from a large circular make-shift table, then retrieves a ragged cloth from a small rectangular box next to him. It looks old, worn by the ages. The Hundri begins to unwind the cloth layer by layer, and I see a glint of sunlight bounce off as he reveals a long, double-sided twisted dagger that looks to have a residue of dried blood coating its exterior.

"Tex, she's not a hostage. She's a sacrifice."

"But it's just a defenseless child. We can't just let them murder her, Beck," Tex says as he heads towards them. "We have to do something." His eye looks at me, and then back to the child.

I shove Tex downward. "Hold it!"

"What?" he interjects, his voice slightly muffled by my hand.

"We can't just walk right up to them."

"But they are going to kill her. We have to do something."

"This could be a good distraction," I offer. "With the Hundris' focus on the child, we could pass through unseen and not have to spill more blood than is needed. She's not our problem. And more of them could come back soon."

"Beck, she's just a kid."

I pause a moment, staring to the area of the coordinates off in the haze, then back to the kid.

"Fuck."

"Obviously, I don't want to let a little girl die right in front of us," I say.

"What would Avery think?" Tex asks.

"Don't..."

"Well, shit, Beck, what's the point of all of this, then? To find Avery again, right? Do you think she would want you to let some kid die in the process? Do you think she'd recognize the man you are?"

"I don't know," I say, staring at Tex, but he doesn't waver. His stare is firm, he never blinks.

I pause a second, looking at the screaming child, then back at Tex as he urges me to reconsider. "Come on, Beck."

The Hundri, swathed in their sun-worn cloaks, arch their arms upwards, reaching for the embrace of the vast desert sky. Their voices emerge not just from their mouths, but from deep within, resonating from their very cores. The sound, reminiscent of an ancient throat-song, harmoniously ripples through the dunes. "Lum'shar Velarr. Dun'ra Ser'ethi. Qui'lan Vizra. Pal'men Tal'kir." It's a persistent, deep drone that seems to vibrate the very sands beneath.

"Tex, can you decipher that chant?"

"Analyzing... The dialect is old, older than Turkken, reminiscent of the language from the plains of Zhal'kor nearly a thousand years ago." He pauses, the ever-present drone of the Hundri's song filling the void. "Translation complete."

"What is it?"

"Watcher's Light. Worlds of Sand. Silence Sight. Receive our Hand."

Repetition of the hymn comes from far and wide as suddenly, half a dozen more Dök Hundri emerge from nearby tents.

"Oh, fuck. Hide," Tex says, and we take cover behind the machine parts as the rest of the Hundri make their way to the camp circle and join in vocalizing the song. It's a ritual, a haunting hymn for the deity of this land.

"Do you think the song is for something?" Tex asks.

"Probably a sacrifice for this land, probably for food or water."

A clunky Hundri walks to the child and retrieves her from the enclosure. The child screams for her mother and father, pleading with the Hundri to let her go. She violently kicks and punches at his chest as he puts her flat onto the slab of the table, strapping her arms and feet down ritualistically.

"We can't just sit here, Beck; we have to do something *now*."

"I know, let me just think a second." I pause, thinking of a plan. "Can you use your thermal laser to cut through the ropes and free the kid if I create a distraction? I have a plan, but if it falls to shit, be ready."

"Copy," he says.

"You ready?"

Tex discreetly makes his way around the Dök Hundri, covering himself with nearby low-hanging cloth strung up to the tents.

I take a step out and start making my way towards them. *This is a bad idea,* I think as I walk cautiously towards the ritual.

The ground is hard here—a rough dried riverbed, cracked and torn from years of sun damage, unlike the surrounding loose, heavy sand. The Hundris' unison song increases in volume with each pass of the hymn.

Even being outnumbered, I'm composed. I clench my fists, take a small breath in, and exhale unhurriedly. "Dök Hundri," I shout.

The chanting abruptly stops as the Hundri turn to see who yelled their name. The knife-wielding Hundri lowers his blade and shouts to the others, and in mere seconds, the sun glares off several precisely deadlocked mid-range barrels pointed at me.

"Tex, are you in position?" I whisper, and I hear his crackling response through the comms unit in my helmet.

"Ready," he whispers as he quietly approaches the altar from the back.

The hair-triggered Hundris shout nonsense at me as they take a few steps closer. The nearest one points his rifle towards my chest and cocks the hammer back. "Who is you?! Why have you come here?" the Hundri shouts, his words translated in real time.

"Easy—easy, friend. I'm just looking for passage through this land," I say, and my voice is then translated back to them in their native tongue through my helmet.

The Hundri's language skills seem minimal at best, but he looks to his partner, then back to me, seemingly understanding what I said. "Who is you?" he says, miming for me to take off my helmet.

"I seek passage. I mean you no harm," I say.

"Passage? No passage here. You return. You return now!"

"Take it easy," I say, lowering my arms as a sign of reverence.

The Hundri takes another step and repeats his warning. "You leave now. No passage for you here, stranger."

"I can offer trade and credits," I say as I reach a bit too hastily into my bag.

The sudden movement nearly gets me killed, as all of them cock their rifles and step forward. "Don't move!" the Hundris scream, their fingers slightly pressing the triggers.

"These are for trade," I cautiously say, setting the food portions on the ground in front of me, then standing back, my eye glances to my forearm shield emanator, readying my reflexes.

"Trade for what?" he asks.

"These for passage, and these for the kid," I say as I gently engage my forearm display. A holographic readout of all the credits I have in my account appears above the screen and blinks green, ready to transfer to an account of their choice. That is, if they even have an account or care about credits. I'm sure they know they can buy food and resources with them. They aren't that primitive.

They look at each other, then down to see what I placed on the ground, and then back to me. "No trade, no trade," he says, shaking his head repeatedly, even more agitated.

"This is all I have. Take it or leave it. It's probably more money than you'll ever have."

Seemingly recognizing the information on my account display regarding the ship I pilot, he says something to his comrade, who disappears behind him, pulling out an ancient-looking laptop.

"IPX-7942-XYR," he says as the other enters in the numbers and letters.

Of course, he's running the real intergalactic pilot code he saw on my account, not the encrypted one I have on the *Astra* that makes it look like another ship.

It takes a moment, but the Hundri runs back and whispers something to the maniac with a rifle to my chest.

"You popular, *Astra*. You have big bounty. Some people looking for you for a long time," he says, looking at the background Hundri and signaling for them to hail comms.

"No, you have more. Where is your ship?" he says, pushing the rifle into my chest even harder. "Those guns—you give to us now."

"Tex, get ready," I whisper.

"On your mark," he responds.

As he shifts closer, the Hundri repeats himself even louder than before. "Give us now or die!"

"Listen, shitbreath, I've been reasonable and offered all the money I have, but I will not be handing over my firearms, nor my ship, and if I were you, I'd shut down that transmission before you do something stupid. I'm not the guy you're looking for—trust me," I say, even though I know the Novas Guard have an outstanding bounty out for me, plus Galacom has a bounty out for the real Owen Beck for shit I didn't even do back on Vola Prime. If I'm caught by either, the likely outcome will be death or jail, and neither sound appealing.

This asshole in front of me realizes the bounty on my head is worth more than the credits in my account. This is going to shit and fast.

The threats in front of me are rapidly growing, and I can see the farthest Hundri signaling to someone that he's made contact with the comms receiver and sent out a beacon.

"Last chance—you drop weapons now. No more warning," the Hundri bellows, voice low.

I take a step forward so the barrel of his rifle is pressing hard into my chest, letting him know I'm not scared of them. "Let the kid go and turn off the transponder. I'm not going to ask again."

He hesitates a moment, glancing to his comrades, his confidence diminishing with each syllable I speak. He looks to his left, nodding to his partner to open fire, and quicker than he's even able to lay his finger on his trigger, my sidearm is deadlocked between his eyes.

I feel the slow, gentle breeze brush loose sand around us.

They never stood a chance.

A rebounding boom can be heard from miles away through the canyons as fragments of skull and crimson chunks mist the side of the Hundri's partner's face.

Stunned and dazed, the other Hundri staggers backward for just a moment, looking to his fallen comrade lying motionless in the sand next to him.

As the shocked and disordered Hundri stands still momentarily, a large-caliber round penetrates through the thin opening of his sand visor and out his left ocular cavity, exploding out the backplate of his helmet. The force is so strong that it snaps his head with a violent kick, knocking his feet forward as he falls to the ground. Powder bursts into the air, and I gradually take a few steps forward, smoke billowing from the barrel of my sidearm.

"Now, Tex," I say, and he rushes silently towards the child as I take shelter behind my blue hued forcefield as it ignites in front of me. Gunfire from the Hundris' rusted single-chamber rifles riddles the piles of crates around me, their bullets whizzing so close that their piercing howls scream through the air. Bullets fragment and ricochet off the barrier with enormous force.

I engage the scouting mode on my forearm bracer, and a small corner display illuminates in my holoscreen, allowing me to see everything Tex sees and hears. The child's hands are now free; she removes her gag and looks to Tex as he says gently, "Listen, kid, if you want to stay alive, stay quiet, and follow me."

With the last leg rope cut, the small child nods, uncertain of her future as she jumps from the table and follows Tex behind a few water reserves, hiding out of danger.

I arm my rifle with a press of a button and a voice command. "STARFALL," I say as I lean out just far enough from my shield being riddled with bullets that my holoscreen targeting system locks onto five of the Hundris hiding behind a few vehicles.

"It's almost too easy," I say, only unshielded momentarily. I whip the rifle around, and with a firm squeeze of the trigger, a single spark of light ignites from the end of the barrel, spiraling into the clouds as it breaks apart into five individual projectiles. Quickly changing trajectory, they begin to plummet towards the soil, seeking their targets individually. The heatwave from their detonations scorches the air as each Dök Hundri member bursts into a sea of dark-red liquid, scattering limbs and raining burnt pieces of flesh to the sandy ground.

"*WIDOWRUN*," I say, and the gun switches to rapid-fire. I disengage my shield, and as I advance, I unleash hell, firing a barrage of rounds as it empties the mag almost immediately towards the ruthless Hundris. Dozens of rounds enter the closest Hundri's chest cavity, a mist of blood sprays the surface behind him, and he collapses.

I've lost sight of the two Hundris behind him; I connect comms to Tex and ask, "Tex, do you read?"

"Copy, Beck."

"Execute *Osiris Protocol*," I say over comms.

Tex soars straight up into the sky to scan the terrain, and his targeting system locks onto all remaining targets on the ground. My display interfaces with him, and an x-ray silhouette forms around the Hundri even through their cover, allowing me to see where all of them are hiding.

I lean out from the surface and say, "*STORMFIRE*."

I fire one shot through the metal structure, piercing the hard metal surface, and within a second, a loud explosion rings out, sending shrapnel into the air as a giant flash of fire forms in the distance. The floor rumbles beneath me from the explosion, and an instant later, two Hundri run from behind the piles, ablaze from head to toe, screaming in unbearable pain as the fire engulfs their bodies. As they inhale smoke and their bodies burn to a crisp, they collapse, lifeless, and their screams diminish to nothing.

"Alright, Beck, a few more to go on the ri—" Tex stops suddenly. "Wait, one of them disappeared," he says, and I hear the slide of a rifle as it's cocked right behind me.

"Don't move!" the Hundri shouts.

"Ah, god, I hate that," I say as I make a quick one-eighty and clutch the barrel pointed at my face, and the shot pops off next to my head.

I pull a knife from my boot, lunge, and bury it under the Hundri's jawbone. I stare into his slowly fading eyes as blood begins to pour onto my hand and arm as his body violently locks up. The gurgling and pain fade from his body; pulling the knife slowly downward, I release him from my deathly grip.

He collapses to the sand just as two rounds rebound off my side armor with hard slams. "Shit," I grunt as I get into cover. Dazed for a moment, checking for penetration marks, I shout to Tex, "Do you still have eyes on the kid?"

"Yes. She's found a place to hide."

"Good. Keep an eye on her while I take care of these last few." I groan. I've most likely broken a rib.

"Copy," he says, flying over to the kid.

My attention returns to the last few assholes who scuffed my armor. I try to engage my shield again, but I get an error notice in red on my visor's HUD, "Low Charge."

"Fuck."

Bullets are denting and penetrating the metal structure in front of me relentlessly, and pieces of shrapnel are exploding all around me. They are giving me everything they have and with my shield not working, I'll be too out in the open. They shout to each other as their fallen comrades lay dead around them, they've now climbed above onto the railings of the central water reserve, trying to use its height as an advantage. Shells ring down to the metal walkway below them, clinking as the metal casings hit the rails.

I load the last round and say "VAPOR" into the voice system of the rifle.

With my eye through the scope, I fire a single shot between them, and for a short-lived moment, the Hundri pause, thinking I've missed. They look to each other, then back to me as a single small charge implodes between them, causing everything in a five-foot radius to be pulled into a dark purple vortex, slowly conjoining their atoms and molecules together part by part, spiraling their bodies as they are ripped apart and contorted limb by limb, disintegrating till nothing but their faces remain, both morphing into one, long, excruciating look. As the final face screams its last roar, the vortex shrinks into nothing and vanishes in a small flash of purple light and a poof of smoke.

The last of the gunshots has ceased; it's quiet again.

Standing up slowly, I watch the smoke clearing out from the explosions and fires. I can see the parts of the Dök Hundri, lifeless, emotionless, dispersed throughout the center. Nothing but blood and sand remain.

I take a moment to assess the damage I may have taken. Luckily, those few bullets only struck my armor plating, and I scrape by with a possible broken rib and ringing in my ear from the adrenaline.

"All clear," I say as I walk through the rest of the camp to clear any stragglers.

They reveal themselves inside the empty water reserve.

I make my way over to Tex and the kid. "Well, it looks like you got them all," he says, looking around at the dead bodies piled through the sand.

The kid is standing very guardedly behind Tex. "Hey, kid, you okay?" I say as she rubs her swollen wrists, which are rope-burned from being tied up.

"You forgot to charge your shield again didn't you," Tex interjects, rolling his eye.

"No, I di– yes, yes I forgot to charge it."

"Told you, you need to stop forgetting that dumbass," Tex says as the child cuts in.

"I'm... I'm okay. Thank you. Who are you?" She sounds like she's still in shock, and tears are welling up into her puffy eyes. She stumbles over to me, limping on one leg to relieve the pain from her other.

"First things first, kid—are you hurt?"

"Nothing serious," she says as she glances over her body.

"Do you live around here?" I ask as I rake her for bullet wounds.

"I'm not sure where 'here' is," the kid says as she looks to the east, then to the west, confused and incoherent. "I live in the Deathly Flats, in a town called Dos Calderon. My father is a trader there. They ambushed the town two nights ago, and my father hid me under a truck. I watched as they killed and destroyed most of my home and town," she says, hesitating word by word, throat hoarse from all the screaming and crying. "I don't—I don't know if my parents are alive. The Hundri found me and dragged me out from under our truck, then covered me with a bag before I could see what had happened to them. I was so scared. I could hear the screams and cries of my family fading in the distance as they threw me into the back of their vehicle and sped away."

"If I showed you a map, could you point to where it was?"

"I think so," she says apprehensively.

"Tex, pull up the grid of Turkken. Maybe we can get this kid home to her parents."

Tex stops in front of us, and his circuits project a holographic map grid of Turkken from his center eye, creating a full comprehensive map readout of Turkken's terrain. Looking at the grid, I reach two hands forward, pointing them in opposite directions to enlarge the map section where she'd said she lived. "Is it somewhere in this sector?" I say, pointing to the map.

"Yes, it's in the flatlands, right next to the trenches."

"Okay. So, what's your name? I can't very well just keep calling you 'kid.'"

"My name is Aanos Luna, but you can just call me Aanos."

"Okay, Aanos, let's go back to my ship and get you home," I say, unsure if she even has a home left.

As we begin to proceed towards the ship, I stop for a moment to pick up the rations from the ground, shoving them back into my bag. I flip through them and toss the kid the last of my dried Kuaviberries, and her eyes light up. She probably hasn't eaten in days.

Slinging my rifle onto my back, I say to Tex, "Let's make this quick. Dos Calderon is just a short trek over those flatlands, so I don't think we'll be gone too long, but I'm assuming those Hundri made contact. If they sent out a beacon for my bounty, the Novas Guard and Galacom probably aren't far behind. I also don't think that was all the Dök Hundri. There are way more tents in the encampment than would be necessary for how many we fought."

"She doesn't get my seat," Tex says as he leads the way towards the *Astra*.

"What?" I say.

"*She doesn't get my seat.*" Tex emphasizes word by word.

"Of course, buddy."

Stepping over bodies and the vacant, steaming shells, we make our way out of the camp and back to the ship. I press the button that disengages the turret sentry mode, and the bay door to the *Astra* opens.

I want to be the man Avery would want me to be. So much time has passed, would she even recognize the man I've become? The memories of who we used to be can't define our future, I think as we head up the ship's ramp with the sun in the south. I see the monstrous storm is a few hours away. Hopefully, we'll make it back before it hits.

The cabin door closes behind us, and Tex flies quickly to the cockpit and plops down firmly in his chair, nestling comfortably. Aanos sits in the third seat behind us, and I lift us into the sky on a course to her home, Dos Calderon of the Deathly Flats.

ACROSS THE
DEATHLY FLATS

THE FRAYED CHILD gazes out of the window as the *Astra* soars through the muted greenish skies, planted firmly in Tex's seat. She's rummaged through the limited cuisine choices I have left on the lower deck in the common room, and probably hasn't left me much of anything, but who can blame her? Her giant green eyes blink twice, overjoyed; the food is clearly helping with her starvation.

Tex, in a pout over his seat, offers her some water from his little retractable mechanical arm, and Aanos graciously accepts his peace offering. She clicks the top of the metallic canteen and spins the cap outward, and it locks in place. She vigorously gulps the liquid till there's not a drop left.

A slight turbulence rattles the hull as we break through the sound barrier. The speed of the *Astra* seems to scare her, and she begins to grip the armrests tightly as her eyes wander out to the bleak deserts and graveyards of old forgotten ships and mining equipment that plague the sands—the skeletons of behemoth CoreCrawlers, machines that mined the core, but have been left, broken-down and scavenged bare for parts.

I don't think the kid has ever been on anything faster than a small Sand-Drifter, a Turkken-native transport that employs a compact, yet powerful one-speed engine, specially engineered to operate optimally in the extreme desert conditions. Its engine efficiently converts a variety of liquids into fuels, such as biofuels or advanced energy cells. Many natives use them as conveyances through the harsh, massive plateaus.

As we approach Dos Calderon from the West, Aanos's face grows weary with anticipation, hoping her family is still alive.

"You sure this is the right place, Aanos?" I ask, seeing a wake of smoke and embers appearing on the horizon and feeling doubtful of her future.

"Yes, that's the main road that leads to the town, down to the right," she replied. Her demeanor is overflowing with uneasiness. Her hand is shaking, so she tries to clasp it to her other arm, but it won't cease, and her delicate eyes hide behind her tangled brown hair.

"Just breathe, kid," I say, trying to ease her discomfort.

"I'll try," she says, taking a few breaths in and out; she does seem optimistic about being free of the Hundri.

I bring up the navigation display, reading the underground layout of the great trenches and gorges ahead. "We are about two minutes out," I say as the ship's inner command lights on the unit display flicker from green to yellow, signifying the destination is close.

Smoke begins to billow slowly around the *Astra* as we break into a clearing closer to Dos Calderon. Ashes from the fires ahead coat our outer hull, and the smell of char lingers even through the filtration. Aanos's warm gaze grows cold as she looks to the horizon, watching as the silver steam and golden embers cascade over the land she once knew as her home. Her eyebrows clinch as she squeezes her hands, and her voice stutters as it changes in pitch. "Every-everything's on fire." She stops.

Looking at her, I can't think of anything to say. There's no sugarcoating it. I sit there trying to think of something optimistic to tell the kid to keep hope alive. But what do I say? What do I say to a kid whose parents are most likely dead?

I sit a moment, pondering, as I land the *Astra* just outside the town. At my side, the kid has a rush of adrenaline hit her like a hammer; she can't stop trembling. I can't think of a single thing to say to give her hope, so we stay utterly dead-mouthed as we make our way towards the exit ramp.

"Tex, stay with the ship, and make sure to do the routine checks and give it a once-over. I think I can handle this one on my own."

"Oh…" he says, stopping abruptly, his eye looking back and forth. "Sure thing. I'll just wait here, I guess," he says as he starts to hover backward up the ramp, slowly muttering something inaudible.

Aanos stays close behind me, like a small animal cowering behind its parent in the wild, as we pass the remains of dead bodies in a row through the entry into town. It's a small two-lane dirt road leading to the entrance. The bodies are lined up parallel next to one another, with arms crossed and hands to their shoulders. Two smeared ash marks have been wiped vertically down each dead person's cheek in a sign of remembrance and the soul's journey through the afterlife. She peeks around me, hoping she doesn't recognize any of their faces.

Dos Calderon isn't a significant town. The settlement is filled with traders, mechanics, and terra-farmers, and the buildings range from smaller handmade houses to more prominent edifices assembled from yellow sandstone slabs and makeshift metal supports. Tattered-clothed windows on every structure look handmade and imperfect, down to the crude, uncomfortable-looking rock benches.

The agricultural prospects within this region of Turkken are noticeably challenging due to the inherent deficiencies of its soil composition. Nevertheless, the inhabitants of this location have ingeniously devised enclosed bio-environments to facilitate the farming of their crops. Their innovative water recycling system shows a level of cleverness, wherein all utilize water undergoes meticulous filtration via a purifying mechanism before being efficiently redistributed to sustain the growth and nourishment of their flora. Without such a system in place, viable agricultural endeavors in this environment would be virtually unachievable. It remains a mystery to me as to why individuals would willingly choose to endure the adversities of Turkken.

Now, though, the city is in utter ruins; most of the buildings have collapsed, and families are searching through the remains of their dilapidated lives, saying their last goodbyes to the faces blown apart from rifle blasts or charred nearly to the bone. The Hundri have laid waste to this town; I don't know what the townsfolk are expecting to find in all this rubble. This town has been surviving off very minimal resources as-is, and now, these people have nothing left.

Stepping away from my side, Aanos peeks out from behind me and stops. "What's wrong, kid?" I ask as she rushes away as fast as she can, running full speed toward an ash-covered man kneeling on the ground, embracing a battered dying woman in his arms with a lachrymose pose of loss and suffering.

Aanos cries out to the older man and woman lying on the ground. "Father!" she shrieks as loud as her lungs can expel the words.

The father is stunned at what he sees, staring at Aanos like she was a ghost. Then he starts to weep uncontrollably. Without saying a single word, he fully embraces Aanos, and they grip each other hard as she stares into her dying mother's eyes. Her mother's mouth is filling with blood; she can't speak, so no words are said.

I watch this encirclement of sorrow and love as the background of indistinct deceased are buried and remembered. The bereaved families cry and mourn as the wind brushes against the bodies and embers, a reminder nothing in this life is forever.

Aanos's father gently lowers his wife's head to the gravel as her eyes close for the last time. Expelling one last breath to the air, she fades away—the greatest and most final release. I try to give them their moment, saying their last goodbyes. I'm not sure if I should head back to the ship or stay. Flashes of Avery enter my mind—her gaze fading the same way. It's a pain one never forgets.

Just as I turn to leave, her father tries lifting her mother's body from the ground, but falls to the ground himself. I walk over, resting my hand on his shoulder. "Allow me," I say as his nearly black eyes look to me, then to Aanos.

"It's okay; he's a friend," she says softly.

Looking down to the love of his life, now gone, he nods as his long hair brushes against his bruised sunken-in cheekbones, and he lets her head rest back on the ground, giving her one last kiss on her forehead. "Thank you," he says gratefully.

"Let's get her back home," I say as the father picks himself back up and limps towards Aanos, hugging her once again, cherishing every new second he has with her.

I carefully pick her body up from the gravel, embracing her as we head through the town, carrying her back to their home in my arms.

"They—they took everything. It's all gone," the man says.

"Is the house okay, papa?" Aanos asks.

"They didn't reach our side of town; they went straight to the water and food reserves, killing anyone who got in their way. Your mother..." the hurt man says, lowering his head.

"What, papa?" she says, stopping to face him.

"We thought we lost you. When the gunfire started, we couldn't find you. We ran through the town, but bodies were falling left and right, and that's when we saw you. She chased after you when they took you, and that's when they—" The man breaks down.

"I'm here; we're all together again, papa," she says, wiping his tears as I slowly trail behind them with their loved one in my arms. The mother's eyes are closed, and she looks at peace. It seems like she sustained a wound to the abdomen. Must have bled out slowly, from the looks of it.

Aanos and her father have reached their small sandstone home, and I follow close behind. The roof of the home looks to be barely held up by cracked slabs, and corroded tubes line the outer walls, running to the reserves that supply the town with water. It's a simple house for a simple family.

I follow them into the house and gently lay her body down on a bed, then head back outside.

The father bows his head in acceptance, "Thank you. Thank you," he repeats as he heads over to Aanos at the door of the bedroom.

The gloaming settles like a pall, the once-thriving town reduced to rubble and desolation. I step outside, unable to bear the weight of the grief within, and settle under the skeletal remains of what once was a grand tree. Its lifeless branches seem to reach out, attempting to caress the darkening sky.

Time seems to stand still, but eventually, the door of the house groans open, revealing Aanos. Her eyes, puffy from tears, seek refuge in mine. I can feel the weight of unsaid words between us. "Are you okay?"

"Yes, my father's inside prepping my mother for her burial."

"Keep him safe, Aanos. I have to return to my ship. Your father..." I hesitate, the words catching in my throat. "He needs you. Now, perhaps more than ever."

She nods, her voice barely above a whisper. "Thank you." Just as the last syllable leaves her lips, the imposing figure of her father appears. Grief has carved lines onto his face, making him appear older and wearier.

In the waning light, he approaches Aanos, his arms pulling her into a tight embrace. "We'll lay her to rest tonight, beneath the watchful eyes of the stars," he says. Tears glisten, tracing the pathways of sorrow on Aanos's cheeks. His gaze settled on me, intense and unwavering. "You, stranger from the skies—you have my eternal gratitude. Because of you, my Aanos still breathes." He extends a hand, not as a mere formality, but as a bridge between two souls. "I'm Felix Luna."

"Pilot," I reply cautiously, meeting his grip.

The strength in his grasp intensifies. "I need to know the name of my daughter's savior," he says.

Hesitation flickers briefly, but I give in. "Beck," I say.

"A celestial wanderer with a heart of gold. But tell me, where did you discover my Aanos?"

"The Dök Hundri had her, close to Mount Noragöth," I say, and watch his face drain of color.

"Noragöth?" His voice fills with a cocktail of dread, disbelief, and a hint of anger. "You must never return there."

"Why?" The single word hangs in the air, heavy with portent.

The atmosphere grows dense, every word Felix spoke dripping with a grave forewarning, "That mountain—it's not just stone and rock. It's a tomb. Many souls have sought its secrets, and none have come back to tell the tale. There's an old darkness that guards its depths. My forefathers, lured by the siren call of riches, burrowed into its belly for years. But what they found"—he pauses, pain evident in his eyes—"wasn't just riches. Family tales speak of entire teams vanishing without a trace in the earliest years of the excavation."

I frown, leaning in. "What do you mean by 'something?'"

"My father would share tales by the fire of miners who would be lured away by strange shrieks and sounds through the tunnels. The mines—they melded with Turkken's natural caverns, creating a dark labyrinth that can easily ensnare the unprepared."

Curiosity, mixed with a touch of dread, takes hold. "But what lies within? How deep did they go?"

He looks away, his voice a hushed whisper. "No soul around here has dared to approach that accursed place in a century. They remember the anguish, the waiting for loved ones who never returned. They would say the ghosts of the mountain fed on the souls of those who dared to get too close. Please, if you venture there, tread with utmost caution. The mountain—it's hungry."

A gust of wind blows around us. "Just another day," I reply, trying to shake off the mounting anxiety. "I need to move before the storm sets in."

But Felix is relentless. "Wait!" he says, motioning Aanos forward. "At least take this."

"I really don't need--"

His grip on my arm is firm. "I must repay the debt. Please."

The urgency in his voice is undeniable, a desperate plea from a man well-acquainted with the darkness of the world.

"Aanos," he says, glancing nervously towards the shadow-cloaked entrance of the small stone house. "In my closet, there's my grandfather's box. Bring it to me."

"Yes, father," Aanos responds, her small feet quickly ascending the creaky steps. Over her shoulder, her eyes meet mine, and within her fear, there's a faint glimmer of a smile.

Her quick return is marked by a stumble, the soft thud of her foot catching an uneven patch of ground. Hastily, she rises, wiping away both the dirt from her knees and a lone tear that escapes her eye. She hands me a tattered rectangular box, heavy with history.

I gingerly open it, revealing layers upon layers of old letters and sun-faded photographs. "What's all this?"

Felix steps forward, fingers trembling as he retrieves a fragile piece of paper, edges yellowed with age. "This might be of service, Beck."

I cautiously spread the paper, revealing the intricate lines of a map.

"It's been passed down in my family for generations—an ancient map of the mines of Turkken. Treacherous paths lay ahead, but perhaps this will guide your steps safely."

I study the routes, the sprawling maze of tunnels beneath the soil, then tuck it away. "I'm grateful."

He hesitates, then adds, "If it pleases you, might you accompany us? A burial awaits."

I glance towards the sinking sun, its fiery hues painting the horizon. "I must continue my journey, but thank you."

Felix's voice grows softer, the weight of grief apparent. "May the spirits guide your way, traveler of the night. The shadows grow long, but perhaps in them, there's still light."

Aanos's arms wrap around me suddenly. Her embrace is surprisingly strong. "Please," she whispers, "don't forget us."

"I promise," I reply, even as I feel the weight of unspoken truths between us.

As I step away, the town of Dos Calderon stretches out before me, a landscape painted with melancholy hues. The two figures, father and daughter, grow smaller, but as they disappear into their home, a final gesture—a nod, a fleeting smile—assures me that in the heart of despair, hope remains.

I've grown accustomed to living an existence of isolation. Without Avery, I've found no consolation in existing any other way. At least, that's what I tell myself in an otiose attempt to push off the pursuing loneliness that stalks me.

I head back to the *Astra*, my head low, passing the town folk of Dos Calderon. With a quickened pace, I turn the comms back on and connect to Tex. "Hey, Tex—status report."

"Where the titty fuck were you? I was trying to tell you—I'm picking up something close by on the radar. Not sure if it's a ship. It's too small to be a fighter."

"I'm on my way back now."

"Did you find her parents?" Tex asks.

"Yes," I say, then pause for a moment. "She's home now."

"Good. We should get going."

"Yeah, yeah, I'm nearly there," I say. I can see *Astra* powering up nearby.

The sun's just about down; we probably won't make it to the cave before nightfall, and we can't wait till morning. If the Dök Hundri contacted the Novas Guard, we need to get there first, I think.

As I make it back to the ship, I see a dark shadow stream by as something turns the ecru sand to a dark taupe as it passes overhead.

I swing my rifle into my shoulder with a quick look up and use its scope to further my view. I lock onto the vessel from the ground, and I can see a clear marking on the ship's side.

It can only be one thing: an NG-742 Hunter, a quick stealth reconnaissance drone used by the Novas Guard. If it has made it here, that means the Hundris made contact, and the rest of them aren't far behind.

"Tex, start the ship. We need to get airborne now! A hunter just flew overhead. What you picked up isn't a ship—it's a drone," I say as I grasp my bag, hastening for the *Astra*.

"Copy," Tex says.

Entering the bay door, I climb up to the cockpit, kicking in the thrusters on the panel above while jumping into the vacant seat in front of me. I flip the last few toggles for the engines to align, and with a precise push of a single lever, the ship flashes upward into the air and soars after the hunter drone, and we leave the smoldering city of Dos Calderon and Aanos far behind.

FROM THE CLOUDS
CAME FIRE

AT THE PERIPHERY of my vision, the enemy Hunter-Drone soars, its silhouette occasionally illuminated by the dying sun. The *Astra* vibrates powerfully beneath me, heeding my every directive with surges of raw speed. Hovering scant inches from the terrain, I'm locked in a high-octane chase. The drone, with its nimble dodging capability, becomes a whirl of metal and wires, defying every effort I make to target it. Our velocity is almost on par, its factory engine seeming strangely akin to the *Astra*'s power.

It employs daring tactics to shake me off, diving perilously close to the ground and slaloming between towering rock formations. But its speed, though impressive, is insufficient. As I gain on it, it vanishes from my line of sight, diving into the depths of the Great Canyons that define Turkken's landscape.

Without missing a beat, I pursue, mirroring its path. There it is, threading its way through the jagged embrace of the canyon.

Per request, the *Astra* rumbles, and as the heavy weapons system powers online, two lethal projectiles emerge from beneath its wings. With my eye on the targeting screen, I squeeze the trigger, and two azure-streaked missiles bolt into the sky. They chase the drone with unerring focus, mirroring its every twist and dive, matching its desperate attempts to escape their relentless pursuit.

Just as they near impact, the scout ignites an anti-missile defense system, and a firework show of flares erupts through the sky around it, sizzling and exploding one by one, hailing down in a flurry.

As the missiles veer off course, they connect with the side of the canyon, and a field of loose falling rocks implodes in front of us. "Watch the rocks! Watch the rocks!" Tex shouts.

I yank on the stick through the explosion, causing a high-g barrel roll, and debris from the rock's impact around us; we narrowly escape being crushed as the explosion thunders through the hull. "No shit," I shout as I flight-correct the *Astra*.

"Where did it go?" Tex says.

"Ten-low," I say, pointing to ten o'clock low out the cockpit.

My targeting system activates once more, emitting a distinct ping as it locks onto the ship. Instantly, a vivid blue hologram of the vessel materializes and hovers on my cockpit screen, providing me with a clear visual. Firmly grasping the rugged controls, I execute a sharp maneuver, swiftly veering to the left and slicing through the misty expanse above.

Positioned closely behind the agile drone, I unleash a torrent of devastation from the *Astra*'s under-mounted heavy machine gun. The weapon, boating six barrels and equipped with an efficient air-cooling system, projects from the hull. A barrage of three thousand .50 caliber rounds spews forth at an astonishing rate of fire, obliterating anything it encounters along its destructive path. The once-solid canyon walls shatter under the assault, unable to withstand the sheer power.

The canyon walls crumble around the drone, and as the trail of bullets snakes through the sky, I manage to clip the rear of its right engine, and a green-hued detonation ignites through the cold cirrus.

It's only a matter of time.

Smoke begins barreling around me as the scout's velocity begins to sputter and decrease. The drone is exceedingly hard to track; I'm having difficulty getting a lock on its exact location. However, no matter the tricks and ploys it tries to evade me, I'm close behind it.

I tug back on the controls, and the *Astra* soars into the vapors, nearly causing the ship to skid through the air—a "departed controlled flight," as us pilots call it.

Regaining control, we head towards the thermosphere; the front of the ship is now at a sixty-degree incline. The wind pushes the hull's bottom, and the *Astra* is pointing nearly straight up. I increase acceleration with the afterburners, juddering the craft slightly as I soar out and over the canyons.

I align *Astra* to the skyline, and I can see we are right on top of the drone. The scout ship is banking left and right through the deep trenches below. I ease over the digital target on my display, flipping the toggle on the controls, and the yellow tracker homes in and locks on target; I ease the throttle back just a tad, remaining above it.

"Alpha-2," I say as I click the control's top trigger button.

A bright, blurred purple rail bolt fires from the *Astra* and gleams through the sky towards the drone. The bolt slices straight through the vessel's power core, and a brilliant explosion of destruction and energy stirs the sky as it disintegrates over the desert.

Piercing through the brief grey cloud of smoke, we emerge triumphantly. "Damn, that was a big explosion!" Tex exclaims. "Just like old times."

"Not going to lie, my butthole tightened a little bit," I joke.

"Yeah, I think I spilled lubricant on my seat," Tex says, looking down.

We have a clear heading. I've probably bought us a few more moments with the drone taken out.

I change course direction towards the Dök Hundri sector and loosen my grip, easing into the controls, gradually exhaling the thrill of the chase. I lower the ship's speed to a serene cruise, counting each mountain as we zip past.

Scrolling through the cockpit's mainframe, I say, "Tex, can you add the map to our database?"

"Sure thing," he says as he heads over to my bag. His little mechanical arm quickly digs through my pack hanging next to the door; laying the map on the ground, he unfolds it carefully. A beam illuminates it as he scans the old mining map into our digital database. "There you go, you beautiful man, you."

"Hah. Shut up." I smirk. "Let's land close to where we did before. It's well enough out of the way, and the Novas Guard may not tag our ship if it's under cover."

"I conquer," he says, nodding in agreement with each word.

"'Conquer?' Do you mean concur?"

"Probably," Tex says as he tilts his head in a shrugging way.

I shake my head. I think his processor might be acting up again.

I set the *Astra* down on the sand, covering it under an overhang of jagged rocks. "This should work," I say to myself confidently as it settles.

Tex bustles his way through the cabin's entry, making his way through the loading bay, and I follow close behind.

We head through the Dök Hundri camp for the second time, and I think back to Aanos and Felix. I look down at my new footsteps as they trail through the same pathways, though it is harder to see now, since it's practically nightfall.

The planet's nightly insects, glowing yellow-green-winged bugs, are afoot, circling in patterns around the camp, and distant whistling calls from nocturnal animals travel from the canyons over the fallen Dök Hundri. The rotten smell of death and crisp corpses fills the air. The stench has gotten even fouler. My guess is the nightly beasts are waiting until nightfall to eat the bodies; it's best we don't stay long.

The day is gone, and I take a minute to give the vast summit that lies on the brink of the horizon a once-over. The obscure orange-grey mountain sits spectral and desolate, just an uninviting shadow lasting in the nightly sky. Its gloomy base stretches for miles in opposite directions, fanning over the land. Most of its rock formations seemed jagged and unscalable, making accessible paths and graded platforms a rarity.

The starry sky looms overhead with zero visibility of the Novas Guard, and it seems the sandstorm hasn't made it here yet. Just the light of the two moons will guide our way through the dark, forbidding dunes lying between us and the peak.

I tighten my shoulder bag, and we embark to the crest of Mount Noragöth.

The dark desert sprawls out before me, bathed in a strange, hazy light from the distant stars above. The mysterious cries of unknown nocturnal creatures echo across the stretch of nothing, weaving a haunting tune with the mournful sigh of the wind. Faint cries can be heard through the mountains, and a rattled call is barely audible.

Beside me, Tex hovers. His gentle blue luminescence paints my shadow long across the sands. "Hey, Beck," he says.

I glance toward him. "Yeah?"

A brief pause fills the space between us. "Throughout our journey," he says, his eye light dimming slightly, "I've logged countless data points. But there's one observation I've yet to share."

I raise an eyebrow. "Which is?"

Tex's glow warms, hinting at the drone's attempt to mimic empathy. "Your resilience, driven by this emotion called 'love,' baffles my circuits. Even though I've never interfaced with Avery, I've archived her essence through your narratives. She must have been... significant."

Tightness grips my chest. Memories of Avery flood my mind, and I manage to whisper, "She was everything."

For a moment, there's silence. Then, Tex hums softly. "Your bond with her—I admire it."

A soft chuckle escapes me. "Tex, for a piece of advanced tech, you're surprisingly... like us sometimes."

He brightens briefly. "But..."

His blue eye starts to wander.

"But what?" I say, stopping in front of him.

Tex pauses, drifting closer, his eye shimmering with genuine concern. "I've seen you on the edge, Beck. On the brink. If this Khu'Val ends up being a bust, I don't want you spiraling down again. Watching you drown in despair once was more than enough."

"My direction was... skewed," I admit, the pain of the memory evident in my voice.

"'Skewed?'" Tex emits a sound that, for a machine, resembles a snort. "That's one way to put it."

"I was shattered, Tex," I say. "Lost without Avery. Every lead on Ezrek, every hint of where he might be, vanished like mirages. On the edge of surrender, I found clarity," I say, fiddling with the ring shielded under my side cloak.

"In what?" His voice softens as we continue forward.

Reaching into my pack, I retrieve Avery's worn leather journal, its pages filled with her handwriting. "This. I stood at a crossroads, Tex: Avery's journal in one hand, the weight of my gun in the other. It was her legacy versus my despair. And in that crucial moment, I had a revelation."

"Which was?"

"That maybe I survived everything for a reason. Maybe I was meant to complete Avery's mission or face oblivion trying."

"Well, I'm with you to the end, Beck. Regardless of whether the power is real or not, we will make Ezrek pay for what he did to Avery. At least murdering that murderer with a nice case of murder will ease some of the pain you feel."

"Goddamn right, it will," I say as we finally arrive at the base of the summit.

"Teamwork," Tex says, pausing in the air and slowly looking up the side of the giant mountain to where the tip meets the clouds. "Hope your cardio's up, small legs."

"Why is it always a short joke?"

We embark up the hillside, which is somewhat sloping to start. It truly is one of the highest summits in this sector, and the ground here makes ascension difficult, but not impossible. I have little climbing equipment, so my only option is doing this in a free climb. I first retrieve my cable harness from my belt and insert the anchor into my forearm module. I begin to trudge up the precipitous embankment of sand, loose gravel, and deeply sculpted walls of rock. The flooring is firm, but I notice some areas could give way at any moment, though it seems to have many slim ledges and narrow barriers I can use to balance myself.

I scan the immediate surroundings, and my helmet, with its advanced terrain navigator, immediately kicks in. It senses the low-light conditions and suggests paths that look about as appealing as a bed of nails. Along with best approaches, it provides fun little statistics on the likelihood of me killing myself.

"I should have waited until dawn," I say as I muster the courage to move forward.

"You could use the exercise," Tex says. "Given the amount of snack wrappers I've seen in the cockpit... just saying."

"Really, Tex? Right now?" I reply, trying to negotiate my way without getting stabbed by a particularly pointy rock. "If you want to be helpful, how about you scan ahead?" I suggest, only half-hoping he'd be useful.

I come to a tapered path leading to a level above. The first part of the climb is rocky, and there aren't many ways around it, so it seems to be the only path onward. I tightly mount the slab in front of me, muscling my way up. I peek over the ledge, see an opening, and hoist myself to the next section.

I'm already sweating, and as my shoulder shakes from my old bullet wound, I can now feel a deep burn stemming from the sides of my triceps. The physical toll is unsettling. We've pushed about halfway up the summit. *Shit, I'm tired, and my rib is killing me.*

Taking a rest, I see the following flat only has one way forward—a small, fragile ledge that's barely wide enough to accommodate my feet.

"A break already?" Tex says, casually hovering nearby, making it look easy.

"Eat shit, bolthead," I say as I wedge my fingers deep in the rock before me and test the ledge's durability by tapping my foot lightly, then a little harder. "Seems good," I say. My system says that I have a forty-seven percent chance of survivability of this ledge walk.

"Forty-seven percent, huh?"

"Eh, I've had worse," I say, flattening myself out like a pancake. Huddling parallel to the rock wall, I enter the side-crawl.

I gently make my way across, slowly shifting my position sideways, step by step, looking down into the dark chasm below. "Fuck."

"What?" Tex says.

"I looked down."

"You never look down, you big stupid idiot."

One wrong misstep, and the mountain's judgment will be swift. The sharp rocks below are waiting to receive me at any moment. "Fuck, I hate heights," I say.

"But... but you're a pilot?" Tex says curiously.

"I'm not in a ship, am I, you glorified toaster?" I say, shimmying along the thin ledge.

"I guess? You're a weird guy, Beck. A weird guy."

"Shut up and let me focus," I say. I've nearly made it to the end.

Carefully leaving the ledge, I reach the other side and sharply exhale in relief. The wind up here howls as it brushes against me, tightening my muscles. It is a long way down.

Fuck, it's cold, I think as my hands start to shiver a bit.

Turkken gets too cold for my liking. Even with my undersuit, the temperature radiates through my gloves, and it's hard to grip. The numbness is familiar, like the dead cold of space tingling your fingers.

The jagged landscape spreads below me, an intimidating maze of rocks and cliffs. The data on my visor indicates just one feasible route upward, but it's far from ideal. Taking a deep breath, I take the leap of faith to the next ridge. My fingers grasp onto the ledge, muscles straining to pull me upward onto a narrow platform, barely wide enough for me to stand.

My next grasp misses, and fear surges through me. I try to shift my footing for better leverage, but without warning, the ground crumbles beneath me. A scream tears through my throat, echoing in the barren night sky.

"Tex!" Desperation laces my voice, searching for him as a platform rushes up to meet me.

As the rocks get closer and closer, my visor manages to lock onto an anchor point above, and as the ground grows clear, I fire at the very top of the last ridge, and the line hurls through the air.

Just as I'm about to slam into the rocks below, the anchor penetrates the stones, and with a hard snap, the line goes firm and takes my entire weight.

I clinch the line and crash into the wall with a slam so hard it knocks the air from my lungs.

I gasp, but nothing comes.

I dangle feet above a plethora of razor-sharp rocks, spiraling around the tether. I still have hundreds of feet to the very bottom. I would have splattered about halfway up the mountain. "Holy fuck." I gulp as I look how close I just came to death. "That was too close," I say, feeling relieved as the air begins to return to my lungs.

"Beck!" Tex shouts as he checks on me. "Are you okay?!"

"Yeah. Might have broken that rib properly now."

"What can I do?" he says anxiously.

"Nothing. Just make sure I have a clear path ahead. I'm going to have to rappel the rest."

"You got it, boss," Tex says as he jets upward, his eye frantically looking for any dead ends.

"Looks clear to me. You should be good the rest of the way boss," he yells from afar.

I grasp the wire and start to rappel, masking the pain deep down.

Fuck, my rib hurts every time I breathe, I think. Every inch I move hurts worse than the last.

After a few minutes of this, I think I can see the top. It's close now.

With a few more painstaking pulls, I hoist myself over the ridge and fall to my back. Resting, I press the cable-head release button on my forearm, and the anchor-head discharges from the cable and snaps back into my bracer.

Taking a few long breaths, I stare up at the stars. I've made it to the top.

After enjoying the starlight for just a moment, I roll to my side and groan loudly. Tex comes into view and blocks my beautiful sight with his small, dumb robotic face. "You alive?" he says.

"Barely," I grunt as I make it to my butt. "That could have gone better," I say as I shake off the clinging sand and debris. Tex remains unusually silent. "Tex?"

His focus is clearly elsewhere. With a sense of urgency, he says, "Owen... look."

I lift my gaze, and my breath catches at the sight before me. "Incredible," I say, slowly rising to my feet, my weariness momentarily forgotten.

Before us, concealed by time and nature, stands a majestic ancient ruin.

The initial section of the passage is flat, leading to peculiar formations and pillars that are intricately carved into the mountain, giving the impression of an overhang. These structures exhibit a unique ashy grey color, with deep-rooted cracks tainted by teal and rust corrosion. Enclosed within the ruins is a dark stone crest, while broken columns are positioned in a circular manner, adding an element of symmetry.

The rock pillars themselves are shaped in unfamiliar forms and bear intricate glyphs embedded into their fronts. They appear to be seamlessly integrated into the mountain, creating an immense entrance. Curiously, strange emerald vines twist and weave their way into the surface of the peak, converging towards the entrance. In this mystifying scenery, I notice the presence of yellow-green bioluminescent insects floating through the dense vegetation. The proliferation of this plant life seems highly improbable, as these parts of Turkken lack the necessary conditions for growth without enclosed ecosystems like Dos Calderon; the soil doesn't allow it. So, what the hell is this stuff?

Peering into the shadowed realm of the ruins, I see that a cryptic sigil lies almost concealed on the ancient ground, just within our grasp. Its faint outline is discernible only from the rare angle of the skies above, rendered obscure by the jumble of towering pillars and overhanging rocks.

And another presence pulses here—a magnetic force emanating directly from the mountain; it's making my electronics sputter and misbehave.

It suddenly makes sense why the *Astra* has had such a hard time pinpointing this location. With the relentless interference, it's a wonder it registered anything.

My screen flickers, the terrain reader flashing intermittently on its lower right corner. Again and again, the message loops:

[//:SYSTEM BOOTING// >INITIALIZING//]

[>//:SYSTEM//>REBOOTING]

"Damn it," I say, tapping my helmet in frustration.

Tex's voice breaks the silence. "This doesn't scream 'mining entrance' to me."

"It looks almost untouched," I say, stepping closer to the stone columns. As I crouch, the chilled rock greets my touch. Sliding my fingers over it, I feel the engravings—glyphs I recognize. They are the markings of the Khu'val. My gaze is drawn to the crest's midpoint and the concentric designs on the ground.

"I know these symbols," I say, excitement rising in my voice as the tip of an inverted triangle emerges from the sand.

"Beck, this is ground zero," Tex says, his scanner whirring over the central seal. "We're onto something big!"

"Tex, with the intel we have, can you make sense of any of this?"

He doesn't miss a beat. "I'm on it." I watch as he moves methodically, analyzing each pillar and inscription. His signature blue lights shift to a decoding green. After a few moments, they dim slightly. "Nada. The magnetic field's wreaking havoc on my system."

I retrieve Avery's old journal from my pack, flipping open the leather binding. I have spent years memorizing this journal, which is teeming with notes from incoherent ramblings to crude drawings and pages filled with information. One page holds sketches of the lost glyphs, with logs of what a lot of them represent. It doesn't look like she had all of them that I see here, but at least she had their alphabet and over two dozen or so logged.

She'd jotted a quote of some kind at the top of the page of the glyphs. It reads:

At night, the sight comes without being asked.

By day, we are lost without being stolen.

"What the hell does that mean?" Tex says, his digital eye narrowing in a quizzical expression.

"I'm not sure," I say, still fumbling through the journal. I'm not sure what it means or its relevance.

There are dozens of symbols written on the fronts and sides of the pillars. Each one has a distinct characteristic, with some ranging from having sharp corners and straight lines to many having no edges at all.

Stepping back, I traverse over some boulders stationed in front of the monuments. Walking by each rune-etched monument, I sketch them into the empty pages of the journal just in case our cameras' recordings are corrupted during all this interference.

I finish the sketches, close the journal, and place it back in my bag. "Tex, let's go," I say as I walk under the foliage hanging all around me, pushing it upward out of my way.

As we push our way through the thick, heavy vines, we reach the mouth of the crest. "What the hell?" Tex says.

The entrance is blocked. It looks as if someone blew the opening with some sort of explosives, causing a cave-in decades ago. There's no way through.

"Maybe it was to keep people out of the mines," Tex says.

"Or to keep something in," I reply.

"You're probably right," he says, backing up, looking for any other way into the cave.

"Think we can blow that open?"

"Only one way to find out," he says as I start to back up.

Hiding behind one of the columns, I retrieve an NX-8 detonator from the back of my belt. It's a small explosive device usually used for breaching smaller walls, but it should suffice. Clicking the top of the device, I throw it to the center of the rock pile. It sticks in place and a red light blinks from its core. With each second that passes, it increases in speed, beeping faster and faster.

It explodes gloriously with a thunderous roar, sending rocks and dust everywhere and shaking the ground around us.

Tex and I wait for the smoke to clear and the raining rubble to cease. It's not an ideal way in, as these ruins are probably thousands of years old, but I had no other option.

I glance over the stone as the smoke clears, revealing a wide-mouthed opening leading into the chambers. Walking up to the entrance, I take a long look at Tex, then back to the eclipsed depths of the hollow cavity, thinking of what may lay ahead.

"You first," says Tex, looking at me then back to the hole of darkness.

With the night quiet and the swift gusts creating an unnatural howl throughout the valleys, we make our way inside the maw of the cavern.

Shadows slowly blanket our figures as we disappear into the black void.

INTO THE WIRED ABYSS

IN AKEREON CITY, a decaying metal jungle inside a cursed water world, hundreds of millions of people scramble through their lives, blind to the enormous universe that awaits just beyond these walls. Merely seventy-two hours remain until the job, and I am counting every minute. My heads-up display glows with a readout of ten past six, yet the expected call from Ezrek remains absent. I let my finger skim lightly across the cold, gleaming digital surface of the truck's dashboard, absorbing the blinking traffic reports of Akereon City in a stream of frenzied data.

The holographic city map blinks stoically back, indicating an unsettling stagnation: no traffic movements for the past twenty minutes. Suspended in mid-air, trapped within the confines of this one-way airstream tunnel, my truck is blocked in its path. Of course, things like this always happen at the end of the day. I am nearly back to Takashi Cybernetics headquarters, where I can drop off my work truck, get my car, and finally go home.

A blaring of disgruntled horns and rumbling engines reverberates behind me, the agitated outcry of my fellow skyway commuters somewhat muted by the confines of my cockpit. Muffled, indistinct shouts pepper the backdrop of noise, their originators' frustrations as indecipherable as the words they holler through their windows.

With no idea how much longer I'll be here, I flick my wrist in an instinctive swipe toward the dashboard, awakening the radio from its slumber.

The speakers grumble back to life, a low hum rising from their depths, their voices crackling and droning in response to my summons.

My fingers swipe through the short list of satellite stations offered by the truck's receiver, an add-on feature on this otherwise standard-issue Rifterport 7-series cargo truck. Despite its sleek design, the limited radio selection in this state-of-the-art vehicle leaves much to be desired.

After all this technological advancement, one would assume that, as we moved our transit systems to the sky, it should have eased the congestion from the ground, but we haven't entirely made it there yet.

Yes, automated navigation systems are now as integral to any hybrid flight model as the engines that propel them. And yet, despite these advancements, there are always those reckless individuals who deem themselves superior to AI guidance. Take, for instance, the audacious miscreant ahead of me, who, in his misplaced confidence, disengaged the autopilot, hurtling himself recklessly through the air speedways. Now, his crumpled craft, having collided with a public transit vehicle, clings to the tunnel's precipice, his arrogance entrapping all of us within this airborne gridlock for over an hour.

Looks like I may be here for a little, I think as I change prompts on screen from the monotonous traffic reporter boring my speakers to death to an assortment of music folders that appear on my center dash screen.

With a swift upward swipe, I sift through the digital archives of my music collection, landing on a highlight—a thoughtfully curated playlist crafted by Ave. This special collection was designed precisely for predicaments such as this, a sonic antidote to the mounting frustrations of a stagnant commute. The *Try not to kill anyone* playlist, a name steeped in our shared sense of humor, seems fitting for the moment. With a determined tap, I select the folder and grab the volume dial, cranking it up until the truck's sound system protests its limits.

A prompt materializes on the screen, a little icon inquiring whether I wish to lift the volume restriction. With a satisfying jab of my finger, I enthusiastically select *Yes*.

I lean back into the seat and watch as the ceaseless rush of opposing traffic whizzes by, each vehicle a streak of light and sound zipping past my stillness. The harsh cacophony of horns and city noises dwindles, succumbing to the gentle rise of the first song. The music, like a gentle tide, washes over me, providing solace amidst the urban chaos.

My fingers lightly drum out the rhythm on the truck's controls, synchronizing with the rhythmic pulse of the three-four pattern that underpins this gentle symphony. Avery, ever-attentive to my mood swings, highlighted this piece precisely for those moments when my patience hangs by a thread.

The melody unfolds, a high-octave chorus delivered by a delicately bowed instrument, soaring effortlessly over the steady, graceful progression of the lower, larger strings. It's a musical conversation, a perfectly composed waltz born from the genius of a deceased composer: Nicoli Saviano. Even in death, his musical legacy continues to resonate, calming ruffled souls within the pandemonium of city life.

I know I should at least try what Ave has recommended, so I hesitantly close my eyes and listen to the grand strings of the orchestra, softly strung full-measured whole notes, letting them release the impatience from my body. Each pluck of the strings and Ornahorns releases more endorphins from my spine down to my fingertips. My eyes are still closed, and I feel the music making my anxiety drift away. The elegant breath of the winded instruments creates a call-and-response progression with the keys' harmonic melody. I sit pensively, listening to the song nearing its finale, note after note releasing more and more of my tension, and just as the music is nearing its climax—

Honk! The brusque blare of a horn behind me shatters the tranquil ambiance, jerking me out of my meditative respite.

Startled, I blurt, "What the f—"

An ironic smile tugs at my lips. *Of course.* I laugh. A moment of peace was too much to ask for in this bustling city. Peering into the rearview camera, I zoom in on an irate individual behind me, their flailing hand and angry shouts registering as a distant spectacle.

Drawing a calming breath, I say, "Okay, okay." My hand offers a conciliatory wave as the previously static traffic starts to flow once again.

Reality has reasserted its hold; it's time to navigate the familiar path home.

I cast a wary glance through the windshield, silently questioning when this relentless storm would finally relinquish its stranglehold. Brooding, dark clouds swell ominously among the architectural giants, their murky shadows adding a sense of foreboding to the cityscape. The ceaseless rain performs an intricate ballet against the glass, droplets pinging and ricocheting in an endless cascade down the fog-kissed windshield.

I find myself speculating on the likelihood of a new weather record for Akereon City. With twelve consecutive days of torrential downpour, not a glimpse of sun or blue sky in sight, the city has been cloaked in a chill, misty shroud that saturates every street corner.

Typically, the oppressive grey is broken by occasional flashes of daybreak, but lately, it seems the city has been held captive under the weight of the rain. I can sense a significant surge brewing on the horizon, a gut feeling whispering of more stormy weather to come.

My automated sensors activate, and a one-armed wiper streams across the windshield back and forth from left to right, creating a faint screeching noise, as the bottom material is nearly worn to the metal bracket. The megastructures of Akereon City rush by in a dizzying blur, their imposing silhouettes vying for dominance in the skies of the city's upper west sector. Housing millions within their colossal walls, each structure presents a unique architectural identity, and yet there's an undeniable thread of familiarity running through them.

As I navigate the maze of buildings, East Village's bustling skyline recedes behind me, signaling my imminent arrival at Takashi Cybernetics HQ. Soon, I'll be able to unburden myself of the trusty Rifter and make my way home.

The workday is done, and I'm looking forward to a much-needed shower, not to mention that I'm only running off four hours of sleep. I'm tired—exhausted, even—and this repetitive trip back and forth has been an ongoing thing, day in and day out, for months. Wherever Ave and I end up, hopefully, I won't be flying back and forth as much.

On the verge of returning to headquarters, a call invades the melodic serenity playing through the speakers. The tri-tone octave leap of the ring-tone cuts through the music as an image of Aden Graves materializes on the screen, flanked by two enticing options:

< [ANSWER | REJECT] >

With a swift tap on the answer icon, my fingers glide the screen to the left. Suddenly, the windshield morphs into a vibrant conduit for a high-definition video call. There, in its panoramic grandeur, Aden is projected front and center. His mouth curves into an eager grin as he greets me. "Beck! How you doin'?" His words brim with an infectious enthusiasm.

"Graves, I'm just getting off work and heading home for the day."

"You got a spare hour? I wanted to meet up at The Wired Abyss. I wanted to have one last refresh before, you know, that thing we have coming up," he says.

Of course, he's referring to the job in a few days, but he isn't stupid enough just to blurt out any vital information over an unsecured work channel—actually, he might be.

"Why? The plan's solid; it's been a long day, and I just want to get home, see Ave, shower, and eat. My stomach is yelling at me, and I'm exhausted," I half-heartedly say.

Aden says, "Aw, come on, I won't keep you out too long. Plus, the Abyss has the best garlic noodles in town, you know that. My treat!"

He isn't wrong. I do love their garlic noodles.

I think for a second, glancing at the clock. "One hour. Then I'm gone," I say, scratching my rough stubble.

"Yes! Thanks, Beck. Let's say twenty minutes?"

As I glance upward, the gates of headquarters come into view. "I'll be there in ten," I reply, and end the call.

The viewport flickers into transparency mode, revealing the armored expanse of Takashi Cybernetics as my Rifter glides through the imposing rear gates. Flanking the entrance, guards in full armor and carrying KAR-7 armature cradle rifles capable of punching through most armor come into view. Security's grip here is as unyielding as an iron vice, with credentials and identifications meticulously displayed on my windshield, each complemented by a precisely clipped identification badge. The latter is a temporary loan that must be accounted for at day's end.

My eyes wander over the seamless horde of automatons populating the drop-off zone, an uncanny vision of my impending redundancy. It's a fleeting thought, yet starkly real, shadowed by the reality that android drivers have begun to dominate the roads of Vola Prime.

The diligent eyes of the security check my passes and Rifter's credentials with an almost-robotic precision. I turn my attention to the colossal structure looming over the roadway, tapering inward like a giant monolith of power. A triad of separate structures intersects to form an imposing, triangular leviathan of modern architecture. An unending stream of vessels and freighters, carriers of a myriad of wares, weaves in and out of the gates.

The Rifter begins moving into the large drop-off area, and I park in the designated spot. I start interfacing with my work tablet, cataloging today's routes and mileage, inserting the final log for the day, and clocking out. I push on the door, which opens upward, and then hop out, making sure to grab all my belongings from the seat. I can't tell you how many times I've left my phone in here.

As I start to walk away from the headquarters towards my car, I peer up the center tower to the top three floors of Takashi's penthouse. The rain beats against my face harder and harder as the storm surges from above.

See you soon, I think as I exit the main gate and walk to the employee parking lot.

My old transport sits in the same spot, as always. It's a solid hybrid-flight model, one of the earlier years. But I made sure to get the blacked-out Titaneer model. It is a bit more rugged and fully loaded than the stock version. The engine and exhaust upgrades I have done sound monstrous at an idle. This thing is full of muscle.

I quickly unlock the door and sit inside before I get soaked.

I access the computer mainframe and press the ignition button, and all the instruments light up in a blurred red-and-yellow pattern followed by an engine roar. The panel radiates a dim glow from the car's interior as I lift from the ground, and the landing struts disengage, retracting into the bottom of the vehicle. A loud jet pulse shakes under me as it lifts me higher into the air. Checking my mirrors, I reverse out of the parking structure and head towards The Wired Abyss.

As I glance out the window, I notice the rain never seems to completely remove the grime and despair from the city streets. Puddles and pollution fill the alleys and skies and reflect in the hopeless eyes of each beggar hoping for a warm and dry place to sleep. A Depression era-slum emerges before my eyes, and it isn't getting better. It's a melting pot of different people with no singular cultural viewpoint. Everywhere I look, it's someone different.

Also, my vision is constantly overloaded by the constant barrage of advertisements and holographic displays. Everyone sees something personal—ads for new cars and restaurants, porn, or dark, dirty secrets, all based on user history. Barely anything is private anymore. Most cars are equipped to be tools for the advertisers, broadcasting your location and confidential information and narrowing your ad selections to suit your needs and wants.

I can see the A.C.P.D. is in full force tonight; packs of officers are making traffic stops and arrests every other street. Like the rain, the police are an unrelenting force of nature, making life miserable for the ordinary people of Akereon City. It's best to keep a low profile, as they will happily pull you over for a broken taillight, then plant a controlled substance in your car. Most are dirty, so it's wise to keep your distance as much as possible.

Cameras are everywhere, and you can't hide if you want to—there's facial recognition in every officer's visual display, plus cell phone tracking. You can't even take a piss without someone knowing.

It's just another reason to get the hell out of here.

"Finally," I say as I make it through the underground slums. I pull into the parking lot of The Wired Abyss, shift the car into park, and get out.

"Jesus, this place looks worse than ever," I softly say to myself as I see two junkies being escorted out. Their faces are bloodied and bashed, and as one tries to yell something inaudible towards the two jacked security guards, blood spits out of his mouth to the ground. I'm almost certain there are teeth in the blood.

"Get the fuck out of here, and don't let me see you again," the taller of the two says to the incoherent men as they pass me, heading towards the street.

The underground is a haven for criminals, black-market traders, hacking software and coding, and bad people looking to do terrible things. The Wired Abyss, a spacious hub that takes up almost two entire blocks of the west sector, is the place for them. To be clear, when I say underground, I don't actually mean it's underground. It's more like a giant secure hub of different businesses and merchants, food, guns, drugs, and mischief. The A.C.P.D. never comes down this way, nor would they. They know better than to respond to a call in this sector. Most business owners and criminals just deal with problems using their own form of justice, and the A.C.P.D. lets it happen.

Two security officers dressed in Endonium armor and carrying guns to match stop me as I reach the entrance. The muffled deep rumble from a kick drum escapes from inside the underground hub. "Password," the bigger one to the left says with his hand on my chest.

"Touch me again, and you won't get that hand back," I say.

Looking to the beefcake next to him, he drops his hand and says again, "Password."

"*Pink balloon*," I quietly say. Aden had texted me today's password earlier. He nods and waves me through as he opens the large metal doors, allowing access to The Wired Abyss.

With each stride I take, the pulsating strobe lights and resonant thump of the kick drum amplify, their sonic and visual symphony piercing the darkened corridor. The ambient strains of underwater music grow increasingly distinct, their ethereal melodies shimmering through the dimly lit hallway.

The walls flanking my path are formed of transparent glass, revealing a tableau of cybernetically enhanced women enclosed within their glass cubicles. These boxes are stacked neatly alongside each other, creating an enticing spectacle for passersby. Their entrancing gazes, magnetically drawn to any susceptible nighttime reveler willing to part with a few dozen credits, offer an illusion of companionship for the lonesome.

These digital sirens promise an escape, a momentary break from one's burdens and worries. Their beckoning hands weave a tricky web of seduction, a tantalizing invitation to lose oneself in their digital allure.

"You alone, baby?" One asks very seductively.

But I'm immune to their call. I wave off their enticements with a firm shake of my head. *No thanks.*

The constricting, flickering confines of the corridor abruptly give way to the overwhelming sensory onslaught that is The Wired Abyss. A bustling nexus of merchants, black-market traders, and a dizzying array of exotic food and entertainment options, this place is a hotbed of frantic activity.

The Abyss is a frenzy of scents and sights, each more potent than the last. The aroma of sea creatures sizzling on open grills and soups simmering in deep pots cuts through the air, their bracing pungency lacing the atmosphere with an almost-sour tang. As I edge past food vendors, their vibrant stalls creating a captivating mosaic of colors and smells, I am flooded by the jarring sound of the market.

The pulsating music reverberating from the central system battles for sovereignty with the boisterous noise of haggling voices, each competing for the most advantageous bargains. Adding to the disorderly racket is the rambunctious scampering of stray animals, their unchecked antics further fueling the chaos of the crowded streets.

The mayhem is almost overpowering. Navigating the Abyss requires a particular breed of resilience—one that I've learned to master over time.

The Abyss is an indoor-outdoor hub, but it doesn't feel that way at times. The streets are tight, and the buildings stack over one another, creating a maze of structures. Some businesses lead you indoors, though most of it is outside. Surrounded by giant Endonium walls, it's impenetrable.

I turn to head through the crowd towards where Aden said to meet, shoving through the dozens of shoppers. I pass several table displays that showcase the most advanced weaponry on the market, from handguns to missile launchers, SAR-X10 prototype sniper rifles, scanners, facial recognition jammers, and even Takashi's newest addition, the *HALOFIELD* generators—holographic devices that project an artificial face over one's identity, shadowing them from facial recognition. Hackers and criminals love it—that is, if they can afford something that expensive. I'm talking twenty large or more.

Walking by a few more booths, I stop as a glint catches the corner of my eye. "You like?" says the oleaginous-skinned vendor behind the counter.

"How much?" I say as I walked up to the booth, pointing firmly towards a blade.

"This is a rare item," he says, offering me the item to inspect. "It's from the purest form of Endonium, refined to perfection."

The two-toned gunmetal-grey handle settles comfortably in my palm, its cool solidity radiating an assurance of quality. Tightening my grip, I press the embedded release button, and a compact tanto blade springs forth, the blade's uncurved surface gleaming under the market's fluorescent lights. It measures an impressive eleven inches from handle to tip.

"What's going on with the butt of the knife?" I ask the merchant, my eyes focusing on an unexpected indentation. "And why this odd recess on the edge?"

With a knowing smirk, the vendor says, "Turn the bottom of the handle, but be careful." His hand traces a twisting motion in the air, guiding me through the unknown mechanism.

As I cautiously rotate the handle's base, a brilliant white laser jolts to life along the blade's edge. It hums with an almost-sentient energy, the sporadic crackling betraying its volatile nature. I feel a subtle heat start to radiate from the blade, warming my fingers and adding an intriguing dimension to this alluring weapon. "For those tricky ropes or cables that just won't budge. I'd let that go for a fair price. One hundred credits, no less," the man offers.

"Not happening," I retort, shaking my head in quiet amusement. "I'll give you fifty."

"Heyyyyy, I need to earn a living too," the merchant protests, an odd mixture of indignation and desperation coloring his tone. "How about a compromise at seventy-five?"

"Fifty, or it stays with you," I say, but my words trail off as my contemplation lands on a far more intriguing object behind him. "Where did you get that?" I blurt out, pointing at the item.

"Oh, I see—a man of discerning tastes." The merchant preens, even as he carelessly blows snot out of his nose. With the same unclean hand, he retrieves the object that had caught my eye: a drone. "Do you know what this is?" he queries, laying the drone reverently on the counter. "This, my friend, is a true gem. I wouldn't part with it for less than two thousand credits."

Despite the hefty price tag, the offer is tempting. Drones like this are hard to come by—they're not typically available on the open market. Sure, Ave and I are saving up to get out of here, but she probably won't notice the missing credits for a few days. And after the upcoming job, I'll be swimming in more credits than I can count.

"This," the merchant boasts, trying to tip the scales in his favor, "is a TX-49 sensory drone from Galacom."

I can't hide my disbelief. "Where did you get this?" I ask, unable to keep the surprise out of my voice. "These are exclusive to Special Operation Division members," I point out.

"A reliable source," he replies vaguely, avoiding my stare. "It's in mint condition and completely programmable to your liking! I've had to disable some of the military coding protocols to prevent tracking, but other than that, it's been reset to default coding."

Taking a closer look, I must admit, the drone appears to be in impeccable condition. Excitement stirring within me, I ask, "Can I power it up?"

"Of course." The missing-toothed merchant nods, reaching for the control module to power it up. After a brief moment, the drone stirs to life, its rotors whirring as it levitates gently above the counter. "You'll need to integrate into its database and configure it to your specifications, but as I mentioned before, it's in perfect condition. And here's a deal: if you buy it now, I'll throw in the knife for free. Plus, you'll spread the word about me," he adds, his words racing to seal the deal.

Hard to pass up. "Deal," I say as I grab the blade and sheath to secure it around my leg. "Will you hold on to the drone till I get back? I have something to do first."

"No problem, no problem, but first, payment," he says.

The merchant patiently waits for his payment, so I raise my arm and touch his screen, transferring over two thousand. A chime dings on his display. "Payment Received. Thank you, stranger," the enthused seller says.

"If I come back and you've sold that drone, we'll have problems," I say.

"No worries, friend!" he says as he somewhat crouches behind the counter.

"See you soon," I say, my voice trailing off as I retreat towards the garlic noodle vendor where Aden waits for me.

The condensation from the drab grey air units leaks to the ground next to me as I saunter through a neon-lit alleyway. The pink light flickers as the electric buzz from the open door of a tattoo studio in front of me brings back several uncomfortable memories.

I have several tattoos, each marking different stages of my life, each holding its own set of grueling memories. But one session stands out above all: a relentless, agonizing journey of needle piercing skin, of ink being meticulously buried into my flesh. The design is simple—two parallel, uncompromisingly isometric lines running from my hand, up my arm, all the way to my neck, stopping just below my jawbone. The edges and lines, much like the blade I've just purchased, boast no curves or intricate embellishments—just stern, rigid sharp lines and corners forming with my arm.

In an era where under-skin implants project Holo-Derma imagery that shimmers and shifts, some may call my preference for traditional tattooing archaic. This new fad, with its ever-changing, holographic tattoos, may captivate some, but not me. There's an undeniable allure to the authenticity of a needle puncturing skin, the permanence of ink indelibly marking your body. Some even find the process therapeutic, a calming, meditative practice in an otherwise-noisy world.

Drawing my attention away from the alluring glow of the tattoo parlor, I finally spot the noodle vendor. Beyond the rain-kissed windows, I see him—Aden, patiently waiting.

Just as I approach the doors, three armed guards emerge from the noodle shop, causing the door to creak open. They are quickly followed by Takashi Sato, who halts in front of me. "You," he declares, leveling a pointed finger in my direction.

A wave of hesitation washes over me. I momentarily stop, giving him a slight, questioning nod. "Yeah?" I manage, an undercurrent of uncertainty lacing my voice. But even as I respond, my feet keep moving, carrying me onward, unwilling to face whatever confrontation Takashi Sato might bring.

"You work for me, yes?"

Takashi doesn't know you; he doesn't know you're working with his daughter. Just play it cool, I think as I try to maintain an air of nonchalance. I respond, "I do. Transport Department." My words ebb out slowly as tension coils within me. He stops just outside my personal space, fixing me with a penetrating stare that doesn't waver or stray. Real fucking uncomfortable.

My breathing becomes subtle, measured, aware that any misstep here could rapidly descend into a bloodbath. He reaches up in a calculated motion, plucking my work badge ID off my jacket. "Better put this away. Don't want you losing it now, do we?" he advises, placing it into my palm.

He then gifts me a long, probing stare and signals his guards to proceed. As quickly as he appeared, he vanishes into the thrumming crowd, leaving me slightly taken aback. I stand there for a moment, attempting to digest what just transpired. *Was that mere coincidence or something more? What the fuck was that about?* Shaking off the odd encounter, I pocket my badge and push open the door to the modest, brightly lit restaurant renowned for its top-notch garlic noodles. The tantalizing aroma greets me almost instantly, evoking a sigh of appreciation.

Aden is already seated at the center, his face obscured by his long blonde hair as his fingers blur over the keys of his laptop. He's chosen a spot adjacent to several vacant chairs, arranged in a half-circle around the solitary chef skillfully manipulating a wok.

Sliding into the seat next to him, I briefly catch Aden's attention. "Well, look who it is. Glad you finally made it," he says, a trace of mockery in his tone. Juggling between his chopsticks and the laptop, he inhales a mouthful of noodles with an air of nonchalance. "Have a bite, Beck. Take a load off," he suggests, the tail end of a noodle disappearing between his lips.

"Did you see Takashi in here a moment ago?" I ask, watching Aden make love to his food with a sort of perverse fascination.

"Heh, yeah," Aden mumbles around a mouthful of noodles. "He wanted to recruit me for another gig. Something about a deal with—"

My eyebrows shoot up. "You're kidding, right? You do understand"—I scan the room before leaning closer and dropping my voice—"that we're about to rob this man blind, don't you?"

"Absolutely," Aden replies cheerfully, sucking up a plump noodle with a loud slurp. "So what's the harm in getting paid twice?"

I shake my head, chuckling despite myself. "You never cease to amaze me, Graves."

From the counter, the chef hurls a command in our direction. "You," he barks, jabbing a finger at me. "You order something? Can't just sit here without ordering." His gruff voice echoes through the small restaurant.

"Uhm, let me have a double order of noodles, please. Thank you," I say, getting comfortable.

"Jiro special coming up!" he says as the sizzling of the ingredients fills the small restaurant.

Fuck, it smells good.

"How was work?" Aden says, closing his laptop to give me his full attention.

"Better than being shot at. You could have an out too," I say, shifting in my seat.

Aden pauses, the chopsticks midway to his mouth. He turns to look at me, his expression unreadable. Then he sighs, setting his chopsticks down. "It's not that simple, Beck," he says, and there's a weariness in his voice that I've never heard before. "Ezrek... he doesn't let go. You know that."

"I made it out, Aden. I'm here; I'm safe. You can do it, too." My hand is still resting on his back, and I give him a firm, reassuring squeeze.

Aden is silent for a moment, staring at the bowl of noodles in front of him. Then, very slowly, he nods. "Maybe... maybe you're right, Beck," he finally admits, looking up to meet my worry.

"You can get out anytime—take your cut and disappear. Leave this fucking life behind. With your talents, you could be doing something good. Not wasting your life on Prime."

Aden falls silent, looking down at his near-empty bowl. He's always been quiet, contemplative, not one for expressing his feelings openly. But now, in this moment of vulnerability, I can see him wrestling with his thoughts. It's a hard realization, accepting that your life has strayed far from the path you'd hoped for, but it's a necessary one.

He finally lifts his gaze back to me, eyes a deep, glowing red. "You can't be responsible for me, Beck," he says quietly, looking at me as if he's seeing me for the first time. "You can't protect me from my own choices. But... but I do appreciate the sentiment. It... it means a lot."

Despite the seriousness of the conversation, I can't help but smile. It's a small, pained smile, but a smile nonetheless. "That's all I can do, Aden. Offer my help. It's up to you to take it."

"Order up!" Jiro shouts.

I take a large bite of my noodles, feeling the delicious warmth spread through me, both from the food and the comfort of having this candid conversation with Aden. We've shared many moments throughout the years, but this one seems... different. He has a decision to make, and I can only hope he makes the right one. But for now, at least, we have this moment. And the food's not too bad, either.

With that, the conversation lulls, and we both turn our attention back to the food. But I can see something's shifted in Aden. Maybe it's hope, or maybe it's fear. Only time will tell.

As we polish off the last of our noodles and sink deeper into our chairs, the aftereffect of several drinks becoming apparent, I catch Aden's uneasy drifting stare. The autopilot ride home seems more appealing by the second.

"I'm not sure about this upcoming job, Beck," Aden finally confesses, his words wavering slightly from the alcohol. "Something feels off. It's as if

Ezrek is withholding information from us. Plus, his absence over the past few weeks is... unsettling."

"I hear you, Aden," I respond, matching his somber tone. "Ezrek's lack of presence is odd, but we've dealt with less transparency before. Let's not lose focus on what we've got planned. He's a busy guy. I'm sure everything is fine."

"Can we go over it one more time?"

Taking a moment to ensure our conversation remains private, I lean in closer and begin to articulate the plan. "We're going to make our entrance from the sky, dropping directly onto the rooftop of Takashi HQ. You and Drake will control the operation from the jet, neutralizing security protocols on the top level. The conference being held that night works to our advantage; most of the personnel will be preoccupied. The rooftop is typically patrolled by three teams, each with a pair of guards. Once we've quietly dealt with them, you will unlock the roof access when we plug into their network."

"Our contingency plan is Briggs. If things take a wrong turn, he's there for heavy artillery support. Other than that, he stays in the jet. Upon reaching Takashi's penthouse, Naomi and I will infiltrate, neutralizing any security present. You'll be our eyes and ears in there. Once inside, we get to the meat of the operation. We'll crack Takashi's safe to get to the Master Key drive. It's a treasure trove of his illegal activities—accounts, transactions, hidden assets. He's hoarding millions there. After we secure it, we'll transfer everything to a safe account of our choosing and fade away. It's a clean job if we play our cards right; no one needs to get hurt. Then we rendezvous with Ezrek at the safe house."

Seeing Aden's contemplative face, I reiterate, "Naomi assured us the Master Key is in the office. She trusts Ezrek's plan, and so do I. But what's really eating at you, Aden? What are you truly worried about? We've studied this plan inside and out. It's solid."

Shaking his head, he simply mutters, "It's just a gut feeling. Something about the job..." His voice trails off.

"We've got this, Aden," I assure him, my voice firm. "We're prepared, and we'll adapt if we need to. That's what we do. That's what we've done."

Aden pauses, running his fingers through his unkempt hair. "I don't know, Beck. It's just... Takashi's no fool. He wouldn't keep such incriminating evidence in one place, especially not his own office. And there's something about Ezrek... He's been acting... strange. More reserved, secretive."

I chew on this new information, remembering my own encounter with Takashi outside the restaurant. There's something unsettling about this job; I can feel it too. But what choice do we have? We're in this now, and there's no turning back.

"We're a team, Aden," I say, putting my drink down. "We've got each other's backs. If something goes wrong, we'll handle it. We always do."

Aden nods, but the worry doesn't leave his eyes. We finish our drinks in silence, each lost in our thoughts. But despite the dread that seems to hang over us, I can't help but feel a sense of fellowship. We're in this together, for better or worse.

"I—I think—" He stops, taking in the last of his drink.

"Come on, Aden, spit it out."

"Nothing. Never mind. I think it's just pre-job nerves getting to me."

"You sure?" I ask.

"Yeah, I just want to finish our drinks and hang with you for a little, if that's okay?"

"Of course," I say as I grab his shoulder and smile.

That's how the rest of the night goes. We nurse our drinks, indulge in good food, and enjoy each other's company. There's laughter, old stories rehashed, jokes about past mishaps, and even a few moments of introspective silence. Despite the shadow hanging over our heads, tonight is about living in the moment. It's about good company, comfort food, and, for once, not worrying about the world outside.

I know Avery is waiting for me to get home, but I send her a message that I may be out late with Aden. I'm worried about him. He seems much more frail than usual, like a strong gust of wind could push him over. He's a good man, a good friend, and he deserves so much better than what life has dealt him. He's a pure soul, which is hard to come by nowadays. Whether I like it or not, he's probably one of my best friends. With everything we've been through and how much we've lived through, we have a history together, and it's hard to watch as he slowly kills himself day after day, but no matter how many words are spoken to the ears of an addict, the words simply fall to the ground, then wash away in the harsh Akereon rain.

Aden reaches for his cred-chip as we prepare to leave, but before he can even say, "I've got the bill," I spot movement in my peripheral vision—two men converging on us. A quick appraisal, and my gut clenches—gun in one hand, knife in the other.

Casually, the larger of the two men saunters over, muscles straining under a tight shirt, his hand heavy on Aden's shoulder, pushing him back into his seat. The cool steel of a blade presses subtly against Aden's side. "Where you off to in such a hurry, Graves?" he asks in a thick, menacing tone.

From behind the counter, hands raised in a placating gesture, Jiro, the seasoned vendor, sensing the tension, blurts out, "No trouble!"

But the thug's partner isn't in a mood to negotiate. "Just keep that trap shut if you value your life," he snaps, brandishing the knife at Jiro, who wisely recedes against the wall, hands still raised.   I keep my composure, my eyes locked on Aden as he addresses the thugs. His voice trembles, but there's a hidden message in his words. I understand. I remain seated, following his silent cue.

The barrel of a gun presses against my back, a reminder of the danger we're in. I take a slow, deliberate breath, feeling the weight of the situation. With my hand discreetly hidden, I touch the handle of the knife strapped to my ankle, its presence reassuring me.

In this tense moment, I can't help but feel a surge of satisfaction. The investment in the knife has already proved its worth. It's a small comfort within the danger that surrounds us. I stay patient, waiting for the opportune moment to act.

I watch as the tension escalates between Aden and the heavy set, greasy man, the air crackling with animosity. It's clear that Aden's involvement in some shady dealings has caught up with him, and the consequences are unfolding right before my eyes.

My grip tightens around the concealed knife, ready to intervene if the situation takes a violent turn, but for now, I maintain my position, remaining seated as instructed.

Aden, displaying a surprising confidence, retorts, "The code was flawless, Greko. If there were issues, it was your incompetence, not my work."

Greko's face contorts with anger, his voice growing more menacing. "I want my damn money back, or I'll make sure you regret it," he says, his face inches away from Aden's.

"Listen, guys, why don't you sit, relax, and have some noodles before this ends with you in the back of an ambulance?" I say as I stand with the gun in my back.

"Big words, coming from such a small fry," the thug behind me taunts, a smirk forming on his face.

Aden, ever the quick-thinker, interjects, "Nah, look at him. He's in shape, just a little shorter than us." He gestures toward me, a mischievous glint in his eyes.

The bigger thug raises an eyebrow, considering Aden's observation. "Well, I mean, he's average, isn't he? How tall are you?" he asks.

Caught off-guard by the unexpected topic of conversation, I respond with a deadpan expression. "Oh, you know, the usual. Just your run-of-the-mill average height. Not too tall, not too short. Just right." I shrug, playing along with the absurdity of the situation.

Aden tries to redirect the conversation, sensing the tension still simmering. "Guys, guys, let's focus here. I'm sure we can come to some arrangement, right?"

I seize the opportunity to inject a touch of humor. "Yeah, I think we're getting a bit off-topic, gentlemen. Why don't you leave now, let us finish paying Jiro, and we can take this outside for a proper debate on height and its implications on criminal negotiations? Sound fair?"

Their perplexed expressions give way to a brief moment of levity, and even Jiro chuckles nervously behind the counter.

"Enough chit-chatting. Pay us now, or else," the gunman demands, putting his hand on my shoulder.

With a swift and forceful motion, I wrench the thug's arm off my shoulder, propelling him forward. His face collides with the sharp edge of the bar, resulting in a gruesome explosion of teeth and the shattering of glass plates. Blood streams down his face from multiple lacerations, then he screams in pain.

Caught off-guard by the sudden turn of events, Greko releases his grip on Aden. Sensing the opportunity, my blade slices through the air, coming to a halt just inches away from Greko's throat. "I think we've had enough talk, don't you?"

Greko, visibly shaken and confused, mutters, "Who are you?"

A sinister smile curves on my lips as I press the blade harder against his throat. "The wrong guy," I say. "Touch Aden again, and it'll be the last thing you ever do."

Releasing my grip, I allow Greko to stumble back, his focus shifting to his battered and barely conscious companion.

"My fucking teeth, man." The bloodied-face man can barely speak as his lips and gums pour red.

"Go," I demand. Greko carries his friend away, whining and licking their wounds as they fall out the double door yelling, "You'll pay for this!" It's the same jarring nonsense every thug and degenerate comes up with, and they disappear into the sea of people.

"Ah, fuck, man, I'm sorry," Aden says as he starts to pick up the mess on the floor.

"No problem, buddy, just get the next ones," I say, helping him pick up.

"The n-next ones?" he says, stuttering.

"The noodles."

"Oh, the noodles!"

"I'll always have your back, Aden, but a problem with coding? What the fuck?"

"If there was a problem, it was that they are too dumb to know how to use the software properly. My part was perfect. Not my fault they're idiots."

"Just stay out of trouble, okay?" I say, brushing him off. Turning towards

Jiro, I apologize. "Sorry, Jiro."

"No problem; people come around here causing problems too much."

I notice Greko's friend dropped his wallet, so I pick out his cred-chips and throw them to Jiro. "Here's a little extra for you. Those should pay for the damages." He nods in compliance, thanking me.

"I'll see you in a few days, alright? Stay clean," I say. "Call me if you need anything, and tell Ezrek to call me if you hear from him," I say, giving Aden a hug and heading to the door.

"Hey, Beck," Aden calls out, catching my attention.

I turn around, curious to hear what he has to say. "Yeah?" I reply.

Aden takes a moment, his words carrying a weight of concern. "Just... just be careful out there, okay? Watch your back."

"You too, brother," I respond. With those parting words, I make my way towards the vendor to collect my newly acquired drone.

Leaving the anarchic atmosphere of The Wired Abyss behind, I embark on a twenty-minute drive towards my apartment building. The anticipation builds as I pull into my garage and step out of the car, the drone resting on the seat next to me.

I set the drone on the top of my trunk and search for the power button on the control module. Finally finding it, I press the button, and the center light flickers before gradually brightening to a soothing vivid blue. The drone springs to life, hovering slightly above the trunk, its unwavering blue optical lens fixed upon me.

"Well, that's comforting," I say, only to be interrupted by the glitched voice of the drone. It stammers its introduction, its voice bit-crushed and glitching.

"Hello. My n-name is TX-49, I am your division s-scouting drone. How may I assist you today?"

Not a good start, I think, adjusting the control module. "My name is Owen Beck. I am your commanding officer. What parameters are you assigned?"

I inquire, genuinely curious about the capabilities of this particular model.

The drone remains silent for a moment, as if pondering its response. Finally, it turns its attention back to me and repeats its initial statement, as if stuck in a loop.

I let out a sigh, realizing that the drone is indeed faulty. "Looks like I'll have to open you up tomorrow and see if I can fix you. Otherwise, I'll have to pay a visit to that merchant," I say.

"You're faulty," the drone quietly responds, catching me off-guard.

"What?" I ask, peering at the drone in confusion.

Once again, it repeats its introductory statement. "Hello. My name is TX-49, I am your division scouting drone. How may I assist you today?" It just stares at me with its blank eye. Frustration washes over me, and I decide to power it off, closing the trunk with a defeated sigh.

A THIEF'S END

AS I PLUNGE through the icy curtain of the night, my eyes closed, locked away from the rushing world outside, the blustery wind whips around me, stiffening my muscles and serenading the thrill of the descent. Opening my eyes, I see a holographic emblem of a cybercafe reflecting atop a building below, stirring memories of a time when life was simpler. The image of Avery surfaces, as vivid as the day we met. Her smile, radiant and potent, had the power to unravel the galaxy. Her hazel eyes, brimming with warmth, held mine. Time stalled, the world blurred, and I understood what I truly desired—a lifetime entwined with hers.

The city's skyscrapers morph into an impressionist's painting as I snap back to reality, blinking against the distortion. Takashi Cybernetics, the pinnacle of my focus, comes into sight. With a quick movement, I adjust my plummet, bracing for impact. My cable stretches taut, then disengages with a muted click, the sound devoured by the night. I land and settle on the drenched rooftop, a whisper behind my team member, Naomi Sato.

"Good luck," Kruger says over comms.

"Keep your eyes open," Aden responds.

Silence dominates, even as the relentless rain drums against our rifles' cold, slick barrels. Peering through the water-speckled scope, I spot two guards, their shadows hulking beside the railing opposite the grated catwalk. Thunder roars in the distance, its deafening upsurge shrouding our stealthy progression. A lightning spear cleaves the sky, bathing us in a brief glare before our shapes disappear into the shadows.

My fingers curl around the stippled grip of my weapon, a familiar sensation grounding me as the city's luminance spills across the undulating clouds above. Aerial billboards float listlessly, their vibrant purple and yellow lights carving rhythmic figure eights in the gloom. I commit the pattern to memory, anticipating each loop with precision.

Naomi goes first. As the rotating lights reach the apex of their rhythmic loop, she springs into action. A fleeting silhouette against the urban backdrop, she dances between beams of purple and yellow, her body low and her steps soundless on the wet metal. Just as the lights sweep back, she rolls under the cover of a maintenance alcove, vanishing from sight as effectively as a specter.

My heart is steady and slow. I watch for her signal—three quick taps of her gloved hand against the alcove's rim. It's my turn now. With a slow breath, I move. I feel the lights almost graze my back, an electrifying presence urging me to move faster, to be swifter. A half-second's miscalculation, a single faltering step, and the mission could be compromised.

Finally, I slip into the same alcove, pressing myself against the cold metal wall. Naomi and I exchange a glance as our bodies press against each other's. "Don't even think about it," she whispers.

"Wouldn't dream of it," I respond softly as we break cover and head beneath the catwalk.

"You have one incoming," Aden says.

"Hold." I signal with a quick hand gesture, prompting us both to duck and meld with the darkness. Crouched beneath the skeletal bridge, we wait as the rhythmic clanging of the guard's armored boot rings overhead. We remain motionless, our breaths held captive, as we allow the guard to lumber by us, oblivious to our presence.

As soon as he passes behind us, I pivot, dispatching a single sleeper round through the metal grating into his neck. His collapse is quick; he falls over the railing, and his body crumples to the cold rooftop, incapacitated. The splash and thud are dampened by the storm and thunder. Naomi then drags his body under the catwalk and out of sight.

I divert my focus back to our primary objective—the hidden elevator. The architectural blueprints of the building spark to life in the heads-up display of my optical eye tracer, showing the outlines of our battlefield. The public access point on the northwest end is indicated, but that's a path we're not treading tonight. A secret route is our target, revealed only by Naomi's reliable intel—Takashi's private elevator, discreetly tucked on the opposite side of the roof beside a personal aircraft landing port, veiled under the guise of metallic stairs that official blueprints won't acknowledge. This concealed route is our expressway to Takashi's inner sanctum—his office.

His penthouse is a fortress, a self-sustaining entity disconnected from the building's primary power grid and network, powered by a concealed source deep beneath the structure. Graves can't infiltrate this building unless we plug his network link device into Takashi's elusive network.

Naomi and I diverge, each of us assuming responsibility for opposite sides of the rooftop, our paths parallel yet distinct.

"Five," I whisper, my grip tightening around the trigger housing, counting the threats in my field of view.

"Six, you idiot." Naomi's voice crackles through the comms, laced with her characteristic abrasion.

"Yeah, I count six, Beck," Aden says.

"Getting soft, Becky," Kruger says, chiming in with Aden.

Rolling my eyes, I revise my count. "Alright, let's say five and a half. Ex-military, private sector."

A weary sigh from Naomi graces the comms, possibly accompanied by an eye roll of her own.

From the corner of my vision, I catch the silhouette of two guards and a drone appearing from the north. The drone hovers just above them, its scanning beams sweeping the landscape like a lighthouse beacon—a big upgrade from my TX-49 model purchased from The Wired Abyss. I left it at home since I haven't uploaded the new sub-specs. Another item on my to-do list is if we survive the night.

"There, Naomi. You're right over it," Aden says.

Naomi crouches down to the rain-soaked rooftop, retrieving a compact grey datalink satellite from her pack. It unfolds like an origami model, its four segments splayed out meticulously. Swift and silent, she cracks open an electric module unit underfoot with a small blade, hitching the satellite to the building's nervous system. Her nod, brisk and sure, signals the next phase.

"Graves, initiate the upload," I say, my eyes not leaving the leisurely patrol of the guards ahead. "Cillian, move into position."

"Copy," says Cillian in youthful, high-pitched affirmation. High above the sweep of rooftop scanners, remaining a ghost in the stormy night, he vertically aligns the jet to us, and the satellite beneath us whirrs to life, initiating a concealed handshake with the veiled ship above. The elements show no mercy as the winds whip into a frenzy, rain hammers the rooftop, and thunder growls in the distance. The storm is the perfect heist distraction.

"Anytime," I say, the tension curdling in my gut. The guards haven't headed this way, yet.

"Just another second," Aden says.

On my helmet's display, an upload icon signals the start of a silent assault, a virus slithering its way into the heart of Takashi's network, puncturing their firewalls ruthlessly.

"Next time, present me with something actually worthy of my skills," Aden quips, a smug tone in his voice.

A progress bar materializes on our digital screens, commencing at zero. The progress inches forward incrementally, advancing exclusively in even numerals.

"Incoming!" Aden announces.

Stealthily, I cast a furtive glance, sufficient to validate that a drone has deviated from its assigned trajectory and is now directing its course towards us. "T-minus ten seconds," I say softly as Naomi extracts a miniature orbital drone from her utility belt and hurls it into the tempestuous skies.

The device springs to life, gyrating before it activates and ascends into a protective hover above us. It conducts a comprehensive scan of the rooftop, drawing each guard and drone with radiographic accuracy, highlighting them in a crimson hue on our visual interfaces.

Five seconds, Naomi's open hand signals.

Anchored to our rooftop vantage point while the upload continues, we find ourselves ensnared in a strained hush. The coarse urgency in Kruger's voice shatters the quietude, resonating through our communication devices. "Hurry the fuck up!"

"Not helping," I say as the drone approaches our position, the whine of its rotors amplifying. I hide behind a corner and glance out to see its position. It's nearly here. "Naomi, hide!"

The display flashes "95%" as the drone's whirring and trilling become tangible presences; It rounds the corner and stops just in front of me, making a loud mechanical drawl. *Damn it.*

A luminous azure scanner covers me, contouring my physique from head to sole. I regulate my respiration, my palm poised above the switch to engage my rifle's live rounds, every tendon taut in anticipation of an imminent explosive clash. My finger lingers over the trigger, a mere fraction from initiating a hail of gunfire.

I inhale profoundly. *Maintain composure.*

And then, as if by providential grace, Aden's voice pierces the tension. "Upload finalized."

There's no opportunity to exhale a sigh of relief as the drone concludes its assessment. An odd approval signal emanates from its metallic frame, transitioning from blue to green. It momentarily hesitates, seemingly bewildered, then proceeds to the opposing end of the rooftop. We recommence breathing. *That was way too close.* I relax my grip.

The team is now seamlessly integrated into their data flux, rendering us invisible to drones and visual monitoring. "I looped the feed inside. You are good to go," Aden says.

We establish a connection to their network. Courtesy of Aden's innovative programming, the malware has substituted our DLPNs—Data-Link-Protocol-Numbers, unique identifiers allocated to each citizen of Vola Prime—with those of the rooftop guards.

As we look ahead, the faint outlined path in our visors shows where the hidden elevator is, down a short metal staircase next to the landing pad. Heading toward it, we hear two guards talking, and we both press our bodies against the pitch-black.

"Man, did you catch that weather reporter on VPWN-7 last night? Quite a storm, right? Fuckin jugs on that one," one guard says, his voice tinged with a thirsty note.

"Nah, I've moved on to the digital age. Don't even need to step out of my bedroom."

"Gross, dude. You need to get out more," his companion grumbles, pausing on the edge of our hiding spot, blissfully oblivious to our presence.

"Hey, my free time is my business. Do I rag on you about your obsession with vegetable gardening? No, because I respect your passions, Sam," the other guard retorts, his tone borderline petulant.

"So, your passion is virtual porn?" Sam inquires, disbelief bleeding into his voice.

"Don't knock it 'til you've tried it." He then proceeds to pantomime a martial-arts move just inches from Naomi and I.

"Fuck this," she snaps, her patience wearing thin as she appears from the shadows.

"What?!" the guards yelp, spinning around in surprise.

In a sudden, fluid motion, Naomi springs from her crouch, grabbing the first guard by his collar. She vaults over him, and his face smashes into the floor with a sickening thud. The sound of five, maybe six, teeth scattering across the rooftop is followed by the dull thud of his unconscious body.

The second guard's terrified hands fumble for his weapon, but Naomi's already on him. She whips out a compact electromagnetic baton and slams it against his neck. A high-intensity current zips through him, his body seizing before he urinates his pants and slumps onto the ground unconscious.

"They're not...dead, right?" I ask, glancing at the downed guards.

"Probably?" Naomi shrugs nonchalantly, landing a casual kick on the unconscious guard. "He's still breathing," she adds dismissively.

After dragging the guards into the shadow of a nearby exhaust, we're about to return to the secret entrance when Naomi stiffens.

"Another duo of guards—ten o'clock." Aden's voice comes through, tinged with static. We hide behind some conditioner exhaust fans, crouching with our trigger fingers ready.

The rooftop is slick with rain, reflecting the pale light from the city. The wind whips around us, carrying with it the smell of wet concrete and the distant hum of traffic. We exchange a quick glance, ready to strike.

A helmeted guard's voice, distorted and deepened by a vocoder, slices through the night air. "I swear I heard something." Their advance is methodical, painstaking; every nook and cranny is inspected with a heightened sense of caution, the beams of their rail-mounted torches methodically dissecting the darkness.

In the stillness that hangs heavy in the air, just as the guards break the corner, the sound of two soft clicks fills our ears as we press down on our triggers, delivering blows that render the guards unconscious. They crumple to the ground, becoming nothing more than lifeless forms on the rain-drenched metal. We are nearly to the elevator.

As the guards lie motionless at our feet, I get a read. "Where's the drone?" I say, activating my neck comms.

"Next to the last guard."

"Let me have a go," Kruger interjects from the ship, his voice tinged with ennui.

"Keep comms clear," I caution as we press ourselves against a wall near the final guard.

He's unaware of our proximity, and has the drone by his side. I seize the moment. Vaulting over the metal staircase, the clatter of my boots on the landing makes the guard twitch. "Huh?" he mumbles, the sound muffled by his vocoder.

Before he can swivel completely, the stock of my gun smashes into his jawbone, sending him crumbling to his knees. Alerted by the commotion, the drone activates its weapons and pivots towards me, but hesitates as it scans my coding. In that instant, Naomi lunges, her blade skewering its base plate and core processor. Sparks scatter like fireflies as the drone scrapes across the rooftop, fizzling and popping before succumbing to darkness.

Wiping droplets of oil and lubricant from her blade, Naomi shatters the silence. "That wasn't so hard."

I exhale a breath. A smirk creeps onto my face, despite the lingering anxiety that tints my words. "You didn't have to do that. It wasn't a threat," I quip.

"This is my night of fun, don't ruin it."

I scoff.

"All clear," Aden chimes in. "It looks like we have a clear route. However, I'm not picking up a feed for Takashi's office."

"Storm is picking up, let's keep it moving," Cillian says from the ship.

We can see a white, x-rayed elevator frame through the wall through our displays. Aden has dug into the network.

The concealed metal panels smoothly retract, splitting apart to unveil a luxurious private elevator adorned with a lavish gold couch and delicate white-marble inlays. Its exquisite craftsmanship astounds me—every inch of the elevator trim is meticulously handcrafted from the finest refined Endonium.

Ready to go, I signal to Kruger. He descends from the jet with a faint rumble, landing just behind us.

"Let's go," Naomi asserts confidently, stepping into the elevator.

"Make room," Kruger remarks, joining her inside the elevator.

I hesitate for a moment looking up to Aden and Cillian where the jet hovers, then back to Naomi and Kruger. I can't help but think back to just before I left Avery, thinking I should have stayed.

"Beck," Naomi says, breaking my drifting.

Regret gnaws at me.

"It's now or never, Beck. This is your chance to leave with Avery," Naomi suggests, her words uncharacteristically loaded.

Standing in the hidden elevator beneath the colossal landing pad, Kruger and Naomi fix their gaze on me. The rain momentarily subsides, and the wind whispers through the city's structures. Closing my eyes momentarily, I inhale deeply and step into the elevator. The doors seal shut behind me.

"I should have stayed," I utter under my breath.

"What did you say?" Naomi asks.

I turn to face her. "Nothing," I say as my eyes dart around the elevator.

It's filled with the intoxicating aroma of rich pelt, saturating the air as it descends silently, devoid of any audible mechanical sounds. There is no discernible movement that could be felt either. Puzzled, I lean closer to the wall and ask, "Is this thing even on?"

"Look at the screen above you," Naomi retorts, pushing me behind her to take the lead.

Glancing up, I notice the elevator indicating its descent to the penthouse. "I knew that," I say, clearing my throat to mask my momentary confusion.

The journey is brief, and soon we feel a subtle shift in movement. "Here we go," Naomi whispers as the elevator doors split in the middle, accompanied by a harmonious tri-octave note, revealing Takashi's dark private office.

We quietly step out into the darkness, sweeping the room with our infrared optics, methodically clearing each corner. Floor-to-ceiling windows encompass the entire space, offering a nearly three-hundred-and-sixty-degree panoramic view, except for one wall that leads to his top-floor living quarters. The sheer size of Takashi's office dwarfs my loft apartment at least twenty times over. Vola Prime's most exquisite furniture resides within its walls, ranging from rare paintings to a raw Endonium-stringed instrument positioned near the rain-streaked window. I can sense that many of these custom items are illicit imports from far-flung planets. It's no wonder that most of the population despises him, including his daughter.

We take a moment to absorb the luxury surrounding us, aware that beneath this elegant façade lies a man who lives a life others can only dream of in their wildest fantasies.

A low, chilling laugh cuts through the previously dead silence within the office, causing an abrupt shift in the atmosphere. The lights flicker on suddenly, illuminating the room. Startled, I speedily turn my eyes toward the source of the sound, whipping my rifle into a defensive stance.

An older man's voice resonates from behind the still black leather chair, flatly addressing Naomi. "Hello, daughter." Chuckling lightly, he adds, "I see you've brought some friends. How amusing." With his words, he turns his chair to face Naomi directly.

Kruger and I exchange puzzled glances, our rifles subtly trained on Takashi, unsure how to proceed.

"Father." Naomi sighs, acknowledging his presence. She gestures for us to lower our weapons. "I can handle this."

Takashi, fingers interlocked on the black transparent desk, says, "Confident as ever, Naomi. But you never got it, did you? Never understood what I was building. You turned into my Achilles' heel. Took from me the only person I ever cared for. I can't forgive that." His voice trembles with barely contained fury.

"Mom's death wasn't on me. I spent my life trying to prove myself to you. But growing up, I realized I'd never be enough. Not for you, not for your empire. You tossed me aside like I was nothing," Naomi shoots back, disappointment seeping into her words. "Apologies for the letdown. Why are you here? Didn't you have some bullshit humanitarian award to receive?"

"I received a tip from an anonymous sender. Had to see if it was true." Takashi rises from his throne-like chair and reaches under the table.

Anonymous sender? I think.

"Don't move," Naomi warns, drawing her blade. It gleams faintly pink, reflecting the nearby holo-fronts.

"Too late." He smirks, pressing a button.

The doors fly open, revealing four armed guards. Their shouts for us to drop our weapons reverberate through the room. Outgunned and with my rifle on sleeper mode, I have little choice. Kruger and I drop our rifles and slide them away. *Fuck.*

Takashi, hands running through his slick gray-and-black hair, watches, waiting for Naomi's move. "Planning to kill me, Naomi?" he asks.

Naomi's hand drifts to her belt. "Crossed my mind, yeah."

Takashi nods at the guards to cuff Kruger first, apparently deeming me less of a threat. Naomi tightens her grip on her blade's cloth handle and raises her voice. "I never wanted anything from you!"

"Guys, report." Aden chimes in, wondering what the hell we are doing.

"It's getting pretty rough out here, guys. I don't know how much longer I can hover here," Cillian says, his voice carrying slight concern.

"We are burned," I quietly respond.

I stay quiet as a guard shoves me from the back. "Shut up!"

"What? Should we abort?" Aden responds.

A self-assured smile plays on Takashi's lips. Basking in his elitist demeanor as he adjusts the tie of his expensive traditional wear, he commands, "Arrest them all."

As the guards move to apprehend Kruger and me, Naomi swiftly turns around, throwing a round, spiraling razor-sharp disc through the air. It follows a one-eighty pattern, slicing through the space from left to right and embedding itself in the wall behind the last guard holding me.

All four guards appear confused, their gazes darting between Naomi and Takashi. Meanwhile, Takashi stands across the room, shocked. The guard above me looks down, his eyes wide with disbelief, just before the top of his skull slides off, revealing his perfectly sliced brain. His lifeless body collapses to the ground. The other three guards meet similar fates, their torsos or necks split in half, their heads decapitated and their bodies dismembered. Fragments of their remains fall to the ground.

"What...what did you just do?" Takashi stammers back from his desk.

Holding the blade's tip towards him, Naomi demands, "The master key. Where is it?"

"So that's what you want. I think you know where it is," he replies, turning away from the desk towards his black armoire. "However, I don't think it will be of much use to you."

Naomi questions, "Why's that?"

Kruger and I grow increasingly restless as we sit here, feeling the walls closing in around us. "Naomi, let's just go," I shout.

I stare at a dead guard, his face twitching faintly as blood still pools from his mouth. This situation is going to shit fast, and we are right in the middle of it. I load a tranquilizer round into the chamber of my rifle, aiming it toward Takashi.

"Don't you fucking dare," Naomi warns, her gaze cold and unwavering as she glances at me. Reluctantly, I lower the barrel to the floor, exchanging an anxious look with Kruger.

"What the fuck?" I whisper to Kruger, and he shrugs.

"Do you think your friends can help you? You're already as good as dead. I wouldn't let you simply walk out of here. The A.C.P.D. is on its way as we speak. Besides, you just killed four of my men. That's a life-penalty offense on

Grievous Grey," Takashi reminds us, his tone tinged with a chilling certainty.

"Who are you?" Naomi motions to her father. He doesn't seem to understand the question, so she asks again. "Who are you?"

"I am Takashi Sato, and you, daughter, are no one, and will never be part of my legacy."

Confused by Naomi's words, through all the chaos and disbelief, I only have one thought: never seeing Avery again except through the laser cells of Grievous Grey.

"You want what? The near-billion I have on the master key?" Takashi says stepping toward a large black ornamental inlayed cabinet. Naomi's blade tip following him at every step.

"Among other things," Naomi responds.

"Near billion... what–?" I say with heavy confusion.

I exchange a bewildered glance with Kruger, who maintains his aim, unsure what to make of this unexpected turn of events. The plan was supposed to involve stealing ten million, not this astronomical sum.

Demanding the master key again, Naomi points her blade toward Takashi. In response, Takashi suddenly retrieves an antique sword from the cabinet, prepared to defend himself. A tense standoff ensues.

Naomi chuckles, a flicker of amusement in her eyes. Takashi asks her, "What's so funny?"

She simply replies, "You."

Without hesitation, she draws her pistol and fires a single hollow-point round. The bullet pierces through the air, striking Takashi squarely in the center of his forehead. His brain matter and blood splatter across the giant oil painting behind him, staining it with a macabre beauty—a streaming texture against the burnt sienna sunset.

For a moment, Takashi stands dazed, his hands flapping and grasping at the wound. His eyes trail to the back of his head before he collapses lifeless onto the floor. Naomi breaks into laughter, holsters her sidearm, and steps to Takashi's inert body.

"Sorry father."

My shock and confusion intensify as I witness the unexpected turn of events. Blood continues to spew from the back of Takashi's head, staining the white shag rug that surrounds his desk. Racing over to his lifeless form, I struggle to comprehend the gravity of the situation.

"What the fuck, Naomi?" I say, desperation seeping into my voice. "We need to abort, *now*. This wasn't the plan. No one was supposed to be here!"

She remains unfazed, stepping on Takashi's convulsing body as she approaches the painting. "This is all part of the plan," she calmly responds, removing the painting from the wall and shattering it on the white marble floor. In its place, a safe emerges—the top-of-the-line, impenetrable RE-X5000. No amount of skill or tools can crack this safe; only a DNA sample, voice lock, and thumbprint can unlock its door.

Naomi retrieves a smaller blade from behind her waistline, slicing Takashi's thumb off with one clean motion. She places the severed and bleeding thumb on the biometric scanner and pulls a small audio device from her belt. She plays a recording of Takashi saying "Takashi Sato" from their verbal exchange from earlier, causing the safe to open with a rugged metal clunk and a chime. As the door slowly swings open, the master key drive is revealed, sitting in the center.

"Easy peasy. I knew I could get him to say his own name. He was always so egotistical," Naomi remarks, retrieving the drive. I keep my aim towards the door, on high alert, anticipating more guards bursting in and escalating the situation at any moment.

She plugs the master key drive into the desk, illuminating a screen in the center. Sliding through the files, she navigates to a subfolder within Takashi's empire that contains all his black-market deals and hidden assets.

"The plan is still in motion, small fry. Nothing changes," Kruger interjects, guarding the door.

"What's going on, guuuuuys?" Aden says.

"Master key acquired. Prepare for download," Naomi replies.

"Well, whatever you are doing, you better make it fast. The police are swarming the building, and are currently in the lobby."

"Nearly a billion? This is fucked, we are burned. We need to go, now!" I demand, feeling the pressure mounting.

"Just a few more seconds, Aden. Are you in?" Naomi asks as the master key's light shifts from white to green.

"I'm in," Aden confirms.

"Hurry," Kruger says as he open fires on incoming guards from down the hall.

His belt-fed heavy rifle explodes rounds down the pathway, ripping apart furniture and bodies. I pin next to the door as return fire explodes into the penthouse.

"Just another second, annnnnnd credits transferred and...encrypted to our servers. Meet on the roof. Police air support will be here in two minu—" Aden's comms cut off abruptly.

Naomi unplugs the drive and secures it in her waistband pouch before leaving the desk. "We better move quickly," she says.

"What the hell is going on, Naomi?" I shout, confusion and frustration evident as I follow closely behind her. Kruger remains, providing cover as we enter the elevator.

"Ezrek will explain everything. Don't worry," she assures me, pressing the elevator button.

"No, you need to explain now," I say. It only takes about twelve seconds to reach the roof, but the silence feels like eternity.

As the elevator doors open to a heavy thunderstorm on the roof. Naomi forcefully shoves me out of the doorway without saying a word. The tension is as thick as the clouds above as Kruger heads towards the hovering jet at the roof's edge. "What the fuck, Naomi?"

"Just go. We need to get to the rendezvous."

Something is up. I have a real bad feeling right now.

As we approach the ship, I spot Ezrek holding someone near the edge of the roof.

Confusion floods my thoughts. *What is he doing here?* I wonder, seeking confirmation from Kruger and Naomi, it indeed was Ezrek.

"That's far enough." His voice crackles through the comms within the loud rain and thunder.

I come to an abrupt halt, a flash of lightning illuminating the roof. Ezrek removes the black hood from the bound, bloodied figure on their knees. A shiver runs down my spine as I recognize her. "Avery," I whisper, my voice barely audible above the storm.

Through the rain and lightning's crashing, her frightened eyes meet mine.

"Well, well, Becky Boy," Ezrek's voice slices through the storm, low and venomous. "I knew you'd always come crawling back."

"Z? What are you doing."

Our words hang in the air, sharp as the jagged bolts splitting the sky. "You think you can just walk away? From me? From what we built?" He steps closer, his silhouette towering in the storm. "Do you honestly believe you're better than this? Better than me?"

My anger boils as I prepare to confront him, but before I can utter one more word, Ezrek interrupts with a sinister tone. "Oh, did I forget to give you my parting gift?"

Two loud bangs echo behind me, shattering the illusion of thunder. I try to form a response, but my voice fails me. Attempting to take a deep breath, I find myself unable to do so.

Glancing down, I see two exit wounds in my chest, blood gushing onto the rain-soaked rooftop. Naomi emerges from behind me, gun in hand, and I hear the unmistakable click of the hammer being pulled back for the third time. It rips through my shoulder, causing my legs to buckle, and I crash to the ground.

Raindrops bounce off my black tactical vest while my mind races, unable to process what is happening. Blood pools around the gunshot wounds in my chest and shoulder. The city lights flicker across the rooftop, casting distorted reflections as I realize my rifle lies just out of reach, drowning in the rain.

Suddenly, as I try to get up, I manage to brace myself with my arms but Naomi's foot crashes into my spine, sending me face-first into the roof's hard surface. Water splashes upward, blurring my vision, and at that moment, I catch a glimpse of Avery's face in the distance. "Av—" I try to yell, reaching for my rifle in front of me. It's so close my fingertips touch the handle.

"Ah, ah, ah," Naomi replies, kicking the rifle away with one swift motion, and it slides under a few exhaust units.

"Let him up; he needs to watch. I don't want him to miss a thing. I've been waiting for this for too long," Ezrek says, holding Avery by the back of her hair in one hand and waving a long-barreled silver revolver in the other.

Naomi props me up to my knees, holding my arms back as Ezrek's shadowed figure steps in front of me. "You're not going to want to miss this," she says, prying my heavy eyelids back.

Tears began welling in my eyes as I see Avery in sheer terror, confused about what is happening.

"Don't—let her go," I mumble with the energy I have left.

"You think you can just walk away? After all the years we've been together, Becky boy?"

I try to respond, but no words escape my lips this time, just a wet cough of red.

"We are allllll gathered here today to witness the fall of our prestigious commander, our one and only Owen Beck, a little boy orphan who grew up with nothing and turned into EOS's best pilot Galacom has ever seen. Just when the getting was good, you what? Had a change of heart? For what? For her?!" Ezrek yells, grabbing Avery under the chin to make her look at me, bleeding out, barely able to keep my eyes open. I'm fading slowly. My vision is hard to retain.

"Help! Why are you doing this?!! Wh—" Avery screams before Ezrek puts the gag back in her mouth.

"I'm sorry, sweetheart, but I don't think he can answer you now. He's losing too much blood. How much longer do you think he has, Sato?" Ezrek's voice carries through the pouring rain and thunder.

"From the looks of it, five, maybe seven minutes tops," Naomi responds.

"Well, we better make this quick. Set the charges for three minutes. I wouldn't want Owen to miss the fireworks," Ezrek declares, tightening his grip on Avery and forcing her to witness my bleeding state.

"Wh—why?" I stammer, blood dripping from my mouth.

"What was that?" Ezrek retorts, hurling Avery to the ground before walking in front of me. His voice drips with contempt. "I didn't quite hear you, you piece of shit."

"Why, Z?" I say quietly, seeking some semblance of understanding.

His tone softens, and he kneels before me, an unsettling intimacy in his dark sunken eyes. "Stealing credits was only the beginning, Beck. We could have had it all. I found something—something we could have shared, a power I never knew existed. I needed what was on Takashi's private server, and the only way to get it was with his Master Key. A revolutionary technology, he only saw the small picture. I saw its true potential. Think, Beck—an army of mindless soldiers, not scared, not hungry or tired, no memory of anything but warfare, the best parts of machine and men—the perfect soldiers."

"You are fucking insane," I manage to cough out, my voice strained.

"Insane?" He sneers, cocking the hammer of his revolver.

I glimpse my rifle tucked beneath the exhaust units, an idea forming in my mind.

"Hold him up," Ezrek commands, gesturing towards Naomi.

"Get up," she yells, hoisting me against my will.

"This is your fault, Beck. This is all your fault," Ezrek says, his words heavy with blame. He walks over to Avery and presses the cold metal barrel of his gun against her temple.

"Don't," I say serenely with the last of my energy, our eyes locking in a desperate plea.

An instant passes, the rain intensifying, beating relentlessly upon the rooftop. Then, a deafening bang reverberates through the air. Blood sprays against the side electrical unit as Avery's lifeless body collides with the rain-soaked rooftop.

"*No!*" I shout, summoning the last remnants of my strength to fight off Naomi. But I have lost too much blood. My efforts are futile.

I collapse onto the ground, my face mere inches from Avery's blood-soaked face. Blurred and fading, my vision struggles to hold on.

Her eyes are lifeless, leaving behind emptiness.

I slowly try to crawl towards Avery, reaching out to grasp her hand, my movements laborious amidst the pooling blood and rain. Coughing, I repeatedly utter her name. "Avery."

"Take her body, but leave Owen. We need him alone on the rooftop when the cameras kick back on. He deserves his explosive exit. He was always one for a fiery ending," Ezrek commands, pointing towards Avery's lifeless form.

Naomi complies, gripping Avery's feet and dragging her onto the jet carelessly, a trail of blood marking their path. A feeble moan escapes my lips as I reach out toward her departing figure. A deep-bellied primal scream tears from my lungs, nearly rendering me unconscious.

"This could have been avoided," Ezrek says, water droplets falling from his shaggy black beard. I manage to see two men emerging from the bay of the jet. "Is everything ready?" he asks the men. It's the cops from earlier.

"Yes, sir."

"Good."

Z seizes me by the back of my head, lifting it from the rooftop, and whispers as his voice turns sinister. "I've just taken the most important person in the world away from you, just like you did to me. Farewell, brother. There's no winning this time. Enjoy the light show." With a forceful thump, he releases my head and walks towards the jet, Naomi and Kruger following behind him.

"So long, Beck. Maybe you'll see her again in your afterlife," Ezrek taunts as the bay door closes. "Let's go!" he shouts, spinning his pointer finger in the air to signal to fall back.

The bay door finishes closing, and the jet speeds away.

I'm alone, surrounded by a pool of blood where Avery's body had once lain. Tears stream freely down my face, hot streaks cutting through the cold rain. Rage burns deep within me, but it's smothered by the suffocating weight of loss. I could lay here, let it all end. What's a life without her?

But survival instinct claws its way through the despair. With a trembling breath, I force myself to move—first to my knees, then to my feet. Every motion feels like dragging a mountain, but I refuse to stop.

Slumping against the rim of the roof, I grip the edge for balance and peer down at the city streets far below. The police haven't reached this side—not yet.

"Come on, Beck. You can do this," I whisper, the words drowned over the storm, more a plea than a command.

My gaze catches on one of the charges blinking on the side of the roof, its rhythm quickening with every second. Time is running out.

Desperation sharpens my focus. I scan the rooftop and spot a scaffolding elevator dangling precariously against the building's side. It's a gamble—a leap of faith.

Without hesitation, I hurl myself over the edge, my stomach twisting as I land hard on the flimsy metal platform. The structure groans under the impact, but it holds. My hand slowly lifts, slamming the green lever, and the platform lurches downward, groaning against the storm.

The elevator hurtles downwards, shaking violently as it passes several floors a second. Suddenly, about at the midway point, a loud explosion erupts above me, causing the elevator to veer wildly from side to side before crashing against the building's structure. The detonation obliterates the top floors of Takashi's penthouse offices, erasing any trace of our presence.

A metallic twang cuts through the storm as the pulley system creaks ominously. My heart sinks as one of the cables snaps with a sharp crack, and the entire mechanism shudders violently. Above me, flames consume the rooftop, sending waves of heat and smoke cascading into the night.

The elevator plummets, the frame groaning under the strain, and I cling desperately to the railing, my fingers numb and slick with rain. Another cable whines, then snaps, and the platform veers wildly, accelerating toward the ground.

With a sickening lurch, the final cable tightens, straining against gravity's pull, before it gives way entirely. I'm thrown from the collapsing elevator, weightless for a heart-stopping moment before I crash into a protruding awning. The impact jolts the breath from my lungs, and I slide helplessly off its slick surface, landing hard on the wet pavement below.

The storm rages overhead, unrelenting in its fury. Above me, fire and smoke churn into the night sky, the ruins of the rooftop burning as if to erase everything that had happened there. I lay motionless in the narrow back alley, my body screaming in pain, the rain mixing with the blood pooling beneath me.

"Ave..." I whisper hoarsely, her name slipping through my lips like a final plea.

Darkness closes in, swallowing the flames, the storm, and everything else.

CREATURES OF
THE DARK

"DID YOU HEAR ME?"

Snapping out of it, I answer, "Sorry, what did you say?"

"Did you hear *anything* I said? Where do you go? I swear, I just talk to myself sometimes," Tex says, ducking low to clear sharp, low-hanging stalactites.

"I just drift occasionally. I was thinking about when I bought you and about the night I nearly died. It's a good motivator," I say as we head deeper into the cave.

"Oh, yeah, I can only imagine—from the shifty old peddler with the bum eye, right?" he asks.

"That's the one."

Hidden from the solace of light, we journey onward. We must be at least a third of a mile underground so far, lost in a labyrinth of black stone corridors. The passageway tapers the farther we trek down, and I run into difficulty as I squeeze through the deep, constricted vertical openings.

A faint glow of winding light trails over the cave's inner walls. Disengaging my night vision, I see it's a soft cyan hue. It lights the way forward with a subtle radiance.

The cave is flourishing, with the proper conditions and temperatures to allow life to find a way to thrive—a hidden blossoming ecosystem lurking deep inside this desert planet.

"How can this be?" Tex asks.

"I have no idea," I say, reengaging my night vision.

I remain utterly baffled by the origins of this bizarre occurrence. Swarms of alien insects, each boasting hundreds of spindly legs and bristly antennae, scuttle through the crevices of the walls, venturing deeper into the abyss. These creatures, unlike anything I've ever seen, display an array of luminous colors that dance across their exoskeletons as they move in a synchronized pattern. Among them, smaller critters, their bodies adorned with iridescent scales, flit through the air, their wings fluttering hums in the dark.

The stone underfoot is slick and damp, so I tread with deliberate care, each footfall a risk amid the trickle of liquid seeping through the fissures. A misstep could easily send me skidding into a chasm—or, worse, skewered on the sharp points of the jutting rocks. Every move matters in this treacherous terrain, each step a precarious foot between survival and disaster.

Strident stalactites hang from the ceilings, and broken-down stones lay forgotten throughout the passage before us. I can feel a warm breeze brush my hands, even through my division-grade combat gloves, and it's like the cave is alive—I can feel the air breathing in and out from somewhere behind us. This subterranean world appears unspoiled by anyone's touch, frozen in a time capsule spanning countless centuries. Yet here we are, inching further into its belly.

Tex and I eventually navigate our way to the end of the initial tunnel. We are met with a trident of miner-made pathways, each eerily identical to the next. Peering down each one, I'm struck by a sense of disorientation—each tunnel is a mirror image of the others. I squint into the depths of each, but my choice is far from clear.

"Tex, picking up any signals in here?" I ask softly, my voice dull off the cavern walls.

"Nothing," he replies, his eye scanning the shadow-laden chambers. "My night vision isn't fully operational—it's on the fritz—but I can still interpret the mining map Felix handed over, along with my weapons system and flashlight." Tex takes a moment, scrutinizing the murky surroundings. "Probably some residual effects from the magnetic interference we encountered on the mountain's peak. My normal vision mode seems to be working, though. The interference is probably all around us."

"My night vision is doing the same. Let's switch to our flashlights," I say as I disengage the scrambled green-hued night vision and power on the flashlights. The beams cut through the dark, illuminating the paths before us. "Which way?" I ask, anxiety edging my voice.

"The middle passage will take us further into the depths," Tex responds. "But the miners' notes are incomplete. It marks the mining tunnels, and some natural paths they plotted, but then it just... ends."

"I'm certain there's something more down here," I say, an unexplainable intuition nudging me. "Something they didn't, or couldn't, map out. Why would the Val'Ara be etched into the top of the mountain? The Khu'Val left something here."

The extent of the underground system before us remains a mystery. Has it burrowed a mile deep or twenty into the heart of this planet? We're embarking on a journey into the abyss, and the uncertainty gnaws at my resolve. Yet retreat isn't an option. Not when we are this close. I can feel it.

Our trudging echoes hauntingly in the sprawling caverns, the sounds bouncing back to us like ghostly reminders of our solitude. Then, instinctively, I halt. "Hold." My raised fist signals a command to stop.

Tex freezes.

We wait, unmoving, for what feels like forever.

"What?" His whisper slices through the stillness.

"Quiet," I reply.

The silence is punctuated only by our tense breathing as we strain to listen. And then it comes. The faint but distinct *click-click-click* rattles down the tunnel—the sound of something scraping against rock follows, insidiously close. We are statues, partially paralyzed by the chilling realization that we aren't alone.

The inadequate light from our flashlights does little to dispel the inky darkness of the tunnel stretching ahead. Its intimidating expanse seems to consume any sense of direction or safety.

Click-click-click. The anomalous rhythm reverberates once more, joined by a hollow, guttural intake of breath.

It's a sound that burrows under your skin, unsettling and unplaceable. More than mere clicks, there's an undercurrent of a gasping wheeze, like a creature clinging desperately to its last moments of life. My ears strain against the suffocating stillness, trying to trace the source, but the calm is only punctuated by the sporadic dripping of water.

"What the fuck was that?" Tex whispers, an undercurrent of fear weaving through his voice.

"Keep focused," I whisper back, louder than I intended. We continue our cautious advance, the clicking sound seemingly absorbed by the sounds of the tunnel. The absence of it is oddly more unsettling, but we keep pressing on, every sense strung tight.

Determined to lighten the mood, or perhaps to distract himself, Tex ventures a change in topic. "So, what's the story with Dos Calderon?" His voice hovers just a bit above a whisper.

"What are you on about?" I reply quietly, keeping my attention ahead, clearing each little chambered hollow we pass. The dark abyss of the tunnel feels like it's closing in on us, the unknown lurking just beyond our limited range of our flashlights.

"I don't know; you just seem... more reserved than usual. It's hard to get a read on you with that brain hat of yours." His voice lowers slightly, a note of concern underlying his words.

He is, of course, referring to my helmet, which I scarcely remove these days. "Well, I just experienced the anguish that Felix is enduring—the loss of a spouse, the disappearance of someone who means the world to you. His universe is collapsing around him," I say, cautiously avoiding a cluster of pointed stalactites overhead. "It brings to mind a discussion I once had with Avery. The notion of having children never appealed to me until I crossed paths with her; suddenly, it felt like the most natural thing in the world. Then, to have that dream ripped away from you... The only way to reclaim that lost future is to bring her back."

"I believe Avery would have been proud of you, despite the trail of battered and bloodied bodies you've left in your wake, Beck. You managed to rescue the only thing Felix had left in this world: his daughter. Avery would agree."

Several seconds pass. "Yeah, I suppose," I say.

"It's just been five years of this, Beck, and if this lead doesn't work out, that's it—that's everything we have. There are no more clues, no more leads; we'll have nothing left if this doesn't pan out."

"Something will be here," I say reassuringly, heading in front of Tex, eager to step up the pace and get away from the noise.

The sound of rushing water grows louder as I grip the rugged rocks before me, pulling myself through a narrow gap, mindful not to scrape my exposed skin against the sharp edges. I plant both hands on the uneven surfaces of the cavern walls, hoisting myself through; I land feet-first with a muted thump.

As I rise from the ground, I discern what I believe to be the same clicking sounds emanating from the tunnel ahead of us, but this time, they are much closer. "Hold!" I signal once more.

Clutching the stippled grip of my rifle, I brace myself for any eventuality.

A series of clicks and scrapes resonate from the darkness ahead. We aim our flashlights towards the source of the noise. Something darts rapidly across our field of vision; I sweep the stony cave with my flashlight in an attempt to identify the creature, but it has vanished.

I whip my rifle into my shoulder and creep forward, aiming at anything that moves.

"I definitely saw it that time," Tex whispers, surveying the void before us.

"Defense mode," I whisper, and Tex's body shifts and contorts on itself, growing to nearly double his size as a turret ejects from his bottom panel and loads. His triangular blue eye turns fiery red-orange, scanning each nook.

"Picking up anything?" I ask, glancing at the readout on my forearm that displays what he's detecting.

His scanner ignites a red hue as it marks each location. "No heat signatures anywhere," he reports, deactivating the gridded model.

I allow myself a moment to decompress before loosening my grip on the textured handle. "Whatever that was, it's fast."

Suddenly, a spine-chilling shriek reverberates through the tunnel, echoing off the walls. "What the fuck?!" Our flashlights both point to the end of the path. I fire two shots into the void, hoping to hit something. The cracks of the incredibly loud sound, muffled by my helmet's high-decibel feature, startle Tex for a moment.

"Warn me next time!" He whisper shouts.

I narrow my eyes and regulate my breathing. I detect a fleeting movement of darkness against darkness, blending into the shadows. "You picking up anything?" I whisper to Tex.

"Nothing," he whispers back as he charges his high-intensity plasma laser.

Are my eyes playing tricks on me? Hesitating, ready for whatever it was to show itself, I wait.

Liquid drops from the slide of the rifle, splashing to the floor below. "Steady," I whisper.

We wait for five minutes, not moving a muscle, and still nothing.

"What the hell was that?" Tex says, finally breaking the silence.

"Probably just a bird," I joke.

"A bird? Are you fucking kidding me?!" he shouts back in a quiet yell.

"Obviously, it's not a fucking bird, Tex; lower your voice. Is there a different route we could take?" I say, as I see a few different pathways coming up.

"Yeah, lets hang a left, that leads around back to the center," he says. "Do you think that's what Felix was talking about?"

"You listening to my conversations again?"

"Huh? What's that?"

"Don't act like you didn't hear me."

"Oh, no, of course not. I wouldn't do that to you; what kind of person would that make me? Well, yes, but that's just because I like to know you're safe," he says unsteadily.

"We've talked about this, Tex."

"I know, I know. I promise I'll try to not not listen to your conversations anymore."

"That's a double negative."

"You're a double negative."

"Just shut up and clear ahead for me."

"Whatever you say, Cap'n."

We walk through the long tunnels for a half an hour with only the sounds of ourselves and the small critters making their appearances.

"Yuuuuuuck," Tex says.

"We still heading in the right direction?" I whisper to Tex, ignoring his previous statement.

"Yeah. If we keep heading this way, we should be on the right path back to the center route. We should be coming up on it twenty paces."

"Got it."

The same faint clicking sounds trail through the empty holes in the walls as we pass more and more pathways. Falling pebbles and debris echo around us; something is definitely moving closer. It sounds like it's coming from all around us, pinging off the walls. This place is a confusing maze of dead ends and encircling passages on both sides, and we could be surrounded and not even know it.

It's only a short duckwalk towards the end of the tunnel as we come to an uneven oval keyhole about twenty meters down. The small opening in the wall is big enough for us to climb through.

"Think you can fit?" Tex asks as his eye drifts down to my stomach area.

"Eh, probably?" I say, looking at the hole and adjusting my combat belt.

"I'll go first to make sure it leads somewhere," Tex says as he heads through the small gap in the rock first.

I inhale a breath as he slowly disappears into the shadows through the hole. I stand patiently at the end of a passage, waiting for his confirmation. Now, the lonely chamber is completely quiet. I can feel my heart slowly thumping in my chest. "Tex, hurry up," I say, but all I hear is static in return.

In a low, raspy tone, I say, "Tex."

There's nothing but low static. *Where the fuck is he?* I think, tapping the side of my helmet. Maybe my comm unit is down. "Tex, status?" I repeat a little louder, and I get silence.

Click-click-click.

I freeze. The noise is coming from behind me.

I spin, bringing my rifle up with my eyes down the sight as fast as I can.

I discharge a single sun-flare round down the tunnel. Its trajectory halts midway as it collides with one of the creatures, dropping to the ground and casting a ghastly illumination upon two horrifying figures before me. The silhouettes of the creatures contort in the flare's red hue as they screech and snarl on all fours down the tunnel. Their elongated, sinewy arms invert at the joints, and their legs, twice as long as mine, click and draw in the air. Saliva cascades over their jagged, serrated teeth as they arch their bony spines downward, inching forward as they prepare to charge.

Uh, shit.

I enhance the image with my optics, and the creatures come into sharp focus as they click and shriek down the tunnel. Their claws scrape against the rocks beneath them, honing their edges as they flare their nostrils, slowly drawing in my scent from a distance.

"*DEADWEIGHT,*" I bellow into the rifle, preparing to unleash a barrage upon the abominations before me.

The smaller creature unleashes a deafening roar before charging at me on all fours.

It bounds with terrifying ferocity, shrieking voraciously as it effortlessly skitters along the tunnel's side, up the walls, and onto the ceiling, embedding its razor-sharp claws into the solid rock with each leap.

I tweak my zoom, cock the rifle, and depress the trigger, sending an anchored tether spiraling into the air. The spinning projectile activates as it ensnares the creature's legs, binding them together and sending it plummeting from the ceiling. It smashes onto the ground with a resounding crash and skids to a halt mere inches from my boots.

Its bifurcated tongue flicks out, dripping with saliva, and it emits a horrifying snarl as its maw snaps towards me. Stepping over the fallen beast, I discharge a single round into its cranium, causing its brain matter to splatter onto the ground. Sapphire-hued blood gushes from its translucent grey mucus-like skin.

Before I can take a closer look at the downed creature, the other one, enraged by its companion's demise, hurtles towards me at breakneck speed.

I aim the rifle and fire a solitary shot. It misses as the creature agilely vaults to the tunnel's side, propelling itself forward with each powerful leap, and I depress the trigger once more. My shots only find empty air.

Damn it. The creature is much faster than I anticipated. *Time to bring out the big guns.*

I switch to armor-piercing and unload on the fucker. Wall pieces blow up around the creature's face as it gallops even faster, but I manage to clip it in the shoulder just as it leaps toward me.

"Shit!" I belt out as the grotesque jaws of the creature clamp down onto my forearm armor. One of its sharp teeth squeezes through the slit of my armor plating and punctures just below my elbow.

"*Tex!*" I groan from the pain as the force of the beast knocks me backward onto the ground, and it puts all its weight on me. Mucus spills onto my faceplate as it frantically tries to claw at my torso.

Damn, it's strong—much stronger than me, I think as it anchors me to the floor like the weight of a freight cruiser. *What do I do?* It's like trying to lift three hundred pounds with one hand. It isn't going to happen.

It lunges again and again, nearly ripping my throat out. I push upward as hard as possible, keeping its contorted razor-sharp teeth from my neck. Its scent is overwhelmingly bad; it smells like old sewers covered in even more rotten shit.

My knife is too far down, and if I release either hand, I'll be dead.

I push the beast up as hard as I can as it keeps aggressively biting its way closer and closer to my neck, and with a final struggle, as my arms are about to give out, a single thought enters my mind. *This is how I die—mauled alive and turned into this creature's shit. It was all for nothing.*

It belts out a final screech as it lunges downward for the kill, but just as it reaches my throat, a perfectly aimed laser beams through the side of its head and out the other side.

Blood and slime began spewing out of its mouth and brain hole, spilling all over the front of my helmet and armor, covering me in a stench worse than death.

A deep, disgusted gag billows from my throat. "Seems about right," I say as I push the heavy beast off me. It thumps to the ground, dead. Lying still for just a brief moment, I let out a hard exhale.

Wiping the blood from my helmet, I flick it to the dark misty ground with a gross splat. "Fuck those smell," I bellow with a dry heave into my helmet.

"You're welcome," Tex says, tired of patiently waiting to be thanked.

"I had that one," I say, wiping the remainder of the innards off my faceplate.

"You suuuuure did, big guy," he says as we look down at the malodorous deceased beasts.

I sneer. "Where the fuck were you?"

"I was mapping out the tunnels below. Mostly dead ends, but I headed straight back once I heard the shots," he says, getting a closer look at the creatures. "What is it?" he asks curiously.

"No fucking clue I've never seen anything like it," I say, quickly retrieving an antiseptic cleanser spray and wound sealant from my belt. I high pressure spray coats the wound and I bite down hard, Tex interrupts and distracts my brain from the pain.

"Where are their eyes? How did they see you?" Tex says, backing away.

The creature has evolved not to require eyes, as its forehead blends seamlessly into the front of its elongated grey face. The animal is enormous. Its head reminds me of a bat, but this is far too big, and its muscular lycanthropic body is perfect for navigating through these tunnels. It's terrifying, to say the least.

"A perfectly evolved predator," I say. As I kneel closer to the creature, turning its dead-weighted cranium, I notice that ears are not evident either.

"Where are its ears?" Tex says questioningly.

"I think it has flaps on both sides of its head that it uses for ears and eyes."

"What do you mean?" he asks, his eye trailing over the beast's cranium.

"Look," I say, mesmerized, as I peel back folds of tissue where their ears would be, revealing a large mucus membrane sliming together with a highly advanced set of eardrums. "This looks like a perfectly evolved auricle. It probably uses echolocation to stalk its prey, which is perhaps why they were clicking and reverberating off the chamber walls. They likely use all these passageways to get around under Turkken—hunting locals, the old miners, whatever they can find. That's what the locals claimed to hear before people went missing. They probably heard the shrieks of these fucking things."

"What could it possibly be hunting? There's nothing down here."

"*I* am," I say as I drop its dead-eyed head to the cave floor with a *thump*.

Then, feeling uneasy, I rasp, "Let's keep moving."

I jump through the opening Tex cleared, which causes me to fall fast at an angle. I slide quickly down a short tunnel that opens to an enormous chamber below, and I eject from the ceiling and land with a loud crash that rumbles through the ducts.

Tex appears shortly after me and hovers to the center of the cavity. "We should give them a proper name, don't you think?" he blurts out.

"We don't need to name them, Tex. We need to stay the fu—"

"I got it!" Tex interjects. "Wait for it...waaaaait for it..."

A moment passes. "Bat-Wolfies," he says self-confidently.

"No."

"Aw, come on. That's the perfect name," he says.

"Let's just focus on not dying down here instead of trying to name the things trying to fucking eat us. The locals already gave their names; they called them the Ghosts. Let's just leave it."

"'The Ghosts?' That's stupid, and I'm sticking with Bat-Wolfies," Tex says condescendingly. "Baaaaaat-Wooooolfies," he says as his voice trails out ahead.

This fucking guy—always with the arrogance.

"I've mapped out all adjacent tunnels through here except this one," he says from afar, heading towards the tunnel to the left.

"What the fuck is that smell?" I gag, nearly vomiting in my helmet again.

"Well, I don't smell, but I have sensors for the harmful gases you produce at night."

"*Ha.* Good one, but no, seriously—the smell is almost unbearable," I say, pressing onward.

As I take a few steps into the cavern, the floor's surface turns from a rigid solid stone to a soft, slushy crunch under my boots. I feel like I'm snapping branches every time I take another step. "What the hell is this?" I curiously ask as I point my flashlight down.

I halt.

"What's wrong?" Tex says, hovering over me.

"Tex," I say with a short breath as he points his light towards mine.

"Oh, shit. That's not good."

Our lights have revealed a small array of people's fleshy limbs and animal bones covered in the white mucus under my feet. That's what that sound was—I had been breaking the bones of the arms and legs I was walking over.

"Holy shit." Tex gasps, looking in a different direction. "Look!"

I hastily leap a few large boulders in front of me, going over to where Tex was looking. When I land, I see a small pile of rotten half-eaten corpses piled atop each other, slowly decomposing. I see severed limbs ripped clean off and faces eaten away, only leaving partial skulls exposed. There are rodents, birds, humans, and even a small child all throughout the den. Thick black blood pools over the rocks. Some of the bones look as if they have been here for decades. Everywhere I look, there are remnants of carcasses; this must be centuries of feeding.

"We walked right into their den," I say, as death shows its malevolent face everywhere we look.

"We should go," Tex warns as I shuffle over some of the decaying parts on the ground.

"My thoughts exactly," I say as I hear a big crunch under my boot.

"Ah, man. I'm pretty sure you just stepped on someone's fucking head," Tex says.

"That would explain the loud crunch-like noise, but we don't have time to be polite," I say.

There are no sounds or signatures of the creatures anywhere. *Maybe the first two were the defensive soldiers protecting their den while the others were away, possibly hunting?* I wonder. I'm not sure where the rest of them are, but I don't want to stick around and find out.

"Which way do we go?" I ask as Tex is flying a bit higher over the mangled bodies. The stench gets worse the farther we trek.

"It's this way, I think. The map is almost to its end," Tex says. "There is an opening on the other side of that small underground stream."

The path ascends upward in a slight winding pattern towards a moderately sized opening, which isn't far now. "Right through here," he says.

We finally make our way across the den and come to a fork at the tunnels. Each opening looks about the same as before; the smell down here is so unbearable I can hardly think straight. Even with my purifier and air filters, there's no getting away from it. It's fucking foul.

"Left or right?" I ask Tex.

"The map ended back there. There aren't any more paths documented."

"Well, it's fifty-fifty. Why don't you take the left, and I'll take the ri—"

I'm immediately interrupted by several bloodcurdling screeches that echo through the tunnels behind us.

"Uhm... Bet you wish you charged your shield now huh?" Tex says, slowly turning around. Our flashlights fan over the openings, and we see dozens of creatures emerging from the shadows, their long, razor-sharp claws sinking deep into the rocks. More appear by the second, and I'm quickly losing count. Ear-shattering cries overwhelm the large chamber.

"We should run," I say, and we hightail it down the right tunnel as the beasts begin running straight toward us.

As we enter the mouth of the tunnel, I retrieve three small mechanical devices from my belt and throw them against the wall in a triangular formation. "These should slow them down a bit," I say as a grid of light illuminates a barricade of laser fields, creating a security wall behind us, even if it's just for a short while. The faint whine of the power cells fills the air. "But don't get comfortable—five minutes, tops," I add as I bolt forward.

I'm running as fast I can, but the long tunnel comes to an abrupt stop in a tapered dead end with nowhere to turn. "I thought you said this was the way, Tex!"

"I didn't say that; you just ran down this one—don't blame me! It was probably the other way!" he says as he vigorously looks in all directions for a possible opening, scanning each wall and the surrounding areas. "Maybe there's a door or something around. Keep looking."

"Dammit!" I say, slamming my hands into the walls, pushing as hard as possible. The wound under my elbow throbs blood onto the ground.

Nothing budges. I'm looking at the walls, the ceiling, the ground, but there's nothing—I can only see a dead end.

"Shit. This can't be it. We can't go back." I drop my head down while I rest one arm on the wall. I slam against it once more, and my fists start to throb from the impacts.

Tex pauses for a moment and then says hopefully, "What do we do?"

For the first time in a long time, I feel defeated.

"The only thing we can do," I say turning toward the long tunnel.

"Do you think we could blow an opening and see if it leads somewhere?"

"I don't even have enough time to explain why that wouldn't work. If we caused a blast here, the whole structure could fail, which could trap us here," I say.

The laser grid hums with fluctuating power, slicing the creatures into pieces as they relentlessly test its durability. Each strike drains the battery faster, a ticking clock we can't afford.

"Well, there has to be something," Tex says, making one last attempt at looking around the walls, gridding out the entire room with his scanner.

I shoulder my rifle, then slowly pointing the barrel down the long dark tunnel.

"We'll make it through this—" Tex starts, but his words falter. His sensors swivel sharply, and his glowing eye dims slightly as he notices the containment grid has failed.

"Oh... no," he mutters, his voice barely above a whisper.

Then it hits—a dissonance of screeches, echoing down the narrow, suffocating tunnel. The sound grows, swelling like an unstoppable tide, the unmistakable anarchy of dozens—if not, *hundreds*—of creatures bearing down on us. The noise is deafening, a thunderous roar of primal hunger and relentless pursuit, shaking the very walls around us.

I switch my sensor to motion detection, and it immediately locks onto the oncoming targets, tracking each one as they slither into view, skittering up walls and across the ceiling. The chamber comes alive with movement, my tracking sequence temporarily managing to keep pace. Every square inch of the dark, cavernous space lights up in a ghostly green hue, the outlines of creatures multiplying faster than the system can process.

The sheer number is overwhelming—an endless tide of motion, the sensors struggling to tag them all. For every target locked, two more emerge, flooding the display in a phrenzy. My gut tightens as I realize we're out of time.

Setting the rifle to full-auto, I press the stock firmly into my shoulder and squeeze the trigger. A relentless stream of bullets tears through the creatures, ripping apart the first wave with mechanical precision. Bodies crumple to the ground, tangling with those behind them as they charge forward, relentless and unyielding.

Tex's energy turret pivots beside me, firing precise laser bursts that carve through the swarm. Spent shells clatter to the floor, a steady rhythm beneath the echo of gunfire and the shrill cries of the creatures. The tunnel is a funnel of destruction, but it's not enough. For every creature I take down, more flood the narrow space, advancing in an unbroken tide.

Almost empty!" I shout to Tex, the weight of my dwindling ammo pressing down. The air feels heavier with each passing second, each breath a struggle against the inevitable.

Tex doesn't hesitate, his energy turret firing with mechanical precision. His glowing eye shifts toward me, the movement deliberate.

"Beck," he says, his tone calm—too calm.

I glance at him, and the realization hits like a punch to the gut. "No, *fuck that*! Don't even say it!" I shout, firing off my last rounds as the creatures tear through the piles of their dead. "We'll think of something else. We *have to*!"

"It's the only way you'll get out of here alive," he says, his voice unwavering.

"Tex, don't even fucking think about it!" I yell, slamming my final magazine into the feed.

The horde surges closer, their shrieks closing in. Time slows as Tex turns to me, a serene moment with a backdrop of nightmares. "You have to finish this, Beck."

"Tex!" I yell, desperation thick in my voice, emptying the last of my rounds into the relentless horde.

"For Avery," he says softly, just as my rifle runs dry. *Click.* The rail locks back, the sound deafening in its finality.

I fumble for my sidearm, but Tex is already speeding forward, his core glowing brighter with each second. The red light at his center pulses, illuminating the jagged tunnel walls as the creatures swarm toward him.

"Tex, don't!" I scream, but he doesn't stop.

With a final glance back at me, his digital eye lingers, filled with a quiet resolve. "It's been fun, my friend," he says, his voice almost... warm.

"No!" I shout, bolting toward him, but it's too late. A blinding white light erupts from his core, consuming everything.

The explosion hits like a freight train, the concussive force hurling me backward. I slam into the wall with bone-jarring impact, the air ripped from my lungs as I crumple to the ground.

Dust and debris choke the air, and the tunnel fills with a deafening roar as the ceiling collapses in front of me. The falling boulders crush the creatures into grotesque smears, their cries fading into gurgling death rattles.

Coughing, gasping for air, I try to pull myself up, but my body won't respond. The world dims, my vision narrowing to a pinprick of light.

"Tex..." I whisper, the word barely audible as my strength fails.

The silence that follows is absolute.

GHOST OF THE GUARDIAN

[//SYSTEM REBOOTING . . .

///PLEASE WAIT...///]

My backup systems engage as my eyes feel heavy. *Wh-what happened?* I wonder as my nostrils widen to the smell of something putrid. My system reboots partially over my eyes, and a green HUD flickers as it illuminates my face, glitching sporadically.

I try to speak, but I cough, and the metallic taste of blood hits the back of my throat—a familiar tinge I know all too well. My face feels flushed, and my head is pounding. *What the fuck happened?*

I wrestle myself up to my knees, seeing nothing but blackness. I start to become more coherent, and I feel a lump in the back of my throat as I say, "Tex."

The detonation must have thrown me into the wall, and the impact disabled my helmet's electronics. As my suit's systems try to reengage, my backup regulator power cell fluctuates, causing a momentary failure, and after a sizzle and pop, it powers down with a dropping tone.

I hit the side of my helmet with two firm thuds as I stand, and the screen flickers on for a moment, then back off. It powers on with another whack, but switches my view modes at random—first thermal, then infrared, then active EM-Field mode.

With a few more hits, all my systems reengage correctly, and I scan the area ahead of me.

Tex! I rush to the boulders of the cave-in, where dark-colored blood pools out from underneath the heavy black stones. I see bits and pieces of Tex scattered on the floor and stuck under the rock. I kneel, and a deep hollow feeling sinks into my stomach as I sift through the rubble and debris; there isn't much left other than bits and pieces of his brain and the creatures' flesh and blood.

My hand stops as I see Tex's cracked optical display next to a severed claw. I pick up his broken eye and stare at it for a moment.

"We could have found another way," I whisper to myself as I look around for other parts.

That's all that's left. He's gone, I think, looking to the collapsed rocks.

There's no way through.

"Come on!" I groan from deep down as I try to make the rocks move. They won't budge. I repeatedly try, using all my strength, even though I know it's a useless gesture; they are too heavy. The remaining creatures' shrieks are now muted by the thick wall of stone. I'm stuck in a tunnel, miles below the surface with nowhere to go.

I fall to my knees, coming to a painful realization—I've just lost my only friend. "You idiot," I whisper painfully, hitting the top of the boulder with a fist.

Sitting with my back to the rocks, I let out a loud anguished cry. The only thing I've found solace in since Avery—he's gone, and I'm now utterly and inescapably alone.

Fuck. We could have figured a way out, I think as I sit there for a few more moments, mourning the death of my fallen friend. I just want to give up.

I'm a fucking plague.

Everything I touch dies. Avery, Tex, Aden—every person I've ever cared about is gone.

This is what I am. This is what I've become.

Death's touch.

I sit for what feels like eternity next to Tex's remains; it's hard to leave, to abandon him here with these awful-smelling creatures. I fiddle with his eye, staring into the blank space where his light would be shining through, hoping by some miracle it will magically turn on and I'll hear his voice again. I realize that now, it's just a piece of broken scraps—no life, no witty comebacks, just nothing.

Taking my focus away from it as tears gently fall down my face under my helmet, I barely manage to say, "Goodbye, Tex."

It's hard to swallow, but I must keep pushing.

Without him, I'd be dead, but I would have fought with Tex to the end, no matter what.

"To the unknown, buddy."

I place the piece of Tex I have back into my pack, and my attention shifts as I hear even more creatures in the distance. The sounds are muffled through the thick boulders of the cave-in, it whispers through the fissures.

I need to find a way out of here. I get to my feet and start looking for a way out of this deathtrap.

Now that my visor modes seem to be functioning correctly, I begin switching through the different types. First, I engage infrared, and a dark emerald silhouette of the chamber glows around me. Looking around, I see that it's nothing but the same, so I switch to thermal. Some of the charred remnants of the blast illuminate from where Tex had been, but that's it—nothing new or out of the ordinary.

Finally, I engage my visor's advanced Electromagnetic Field view, scanning the immediate environment. The advanced visualization displays the subtle changes in the magnetic field around me, turning imperceptible shifts into an array of slow-moving specks and transparent purple waveforms. The magnetic disturbance that had been interfering with our equipment seems to have quieted.

My gaze sweeps from the jagged ceiling to the uneven floor. There, in the wall I'd hit during the blast, I notice a slight discrepancy. *Have those rocks shifted?*

From the wall's small opening, a pattern of purple particles radiates, coiling subtly in a circular motion. Encased in sharp, jagged rock, the gap seems just large enough for my hand. I approach with caution to avoid tearing my suit.

This stupidity is typically where Tex would chime in and say that this is a horrible idea, my arm will get crushed, cut off or mangled, blah, blah, blah—but would insist I try it anyway.

"Here goes nothing," I say, taking a quick breath.

I carefully reach into the soggy, creepy hole, slowly inching in as I feel it tapering, getting smaller and smaller. I am just about to my elbow when I find a long triangular crest at the edge of my fingertips. It feels like a different material than the rocks, so I try tugging on it a bit, but nothing happens.

I turn it to the left—nothing—but as I begin turning it clockwise, it surprisingly starts to rotate. I twist it an entire cycle until it locks into place with a loud clunk.

The heavy wall shifts, and debris falls from the apex as it lowers into the ground. The low rumble and vibrations shake subtly under my boots. It clears and stops with a thud, and I pause.

Casting one final glance towards the pile of rocks where Tex was lost, I find myself enveloped in an unexpected surge of sorrow.

A soft voice in my mind chides me back to reality with the mantra that has pulled me through countless hardships: *For Avery.* These two words, her name, anchor me in my mission, reminding me of the promise I had made.

I take a shaky breath. "Goodbye, Tex," I say into the hollowness, a last farewell to my fallen companion.

I refocus, turning my visual display to infrared. With a deep, steadying inhale, I step forward into the hidden, unexplored chamber, leaving my regrets behind. I'm alone but for the memory of Tex accompanying me into the unknown.

As I walk inside, my screen lights up, revealing an enormous circular chamber carved into the rock. The walls, sculpted from the same rocky material as the outer caves, are meticulously adorned with stone-carved figures shrouded in cloaks. The figures are embedded into the walls at regular intervals encircling the room.

As my helmet's scanner swiftly blankets the darkness in a blue hue, I can discern the magnificence of the design. Eleven colossal figures stand guard over the chamber, a silent vigil in stone. The rock giants, each positioned fifty feet apart, tower over me with a profound sense of authority.

Each of the figures, though shrouded and anonymous, assumes a unique pose. The figures' hands differ in position and gesture, creating a tableau of unmoving meditation, a rock ensemble frozen in time.

In a striking similarity to the ruins we have previously explored, these stone guardians bear the unmistakable glyphs of the ancient Khu'Vala language etched onto their monolithic forms.

Maybe statues of the Khu'Val people? I think, quickly pulling out Avery's journal to sketch them into the pages. "Or maybe their followers?"

One figure distinguishes itself from the rest—a woman. Positioned centrally and towering over the others, she seems to levitate slightly, as though the others are her devout followers—a deity among mortals. Yet the woman exudes an innate beauty. Even after the wear of time, the cracks and lost fragments, her majestic presence sings tales of ancient reverence and adoration.

Unlike her companions, this figure's hood is retracted, revealing a crown of intricate cybernetics affixed to her forehead. Lines of circuitry trail down her symmetrical face, a network of perfect contours etched onto her cheeks and chin. A headscarf, nestled beneath a small isometric crown, frames her appearance. Her shoulders and knees bear signs of mechanical augmentation, imposing sharp angles that accentuate her commanding presence. A form-fitting gown cloaks her form, revealing only her torso and lower body, with slits on the sides unveiling slender, extended legs. Her hands are outstretched, palms facing forward and adorned with two circular symbols. A vision of perfection crafted in stone; she is beautiful.

"They—they're human?" I say, my voice layered with confusion.

My heart surges with exhilaration and bewilderment, but I mask it. Years of hardship, of frustration and despair—they've been worth it for this moment, for this discovery. Tex and I have tracked down something monumental, something unprecedented in our search for the Khu'Val. We are closer to the power—closer than anyone has ever been.

The thought of it brings a joy I hadn't felt in years. How would Avery react? And Professor Williams? The entire galaxy? If I were to share this, my name could be etched in the annals of galactic history.

But as quickly as the thought comes, I dismiss it. *No.* This isn't about fame or recognition. This is about my quest, my singular focus: To reunite with Avery. Nothing else matters.

I reaffirm my tenacity, clenching my fists so tightly that my knuckles crack.

My eyes are immediately drawn to the doorlike structure at the end of the room by the female statue. Bracing myself, I proceed towards it, but a singular floor panel beneath me descends with my step. Simultaneously, the massive entrance wall behind me jolts to life, the colossal stone barricade grinding its way upward until it firmly fits into the ceiling with a resonating crash that reverberates through the entire corridor.

At the heart of the chamber, I notice the Val'Ara etched into the floor, encircling an odd-shaped podium. The statues appear to bow reverently towards this alien edifice. As tall as my waist, the black rock monolith looms ominously as I draw near, and I can't help but notice a slight disruption in my electronic systems.

Switching visor modes, I'm greeted again by a shower of purple particles and ethereal auroras that gather around the square-carved entrance in the monolith. It bears shards of stone meticulously arranged into a peak, giving it an uncanny resemblance to a pedestal.

I take cautious steps forward, my pace instinctively slowing as an otherworldly voice whispers through my consciousness, eclipsing my own internal dialogue. The ethereal feminine voice, resonating with a mystical energy, says, "Lone traveler."

I stop, paralyzed by the sudden intrusion. "Hello?" I say into the vast chamber. My eyes dart all around, finding nothing but emptiness. "Hello?" I venture again, my call swallowed by the surrounding silence.

Regaining some semblance of composure, I speak out once more, assertively this time. "Hello?" A twinge of self-doubt resonates in my mind—*Are you losing it, Beck? You're definitely losing it.*

As I examine the podium further, a subtle glimmer captures my attention. Atop the monument, there seems to be an artifact. It shares the characteristics of the chamber's stones—an identical blackness, but metallic, with the same luminescent teal-glowing energy and traces of jade corrosion akin to the entrance.

Hesitantly, I extend my hand towards the strange shard-like object, and the spectral voice re-enters my thoughts. "Lone traveler, what is it you seek?" she asks.

Taken back, I freeze, my hand suspended in mid-air above the shard-shaped relic. "Who are you?" I yell into the vast emptiness, my voice reverberating off the stony walls before dissipating into nothingness.

The answer returns in the form of the same gentle inquiry. "What are you searching for, my child?"

"I seek the Khu'Val," I reply, standing steadfast before the podium, my eyes unwavering from the imposing door at the end of the chamber. The growing conviction in my voice is a beacon against the creeping tide of insanity.

The serene voice questions me once more, her melodic tone wrapping around her words. "And your purpose?"

"Wh-who are you?" I stammer, my mind spinning in an attempt to make sense of it.

After a lingering pause filled with nothing but stillness, I realize there will be no immediate response. Alone in this primeval chamber, I refocus on the shard object in question. With newfound resolve, I gently lay my hand on its top. The moment my fingers graze its surface, an intense luminescent green energy erupts from the podium. The energy fans out explosively, coursing beneath the floor, scaling the walls, and climbing the ceiling with unrestrained fervor. I watch in awe as this incandescent force intersects and spirals around the chamber, converging on the Val'Ara carved into the ground.

Then, it happens: from the glowing symbol, a shape begins to form. A nebulous, humanoid figure takes shape in the most radiant teal-green light, its emergence transfixing me in place. All I can do is stand there, utterly frozen in astonishment and trepidation. A translucent green hologram takes form from the energy dwelling idle within the structure.

I stumble backward, momentarily stunned. *A hologram?* I blink in disbelief, my hand retreating from the radiating artifact.

Her spectral image becomes more tangible, and the details of her form grow clearer as the energy coalesces. Her cloak, seemingly woven from stardust and cosmic threads, shimmers with holographic constellations, nebulas, and the infinite expanse of eternity.

"Wh—" I choke, shocked by her celestial beauty. Her facial features, although subtly transparent and indistinguishable, radiate a spectral light. Her eyes, devoid of pupils, are as black as the space above, filled with an infinite sea of stars.

The impact of this revelation, this apparition of an almost-divine being, hits me with the force of a supernova. My mind and instincts battle, buzzing with questions and theories, instantaneously thrilled and stunned into taciturnity.

This isn't how we've pictured intelligent extraterrestrial life. Not at all. We've spun countless tales of grotesque, monstrous aliens with giant heads and teeth like tentacles. But here, standing before me, is a wraithlike creature who is as beautiful as she is mysterious, as angelic as she is alien. Her form, stunningly like our own, challenges everything we thought we knew about life before our own.

Overwhelmed by a surge of ecstatic relief, I can barely contain my desire to let out a triumphant scream. Could it be? Are we not alone? Or, more accurately, have we never been alone?

"Remove your helmet, young traveler. There is no cause for fear." Her voice resonates gently in the echoic chamber.

I falter. "It's dangerous without it."

"No danger lies here, my child. Take off your helmet. I assure you: you are safe," she says, voice soothing.

Encouraged by her reassurance, I timidly release the latch of my helmet. It depressurizes with a soft hiss, and I carefully lift it from my head. Taking a cautious breath, I inhale through my nose and feel the cool, clean air chill my lungs. It nearly hurts, it's so brisk. I exhale through my lips, tasting the freshness of the air. It is pure and breathable—devoid of toxins, devoid of that metallic tang. Just clean, fresh air.

I take a few more breaths, calming my rampant nerves before settling my gaze back on the divine figure. "It's you... the Khu'Val," I say, my voice barely more than a whisper.

"Yes," the woman confirms.

A sudden look of relief crosses my face. "Who are you?"

The graceful being seems to ponder for a moment, then with a soft serenity, she speaks. "After an era of forgotten past, I was known as Enohk, the chosen guardian."

"How lo—" I stop myself, feeling my heartbeat quicken in my chest. The question whips around my head as I instinctively step away from the podium, drifting closer to the hologram.

"Time is an irrelevant measure, my child," she states with absolute confidence. "Our kind has experienced billions of years of what you understand as evolution. Our minds have evolved beyond the limitations of forms, into entities that stand the true test of time."

"Are you actually here with me?" I ask.

"Part of me is everywhere, not confined to here or there. I see beyond the common perception, my lost wanderer," she replies, her energetic form seemingly hovering directly in front of me. She continues, her voice soft as a whisper, "What is your true purpose?" She reaches out to touch my face, her holographic hand gliding from my cheek down to the silver ring hanging from my necklace.

"I seek the truth... the truth about the power. If you exist, then that power must exist as well."

"And what would you do with such power?" the celestial being asks seductively, her face inching closer and closer, her supple teal lips nearly meeting mine.

"I've lost someone..." I stop. "I've lost everything," I confess quietly as she stays hovering just before me.

A gentle smile tugs at her lips. "It is love that you seek," she states, her vacant, glowing eyes staring at my ring peeking from my collared cloak.

Transfixed by her vibrant stare, I can only muster a single word in response. "Yes."

"A selfless quest," she says, contemplative.

"The only person who ever truly cared about me is gone. I don't care what becomes of me. If I could bring her back, all of this would be worth it. For another minute with her, I would do whatever it takes."

The ethereal woman's voice softens, probing deeper into my soul. "You must learn to let go of the burdens that bind you, young one. Your heart is clouded with anger, and resentment blinds your mind. Yet I see the purity in your soul, the lengths you would go to bring back your loved one. Even in death, you would lay down your own life for hers. A warrior bound by loss. But the answer you seek is closer than you realize."

"I would do anything... anything to see her again," I say, standing tall.

"You will find the truth you seek, Owen Beck," she says, her figure drifting away from my face. Her hands, starlight incarnate, cradle my cheeks and brush against my short beard. I can feel the warmth of the energy, the innocence.

"You know me?"

"Yes, Owen Beck, I know your story," she replies, her voice serene. "Many are the tales of time I have witnessed."

I stand stunned for a moment. "You've seen my future—"

My words are cut off by the soft whisper of her voice. "I see all, my child."

"How do I find you?"

As she speaks, her hand floats over my forearm bracer, emitting an inexplicable energy. A soft humming sound escalates in intensity, peaking in a bright flash of green light. I glance at my digital reader, watching in astonishment as ancient glyphs cycle across the screen, finally settling on a series of numbers.

"Your path commences in the realm of the unknown," she explains. "In the Uncharted Rim, there lies a planet that conceals itself from all explorers. Your journey will test you, stretch you to your limits. Follow the steps that are set before you, never wavering."

"What is this?" I ask.

"The answers you have been seeking," she replies, a hint of mystery in her words.

Coordinates to a planet in a far-off star system, it looks like, I think, looking back to Enohk. "But how—"

She stops me and points to the formation in the center of the room.

"Patience, Owen Beck. First, the Jadestone Key."

"Jadestone Key?" I ask.

She points to the altar.

I look back at the podium and hesitate before retracing my steps. Slowly, I extend my fingers toward the shard artifact and grab hold of it.

As I start to pull the object, I feel the energy in the room draw into the base of the shard, transferring into the circuitry of its inlays. I yank just hard enough to detach the item from its base.

Held in the confines of my palm is a baffling object. It's a compact corroded jade stone shard, small enough to fit comfortably in my hand, yet intriguingly complex. Its surface is awash with an intricate network of teal circuits that radiate a deep, solemn aura. Its green stone surface is jagged and meticulously carved into a three-point key. The circuity is so flawlessly intertwined with the stone that it's impossible to discern where one ends and the other begins.

"But what does this key open? And why here? Why on Turkken?" I ask, holding up the key. Its ingrained energy radiates through the intricate etchings, casting a mesmerizing glow.

"Long before your time, a civilization akin to your own revered us. Over eons, though, they succumbed to resentment, corruption, and insatiable greed. Here rests an artifact from that era, a piece of the larger puzzle you've now begun to unravel."

"I... I don't understand," I confess, my mind spinning.

"You will find your answers, Owen Beck. Patience," she counsels gently, bowing her head. "Patience," she whispers once more, softer this time.

"What will I find near the Uncharted Rim?" I ask, my hand closing around the key, feeling its strange energy thrum against my gloves.

"You must venture to a planet in a far-flung system, beyond the reach of your star maps. A forgotten world. There, you will discover a hidden temple nestled where the tears of the clouds meet the heart of the water. Your path awaits Owen. You will be tested. To relive your past, to confront your fears, you must delve deep within yourself. A difficult decision awaits you."

What difficult decision is she referring to? "Why are you helping me?"

"There is another whose path strays from the virtue of the selfless," she says. "Now hurry. Take the passage upward and leave Turkken behind. Time is not your ally."

My eyes dart to the door on the other side of the chamber.

"Remember," she says. "At night, the sight comes without being asked. By day, we are lost without being stolen."

"How—how did you know that?" I say as I think back to the words Avery wrote in her journal.

The glow from the key pulses rhythmically, as though resonating with my racing heartbeat. The hologram of Enohk begins to dissipate, her form becoming more transparent until she finally vanishes, leaving me alone in the chamber. That's when her voice fades into my head one last time. "Trust in the Jadestone Key."

I cast a last glance at the space Enohk previously occupied. Her sudden disappearance was as mysterious as her sudden arrival. "Enohk! Wait!" I call out into the silent expanse, my voice echoing back at me, unanswered.

An eerie stillness settles into the chamber, broken only by the sounds of my own ragged breathing and the occasional shifting of gravel beneath my boots. The reality of my solitude hits me, and a chill runs down my arms.

Reaching for my helmet, I secure it back onto my head. The latch clicks into place with a reassuring sound, and the suit's oxygen system whirs back to life, filling my helmet with air. My only viable route is through the intimidating stone-hewn pathway. Its destination unknown to me, it could lead anywhere. Should I trust Enohk? No. But it's the only lead I have.

As I step away from the podium into the dark surrounding me, a disquieting ambience fills the passage. I start to miss Tex more and more every second. With a heavy sigh, I steel my nerves and press on into the passage, the luminous Jadestone Key gripped tightly in my hand and the resonance of Enohk's words deep within my mind.

Just as I step through the threshold, I look back to the chamber and pause only for a moment before I journey upward into the dark.

A DEADLY ENCOUNTER

AFTER AN ARDUOUS trek through the depths of the caverns, I finally emerge at the precipice of an ingenious exit—a massive wall of stone sculpted to blend seamlessly with the surrounding rock face. This natural disguise opens as I approach, triggered by the Jadestone Key's latent energy. I clamber out, feeling the desert heat immediately engulfing me as the stone doorway grinds closed behind me, sealing off the mountain's cryptic labyrinth. One glance at my forearm display confirms my bearings. The Navcom shows that I'm on the opposite side of Mount Noragöth.

Exhausted, I trigger a system check on my suit. The digitized whirl echoes in my helmet as it comes to life. Relief washes over me as the indicators affirm that all the electronics, life support, and other integral systems are operating at optimal levels. I had zero run-ins with the ghosts in the tunnels on the way out through the singular passage that led right out of the mountain.

I turn my attention to the landscape that unfolds before me. The enormous stretch of the desert appears deceptively soothing, its beige waves of sand lying still under the scorching heat. Sunrise paints the sprawling desert in hues of golden-orange, the heat mirages twirling like dancing ghosts over the shifting dunes. As the celestial furnace ascends, the blistering glare intensifies, casting long shadows and etching harsh lines onto the barren landscape. It's morning again. We must have been down there for hours.

The daunting journey back to the *Astra* looms ahead, a gauntlet through the unforgiving Hundri-occupied lands. The dust storm is nearly here. Its mammoth cloud shadows over the horizon.

I have been hidden in the bowels of the mountain for hours, with no indication of when the Novas Guard would make their appearance. It could be in the next few minutes or perhaps hours from now. It's entirely dependent on their distance from the scout ship. Every moment is critical. I have a destination to reach, a mission to accomplish, and the Jadestone Key is only the first step. Time, as I know it, is of the essence.

My eyes drop to the key I pull from my pack—the Jadestone Key. Did it open the temple? Or did it open something else? It sits comfortably in my hand, its existence a blunt reminder of the reality of the experiences I've just witnessed. The ancient artifact with its futuristic shard design pulses with a mesmerizing light, the emerald circuits still seemingly alive with energy.

The realness of it anchors me. No hallucination or vivid dream could reproduce the weight of the relic, the intricacies of its design, the reality of its existence. I think after Tex dying, my brain went into survival mode; Enohk, the chamber, and the caves all feel like a dream that's just on the tip of my mind as fragments, just short recordings of the moments that just ensued.

My data log reactivates in the corner of my holoscreen in a small rectangular box. The log report displays all the data from Tex's and my trek underground. Most of the video data is corrupted or missing. His little icon appears, slowly rotating with a big red X through it. His network connection was severed from the ship.

I miss you, buddy, I think as I place the key in my bag. I have no idea what I will find in the outer rim, and I don't think it's going to be an easy journey without Tex.

Tightening the strap of my pack, I head off into the desert, this time completely alone, without my friend by my side.

As I approach the Hundri camp about an hour later, I stay hunkered down on the nearby ridge to keep out of sight. I lift the Trinocs and aim them towards the site. There's no movement, just bloodied flags billowing in the rising wind.

A deep rumble breaks my concentration as an enormous ship pierces through the heavy blanket of stratocumulus clouds, steadily revealing its immense structure as it descends onto the golden dunes of Turkken.

My breaths come in measured, slow rhythms as I recognize the unmistakable outline. It's a CXT-10—a Novas Guard Transport Vessel, a herald from a larger titan, suggesting that Ezrek's command ship, the *Novascar*, must be concealed somewhere within the solar system.

The CXT-10 is a formidable beast. It can transport an army of soldiers, and it's bristling with deadly weapons, mechanized vehicles, and ample cargo. Its daunting triangular shape casts an alarming, desolate shadow across the entire campsite. Its reflective black-sheened hull is punctuated by slits of menacing red lights, illuminating its edges brightly against the early morning sky.

Ryzer is on that ship. He must be.

Ezrek Valleion's third-in-command, Ryzer, is a force to be reckoned with, frequently accompanied by what some would consider a small army. This lethal Guard moves like a venomous shadow, striking with ruthless efficiency at Valleion's command. I've heard tales that Naomi Sato leads his siege across the galaxy as his number two aboard the *Novascar*, while Ryzer leads his ground squadrons.

Ezrek's search for the Khu'Val has led the Novas Guard to countless worlds, each ravaged in their quest for power. Their brutal invasions spare no corner of civilization, ransacking settlements, pillaging towns, looting libraries, and desecrating sacred temples and tombs. Each footprint they leave is a harsh reminder of their thirst for power, marked by their relentless search for even the faintest trace of the Khu'Val.

In their wake, once-thriving communities are reduced to smoking ruins, colorful towns shattered under the weight of their brutal onslaught. Women are left to mourn their husbands and children are rendered orphaned, their innocence stolen in the face of merciless devastation. Worse still is their chilling practice of abducting young men to be forced into service under Valleion's tyrannical rule, swelling the ranks of his already-formidable army. One can only assume whatever mind-altering tech he got his hands on came from Takashi Sato that night on Akereon.

For the past half-decade, Ezrek has been a phantom presence, lurking in the uncharted regions of space, far away from the settled systems and any type of authority. He has masterfully orchestrated Ryzer and his mindless legion of augmented Novas Guard to pursue every lead, every myth, while he stays in the dark.

Ezrek and the Novas Guard always seem to know just as much as I do when it comes to the Khu'Val; they've convinced themselves the power exists just as much as I have. Maybe Ezrek has found something.

Ever since the night back on Akereon City, he's been a ghost, sending his foot soldiers to do his bidding as he lurks from within his command ship, *Novascar*.

In an effort to stay one step ahead of Novas and Galacom, I've avoided the core planets, sticking to the shadows and navigating the deep unknown territories of deep space. Ezrek, on the other hand, has been making waves, ascending rapidly in notoriety. His name is now carved on the most wanted lists across the galaxy, his vile deeds making him a prime target for Galacom, yet they can never find him, or can't go where they need to look.

The enormous engines of the soldier transport send sand and the smell of the half-eaten dead into the air as it positions its landing struts. Hundri bodies flail as the ship lets out a giant roar from its thrusters, shifting into its deployment position. The wide-mouthed oversized bay doors slowly open, lowering a bridge to the ground below with a slow, elegant descent as it settles to the soil.

I wait. The opening is shadowed in black, and no one exits as the hydraulic gases dissipate in the wind nearly instantaneously.

As I peek out a little further, I hear something deep in the distance—a repetitive thumping reverberating through the ground. A dozen Novas Guard emerge from the darkness and embark down the platform in unison, each foot perfectly mirroring that of the soldier next to him. They march forward, not breaking stride as their black boots reach the hot sands. Their mechanical groans shift and grind until they suddenly stop as the last one exits the platform onto Turkken. Their rifles immediately shouldered, they quickly dispel into six teams of two, heading in different directions, scattering in harmony as they clear each tent and check the dead. Every step is a perfected symphony, flawlessly in sync.

The Novas Guard are the epitome of Ezrek's concept of a perfect soldier—devoid of emotions, thoughts, or any personal desires. They operate entirely under Ezrek's iron-fisted rule, each order executed without a second's hesitation. They've transformed into merciless mechanized beings, a terrifying cohort of faceless warriors prisoner to sacrificing themselves for Ezrek's objectives.

Their enhancements span a broad spectrum—superior optical systems, mechanized limbs, cutting-edge weaponry, and integrated artificial intelligence, all merging seamlessly with their organic forms to create potent war machines. Some Novas Guard are so heavily modified that it becomes difficult to discern where the man ceases to exist and where the machine begins.

I find myself contemplating their humanity. Does any part of their original essence persist within these mechanized bodies? What is it like to exist without a soul and under the unconscious control of a despotic madman? Can they even be considered human anymore?

Ezrek is simply too smart to hire criminals, outcasts, and mercenaries. He figured they would grow weary under his command over time, and they would undoubtedly demand more credits and more power. Our species tend to be greedy, and Ezrek isn't arrogant about this notion. Creating these soldiers has been an excellent way never to have a mutiny on his hands.

The Novas Guard clear the camp, emerging like phantoms dressed in their advanced, militant heavy armor. Each soldier boasts an armor chassis that is sleek, modular, and designed for maximum flexibility, with a midnight-black finish that swallows light. Crimson-glowing trails trace intricate circuits along their armor, threading across their form-fitting chest plates and limbs, converging at their state-of-the-art long-screen combat helmets.

These helmets encase their heads entirely, and their visors span from chin to crown, providing an unbroken panoramic field of view. Despite its cutting-edge design and expansive visual range, the material compromises its protective abilities, offering a somewhat vulnerable point for enemies.

The uniformity among these spectral soldiers is discomforting, but a careful examination reveals subtle distinctions. Each soldier wears an identification number and division insignia—"NG–1304" for the Novas Guard Infantry Division. It's a system of codification, identifying each unit's unique capabilities and roles within their ranks.

Their munitions are as varied and advanced as the soldiers wielding them. Some are equipped with the standard issue CX-308 rifles, lethal tools of precision and destruction. These rifles, while formidable, are outmatched by the heavier arms some Novas Guard wield. The HAR S-4 model, a devastating combination of power and technology, is favored among the infantry. Nestled among them are their heavy gunners, menaces wielding missile launchers and long-range rifles. Their presence alone is enough to keep any opponent at bay.

A bright glint catches my attention from the transport, and with a slide of my finger along the top of the Trinoc, it zooms towards the ship. I see a figure emerge from the dark bay door from the decompressing fog, and the sun slowly reveals the mysterious figure as it steps from the ship.

I knew it, I think as I zoom in even closer. *It's him—it's Ryzer.*

Unlike his Novas Guard counterparts, Ryzer's suit is decidedly less bulky, opting for a more form-fitted design that doesn't compromise on protection. It's marked by a flexible combat undersuit patterned with ribbed sections in a rich midnight grey adorned with sleek medium-gray accents, facilitating optimal maneuverability. The black armor almost seems to shimmer as he steps into the sunlight, and the obtuse-angled glow from the ocular screen on his advanced helmet is menacing.

Ryzer favors close-quarters engagements, his weapon of choice being a holographic energy-based blade. This cutting-edge piece of tech projects a high-energy blade using nano-holographic technology. But he's far from helpless in a ranged fight, with a shoulder-mounted energy pulse cannon at his disposal. This weapon fires a high-powered plasma sphere guided by his visor, making escape from its lethal blast near-impossible if it locks onto a target.

He's dangerous right down to his sidearm, the PX-99 Rapid Fire, which is just as formidable as any of their other gear. The PX-99 is compact yet lethal, with an extended magazine that increases its ammunition capacity significantly. This handheld firearm uses kinetic energy, releasing a barrage of high-velocity rounds at an astonishing rate. Aided by a laser-guided targeting system, every pull of the trigger promises an accurate hit.

In terms of weaponry and armor, Ryzer boasts a technical superiority that mirrors the near-limitless resources at Ezrek's disposal. His suit outperforms mine in almost every aspect: sleeker, more polished, and outfitted with more advanced systems.

Ryzer's formidable prowess is often underestimated due to his less-than-imposing stature. However, he more than makes up for it with his aggression, speed, and keen intellect. Like the rest of the Novas Guard, his face is hidden behind a shield, leaving his expressions and intentions veiled in mystery. That's how Ezrek likes his army—faceless soldiers. However, Ryzer seems different. He's smarter than the other Novas Guards. He seems to have more control over his own actions.

As the Trinocs glitch for a moment tracking through the winds, I look behind Ryzer, and a gargantuan shadow steps from the ship and stands next to him. The heavy-armored juggernaut towers over Ryzer, acting as a bodyguard. It's the Teknaut, T-7. The reinforced vicious version of a Novas Guard thunders down the loading dock behind Ryzer. It's at least three times the size of the average Novas Guard, and absent an organic brain like the infantry series—an unlucky soul ripped apart and put back together into a machine. The T-7 is retrofitted with heavy artillery armor, an advanced integrated tracking system, an augmented cardiovascular system, and muscle enhancements. It's best not to be on the receiving end of its Endonium-reinforced fists.

A Teknaut isn't impossible to kill, just very fucking hard. Its processor is hidden deep within its black reinforced helmet, hiding behind the vertical red slit of light that emanates from it. Your best bet is to go for the one-inch gap in its power unit on the backside of its waist; a version that big requires a little more juice to keep that type of soldier functioning. However, with a few well-aimed shots, you can disable it for a short time—maybe just long enough to run.

As I watch, Ryzer commands the Novas Guard to move through the camp. I don't see many options for a clear route forward—the *Astra* is hidden under the far ridge to the south behind them, and there's no way to get to it besides heading through the camp. The rock formations make it impossible to travel around. My oxygen is running low, and I have no ammunition left, and my shield's dead. I'll have a better chance of survival if I slip through the camp undetected using the sandstorm as cover, so I wait, holding for the perfect moment.

The first part of the yellow storm creeps into the camp, sweeping through the different structures. The wind plays games with the sand, and the sand plays right back with short-lived flurries, shapeshifting sheets of grain scurrying across the desert surface and metal structures, a dense wall allowing people to hide in plain sight. The Novas Guard disappear one by one into the wrathful rust-hued veil.

The wind is picking up a bit now, making it hard to see beyond a six-foot radius—it is a wall of milky powder all around, and visibility is close to none. Each step feels as if I'm trudging through wet concrete, the sand accumulating and creating dunes around my boots. Every so often, my foot sinks into a concealed pocket of soft sand, jolting me forward, throwing off my balance.

Quietly skirting the edge of a water reserve, I spot a lone Novas Guard, his back obliviously turned to me. I make my move, silently approaching him from behind as I draw my knife from the sheath strapped around my ankle. Swiftly, I snatch him into a firm grip, yanking his jaw upward to reveal his vulnerable neck.

I bury the knife's keen edge into the side of his throat. I steadily drive it deeper, effectively silencing any hope of an alarm cry. He attempts a shout, but it's muffled into a choking gurgle, his life force spurting out in thick torrents of color against his pale skin. I lay him on the ground, and his body stops moving. I retract the blade and pick up his rifle as I advance forward. The sand sticks to the fresh blood on my hands as I slide the rail back and load a round into the chamber.

I battle through the relentless onslaught of sand and wind, trudging on, my armor serving as my only protection against the gritty particles seeking to invade any exposed crevice. I find a momentary break near a weather-beaten tent adjoining the reserves. My gaze climbs up to two soldiers stationed on a catwalk above the nearby water reserve. It's the same vantage point that was witness to the Hundris' obliteration mere hours ago.

Taking a brief pause to familiarize myself with the foreign rifle, I engage its silencer mode. A mechanical compressor springs to life, swiftly reconfiguring itself over the barrel's front.

From a slight angle down below, I mount the rifle in front of me onto a tent support line, scoping the two Novas Guard standing back-to-back, my eye on the targets. I wait for a break in the storm as the harsh winds make the weapon bob up and down.

A disruption in the storm suddenly reveals itself. I fire a single silenced round, and it strikes both soldiers simultaneously. The round explodes through the chest of the first and hits the head of the second, causing them both to fall to the grated metal flooring with a loud clatter against the wind.

Well, shit.

The noise of their armor against the metal alerts a few soldiers to the left of us, so I sneak my way under, pressing close to the side of the wall under the catwalk, and stop just as I hear their footsteps closing in on me. One guard says something to the other, but I can't make it out over the storm.

I wait till I see the tip of the first barrel protruding from cover, then quickly grab it. Pointing his rifle upward, I hip-fire several muzzled shots from my pistol into the soldier to his left. Blood sprays onto the silo behind them as the left falls, and I struggle with the right. His brute strength is a match for mine. His mechanical arm breaks my grip and grabs me by the throat. His metallic fingers grasp tighter and tighter, shutting down my airway. I choke for air as he reaches for his sidearm. I lift the barrel of his own rifle under his chin and slam the trigger. Silenced rounds explode from the top of his helmet and pieces of brain and circuitry burst into the air, dropping us both down.

I stare at the disintegrated face as smoke and blood pour from the shattered helmet. His hand glitches as it releases my throat, and I take in a full breath and move forward.

Rubbing my throat, I tread past the looming water silos and edge closer to the cluster of tents on the parched, fractured ground. This ground is much easier to navigate, but the sand is piling up.

As I weave my way through the encampment, nearing the edge towards the ship, a group of Novas Guard huddled around a pile of lifeless Hundri bodies catches my attention. Their obscure silhouettes materialize and then fade back into the dusty swirls of the storm. They outnumber me, and any attempt to gun them down would undoubtedly alert the rest of the camp. So, I stop, staying hidden, straining my ears over the storm to catch their conversation.

"NG-6754 patrol, status," demands the one who appears to be in charge, his voice cutting through the storm. There's no response. The leader tries again. "NG-6754, report."

Receiving no answer, the lead Guard's body language shifts into high alert. He spins in my direction, issuing orders to his comrades. "You four, with me! I thought I heard shots."

With a sinking feeling, I realize they are headed directly towards my position. I duck and press myself against the fabric of the tent, holding my breath as the soldiers, led by the Teknaut-7, stride by, alarmingly close.

Internally, I scowl. *Here we go again.* My hand instinctively reaches for the unfamiliar rifle, fingers checking to ensure a fresh mag is locked.

As I'm bracing myself for the approaching confrontation, I constrict my grip and a deep, digitally synthesized voice rings out from behind me. "Move, and you're dead, pilot. Drop the weapons and step out."

The threatening click-clack of multiple weapons cocking fills the air, each resounding sound a chilling reminder of the dire situation I find myself in. Time stands still, my unease ramping up click by click. One wrong move could be my last.

That distinctive digital voice thunders through the gusting winds once more, jolting me from my contemplation. "Drop the weapon and get on your knees, pilot." Sand spins around me in a chaotic gust, every grain seemingly suspended in time. I can feel the laser sights burning into me, a constellation of tiny green dots tracing over my chest.

"Drop it or die. I won't repeat myself," the voice threatens, its tone cold.

I slowly lift myself into the dying storm, raising my hands and the rifle high into the air in an unspoken gesture of surrender. There's no mistaking it. I know that voice anywhere. It has an elegance to it—he's a man of intellect.

It's Ryzer.

I don't have enough ammunition to take them all on, nor can I escape the barrage of firepower from the T-7; I only have one option. I'm at the wrong end of the barrel, and they have the drop on me.

I don't know how I could have been this stupid. I'm smarter than this.

The rest of the Novas Guard scatter through the grounds as I turn around, and they're all aiming toward one thing—me.

"Easy—easy," I say, unclipping the rifle from the foreign sling and slowly placing it on the ground in front of me.

I kneel as three soldiers and the T-7 advance towards me. Two of them pin my shoulders down while holding my arms back as the third cautiously retrieves my rifle and sidearm from my hip. The T-7 stands idle as it towers over me, ready to rip me in half on Ryzer's command.

"Fuck, you're a lot bigger up close," I say, glancing at the excessively large murder robot. Its figure eclipses the sun, leaving me in a subtle shadow beneath it. Its vertical slit eye scans over me, examining me for weapons and explosives.

"You've been quite the nuisance, pilot," Ryzer says as he dismisses the T-7 and stands in front of me. "We've been tracking the *Astra* for a very long time. You've even been able to elude even our best hunters. Yet here you are. All we had to do is wait for you to come to us."

"What's my bounty up to now?" I ask.

"Ezrek placed a ten-million bounty on your head."

"Ten million, huh? I thought it'd be more. Curious, though—that dead or alive?"

"He wants you alive, or you'd be dead already," he says, convincingly making a familiar gesture with his hand.

"I didn't take him for the caring type," I say, smirking.

"Why—why here? What's so special about Turkken?" Ryzer demands.

"Oh, that's easy. Your wife said Turkken was nice this time of year. I thought I'd give it a visit."

Ryzer looks to the Novas Guard holding me and nods, and the Guard slams the stock of his rifle into the back of my head. *Wham!* The heavy blow sends my vision into a slight blur.

"You," Ryzer says to one of the two who pinned me down, "retrieve his bag and bring it to me."

The Novas Guard takes my pack off my shoulder and hands it over to Ryzer, and his red glowing visor scans over it; he then searches through the inside before turning it over entirely, dumping its contents carelessly to the ground. He sifts through the contents with his feet before pausing for a moment. He slowly retrieves the journal from the ground next to Tex's eye, curiously stares at the cover, then the back, pauses a moment, and then tosses it aside when his eye catches the Jadestone Key shard.

"What is this?" Ryzer says as he picks up the odd key from the sand.

"What's what?" I say, as my vision can barely focus. "I can't see shit."

"This," Ryzer states, holding the key closer.

"Oh, that is just a key to your mom's house," I say.

Ryzer nods again.

This time, the Novas Guard lunges and lands a heavy blow to my stomach, immediately knocking every bit of breath out of my body.

Breathless for air, my diaphragm spasms, and I gasp. "I'm sorry...I meant—" I stop; I can hardly get the words out.

"Good. Now, what is th—"

"I meant your dad's house. Whew!" I breathed in. "I didn't know if I would get that one out." I laugh in between coughs.

"Funny guy," he says.

I laugh a bit with my head hanging low, barely breathing. I can't help it. They can eat shit.

"I'm not going to ask again," Ryzer says one last time in a lower-octave synthesized voice.

"What? Is Ezrek too high-and-mighty to come out here and face me himself? He has to send his errand boy to retrieve his prize?" I say through my gritted teeth as I lift my head.

Ryzer hands the key to the soldier next to me and ignites his holographic blade. It begins paneling upward in an energy-based isometric formation, each panel overlapping one another from the hilt upward until they reach the end, unifying as one solid piece that sizzles with energy.

The tip rises just under my helmet. It crackles and singes as the power fluctuates. Ryzer kneels down as the blade is centimeters from my throat and whispers in a synthetic rasp, "Just give me a reason, pilot. Just give me any reason."

"Just get on with it."

"What's the rush? Oh, and by chance, did you feel a bit of an earthquake a few hours ago?" Ryzer says in a dark undertone.

What does he mean?

My heart begins pumping faster. I don't answer and stay silent.

"Well, our Scout made contact with your vessel *Astra* before going dark near a small city."

Dos Calderon, I whisper in my thoughts. *I put them in danger.*

"Dos Calderon, wasn't it?" Ryzer says, his synthesized voice confirms.

"What did you do?" I demand.

"We looked for answers, and we didn't find any, so we spared the rest of the survivors."

"What do you mean, 'spared?'" I ask in a firmer tone as my fists start to tighten.

"'Spared' as in we wiped them from the face of the planet from the sky. We got what we needed, and shortly after take-off, we created a crater of what used to be Dos Calderon. We did them a favor," Ryzer says as he retracts his blade and places it on his belt. "Death from multiple air-to-ground fragmentation missiles is honorable; it's painless."

"'A crater?'" I inhale as my heart feels like it will explode from my chest.

Aanos, her father, the entire town of Dos Calderon. Dead.

I feel my eyes water as the anger creates an overwhelming pit in my stomach. I bite my tongue as I try to show no sentiment of weakness to the Novas Guard and Ryzer. *Aanos...*

"Take him to the ship," Ryzer demands to the soldiers holding me down.

As the two slowly drag my weighted body towards the ship, another guard grabs my belongings from the sand. I see Ryzer also hand him the Jadestone Key, but my mind drifts, I can't help but think of Aanos and her family, Tex, and, most importantly, Avery. I've failed everyone.

Everyone's dead.

We get closer and closer to the vessel, and as we reach the loading-bay bridge, I hear a loud commotion behind us. "Commander, we have movement to the south," NG-1203 warns his superior.

I turn to look as the Novas Guard rush to get into a defensive formation, each one waiting for Ryzer's command to engage. The winds are calming and the sun glares to the west. I look in the distance, and I can barely make out what it is until a group of tiny black out-of-focus silhouettes begins emerging over the sand ridge from beyond the camp.

From the crest of the hills, an echoing symphony of warrior chants fill the air. As the storm temporarily recedes, shadowy figures spread across the slopes like a dark tide, their numbers seeming to multiply with every passing moment as they call to the vast desert sky. There are dozens, if not hundreds of them.

It's the rest of the Dök Hundri, returning home.

"Hold," Ryzer bellows, his digitized command silencing the chaos as he orders the Novas Guard into their final defensive positions.

Before any of us can react, a single gunshot shatters the desert silence with a thunderous crack. To my left, one of the guards restraining me collapses to the ground, a bullet hole gaping in his chest. A dark pool of blood spreads quickly beneath him, and his rifle lies in the sand beside him, waiting.

I look up, and the other guard who was holding me releases his grip in surprise, swinging his weapon towards the looming threat on the horizon.

"Open fire!" Ryzer commands, his gaze fixated on the fallen Novas Guard. At his command, a hailstorm of bullets crackles through the air, igniting an intense firefight.

The first wave of Hundris chant and charge toward the camp, each round they release sparking mayhem among the Novas Guard. The scene devolves into absolute fucking chaos.

The T-7 takes a step forward, its nine-barreled G14 Minigun smoothly sliding from its back, locking into place over its shoulder. The Hundris' bullets bounce harmlessly off its reinforced armor, leaving only minor scuffs and paint-chip damage. The T-7 emits an unsettling roar, then unleashes a torrent of rounds at the Hundris.

Limb by limb, the warriors are torn apart. The bullets shred through the first wave like paper, disintegrating bodies into unrecognizable pulp, as they wear little armor. Some are cleanly bisected, while others explode under the brutal force.

Time to go, I think urgently, my Navcom scanning the battlefield for a viable escape route.

Ryzer's plasma cannon ignites and rips through a line of Hundri—their bodies mangled, large intestines spilling to the sands. They are being decimated; the Novas Guards' firepower is overwhelming. Their casualties are remarkably minimal in comparison.

Despite the Hundris' lack of precision, their sheer numbers grant them an advantage as they swarm over the battlefield, their forces matching those of the Novas Guards.

It's now or never, I think as I grab a loose fist-sized jagged rock next to my feet.

In an instant, I pivot, delivering a rapid kick to the knee of the soldier next to me. The sharp, sickening crack signals the splintering of his bones in the opposite direction. As he crumples to the ground, I seize the opportunity, lashing out with the sharp rock in my hand. The stone crashes into his windpipe, delivering a fatal blow. A guttural, choked sound I've never heard before escapes him as he collapses, desperately clawing for air that will never come.

I turn quickly to another as I grasp his trigger hand and the body of his rifle tightly; he panic-fires, sweeping across the camp, and his accidental discharge takes out two other Novas Guards in front of us. I shove the rifle body upward, and the metal rail guard smashes against the front of his helmet, exploding the holoscreen visor into his eyes. A bloodcurdling roar, laced with the essence of mortal agony, rips through his throat as jagged shards savage his corneas, plunging him into a world of ruthless darkness. His knees buckle, body convulsing with pain, collapsing under its cruel intensity. I seize his chin and the base of his skull, twisting with a violence that defies all mercy. A sickening snap reverberates through the gunfire, and he collapses onto the war-ravaged terrain, my pack slipping from his lifeless grip.

With a swift motion, I retrieve my gear and the mystical Jadestone Key, retreating into the concealing shadows of scattered cargo crates as a bombardment of deafening detonations ignites around me.

Ryzer, his silhouette outlined by the relentless gunfire, releases a torrent of plasma rounds from his shoulder cannon. The raw power rips through mounds of the fallen, scattering Hundri remnants into the heated winds.

On the blood-soaked battlefield, the T-7, advances, meeting the shattered Hundri frontline. A Hundri rushes the Teknaut with a large sword, and it seizes him by the throat, its raw strength manifesting in a grisly spectacle as he tears the man in half at the waist. A grotesque cascade of entrails and innards spills onto the scorched desert floor, discarded like a hollowed-out shell of a creature.

Ryzer's voice cuts through the battle. "Capture the pilot!" he yells as I navigate the war-torn area, halfway to the safety of the *Astra*.

With my adrenaline spiking, I blind-fire a hasty spray of bullets from the stolen Novas Guard's rifle in Ryzer's direction. The rounds illuminate his small forearm kinetic shield, then fall to the ground as he disengages it. "Don't let him escape!"

The T-7 hinges with a metallic shriek, cleaving through a writhing wall of Hundri and Novas Guards in our path. High-caliber bullets whizz past me, each detonation sending plumes of sand spiraling into the air, accompanied by a lethal hiss.

A resonating blast reverberates in my ears. A split-second glance reveals a gleaming sphere hurtling towards me, splitting mid-flight to unleash a snaring tether, aimed with unerring precision for my legs. The metallic serpent wraps around my shins, binding them with merciless tightness. I'm yanked off my feet, the cruel sound of my own cursing drowning out the world as the tether contracts, dragging me magnetically towards them.

The T-7, out of ammunition, stalls for the briefest moment to reload, and Ryzer's attention is diverted to the Hundri. A moment—that's all I need.

I yank out my blade, rotating the hilt with a sharp twist. The blade crackles to life, energy waves dancing along its edge. It slices through the tether with ease, leaving nothing but molten remnants sizzling in the sand. I rise, sand cascading off me, and charge towards the distant rock formation.

As I near a small rocky ridge, a Novas Guard figure locks into my peripheral vision, lining up their shot. The world slows as they pull the trigger, launching a round that rips through the air. A one in a million shot, slithers right through a crack between my armor plates, the bullet penetrates, lodging the bulky, fragmented round into my oblique muscle. The shot sends me forward, and I flail over the ridge onto the rocks with a hard crash.

I press my hand against the wound in my hip, feeling the hot sting of a bullet buried deep. "Fuckers!" I gasp, my voice a harsh rasp. A dark stain spreads rapidly across my undersuit as my life force seeps away. I apply more pressure, grinding my teeth against the searing pain as I hoist myself to my feet. Each throb sends fresh waves of blood to pool on the arid ground.

Using every ounce of my remaining strength, I stagger towards the waiting *Astra*, my path marked by a bloody trail. Glancing over my shoulder, I find refuge in a blind spot from the enemy's fire.

With a few forearm commands, *Astra* roars to life, engines humming with anticipation. As I limp up the bay door, the craft shudders beneath me, primed for ascent. I collapse into the cockpit, the ship's controls offering an unforgiving embrace.

With a deafening boom, the ship lurches skyward. In the distance, I see Ryzer fire off a futile round, the bullet ricocheting harmlessly off the advanced Endonium hull. I can't help but smirk at the useless gesture.

As the dust storm engulfs the battle scene once more, his figure is the last thing I see before the *Astra* breaks through the cloud layer and vanishes from sight.

Rocketing into the atmosphere, I leave Turkken behind, heading for the pitch-black void of space. I have one fewer ally at my side, a fresh wound burning in my hip, and the Jadestone Key secured in my pack. I leave only a legacy of blood and sand.

I set the coordinates for the Uncharted Rim, pinning my hopes on Enohk's cryptic instructions. As I apply pressure to my wound, blood spurts out, splattering across the console. I survey the mess, a weary sigh escaping my lips.

My vision dims, the weight of my injuries pulling me under. I close my eyes, only for a moment.

STRANGER FROM THE PAST

A FAINT MELODIC tune crackles in the background as I struggle to pry open my heavy eyelids. They resist my efforts, as if weighted down by an unseen force.

My entire body feels like I took a few rounds to the chest and fell off a fucking building or something. Every time I try to shift, I succumb to the pain and give up.

The scent of gauze and disinfectant is coming from below me. I'd know that smell anywhere.

I try to move again, but no luck.

Let's see if words work.

Did I make a sound? I don't think I did. It was probably just a dry rasp noise.

After what feels like an eternity, my fragile eyes open and are greeted by a disorienting haze. The surroundings appear distorted, unfamiliar. Someone has cleaned my wounds and bandaged them very methodically. I am impressed. But I also realize I am practically naked, save for a pair of someone else's underwear, and I'm sprawled on a worn-out tan leather couch.

Bathing the room in a medley of hues is a slender transparent-edged screen playing the news. Several ads and breaking news stories flicker off the touchscreen's surface, bathing the small, dimly lit apartment in an intense afterglow.

Everything reeks of the neglected slums district of Akereon City—the stained shag carpet, the smoke-yellowed walls, the lingering odor of aging, the cramped living room, and the medals adorning the wall. A shiver runs through me as a gust of cold air slips in through the slightly ajar window, settling over my bare feet. It penetrates to my bones, accentuating the chilling feeling that accompanies blood loss.

Peering out onto the balcony, I witness a relentless storm shaking the outdated windows of this mid-level apartment. Questions flood my mind, but my memories remain cloudy, fragmented.

Who am I?

I struggle to recollect, searching my mind for answers. Finally, a name surfaces amidst the fog—*Owen. And my wife...*

"Avery," I whisper, a large ball forming in my throat, constricting my breath. My heartbeat begins to pound out the back of my chest, and my vision slowly begins to clear.

I lost her. She's gone.

I'm never going to see my wife again.

A foreign type of rage and anger progresses through my veins, something I've never felt before. It's more than anger. The pain, the loss, and the unanswered questions ignite a furious storm that eclipses any lingering sadness. The only thing I feel is fury.

I lie there, prisoner to my own mind as it fills with swirling contemplations and unanswered questions. I can't help but dwell on the moment of Avery's death and Ezrek's role in it. The image of her lifeless body disturbs my every thought, etched into my mind like an indelible scar. I find myself lost in a sea of emotions ranging from grief to anger, confusion to disbelief.

The rain beating the windows transports me back to the moment on the roof. Sato had hundreds of millions stashed away. The plan was to steal everything and pin it on me? With Sato dead, there's no one left to search for them, to get revenge. The plan was always to pin it on me. That's what Aden was trying to tell me. Ezrek probably threatened to kill him if he didn't help. But who informed Sato we were coming? And why would Ezrek murder *her*? It doesn't make any sense. Just to torture me? Just one last fuck you? What drove him to do that to Ave? My mind races, searching for any clues or signs I might have missed, desperately trying to unravel the net of deceit and betrayal that has woven its way into my life.

Was it greed, power, or some hidden agenda that led Ezrek to pull the trigger? Avery had been an innocent bystander caught in the crossfire, her life cruelly snuffed out.

The weight of the unanswered "Why?" presses heavily on my chest, each breath a painful reminder of the emptiness left in her absence. I vow to find answers, to confront Ezrek and hold him accountable for the irreparable damage he has caused. *I'll find him Ave, I promise*, I think as tears fall from my eyes.

As I turn my attention away from the balcony, the emergency broadcast on the television interrupts the local station. The news anchor's voice fills the room, pulling me further into the unfolding story.

"Good evening, viewers. This is your anchor, Jack Callahan, bringing you the most recent unfolding events here on VPWN-7. We interrupt your regular programming to bring you the latest shocking development. An immense explosion last week has severely impacted the heart of Akereon City, extinguishing countless innocent lives," he says firmly, neatly arranging his documents before he resumes speaking. "Preliminary indications suggest the epicenter of the explosion was none other than Takashi Cybernetics' headquarters, the iconic landmark at the city's very core. The origin of the catastrophic blast remains shrouded in mystery, yet the death cost is alarmingly mounting, and among the casualties is the head of Takashi Cybernetics, Takashi Sato. If anyone has seen this individual..."

Suddenly, my image flashes across the screen, stamped with the label *Prime Suspect*. "We urge anyone with information to immediately contact A.C.P.D. Owen Beck, former high-ranking commander of Galacom, is being sought for interrogation concerning the blast and the mysterious disappearance of Avery Beck, his wife. The connection between these two incidences remains elusive, but the public is advised to consider Owen Beck both armed and dangerous."

A picture of Avery from her university identification appears on screen next to my military photo. I stare into her eyes as I can feel the weight of suspicion pressing down on me. Panic surges through my veins. "Fuck," I say, trying to move again with my eyes trying to find the door.

Just then, a voice from the kitchen breaks through the turmoil. "You better stay put, soldier, or you'll open up those wounds again."

My attention shifts to the source of the voice, and I see an older man emerging from the kitchen. His weathered face is adorned with a thick, bushy white beard, and his sunken eyes reflect a blend of wisdom and age. He approaches, his slender elderly hands carrying a tray of steaming soup.

"Who are you?" I manage to ask, my throat raw and hoarse.

"Call me Dyce," he says, offering a warm smile. His yellowed teeth tell the tale of smoking for years.

I take in his presence, sensing a kindness that instantly puts me at ease. Dyce sets the tray down on the table and takes a seat in an armchair nearby, muting the television. "I don't mean to pry, but do I have to be worried?"

"Worried?" I say through my swollen, dehydrated lips.

"The explosion," he says, pointing towards my picture on the screen. "I found you practically dead in that alleyway. After I heard the boom, I saw you fall from that scaffolding. I slammed on the brakes just in time to see you hit pavement. I pulled into that alley, and when I got to you, you just kept mumbling the same thing over and over—it was either 'Please, no cops,' or 'Avery,' I think you said."

"I have to go. Please," I say hastily.

"Listen, soldier; you aren't going anywhere in your condition. You're lucky you're alive, let alone speaking."

"I can't stay here," I say urgently, struggling to sit up.

Dyce places a firm but gentle hand on my shoulder, easing me back down. "Easy there, soldier. You're in no condition to go anywhere. You had a collapsed lung, a few gunshot wounds, and several broken bones. You're lucky to be alive."

His words sink in. I'm not going anywhere. Avery is gone and there's nothing I can do about it.

"Did you kill Takashi?" Dyce asks.

I don't say anything. I don't want to reveal too much—not to a stranger whom I just met. I must tread carefully, guarding myself while finding solace in sharing just enough to unburden his conscience for saving me in that forsaken alley. "No," I respond. Sniffling up my runny nose, I refuse to let my emotions consume me entirely. "I didn't kill anyone. You have my word. It wasn't supposed to end this way."

The reassurance brings the man a spark of relief, a reprieve from the weight of judgment. "I believe you," he replies.

"Why are you helping me?" I manage to ask, looking into Dyce's compassionate, weary bloodshot eyes.

He chuckles softly. "Sometimes, life presents us with a chance to do the right thing, even for a stranger. I saw a fellow brother-in-arms in need, and my instincts kicked in."

I pause, overwhelmed by his selflessness. "Thank you," I whisper sincerely. "But... how did you know I served?"

"Your tattoo," he says, pointing to EOS Division's insignia on my shoulder.

"You know what this means?"

Dyce nods, a flicker of understanding in his eyes. "You're one bad motherfucker. Only the best had that mark. Never met one of you in person."

As he reaches for the bowl of soup, I catch a glimpse of a faded tattoo peeking out from under his sleeve. Intrigued, I ask about it. "And that?"

"That?" Dyce says, rolling up his sleeve to reveal a tattoo like mine, but from a different Division. "I served with Galacom back in the day. Those were some wild times. Just a reminder of a life we both lived, huh, ghost man?"

"How—" I stop, as the words are too hard to produce.

"How are you still alive?" he interrupts, finishing my sentence.

I nod.

"With steady hands, a heap of TetraGel, and a dash of luck, I'd say I did a fair job. If I were a bettin' man, I'd wager you'll make it. There's a guardian angel watching over you, son," he says, gently lifting the dressing to inspect my wounds.

My torso is covered in bruises and lacerations. Everything down to my toes screams in pain.

"I was a medic for Galacom for some time, and I know my way around death." The man sits forward and, as his dark eyes tighten, softly says,

"Here. I heated you up some of my favorite soup. Now, I'm not the best cook in the world, but it has everything your body needs to regain strength. There will be time to fight again, soldier. You need to rest," he says, gesturing to the murky brown throw-up in the bowl. "It tastes better than it looks, I promise." He nods to the soup.

He guides me gently back down, holds the base of my skull, and puts the bowl to my mouth. I slurp down the salty meat liquid, nearly gagging as the lukewarm bowl of mush runs down my throat.

Dyce leans closer, holding two blue pills in his hand. Their significance is not lost on me. "It's going to be a long night. I suggest you take two of these and knock out for a while," he says, his tone gentle yet firm.

He tosses the pills into my mouth and picks up the glass of water from the table, placing the straw to my parched lips. He guides me to drink, and I comply, gulping down the water, which soothes my gravelly throat.

"You need to go to the bathroom?" Dyce asks.

Everything hurts so bad I can't even tell. "I don't think so," I say uncertainly.

"Hah." He smirks. "If you piss on my couch again, you're cleaning it this time."

"'Again?' How long was I out for?" I ask, as my sense of time is patchy. I can barely grasp a simple thought.

"Nearly a week. Thought I lost you a few times. Glad you woke up."

"Me too," I say, as my eyelids feel heavier by the second.

"If you need anything, I'm a bit hard of hearing nowadays, so just holler as loud as you can. The bandages should be good for the night; I'll replace them tomorrow. You should try to get some rest," Dyce says as he walks toward his bedroom.

"Hey—" I say, and he cuts me off.

"Yeah?"

"Thank you," I reply.

"My pleasure. Goodnight, ghost man," Dyce says as he enters his room, shuts the door behind him, and locks it.

I guess I would, too.

I'm not going anywhere soon, and I need my strength if I'm going to find that son of a bitch Ezrek.

My eyes feel heavy. Whatever he gave me is working fast, and I quickly slip into a deep sleep.

Weeks go by. I notice that my body has regained some of its strength as I stretch my shoulder. It radiates pain, but I'm hoping it will go away with time. The wounds have begun to heal, but they leave behind fading scars as reminders of the discomfort. It's been weeks of physical therapy, ice baths, and long, painful stretching sessions, but I'm finally starting to feel better.

Across from me, at a small, dingy circular foldable table, sits the old man who saved me that fateful night, Dyce. His eyes light up with a warm smile as he notices my consciousness returning. "Ah, welcome back, Owen!" he says. "Let's play, airhead."

"Sorry," I say, returning my attention to the game. He waves off my apology, reaching across the table to grab more pieces for this "intriguing" board game I've never played.

The game's design is simple enough, but Dyce has had to explain it a few times. "One more time? I think I'm getting it."

"Ugh, okay. From the beginning?"

"If you wouldn't mind," I say.

"Fine," he says, organizing his pieces. "The board game is called *Satori Stones*. It is a very old game my mother taught me. It beautifully embodies the concept of duality and harmony, using these black and white stones and paper cards to create a simple yet very serene experience. The objective of the game is to find balance between opposing forces represented by the black and white stones. The game board consists of this circular grid divided into sections that resemble the interlocking flowing halves of a circle. Each player begins with a set of stones—these," he says, pointing to the pile, "either black or white, and this stack of cards."

"Okay," I say, slightly unsure.

"The game starts by placing a neutral pebble—this one," he says, holding up the grey one known as the Balance Stone and placing it in the center of the board. "Players take turns strategically placing their pieces on the grid, trying to create a balanced pattern by surrounding the Balance Stone with their own colored stones. The challenge lies in maintaining the delicate equilibrium while strategically blocking your opponent's moves. Ultimately, the winner is the player who achieves the most harmonious and balanced arrangement of stones on the board while effectively countering their opponent's moves. These paper cards, known as Harmony Cards, add an element of surprise. These cards can be played during a turn to influence the positioning of the stones or disrupt the opponent's plans."

"How so?" I say, a little confused.

"Some cards may allow players to swap stones, create temporary barriers, or even alter the grid itself. As the game starts, we must carefully analyze the ever-evolving pattern on the board, anticipating each other's moves while ensuring our own stones maintain balance. The placement of each stone impacts the overall harmony, and the strategic choices made by a player can shift the delicate symmetry in their favor or disrupt their opponent's plans."

"Perfectly not confusing," I say, staring at him blankly.

As the Satori Stones adorn the board, Dyce and I delve into a conversation about our favorite intergalactic cuisines. We share stories of exotic dishes sampled during our respective travels across the cosmos, reminiscing about the unique flavors that have tantalized our taste buds. Dyce recounts the time he savored the delicate essence of Nebulon Spice Soup, a concoction known for its celestial aroma and mystical properties. "That shit was spicy," he says. I, on the other hand, amuse him with tales of indulging in Lunar Blossom Noodles, which are infused with the essence of moonflowers and accompanied by the crispness of Telos Valley greens. Our mouths water as we exchange descriptions, imagining the vibrant colors and scintillating flavors that accompany these delicacies.

Dyce's face breaks into a tricksy smile as he makes his move on the Satori Stones board, strategically placing a white stone amidst a cluster of black ones. "Ah, Owen, don't underestimate the power of balance," he says. "Life's a lot like this game, you know. It's about finding balance, navigating the delicate placements of rival stones. Sometimes, a seemingly insignificant move can shift the tides and lead to a remarkable outcome. So, tell me, my friend—what move will you make to tip the scales in your favor?"

I ponder his words, my concentration now fixed on the board before me.

"What's your next move, Owen?"

With a determined smirk, I strategically placed a black stone adjacent to his white one, subtly disrupting his carefully constructed harmony. As I make my move, a silent challenge passes between us.

As we sit there, occupied by the game, the wounds within me may still ache, and the pain of my wife's loss remains a constant companion as I stare at my ringless finger, but I am not alone. Dyce's presence, the growing friendship we share, reminds me that even in the darkest of times, there are soldiers' bonds that can lift us up and help us find strength anew. But I sit there and wonder his words, *what's my next move?*

Weeks have turned into nearly three months. As I continue to recover, a deep connection has formed between Dyce and me. He's become more than a caretaker; he's become a mentor, a confidant, and a true friend. We've shared our war stories, baring our souls and recounting the triumphs, the losses, and the invaluable lessons we have learned throughout our lives. In Dyce's presence, I find solace and the strength to face the challenges that lie ahead. He lives alone, surviving off his pension, with no children, and he lived a minimal life. I feel bad for him, he's so alone.

However, as my physical strength returns, so does the weight of my obligations. The walls of Dyce's modest dwelling seem to close in on me, reminding me of the unfinished business that awaits me out there. The authorities, relentless in their pursuit, are still hot on my trail. I'm a wanted man not only for the explosion and the death of Sato, but also the disappearance of Avery, and time is running out. My face is plastered everywhere. There is no way they would find me here, but how long can I stay hidden?

"Thanks for dinner. I'll cook the next one," I say, clearing our plates from the dinner table.

He stands in the kitchen cleaning the pots and pans, his thermal sleeves pushed to his dry elbows. "Sounds good, star man."

The residual heat from dinner lingers in Dyce's kitchen as I step out onto the balcony. The apartment, a humble speck on the fringe of Akereon City, is a short throw from the glitzy heart of the Osaka district.

From here, the city looks like a setting straight out of a neo-noir thriller, the reality of its grimy underbelly hidden beneath the glamour of neon lights. Buildings, both old and older, are stacked haphazardly, their silhouettes creating a serrated skyline against the rainclouds' heavy grey.

The rain has started in earnest, droplets turning into a relentless torrent that wash the city in a cold, persistent shower. It paints the cityscape in varying dreary shades, creating a sheen that lends a deceptive gloss to the otherwise worn-out structures.

When will it end? I think as I lean on the railing. The patter of rain on the concrete below merges with the city's incessant whine. There's a peculiarity to it, a subtle undercurrent of danger that mirrors the predicament I'm in. It's like the calm before a storm, the city holding its breath as if aware of the conflict that's about to unfold.

Below, the city goes about its nocturnal rhythm, unfazed by the downpour. Automated taxis fly past, their headlights creating a moving lightshow on the rain-slicked streets. Far-off music drifts up from a neon-lit nightclub, a lively beat that's at odds with the serene drumming of rain.

Looking out at the city, I suddenly know it's time to go. Time to leave Dyce, Vola Prime, and everything I know behind to find that son of a bitch Ezrek and make him pay for what he did to me. A sense of resolution washes over me. It's time to face my past, to dive headfirst into the unknown that awaits.

I open the balcony door and step inside. Dyce is sitting at the kitchen table with a small box in front of him.

"Dyce," I say, walking over to him.

As I approach, I know that our time together is coming to an end. I need closure, a resolution to the mysteries that plague my existence, but a part of me doesn't want to go. I don't want to leave my friend.

"Sit down, Owen," he says with his hands atop the small metal lockbox. "It's time," he says, opening it slowly.

I stay quiet, wondering what's in its confines.

"Owen, this was always temporary. I was just waiting for the right time. I think that's now."

"What do you mean?" I say.

"I was just waiting for you to tell me you were ready. We can sit here all the while, playin' games, drinking, reminiscing, but you don't belong here. You never did."

"I know, Dyce. I can't ignore the pull any longer. I must face it. It's been too long."

He reaches into the metal box and reveals a sleek, compact pistol—a snubbed-nose eight shooter that looks older than I am.

"You have a choice, Owen," he says, placing the gun on the table. He slides it, and it stops just before me.

"What choice?" I say, staring at it, then back to Dyce.

He sighs. "The pain you feel now won't be alleviated by chasing ghosts of the past. She would've wished for you to cherish the memories, to embrace the present and find your way forward. Think, Owen—do you wish to be an old soul, burdened with regrets of a life never fully lived?"

Unsure of what to say, I stay silent for a moment, but suddenly, I muster four short words. "I made a promise."

He stays silent for a moment. "I thought you'd feel that way. I want the best for you, my friend. I just don't want to see you go down that road and lose yourself—or, worse, end up on my damn sofa again," he says light-heartedly, trying to soften the mood.

I accept the weapon, feeling its weight in my hands. "Solid," I say.

"They don't make them like that anymore. That is an earlier model standard issue."

As I tuck the pistol to my side, Dyce's stare bores into mine. "If this is the path, I can't stop you. But let me help you one last time."

"What do you mean?"

"There's someone you need to find—a man named Léon. He owes me a favor, and I believe he can help you. You aren't safe walking the streets—not with all the cameras and digital scanners, regardless of how long it's been. The second they scan your retina or NetCode, you're done for. A.C.P.D. will be there in three minutes or less."

"Agreed. Who is Léon?"

Dyce's voice lowers. "Léon is an old friend, like us. He served with me, and he owes me one. Hell, he owes me two. He's currently running a transport cargo ship—livestock. If he's there, he'll be docked at the spaceport. I'll shoot him a message to let him know to look out for you."

"Livestock?"

"He's a smuggler. He will get you to where you need to go."

"The spaceport will be swarming with police. It always is."

"I thought you were slick."

"I am."

"So, it shouldn't be an issue for you to get down to the cargo levels unseen, right?"

"Right," I say with a small scoff.

"Find Léon, get off world, and never look back, my friend."

"I won't forget what you've done for me," I say, reaching for his hand.

A somber smile tugs at Dyce's lips. He knocks my hand out of the way and reels me in for a hug. "You don't need to thank me."

"But I have to thank you, Dyce," I insist, my voice steady and determined. "If it wasn't for you, I don't know where I'd be. You've given me more than just a chance. You've given me hope and strength to keep fighting. And I won't forget that."

A touch of sadness seeping into his voice, Dyce replies, "You've given me something too, Owen. Having you here—it's been like having a piece of the old times back. It's probably been good for me to be honest."

"Farewell, Dyce."

The goodbye feels heavy, like an anchor pulling at the pit of my gut.

"So, where's your first stop?" Dyce's query breaks the silence, his voice tender with concern.

I pause, my mind swirling with a deluge of possibilities. Gathering my belongings, I stuff them into Dyce's weathered black duffel bag. I toss the pistol on top of everything else and zip the bag securely. Pulling a tattered scarf over my face, I move toward the door.

He stares, waiting for my reply, his question ringing in the stillness of the room.

In the doorway, I halt, the sound of relentless rain serving as the only backdrop. I glance back over my shoulder, meeting Dyce's gaze. Through the fabric of the scarf, I utter a single word just loudly enough to reach him.

"Home."

A ONE-WAY TICKET

MY LEGS BURN as I climb the tall, narrow old fire escape. It took a little longer to get here, having to take back-alley paths. I can't shake the feeling someone is watching me—brief flashes of light illuminate my shadowed figure only momentarily as cars and transports speed past. After a few minutes and a few hundred stairs, I reach my apartment window. I gently break the glass with my elbow and reach in to unlatch the locking mechanism. I lift it slowly to mask the noise, and the city racket and thick sporadic rain partially covers it. It sticks at first, but then slowly creaks open, and I clamber through.

Dyce's heavy eight-round pistol points into the dark apartment; thick drops of water fall to the floor from my hands and clothes. I cautiously step through the living room, shining a small flashlight through the darkness. Fluorescent-orange crime-scene tape reflects the beam; evidence tags are everywhere. *What the hell happened here?*

The apartment is in shambles. My heart drops as I look around at our scattered belongings—overturned furniture, drawers broken on the floor, kitchen cabinets hanging open, their contents spilled out onto the counter; the loft has been turned inside-out. It's a violation. The feeling of home and safeness is gone.

I lower the gun. No one has been here for days.

As I scan the room, I don't see any sign of gunfire, just a heavy scuffle and A.C.P.D. evidential remains. My guess: The receptionist allowed the two men dressed as police officers to enter the lobby and gave them a key to the apartment. While Avery was sleeping, the two entered the room, beat her, and kidnapped her into a nearby ship, then transported her to Ezrek on that roof.

I sit for a few minutes, racing over different scenarios in my head—various places I should go if Léon can get me offworld and what friends I still have left out there among the stars, if any at all.

I stop when I have a sudden thought. I walk over to the bookshelf in disarray and begin digging through the stack of literature, tossing book after book, wondering if it's still here, and as I get to the last few, I see it turned over.

I pick it up and flip it to the front. It's *The Water's Edge* by Clive Ivory.

The discovery feels like a punch to the gut, leaving me reeling in disbelief. It's all there, hidden within the hollowed-out sanctuary of an old book: my ring, Avery's small, dark leather journal—her entire essence captured in bound pages. And beneath it, a trove of memories and might-have-beens: a holographic photo capturing a moment of pure happiness, a stack of credit chips untouched and a computer drive.

I draw the photo nearer, our captured smiles—a bitter reminder of a happiness now lost—mocking me silently. Clutching her journal, a wave of deep loss washes over me; it's as though I'm holding a fragment of her very essence. Yet, I can't bring myself to open it. The fear that turning these pages would unleash an overwhelming deluge of grief holds me back.

The misery and anger ignite every cell, driving me to my knees, a broken figure swallowed by grief. For a fleeting moment, the thought of surrender, of joining Avery wherever she may be, tempts me with its finality. The possibility of an afterlife without her seems more bearable than a reality that's been cruelly stripped of her presence. Her name slips out in a hushed breath, filled with longing and sadness, my hand quivering as it pockets the photograph.

"I failed you. I'm sorry," I say, a silent pledge to her memory, as I slip the ring onto my finger, a symbol of vows that feel as distant as the stars. Yet, as quickly as the darkness envelopes me, a flicker of resolve pierces through. The despair recedes, leaving a glaring clarity in its wake. I rise, the decision made. Life presents a few pivotal moments, crossroads that define us. I've reached mine, and the path I choose now is one of transformation, of becoming the man Avery deserved, the man I must be to honor her memory.

The wail of sirens outside snaps me back to the immediacy of my situation. I pack the essentials: a duffel bag of clothes, the credits and drive hidden within the book, and protein squares crammed into the spaces in between. My ring, a loose reminder of the weight I've lost, refuses to stay on. Resourcefully, I thread it onto one of Avery's necklaces, securing it around my neck.

I look to Avery's nightstand, at a small bowl where she would keep her ring when she slept. It's gone.

Shit. Someone took it.

Just as I turn to leave, I hear the door console chime, followed by muffled voices. The deadbolt unlocks and the door creaks open. A flashlight beam cuts through the dark flat as I silently grab my pack from the counter, quickly duck into the kitchen, and press against the wall, out of sight. *Ezrek's men?* I grab the eight-shooter from my back waistline.

The rain from the open window falls inside the apartment as the flashlights dance around the room. Their radios signal a call coming in through dispatch; it's A.C.P.D.

Holding my breath, I cautiously unlatch the kitchen window to the fire escape on the opposite side from which I came. I've never heard my heart beat louder.

"What are we doing here again?" one of the officers asks, making his way into the living room. His back is to me, and he hasn't seen me yet.

"Something just doesn't add up," the older-looking detective says. His tapered dark brown trench coat gives him the appearance of an experienced detective. They start moving toward the bedroom, searching. "This highly decorated soldier, goddamn war hero, just breaks into Takashi Cybernetics, kills Sato, and, what? Gets in a firefight with security and then blows himself up on the roof? And his wife disappearing? Doesn't make any fucking sense."

"What do you think happened, Detective Bishop?"

Detective Rylan Bishop. The name is familiar; I've heard it before. Before joining A.C.P.D., he had served in the Galacom forces.

"I've got a theory," Bishop says.

"And that is?" the accompanying officer asks, his silhouette discernible as I stealthily observe.

"Owen Beck. I believe he got mixed up in something, and it went bad."

"You think he wasn't the only one up there?"

"It's odd, isn't it? How the security footage miraculously comes alive just as Owen is on the rooftop, wounded and moments away from the explosion," Bishop retorts. "And there are whispers in the streets. Credits, Endonium, and a shitload of advanced tech have vanished. Military-grade. I'm willing to bet that it ties back to Takashi and that blast."

"What's our next move?" the younger officer inquires.

"Start by being observant for once. See what you can find, Rook. Maybe we missed something."

My pulse quickens as I cautiously edge the kitchen window open wider. "Check the kitchen," commands Bishop, moving in the direction of the bedroom. The rookie's flashlight sweeps the space, narrowly missing me. *Damn.* I power through the open window and conceal myself against the wall just outside. I strain my ears to listen over the rain's patter on the metal stairs.

The echo of footsteps grows closer as the officer steps into the kitchen. "Rookie, anything?" Bishop asks loudly, rummaging through the clutter in the other room. "One second. I have an open window here," the rookie responds, flashing his light around the empty kitchen and to the window in the living room. "Was this left open?"

As the cop presses his head slightly out the window, peering down the fire escape, I seize the moment. I emerge from concealment, the cold pistol in my hand serving another purpose. Before he can react, I strike, knocking him out cold with the butt of the gun. He crumples to the ground, unconscious, and I catch him just before he slams down.

I silently maneuver his body onto the metal grating, ensuring he's hidden from prying eyes. The relentless rain continues to fall, providing cover for our clandestine encounter as I cautiously make my way back into the kitchen.

Rain's steady rhythm is the only sound filling the loft until Bishop's voice cuts through, curiosity laced with concern. He's oblivious to my presence, his attention fixed on the clutter of papers beside the bed. "Hey, Rook, you find anything?" he asks, his back still turned to me.

The loft drowns in the relentless patter of water against metal.

"Hey, Ro—" Bishop starts again, but his words are cut short as the cold muzzle of my pistol finds the base of his skull. He freezes, every muscle taut with sudden realization.

"Get up, slowly," I command, my voice a low rumble against the rain's symphony.

His compliance is immediate, hands raised in surrender. "Whooooa, easy, now. Take it easy," he pleads, turning slowly to face me, his eyes wide with shock and recognition. "Owen. Think this through. This is a mistake."

I look at him—really look—and I see more than just the man standing before me. He's big, not just tall, but with a presence that fills the space between us. A five o'clock shadow roughens his jaw, adding a layer of ruggedness to his appearance that's hard to ignore. His right leg, a cybernetic replacement, catches my eye—a visible marker of his sacrifice in the war for Galacom.

His hair, a rich shade of brown, seems almost carelessly tousled, as if to soften the harsh lines of his face. And his nose, long and pointed with a bridge you can't help but notice, gives him an air of distinction, of character.

Inhaling deeply, I brace myself for the revelation that needs to come. "I was framed," I say, each word deliberate, slicing through the tension. "The accusations, Avery's death, Takashi's murder—it was all orchestrated."

Confusion flits across Bishop's face, replaced quickly by a dawning comprehension. "What happened to Avery?" he asks, voice low, eyes searching mine for truth. "Who's behind this?"

"Ezrek Valleion," I say, the name heavy with betrayal and anguish. "He's the puppet master, pulling strings from the shadows."

His skepticism is unmistakable, even with the gun still aimed at him. "Hard to see your innocence with that gun aimed at me. Is the rookie okay?"

"He'll live," I assure him tersely.

"Put the gun down, Owen. We can talk this out. If you're innocent, I can help. If Ezrek is to blame, I'll see to it he pays for what he's done," Bishop says, his voice steady, betraying neither fear nor anger, only a genuine desire to understand, to help.

But deep down, I know the paths we walk are too divergent, his faith in the system unshaken, while mine has been shattered into a thousand irretrievable pieces. "That's my job, and I won't fail again," I assert, my voice low, the weight of past failures heavy on my shoulders. This mission, this quest for justice—or perhaps vengeance—is mine alone to bear.

With a calculated, regretful motion, I strike Bishop—a precise, controlled blow that sends him slumping to the ground, unconscious.

I move quickly, efficiently, gathering my scattered essentials. Every second counts as I sling my bag over my shoulder, casting one last glance at Bishop's prone form. There's no time for hesitation, for second-guessing the path I've chosen.

I slip through the window, the cool night air brushing against my skin. The fire escape creaks under my weight, a precarious melody to my hurried descent. Below, the city lives on, oblivious to the drama unfolding in its shaded crevices.

The crowd swallows me whole as I break from the alleyway, my feet carrying me hastily, my movements deliberate to avoid drawing attention. Yet, I can feel the weight of countless eyes, not on me, but on the digital renditions of my face already plastered on every holoscreen, every wanted poster. *That was fast. I should have hit him harder.*

The specter of arrest hangs heavy in the air, pushing me to flee off-world with urgency. Grievous Grey prison isn't even an option—I refuse to waste away in confinement while Ezrek roams free.

My mission now is clear: regroup, hunt down Ezrek, and bring him to justice. But before I can pursue that vendetta, I must vanish, out of reach of the law's grasp.

The timeworn OsakaLine emerges as the best route across town, as Dyce suggested. It's a low-profile path, less surveilled and less likely to draw attention. Walking would take too long and pose too many risks, while driving my car is out of the question due to the random retinal scans scattered throughout the city.

As I round the corner, the parking structure stretches out in stark lines, illuminated by strips of cold, steady light embedded in the ceiling. My garage sits on the far left, its smooth, gunmetal-gray door catching a faint metallic sheen. The lock panel blinks expectantly, a single green light waiting. I press my hand to the scanner, and it scans in silence before the door releases with a compressed hiss, sliding upward in one fluid motion. The interior is pristine and utilitarian, the walls lined with brushed steel panels that reflect the glow from recessed lights. My matte-black car sits at the center, its sharp contours and angular design giving it an air of readiness. The faint hum of the structure's ventilation system fills the air, steady and mechanical.

As I pack the oversized duffel bag with more hardware scattered across the workbench, the faint scrape of movement from the trunk freezes me mid-motion. My hand instinctively reaches for one of the pistols I'd just secured in the bag. The cold weight of the grip steadies my racing pulse as I draw it, pointing the barrel toward the trunk. Each step I take toward the sound feels deliberate, the faint creak of my boots on the polished floor the only noise. I stop just short of the trunk, the pistol unwavering in my grasp, and exhale slowly before reaching for the release latch.

Suddenly, the TX-49 drone appears. "Oh, hello. Didn't mean to scare you. It was getting hot as balls in there."

"Uhm…" I say, lowering the pistol, confused.

"Where am I?" he asks, his digital eye blinking as he looks around.

"You're in Akereon City of Vola Prime, in my garage. Do you have any directives loaded into your software? How did you wake?"

"Let me check," he says, pausing for a minute as his blue light turns green. "No directives assigned yet. Are you my commanding officer?"

"Yes, I'm Captain Owen Be—" I pause, putting the gun back in the duffle bag. "Just call me Beck for now."

"Beck priority one programmed. So, what's the grand plan, Mr. Mysterious?" His voice echoes with a hint of mischief.

"Sorry, what was that?" I can't help but raise an eyebrow, puzzled by his tone.

"Why do we find ourselves in this dimly lit garage, shrouded in secrecy? Oh, I get it—we're playing 'enigmatic wanderer of the night.' My turn then." His voice drops to an impossibly deep mimicry. "Behold, I am Beck, master of the art of dumpster diving for apparel."

"Have you glitched out on me?" I chuckle, despite the situation.

"Judging by yourself, two-eyes. I, on the other hand, am a masterpiece of engineering," he quips back, his tone brimming with faux arrogance.

"Looks like someone needs a diagnostic check. But that has to wait; we've got a planet to dash from, and you're my new ticket out."

"How may I assist you, Captain?" he inquires, suddenly all business—or as close to it as his sarcastic programming allows.

"Nice to know some semblance of order remains in that circuitry of yours," I comment, half-amused. "We need to get to the spaceport and off-world. The OsakaLine is the only way, although once we get there, the place will be swarming with police and eye-scanning software. I'll need you to be my eyes."

"Easy as cutting off a wiener."

"Uh, not sure I understand the analogy, but I appreciate the optimism. What do I call you, anyway?" I ask.

"I don't have a name, but my model number is TX-49 and a bunch of model series numbers you probably don't care to hear," he says, hovering over to me.

"Well, that will get annoying to say all the time." I pause momentarily. "It'll come to me. Get in the bag for now, and I'll power you on when we get to the station."

"No problem," he says as he gets into the bag, then powers down.

I look at his casing and see the numbers of his TX-49 designation have worn off a bit. The letters *TX* are all that remain.

I smirk as I zip the bag up and toss it over my shoulder, getting ready for the long walk to the rail station. I throw the keys into the car's trunk and slam it shut, leaving the car behind to head out on foot. As I stare at the shutting door of the garage for the last time, I have a brief moment of stillness before heading off into the night.

With my drone and duffel bag slung over my shoulder on the rail plat-form, I patiently wait for the train. I hide my face from the several separate surveillance cameras at the station. Staying invisible is the only thing that will keep me alive, so I hide in the crowd of vagrants and misfits.

The OsakaLine arrives on time. The old grey-toned Endonium train stops, and the heavy metal doors open with a loud creak and scraping noise. I step inside, and the lights flicker as I find an empty seat close to the exit. The rugged, dirty benches reeked of homeless and leftover secretions.

The port is the last stop. As I think about the city's map grid, I know I have some time to rest if I can get over this smell. I lay my head on my arm on the seat in front of me and close my eyes; it's hard to get comfortable, but with some proper adjustments, at least an hour goes by as I sleep lightly, ignoring the dampness of my clothes as the cold water seeps through them. The water-resistant cloth can only withstand so much soaking.

The old OsakaLine windows reveal blurred buildings, and different-col-ored lights from billboards illuminate the dim cabin every half-block, besides the entire-block holographic video of Takashi Sato's remembrance. His face scours the sky, as his legacy is shown on a loop thirty hours daily. They're using my military photo I.D., and my giant wanted face is plastered next to his in connection with the explosion. *"Takashi Sato, Father of Naomi Sato, Dead at 57. A.C.P.D. is searching for ex- Galacom Captain Owen Beck in connection with the murder. Please call A.C.P.D. with any information. We are now receiving reports he is alive and last seen in the stacks downtown."*

The raging explosion turned into a smoking wet debris field within an hour. The flames were put out in a night as the storm of the century surged over them, washing away any usable concrete evidence. They have yet to uncover Takashi's body. I doubt there was anything left to recover. The explosion demolished everything, and I don't just mean the building.

With only a few more stops till the port, the doors open, and a small but loud group of people enters my car, breaking me from my light sleep.

I try readjusting to block out the noise, and that's when I take a breath in and wince. A familiar scent overshadows the previous smell of piss and the non-showered—a sweet, sugary floral smell with a hint of spice. *That perfume... I know it from somewhere,* I think as I slowly look over my shoulder to the end of the car and see a girl sitting at the back.

What are the odds?

It's the pink-haired receptionist from my apartment.

I quickly turn back and stare forward. With my free hand, I pull my tattered brown scarf a little higher, and the material scrapes against my short, thick stubble. I slowly stand, trying not to bring any attention to myself, and make my way to the back of the car. I shadow myself in the darkest section away from the windows as I indignantly watch her sit there with oversized red headphones on, eyes glued to the screen in her hand without a care in the world. She indifferently picks at the frays of the neon-pink fishnet stockings covering her thighs. They vomit into my eyes, as they are the same color as her hair. I watch as the frayed strings fall to the floor by her new high-top platform boots and brand-new designer bag.

She was just a pawn—she's a nobody who wanted to make some quick credit chips.

But all I can focus on is the overwhelming sense of ferocity consuming me from my core. My shaking hand enters my coat pocket, feeling for the gun I already know is there. My fingertips touch the cold wooden handle, and I grasp it tightly. Unsure of what to do, I do the only thing I can: I watch, and I wait.

We only have about ten more minutes to get to the port. I bet that's exactly where she's headed. She has luggage and a look of relief as she sits there alone. I nearly muster the anger to walk over there and put a bullet between her eyes, but just as I have that satisfying thought, two loud, obnoxious, and intoxicated men enter the train. I watch as they enter the aisle, leering at the limited women aboard the car. They stop as they sight the beautiful pink-haired woman and stumble toward her. "Of course," I whisper, thinking of a way to get her alone.

The two men wave, trying to get her attention, rambling something incoherent and bothering her. She looks down, ignoring them completely, so they move closer as she stares at her phone. The two men, clearly annoyed, whisper something to each other, then tap on her thigh. She looks at them as she takes one headphone off her ear. With an unpleasant look, she says, "What?"

"Hey, beautiful! Where are you going all by yourself this time of night?"

"To the corner of fuck off and leave me alone," she says, turning her attention out the window and replacing her headphone.

"Aw, come on! Don't be like that. We just wanted to see if we can buy you a drink or if you wanted to get Frosty," one of the men says, offering an inhaler of Frost. "We'll take care of you."

Without missing a beat, she says, "Fuck off!"

The two men's demeanors change from lust to irritation as their little egos bruise from her rebuffing their inappropriate advances. They try getting her attention one last time, but she immediately stands and walks between them to the next car—straight toward me. I turn to hide my face as she walks behind me, and the junkies follow closely behind her. They shout all types of vulgar sexual things about their dicks, even though she can't hear a word of it. She opens the sectional doors and heads into the next car, and the men follow right behind her.

I wait for the right moment and loosely follow behind them, slipping into the space between cars as the train rumbles along. As I exit the car, I can see through the window that the men have surrounded the pink-haired girl, acting as a barrier so she can't escape. Her face grows tired as she reaches around to her back, pulls a short butterfly knife, and whips it to one of the men's throats. I see her mouth, "This is your last warning."

The two irate men let go of her just as the train comes to a stop. The platform doors open, and the two men back up slowly as they yell something in a dialect I haven't heard before. They exit the train, and the doors close. The woman shuts her butterfly knife and sticks it back in her pocket as I wait patiently outside the cars. I position myself on the outside corner, noticing she's about to return to the first one.

The door opens, she steps through, and I grab her. I quickly retrieve her knife and throw it over the side as I slam her into the cabin's hull. She screams as I pin her body against the metal. "What the fuck? Fuck you! What do you want? I'm tired of you assholes!" I keep her pinned as she tries to get me to let go. "I'm going to fucking kill you," she yells, but the noise of the speeding train hides it.

"I'm not here for that," I bellow through the fabric.

"Then what the fuck do you want?" she chokes out as I take hold of her neck.

"Payback," I say as I reveal my face.

"What—Owen..." She can barely speak as her curious, squinted eyes go wide with fear.

"Where the fuck is Ezrek? I'm only going to ask you this once," I yell over the sounds of the brakes screeching and stabilizing the cars.

"I—don't—know," she says, choking.

I release a little pressure as her eyes roll to the back of her head. I need her conscious. "Where is Ezrek?" I demand again.

Her eyes snap back to mine. She catches a slight breath and says, "I got paid to let in Ezrek's men, and that's it! I didn't know what he'd do to Avery! I'm sorry! Please don't hurt me. I'm so sorry! I didn't know what they would do!"

"I'm not going to ask again," I say.

"He's gone. Already off the planet," she says with terror in her eyes as my hand begins tightening again.

"Where?" I shout one last time, my voice echoing against the clamor of the train as we hurtle down the metal track above the bustling streets below. Her cries and pleas are drowned out by the cacophony of the moving train.

"I swear to you, he's gone. The whole team left off-world. They took the credits and ran. Please! I don't want to die! I promise that's the truth. You don't want to do this. Think of Avery!" she pleads, desperation lacing her words.

An icy serenity envelops me, time seeming to slow to a crawl. With a piercing gaze, I meet her eyes. "I am."

But before I can react, fate intervenes with cruel swiftness. The ground beneath us shudders as the train hurtles forward, and in a split second, she stumbles, slipping from my grasp. Panic grips me as I reach out, but it's too late. An enormous rail of cold metal looms like a ravenous beast, and her petite form is swept under with a sickening crunch.

The force nearly pulls me under too, my hands barely grazing hers before she disappears into the abyss beneath the train's wheels. A gory mist tinges my face, and I'm left rooted to the spot, hands trembling, gasping for breath.

As I glance around in a panic, paranoia creeping in, I realize our struggle has gone unnoticed by the oblivious passengers. With a heavy heart, I turn my attention to the empty car on my right.

I use my jacket like a threadbare cloth, wiping the damning evidence off my hands before zipping it up to mask the remaining stains. Then, moving into the empty carriage, I take a seat.

Over the transit's intercom, a voice rings out. "Welcome to Akereon City Spaceport. We hope you enjoyed your stay here. We'll see you soon," says the automated voice, tinny through the deteriorated speakers. Adrenaline still coursing through me, I find it hard to sit still.

As the train grinds into the port, the high-pitched squeal of the brakes reverberates through the carriages, shaking them violently until they halt. The doors hiss as they open, and I step onto the platform, finding myself in the lesser-known back end of the station.

I pull up my scarf as I navigate through the throng of commuters. A sign positioned conveniently over the ticket booth about thirty paces away catches my eye. Its bright yellow block letters spell out *Cargo Deck—Lower Level*.

I wade through the densely packed crowd, a swirling mass of humanity with their own stories, their own destinations. Around me are daughters leaving for school with teary farewells and husbands preparing to embark on deceit-filled business trips. I catch the hollow gazes of corporate men, their wealth fronts for troves of lies and betrayal. They don't deserve the affection they command. The raucous laughter, the tearful goodbyes, the raw emotion on display is a dark contrast to my own life—one now marred by a cold, brutal act. I am the anomaly among these everyday people.

To them, I am just another traveler. But I can't help but feel alien, detached from the normalcy around me. The guilt that gnaws at me serves as a constant reminder that I am now a stranger among them, utterly alone.

I push forward, keeping my gaze low, making my way toward the cargo dock, hiding my eyeline from the cameras and trackers as I move toward Léon. As I weave through a narrow gap in the flow of people, a sign for the restroom passes overhead, snapping me back to reality. I glance down, and my stomach turns. The stains of her blood, still slightly speckling my hands, have resisted the light rain. I need to clean up and reassess.

Stepping inside the restroom, I quickly swipe the console, ensuring the door is locked from the inside. I stare into the mirror, my reflection confronting me with a glaring reality. *What have I done? What would Avery think of me?* But I shake off the thought. *No, Owen. This is not the time for regret or remorse. Own that shit*, I command myself.

My hand, frozen under the icy cascade from the faucet, snaps me back from the edge of introspection. I draw a slow, composed breath. The undercurrent of fear that gnawed at me is replaced by an unusual tranquility. I scrub the stubborn scarlet stains off my hands, and the water swirls them away into oblivion before I twist the faucet shut.

As I airdry my hands, I reach into my duffel and activate the drone. It beeps as it comes alive, hovering out of the bag to float obediently beside me. "We at the station yet?" he asks, his voice powering on.

"We are, Tex."

"Tex? What does that mean?"

"That's you. I thought it'd be faster," I reply, keeping my tone casual.

"Mm. Not sure I'm fond of it," he says.

"We don't have the luxury of time right now," I cut in. "I need you to scope out the platform. Identify any police officers or officials in the vicinity. Tap into comms channel seven." I pull out a forearm display and comms device from the bag, strapping it to my wrist. With a few clicks, I activate it wirelessly and sync it with Tex. The next phase of our plan is in motion.

"How about Max Power?"

"Huh?" I say, throwing my bag over my shoulder.

"For my name."

"That's not even a name; that's an electronics setting. I'm calling you Tex."

"Fine, but we are circling back to this conversation."

With my face concealed under the cover of my scarf and Tex discreetly hovering behind, I walk casually out of the restroom. Tex hovers away from me upward into the sky as I merge with the thrumming energy of the central platform, where a sea of travelers ebbs and flows. My eyes skim over the series of monitors dotting the area, each broadcasting one of three channels: the news, a live feed of the station, or the departure and arrival times. Images of Akereon's most wanted fugitives flicker unpromisingly across several screens. I count seven cameras just in this section alone.

I see a line of A.C.P.D. officers stationed at the entrance of each ship, their retinal scanners inspecting every passenger meticulously. Robotic canine units patrol the area, their noses attuned to the scents of explosives and contraband. The crowd's constant murmur, coupled with the relentless announcements blaring over the intercom, makes the space feel oppressively tight.

"Tex, you copy?" I say, securing the comms device in my ear with a swift finger motion.

Tex's voice cracks through. "Copy, Beck."

My pulse quickens as I spot a group of police officers near the cargo entrance on the opposite end of the platform. I hold my breath, hoping they'll move on, but they stand their ground, scrutinizing each passerby's I.D. chip tag through their holographic visors. They're performing random screenings, hoping to catch criminals in their dragnet. I must remain calm and composed; any sign of nerves could give me away.

The shrill whistle of wind penetrating the comms is accompanied by a faint shimmer of metal in the sky, a signal that Tex is in position. His voice crackles through the speaker. "Initiating platform scan."

"I need a clear route to the cargo hold transport ships, Tex. The entrance is across the platform. Our guy, Léon, is somewhere down there. He's our exit strategy."

As I blend into the pulsating crowd, Tex's sluggish scan of the platform puts my patience to the test. "What's the holdup?" I ask, striving to keep my tone even.

"The police have deployed their own drones, and security is tighter than a drum. It'll take a minute," he informs me.

"We don't have a minute, Tex," I say impatiently, biding time. "I have a few officers heading my way." I retreat around a large advertisement display in the middle of the station, pretending to observe the local commercial.

The officers walk side by side as they pass the tall display.

"Tex…"

"Got it," he says.

Tactical information floods onto my display. "Four officers are posted by the gates, eight more are carrying out retinal scans with their canine units, and a pair of undercover agents are stationed at each entry and exit point. The area under the platform near the cargo bay is clear, but there are workers scattered around. I've updated your forearm display. You should be able to see all targets."

The small rectangular screen flickers to life on my inner wrist, revealing an X-ray view of the station with all potential threats digitally highlighted in blood-red. The only route to the lower decks appears to be the heavily guarded door. No civilian is allowed past that point.

"Can you divert those officers from the cargo bay door?" I ask, positioning myself next to a waiting area to blend in.

"Alright, I have an idea." Tex's voice crackles in my ear. "Hold tight."

A few moments pass, and then suddenly, an earsplitting alarm begins to wail, echoing around the cavernous station. Passengers jump, startled, covering their ears as the shriek of the alarm rips through the air. Simultaneously, Tex projects a holographic image of a man brandishing what looks like a weapon on the opposite side of the platform, waving it in the air, causing the crowd to scatter in panic.

"Officer!" Tex yells loudly at the guards near the door, creating audiovisual chaos. "Threat detected at Section C6!"

The alarm, the apparent threat, and Tex's panicked announcement all converge into a perfect storm of diversion. The officers at the door spring into action.

"You three, go check out Section C6! I'll stay here!" the lead officer commands, pointing in the direction of the chaos.

With an obedient nod, three of the officers sprint off, leaving the door in the care of a single officer, who's distracted and on edge. It's just the opportunity I've been waiting for. As the last of the officers disappears into the crowd, Tex's voice comes back, smugly saying, "I thought of something."

Feeling the adrenaline pump through my veins, I slowly reach into my pack. My fingers brush against the cold metal of a small, circular device—a sleeping agent ring. I pull it out, keeping it hidden in the palm of my hand as I make my way toward the lone officer.

"Excuse me, officer?" I call out, my voice calm and steady despite the chaos unfolding behind us. As he turns, his visor flickering with real-time data, I quickly bring my hand up, flinging the device against the side of his neck. It attaches with a faint click, barely audible over the alarm. Startled, he looks at me, confusion and suspicion flashing in his eyes. But it's too late. The device quickly releases the agent into his system. His eyes roll back, his body goes slack, and he crumples to the ground soundlessly.

Reacting quickly, I catch him before he fully hits the ground, doing my best to make it look like he has merely stumbled. I glance around, making sure no passerby has noticed our exchange. Reassured by the preoccupied crowd, I move with the unconscious officer through the now-unguarded door, slipping us both out of sight and deeper into the maze of the cargo dock.

"Tex, you read? I'm in."

"Nearly back. Had to lose the cops in the crowd first."

I go down the stairs and open the door to the lower levels. Tex is there to greet me. There is an array of open tunnels and sections leading to the cargo bay. It's much easier for a drone to get around. "What took you so long?" he says.

"Unfortunately, I don't have the luxury of zipping around like you do. Let's find Léon before someone discovers our surprise upstairs," I reply as I hear the alarms shut off.

"Shoot. They are probably sweeping the station now."

"Let's hurry," I say as we continue forward.

The cargo bay is a hive of activity, with workers donned in bright orange jumpsuits and sturdy hardhats, hustling to load and unload cargo from various ships docked across the bay. The alarms have stopped, "Which way,

Tex?" I say, as Tex uses his facial recognition for any sign of Léon.

"Not sure yet," he says, logging every worker.

No one notices us; they just don't get paid enough to care. Workers shout at each other as they load and unload priceless paintings, luggage, livestock, and refined and unrefined Endonium into the transit ships above.

"That's him—the one with the spectacular mustache and loose-fitted glasses," he says, hovering toward a lanky man taking a smoke break.

The man notices me and stares as we approach him. He seems on edge, and his demeanor tightens until he speaks. "Who are you? How did you get down here?" he says with a troubled tone.

Suddenly, a deeper alarm blares through the station, and the once-white fluorescent lights dim to a spiraling red as the station locks down. *Shit, they probably found the downed officer.*

"Who are you? Security!" the man yells.

"Listen! Dyce sent me. Said you could help me get off-world," I say.

He quiets, becoming more relaxed.

"He mentioned you can help me. I need to get out of here, now," I say as I hear commotion from where we came in. I turn around and notice the three officers Tex led away have entered the platform. "Please. You're my last hope."

"I got his message. Follow me," he says as he leisurely gets up from the cargo boxes where he rests and leads me straight into the closest ship's cargo bay.

"Holy hell, what is that smell?"

"This is a livestock transport to the Erogan system, and it's a forty-six-hour journey from here," he says as we see the officers making their way over.

Tex and I enter the cargo bay and see several furry large-mouthed creatures as they try to get comfortable in their crates. Beady eyes glare as dozens of quadrupedal farm animals are stacked high in a line throughout the bay. The smell is foul, nearly unbearable. The sound of the animals shrieking and roaring is deafening. No wonder they put them on the lowest levels. The smell alone could kill.

"In here," Léon says, opening the backside of a giant animal's crate. "Take this," he continues, handing me a black bag he grabbed near the entrance.

A hidden compartment? "What's this?" I say.

"Survival," he says as he points to the small secret space inside the animal crate. "You don't have time; the police are nearly here."

"Thank you," I say as I get into the small compartment, which is barely big enough to fit one person.

Tex hovers behind me and settles next to me. "Gross," he remarks.

"You can stretch your legs after take-off. I'll come get you when it's time. You'll just have to get back in the crate closer to the surface, then wait until the ship docks and we unload the crate. I moved the contraband out of the back out of this false backing in case you showed up. You'll have to stay in there till we get through customs," Léon says, sliding the compartment door back into place. There is a small break in the lining so that I can see a tiny sliver outside just at his thigh line. I hear a click, and the light disappears from the space. I'm sitting in darkness with Tex and the horrid smells of piss and shit.

The animal shifts and shakes the crate as the three police officers enter the bay. I hear their footsteps growing closer to the container as they speak. "Sir, have you seen anyone strange down here? We have a code four, officer down. Anything strange at all?"

"Strange? Besides you three? No, sir," Léon says as he steps away from the crate.

"Step forward for identification," one officer demands with an entitled tone.

I hear as they grab Léon and struggle with him. "Get your hands off me. Are you kidding me? I'm just trying to work."

"You wouldn't mind if we cleared this compartment then, would you?" a synthetic vocoder voice says.

"There isn't anything in here but livestock and shit, man. I'm just trying to earn a wage here. I haven't done shit. This is my ship, and I was getting ready to leave," Léon says with a somewhat shaky tone.

"247 to dispatch. The suspect may be in the cargo bay. Please send additional units to my location."

I gesture to Tex to be quiet, and his glowing lights and eye dim before shutting off completely.

The police search the room from top to bottom. I try to stay frozen as I hear them tossing and turning cargo around me. Heavy footsteps approach the crate, and a flashlight beam cuts through the slit momentarily. I can tell the officers have cleared each animal stable and crate, but my ability to see is minimal—that is, until one officer stands directly in front of the secret compartment with his weapon drawn. "Sir," the officer yells over the animal noises.

"What is it?" says the officer.

I stop breathing to hide the noise and silently reach for my pistol.

The senior officer walks over to him, and I hear him step closer and closer until he reaches the other officer. "What?"

I slowly exhale as I tighten my grip around the pistol.

"Sir, there is nothing here, and we have nothing on this guy, and his ship's clean. Let's get out of here. I can't breathe in here with all this shit."

Looking out the small sliver I can barely make out Léon and two of the officers. "Agreed. Let's move out," he says quietly as their attention shifts back to Léon. "Sorry about that," the officer says, letting Léon up from his knees. "Thank you for your cooperation and have a pleasant evening."

Léon grunts. "Just get the fuck off my loading bay."

"Let's go."

The officers retreat to the platform, and I hear one say, "Keep searching. They must be down here somewhere."

I sit quietly in the dark as the voices trail into silence, and Léon taps the top of the crate.

"That was close," Tex whispers, his digital eye pulsing softly in the darkness.

"Fucking A.C.P.D," Léon says, brushing off his knees.

"Thank you again," I say quietly.

"Anything for Dyce. I'll be back soon," he says, knocking on the top of the crate before exiting the platform, shutting the bay door behind him.

The hinges unlock and groan heavily as the door closes. The ship's thrusters ignite as the fuel cells engage, and the mechanics unlatch the cargo cruiser vessel from the dock. I hear the thrusters surge, probably indicating we've left port. I can only imagine we are leaving Vola Prime far behind.

I sit in this small dark box that feels more like a coffin than my salvation. It's hard to leave the memory of Avery, to leave everything I've ever known behind. I have nowhere to call home anymore. It's the hardest thing I've ever done, but I deserve all this. Owen died on that rooftop with Avery.

"Hey, Beck?" Tex softly says.

"Yeah?"

"What are we going to do after we get to Erogan?"

I stay quiet for a moment, thinking before I respond.

"We need a ship."

THE TITAN'S GAMBIT

AS BLOOD CONTINUES to seep between my fingers, I start priming the sub-light drive. I feel fortunate to have made it out of Turkken alive with only a gunshot injury, broken rib, and forearm wound. I press firmly on the wound and groan from the discomfort, as it only worsens with each breath. It looks like a through and through, but from the amount of pain and blood, I'm guessing shrapnel has lodged itself deep within the muscle tissue.

It's urgent, but fleeing the sector takes priority. The *Novascar* could arrive at any moment. Endonium ship or not, I could never survive a head-to-head with a fleet of Novas Guard fighters—Galacom, maybe, but Ezrek's tech surpasses most. *Just what I need*, I think as I glance down at my hand, which glistens a deep red.

The dim, fading rays of Turkken's sun, Bode-5, fill the cabin, casting an illuminating glow on Tex's empty chair behind me. I can't help but feel the weight of loneliness, adrift not only in the massiveness of the galaxy, but also in the fucked-up depths of my own mind. Aanos, Felix, and the people of Dos Calderon are in my thoughts. Tex was wrong—happiness feels undeserved, as if I'm fated to be deprived of it. Ave, the kindest of strangers, is an elusive dream. It seems that death follows me relentlessly, claiming the lives of those I hold dear. As I prepare to venture to the coordinates Enohk bestowed upon me, that will likely take me through a jump point toward the

Uncharted Rim, I do so without my friend by my side.

Unexpectedly, a different sense of unease fills the small cabin. My eyes are drawn downward. A bright, blood-red blip emerges ominously at the ships six o'clock. As I probe the anomaly, the screen pulsates and projects a holographic model, a ghost from my past I've been relentlessly hunting for years—the *Novascar*. The phantom has taken form. They have, at last, tracked me down.

The massive black Warcruiser ship manifests on my display, a shadow carved into the fabric of space. Closer inspection reveals the ship's exterior as a sleek expanse of black alloys, undoubtedly Endonium, punctuated by red running lights throughout its hull.

Measuring a staggering three thousand meters in length, the *Novascar* 's sheer size engulfs the surrounding starscape, overshadowing everything in its vicinity. Its design is sharp, with angular edges that cut through space like a blade and converge to form a streamlined prow. A central spire rises from the *Novascar*, housing the bridge that serves as Valleion's command center. Encased in a dome of darkened glass, it offers a panoramic view of the cosmos, keeping everything under its master's vigilant eye.

The ship's exterior is fortified with a staggering array of weaponry, each system strategically positioned for optimal performance. Plasma turrets, ion cannons, and missile launchers are scattered across its surface, while powerful kinetic shields serve as the spacecraft's first line of defense.

"Ezrek…"

Clenching the throttle, I channel every atom of available energy, thrusting the propulsion system to its absolute limits, quickly soaring away from the *Novascar*. The deep, throaty roar of the engine rumbles through the hull. My hand, steadfast on the controls, vibrates in resonance with the raw power. I need more time to prime the sub-light drive.

Each beat of my heart mirrors the rhythm of the *Astra*'s engine, the pounding pulse to a ticking clock. Warning sirens rip through the cockpit, punctuated by the flash of red emergency lights flickering off the glass panels. *They are trying to get a lock.* The *Novascar* has activated its weapons system, but they are out of range. My gaze suddenly whips back to the viewport

HUD as the jump point coordinates lock.

A green autopilot notification prompts. TC-X10, the wormhole jump-point about four hours away, nestled within a formidable field of gargantuan asteroids, the largest I've ever seen. It's risky, yes, but with sparse alternatives to reach this sector's outer rim, it emerges as my only viable option. The next closest jump-point looms a daunting six weeks away, transforming TC-X10 into a desperate gamble I'm forced to stake. One wrong maneuver out there, and it's game over.

As the *Astra* soars away and the intimidating radar blip begins to fade, the navigation signals with a new alert—the sub-light autopilot course is primed and ready. I reach for the drive switch, lift the yellow casing, and flick the toggle.

Nothing happens. "Come on!"

I attempt it a few more times, switching it back and forth, but to no avail—just hollow clicks. Then, a prompt appears on my screen, indicating that a sub-backup protocol for autopilot is attempting to override my system. "What the hell?" I say under my breath. I quickly input my authorization code, *09-0C518-4X29-79*, into the keyboard.

As rapidly as it emerged, the message recedes, restoring the system to its normal state. *That was weird*, I think.

I clutch the toggle once more, inhaling deeply as I flip the switch. I try the button one last time, and the fusion engine activates, igniting the *Astra* into an accelerating blur away from the *Novascar*.

Gracefully streaking through the infinity of space, the *Astra* maintains its planned trajectory. My speed magnifies with each passing second, culminating in a surge of momentum until it plateaus at a fraction of the speed of light. I cast a glance down at the radar; the blip of the *Novascar* diminishes slowly until it vanishes from the screen entirely in a flash.

I've lost them—for now.

I take a second as my vision blurs slightly, clouded by the loss of blood.

After ensuring the *Astra*'s safety for a few more minutes and with autopilot engaged, the tension in my fingers gradually ebbs away as I relinquish control to the ship's advanced navigation system. In one fluid motion, I spin the pilot's chair around, the soft hum of the ship's systems serving as a soothing backdrop to the shitshow that unfolded moments before. I sluggishly stand and make it to the stairs leading down to the common area, but suddenly, a hard cough escapes my lungs, and blood hits the back of my teeth. As a jolt of unbearable pain scorches into my hip. It buckles my right knee and I fall headfirst down the hard, sharp stairs.

My helmet is the first to meet the welcoming floor as I crash loudly and harshly to the ground below. With a jarring thud, I come to rest onto the cold, unyielding surface, pain erupting through my body like an unwelcome guest.

Slowly, carefully, I coax myself to rise, each minor contortion sending a fresh river of red coursing down my leg, pooling on the floor beneath me. "That's a lot."

I slam my bloodstained glove against the command console to my right, leaving a streak of red across its smooth surface. The cold, sterile white room illuminates as the lights flicker on after two or three attempts, and another deep cough expels from my lungs. The hum and bright glow of the lights rapidly fill the compact room. I slump onto the long white surgical table, shifting upright with effort. Carefully, I unfasten my helmet, and the subtle click of the release mechanism echoes sharply in the quiet of the MedBay. As I lift it off, my vision expands, freed from the confines of the helmet's visor. The world appears painfully clear and coldly clinical. I set the helmet aside, its metallic surface reflecting the harsh light of the room. I scowl, bracing myself for the task ahead.

The *Astra*, unfortunately, lacks the luxury of the fully automated medical pods found on larger starships or cruisers. Such advanced AI robotic systems come with a hefty price tag—one that exceeds my limited resources. Instead, I've equipped the *Astra* with a more rudimentary setup, ensuring I have the essentials on hand for emergencies like this. Mountains of gauze, a variety of tools, and an array of medical solutions fill the storage compartments, ready to be utilized in times of need.

I position myself flat on the matte-white gurney and rest my head for a moment. I press the grey button on the right of the bed, and an extended white circular device at the base of the table powers on and begins quickly spiraling around, slowly making its way from my feet, up to my waist, then over my head. It creates an x-rayed scan of my body and vitals on the screen to my left.

[://Foreign Object Detected//], the screen reads as it zooms in on my hip area, showing a dark object next to my right iliac crest.

"There you are," I say, pulling the screen closer. I can see a dark, shadowy piece of the bullet wedged under the muscle, but luckily, no severed arteries or shattered bones. It looks like the wound is a clear through and through besides the small fragment.

While I'm not a trained surgeon, I have received comprehensive training in various medical procedures and field medicine. Trauma management and self-care techniques have saved me more times than I can count. However, my knowledge of a wound like this is average, and I will likely be improvising some of this.

I reach to my right for the medpack and grab the drip bag, along with the necessary supplies. With careful hands, I hang the bag above me, allowing clear liquid to flow through the tubing. I prepare the short needle, inserting it into my forearm and securing it with tape to ensure it stays in place. As I press the satin grey center button of the medpack, its two metal latches unhinge with a subtle click, revealing its small array of contents.

The lights flicker as I fumble the gauze, haphazardly knocking other miscellaneous items to the ground. I grab what is needed and press the top right of the tablet, and a mirror ejects from the side of the gurney to just above me. I pull it close, just low enough to see the injury, and the clear light ring around it brightens the area.

With my hand on the numbing agent device, I pull it from the tray and put the tip to my mouth. I pry off the cap with my teeth, and the two-inch needle tip glistens in the fluorescent lighting. I lunge it into my stomach four times—one above, one below, and one on each side of the wound.

I moan, spitting the cap out. "Mm, shit. That's a big needle."

Grabbing the sterile solution, I point it toward the wound, and the device emits a concentrated pre-spray mixture of microbial cleanser. A faded, muffled yell escapes my mouth as I bite down hard—so hard my teeth feel like they will crack under the immense pressure. The metal bed creaks and moans under my weight as I shift in pain. "Guess those numbing stabs are taking a while to kick in," I grunt, as I still feel everything.

I recall the instructions of Dr. Helena Rose, the Chief Medical Officer of the Elite Operations Specialist Division. I remember her saying that using the wide forceps would be necessary to gently open the walls of the wound, while the thin-nosed straight tool, commonly known as "the grasper thing," would aid in retrieving the embedded fragment. *What's the worst that could happen?* I think as I look to the screen to help monitor the retrieval.

"It's now or never," I groan.

I take a breath in and gently open the wound with the wide forceps. The numbing agent seems to be finally working, as I don't feel much of the sharp pain anymore; it's dimmed to a dull steady discomfort and pressure.

Fuck. My hands are shaking. "Mm, that's a lot of blood," I say as I look down at the spurting wound.

My vision slowly fades as I feel a hard surface under the muscle. Taking a few more sharp inhales and holding them, I grip the handle and give a few hard tugs, but the fragment is stubborn, so I release my breath and try again.

With the forceps in a tight grip, I take one last deep breath and tug as hard as I can on the fragment, which dislodges from my hip and comes out of the wound, followed by a stream of red.

A deep yell reverberates through the room as I'm finally able to catch a breath.

I drop the tools into the tray next to me and sink into the table. "Hooooly shit." I sigh as a giant wave of relief washes over my entire body.

I rest for a few seconds before the display prompts another message in red.

[://SYSTEM INITIATED...] [://Processing...]

[://Object Status: REMOVED]

[://Recommendation: Apply TetraGel for optimal integration.]

[://Continue Monitoring? Y/N]

I reach for the TetraGel device from the table and inject gel into the open cavity, and it immediately begins solidifying from the inside out, forming around the wound to stop the bleeding. The gel acts as a regenerative liquid packed with amino acids, proteins, and a synthetic makeup of tissue and skin. Its compound makeup of healing agents instantaneously begins to heal muscles and tendons and to regrow damaged tissue.

I lay still for a moment as I give myself a much-needed break, letting the TetraGel do its job. *I need to clean up all this blood*, I think, looking around the table.

After several precious moments of rest, my hand remains anchored to my hip, applying pressure to the wound. The pressing dulls the pain, making it manageable even as the numbing agent reaches its limit. The TetraGel is hardening, gradually solidifying over the injury—a comforting, if alien, sensation.

Turning my attention to the HUD on my forearm, I check our arrival time. It indicates three hours until we reach the jump-point, and thankfully, there are no new warnings. The *Astra* alerts me to oncoming collisions or common space debris and will adjust the flight plan accordingly. Its autopilot software is as good as it gets—a very safe system, but not perfect. I'd better not be away for too long, as catastrophic malfunctions happen occasionally. But for now, the ship flies peacefully along its set course, granting me a temporary reprieve from the pursuit of the *Novascar*.

I decide to seize the moment. A quick shower to wash away the grime, blood, and sweat of Turkken, followed by a well-deserved nap, seems in order. Fatigue has long-since set in, the toll of over a day spent in constant vigilance. The word "exhausted" falls short of capturing the sheer depth of my tiredness.

I rise from the surgical table and stand. Each step towards the shower and the promise of rest feels like a minor victory.

I needed to regain my strength. Who knows what I will encounter on the planet?

After agonizing steps down the metallic stairs, I navigate my way through the common room, my destination the small stash of rations tucked away in the galley. Each painful step is a cry for the absence of Tex. He'd make this so much easier; I could just relax.

Mustering enough energy, I manage to consume several protein packs and the last of my dehydrated Merochi fruit. The packs are sustenance, and I'm grateful for it, no matter how tasteless and unappealing it feels. With my basic nutritional needs met, I begin the painstaking journey back to my quarters.

I press the dial adjacent to the diagonally split door. It glides to the left with a hiss, permitting entry, then promptly slides closed behind me, sealing me within my personal sanctuary. I shuffle towards the bathroom, initiating a hot shower. The comforting warmth of the steam fills the confined space, creating a foggy veil over the mirror.

Wiping away the condensation, I confront the weary apparition staring back at me. I appear revolting—a ghostly figure stripped of vitality, my eyes hollow, my expression desolate. I barely recognize the person in the reflection. It's like I'm gazing upon a stranger. My lean chest and abdominal muscles are more apparent as they lead down to my semi-kempt pubic hair. I'm losing weight from not eating enough.

After a rapid rinse, I brush my teeth and attend to my blistered, bleeding feet. I tentatively apply a fast-acting soothing TetraGel ointment, wincing as I bandage the raw areas where my armor and boots have chafed mercilessly against my skin. The pain is incredibly annoying to add to the gunshot wound.

Finally, I collapse onto my bed, gingerly positioning cold compresses over my hip, ribs, shoulder and face, hoping to soothe the inflamed tissues. The coolness is a balm to my heated skin, easing the tension from my body. As the discomfort begins to fade, I surrender to the seductive call of sleep, letting it pull me under into a restorative slumber.

"Avery!" I yell, grabbing the ring on my necklace as I am rudely awaken from another nightmare.

A distant repetitive sound rebounds through my quarters as the *Astra* disengaging from sub-light speed suddenly awakens me. *Where is it coming from?* I wonder. The jolt is so abrupt I nearly fall out of my bunk. *What was that noise?*

The ship's flashing yellow lights spiral as the alarm blares through the corridors.

"Now what?" I say with an irritated tone as I jump from the barracks and limp towards the controls.

Once at the flight deck, I begin to shut down the alarm system on the overhead console and sit down as I decrypt my system logs. *Where the hell am I?* I think as I skim downward. *About fifteen minutes from the jump point. The incoming threat disengaged the navigation.*

The radar map pings, and as I look down, a tiny red blip illuminates on screen.

It's a ship. Shit, is the Novascar again? How did they catch up to me? I wonder as I flip the defensive system toggle into position and the lower rail-gun releases from the bottom of the hull. It spins around, locking onto the enemy behind me.

As I squeeze the trigger, my finger halts upon witnessing the holographic rendering of the unknown vessel glitching into multiple enemy ships on my console. These vessels lack any emblems or markings, and their Galactic Netcodes are encrypted with zeros. The targeting system illuminates in green, but something feels different—they haven't opened fire. It's not the Novas Guard.

From the image, I can tell the vessels are a small fleet of Axis-7SR's—a high-speed and weapons-loaded model. If I had to guess, based on their gunmetal grey coloring and yellow accents, encrypted identification, and lack of symbols, they can be only one thing.

"Bounty hunters," I say as I hastily return power to the afterburners and speed away. The hunters must have received the Dök Hundris' off-world beacon and tracked my NetCode.

"This is the last thing I fucking needed." I scoff because, as of now, not only do I have the Novas Guard up my ass, but I have bounty hunters to worry about too, and don't get me started about Galacom, who probably aren't far behind either. They usually like to make a late entrance—small bounties aren't usually a huge red flag on their radar, but they'll send out small patrols to investigate.

My options are limited. It seems inevitable it'll end in a pursuit or dog-fight. I don't have the time for a pursuit, but their ships are formidable opponents for the *Astra*, as bounty hunters custom-fit their vessels for space combat. Without the necessary components to repair the ship, I'd live, but it's preferable to get the hell out of here relatively unscathed.

I quickly think over my limited options as I keep a small distance between the hunters and the *Astra*. Then I quickly remember what's lingering just in the distance before the wormhole. *This is a bad idea*, I think as an alarm triggers in the cabin, signifying the hunters have activated their weapons.

I rapidly navigate through the Navcom screen, and after several scans, I finally find what I'm looking for: it's one of the most widespread and dense asteroid fields I've ever seen. The rocks range from small, pebble-sized stones to near-dwarf planets, which are massive. Although it will make maneuvering difficult, it should slow down the hunters just long enough that I can outmaneuver them or get lucky enough that they make a mistake.

Or it'll kill us all. *Whatever.*

It's not the odds I'm looking for, but it will have to do.

As I charge headfirst towards the field, my ship's navigation system buzzes in alarm, painting a rapidly evolving nightmare of colliding trajectories on my viewscreen: Enormous asteroids lumbering along their slow, majestic orbits, smaller ones zipping around like frantic birds, and dust and pebbles filling the gaps in between, forming a lethal hailstorm of rock and ice.

One misjudged inch, and it will all be over. But fear isn't an option. I stifle the tremor in my hand and grip the controls tighter. The hunters' ships inch closer, their predatory silhouettes growing larger in the rearview scanner.

I punch a quick risk assessment into the Navcom, feeding it the parameters of my insane plan. It blares in protest, flashing hazard warnings in an array of colors. I override it. Calculations whir on the screen as it maps out the most improbable flight path in the galaxy.

And then it's go time. I slam the thrusters to full power, jerking me backward with a force that feels like it might rip me apart. The ship creaks and groans, echoing my own tension. Rocks blur into streaks as asteroids whiz past the viewport, close enough to touch. I feel every ounce of resistance as I push the *Astra* to its brink.

Behind me, the hunters hesitate, their ships faltering at the field's edge. Then, one by one, they follow. I can almost feel their confusion, their surprise as I carve an impossible path through the rocks. The field is dense, chaotic, and the ship fights for every inch. Sweat drips from my forehead, and my knuckles are white on the controls.

I watch the rear display as the first ship closes in but gets careless and clips an asteroid, spinning out of control before a larger rock finishes it off. The second hunter, smarter or perhaps just luckier, manages to evade the condensed cluster, but it's thrown off my tail. The other ships vanish from my scanner only for a moment before soaring back to the chase.

As I push the *Astra* deeper into the field, weaving between the rocks, I see a mountain-sized asteroid looming ahead—a titan among the rest. It's too late to change course. There's a tunnel through the center of the large icy stone—a mere scratch in its mass, but to me, it looks like the eye of a needle. I tighten my eyes, lock onto the passageway, and aim for it. The adrenaline in my veins drowns out the fear, the doubt. All that's left is the rock, the ship, and me.

With a breathless gasp, I plunge into the tunnel. It's narrow, claustrophobic. The walls rush past in a blur of grey and brown, barely missing the edges of the wings. I grip the controls tightly, and then, as suddenly as it began, it's over. I burst out the other side, a spray of rocky debris spewing out behind me.

The scanner shows the hunters veering away, caught off-guard by the unexpected maneuver. They scatter, and some manage to avoid the massive titan, but at least three fighters explode on impact, leaving their formation in shambles. There are only two left.

I can't help but laugh, a wild, triumphant sound. For a moment, it looks like I've lost them. But the joy is short-lived. The scanners show them regrouping, picking up speed. Their numbers might be diminished, but they're not beaten yet.

I press on, swerving around rocks and through narrow gaps, putting more distance between us. But I can't let up—not yet. Not until I'm safe.

The hunters finally smarten up and tail me at a safe distance, prompting me to let loose a few rounds from my railgun. However, their nimble vessels and the chaotic environment hinder any effective lock-on. My shots only detonate asteroids, the ensuing rubble forming a turbulent barrier in their trajectory.

Undeterred, the hunters counter with a barrage of machine-gun fire that tears through the field, reducing asteroids to incandescent showers of debris as I bob and weave through the hazardous arena. Small shards ricochet off the *Astra*'s canopy as we race onwards. Streaks of luminous yellow gunfire skim past the wing, prompting a sharp roll to the left.

Suddenly, an immense blast rocks the rear of the ship. The *Astra* shudders violently, nearly flinging me from the pilot's seat onto the console deck before me.

"Incoming. Incoming," warns the ship's computer.

"Little late on that one, computer," I reply as I resettle myself and fasten my safety harness.

Two golden blips representing plasma missiles emerge on the screen, their quick, predatory movements zeroing in on the *Astra*'s blue icon. I send the ship into an unbroken barrel roll, spinning end over end. The missiles mimic the maneuver, weaving around each other as they chase us. I spiral the ship downwards through the rocky belt, the force pinning me against the seat.

With the enemy projectiles nearing, I engage the speed brakes, initiating a synchronized burst of counterthrust. The sudden opposing force acts as a potent brake, reducing the *Astra*'s speed and altering its flight path to an abrupt stop.

My maneuver successfully derails the targeting of the incoming missiles, causing them to pass over me and explode into each other.

As the explosion reverberates through the asteroid field, I seize the opportunity to evade the hunters. The *Astra*'s systems recover promptly, allowing me to maneuver the ship swiftly into the heart of a massive asteroid. Its sheer size and rugged exterior provide excellent camouflage, and the *Astra* blends seamlessly with the surrounding dark stone. I activate the ship's stealth mode, further obscuring its radar presence from the prying sensors of the pursuing hunters.

I can see them faltering on the scanner, their movements erratic. They've lost sight of the *Astra* and are scouring the field, trying to reacquire their target. "Let's hope this works," I say.

I flick a switch, launching a decoy beacon. Programmed to replicate the *Astra*'s unique energy signature, it blinks to life after a calculated delay, soaring into the void. The hunters' ships, eager for a target, swerve sharply, their sensors locking onto the phantom readings. Like predators scenting blood, they veer away from my position, chasing a shadow.

Nestled against the jagged surface of the asteroid, I hold my breath. With the *Astra* powered down to minimal life support, we are indistinguishable from the countless cold, dead rocks drifting in this desolate field. Time crawls. The faint vibrations of the hunters' thrusters echo faintly in the vacuum, but I remain motionless, watching as they dart farther from my hiding place.

I count each passing moment, the tension a tight coil in my lungs. Slowly, the hunters' signals diminish, their suspicion dissipating as they pursue the ghost I've sent them. One by one, the threatening blips on my radar fade until the screen is silent, blank.

I exhale quietly, resisting the urge to act too quickly. Minutes tick by as I ensure the field remains still, undisturbed. Only then do I power the *Astra* back up, the cockpit coming alive with a low hum and a series of soft, comforting beeps. The engines spool up with a faint vibration, their glow a pale ember against the asteroid's shadow.

Carefully, I guide the *Astra* away from the rocky expanse, emerging from the field on the opposite side of where I entered. The hunters are gone, their pursuit diverted. The void feels vast and silent again, yet my focus remains sharp as I set my sights on the jump point.

The Gravitron-Ring looms ahead, its immense structure impossible to ignore. Segmented layers of metal spin with mechanical precision, each piece interlocking in a rhythm that feels deliberate and exact. Lights flicker across its surface, marking pathways of energy and motion, their patterns mesmerizing in their complexity.

At the center, the wormhole shimmers—a sphere of warped space, its edges bending and refracting light like ripples on a dark lake. Through the distortion, I can see another star system. A red sun glows faintly against a backdrop of swirling nebulae, its light refracted into ragged shapes. Strange constellations appear and disappear as the view shifts, flickering like images on the edge of a dream.

As I approach, the ring reacts to my presence. Its outer layers grind and shift, mechanisms aligning with precision as sensors lock onto the *Astra*. A deep, resonant hum fills the void, vibrating through the hull of the ship as the wormhole stabilizes. The swirling portal grows brighter, its turbulent energy stretching into sharp definition, offering a glimpse into the unknown.

I maneuver the *Astra* closer, the wormhole dominating the viewscreen. It feels both ominous and inviting, a doorway into uncharted possibilities. A strange weight settles in my chest as I align the ship with the rippling core, the lights of the ring reflected in the cockpit's glass. This is it—the point of no return.

Then, with one final thrust of the engines, we plunge into the wormhole.

There's no jolt, no sense of falling or motion. It's unsettlingly smooth, as though the *Astra* has been swallowed whole. The cockpit goes quiet, save for the steady drone of the ship's systems. Through the viewscreen, the rippling stretches and bends, light refracting in impossible ways. My mind struggles to process what I'm seeing, it baffles me every time—a kaleidoscope of warped starfields and blurred horizons, like reality folding in on itself.

Then, without warning, it's over. The *Astra* emerges into open space, a new star system materializing before me. The transition is so seamless, it feels almost mundane, as if I've simply passed through a veil separating one reality from another.

I sit motionless, staring at the unfamiliar stars ahead. The Gravitron-Ring made it... ordinary. Practical. Yet the sheer scope of what I've just experienced is anything but. I've escaped the hunters, crossed the galaxy, and for the first time in days, the load pressing on my chest lifts. For now, I'm safe.

I adjust the Navcom relay back to the coordinates, since electronics can get a little finnicky when using wormhole travel. I begin to steadily pass the gargantuan red sun, and the location of the uncharted planet illuminates on screen; I'm getting closer, but it's still going to take several weeks to get there.

I kick in the sub-light drive and accelerate far away from the jump point, heading towards the Uncharted Rim.

INTO THE UNCHARTED

THE COLD, EMPTY ship seems more desolate than before. I once thought that Tex would always be my diversion during lonely journeys. Now, the deep silence is all too consuming. Routine tasks, once taken for granted, now serve as my distraction. Ship maintenance, cleaning, exercise—all these activities give me purpose in the cosmic nothingness.

The *Astra* effortlessly glides at sub-light speeds across the mysterious sector, and I find some solace in the fact that my wounds have healed, all thanks to the TetraGel and rest.

In the rear of the ship, I sit at a compact workstation with Tex's remnants beside me in a pack. Their presence lingers, heavy and unspoken, a weight I refuse to acknowledge. I keep my gaze fixed forward, unwilling to let my eyes betray me. To divert my attention, I delicately place the Jadestone Key onto a specialized platform. As the room fills with the buzz of the analytical instruments and the holographic displays spring to life, I find myself lost in the mesmerizing teal aura of the key.

"What the hell are you?" I say, staring at the readouts.

What is this key? And what does it open? This is going to be a very long flight.

Days have melted into weeks. The outer rim of the system beckons, with the luminous light of a nascent sun painting the sector. Each solar flare that bursts forth from its surface is a spectacle of nature's fury, showering the universe in hues of deep crimson and vibrant orange. The Endonium hull of my ship keeps the deadly radiance and scalding heat at bay.

But while it's designed to shield me from the external dangers of the universe, it can't protect against the growing despair within.

I pore over the ship's navigation system, watching the holographic coordinates flicker. Each calculation and recalibration brings me closer to the threshold of the sun's habitable zone, where conditions might be just right for life. But there's no trace of a planet, no hint of the mysterious location Enohk mentioned. Doubt clouds my mind. Could she have misled me? Was it all a ruse? I have combed through countless archives and deciphered age-old cryptograms, and yet I've found no reference to the elusive Jadestone Key or its temple.

Here I am, adrift in the field of stars, the gulf of space stretching endlessly in all directions. Reaching an outpost station or a jump point would take weeks, if not more. And with each passing day, my provisions dwindle, consumed by the gnawing hunger. The ship's advanced scanners, my trusty eyes in this abyss, show no planetary bodies. Only the same enigmatic readings from the coordinates keep flashing, a cryptic beckoning that promises either salvation or further torment.

As I edge closer, the ship lurches unexpectedly. Systems flicker and falter, and in an alarming instant, the main console plunges into darkness. A ripple of panic courses through me, but my instincts, honed over countless missions, kick in. Nimbly, I divert the power, sidestepping the compromised circuits. Auxiliary engines purr back to life, and the console gradually illuminates, drenched in a cautionary shade of red. Then, with a reassuring beep, the system stabilizes and resumes its regular operations.

"That was weird."

Lost in thought and reevaluating my situation, minutes pass. The emptiness seems to swallow hope, but then, the unexpected happens—a faint blip echoes on the radar. Reacting instantly, I throttle down the afterburners, allowing the *Astra* to coast gracefully through this star-studded sector.

There's another signal—sharper this time.

Emerging from the blackness, a planet gradually becomes discernible.

She was telling the truth, I think as I stare wide-eyed at this lonely planet, barely touched by the light of its young star, partially hidden by a neighboring moon.

As I draw closer to this mysterious sphere, I'm in the perfect range for atmospheric analysis. The readings flash on my display: oxygen levels are higher than average. It's as if this planet has been untouched, waiting for me. Most planets we know would have us fumbling for our respirators, but this one is an exception. It feels welcoming, devoid of deadly toxins, dangerous radiation, or hazardous gases. The screen shows a green light, a rare sight in this giant galaxy.

In my time searching the expanse, I've encountered countless worlds that are inhospitable to human life. Yet each of these planets carries its own unique form of life—alien creatures that have evolved to thrive in conditions we'd find intolerable. I've seen worlds where acid rains from the sky or where the atmospheric pressure would crush you in an instant, and others where the air is a cocktail of toxic gases, lethal to us, but a breath of life for the exotic creatures that call these places home.

That's the paradox of the universe: even in its most extreme corners, life finds a way. But discovering a world suitable for us, for our species—that's like finding a needle in a cosmic haystack.

And now, here before me floats an anomaly: an uncharted planet in the middle of nowhere, its atmosphere brimming with oxygen and life on the surface.

However, the silence from the planet is deafening. No intelligent life seems to be having a conversation. There's a conspicuous absence of radio waves, no welcoming docking ports, not a single contrail in the sky. It's vacant of all human existence.

Only one moon is neighboring this small world—no rings, asteroid fields, or other planets. It's just a remote giant moon-sized ball floating through space alone. I've noticed the farther you tend to trek through the uncharted rim, the less dense systems seem to be, which fuels the notion that the universe is forever expanding, which can be even more terrifying—the idea that I could travel infinitely and never reach an end. I try not to think about it too much.

Strange—why would the Khu'Val build a temple in such a remote place? What are they hiding? Unsurprising this planet has managed to escape discovery for so long. It's so far out of the way, you'd have to be lost to stumble upon it. It's lightyears from anything. I couldn't even get a reading till I was close enough, I think as I feel the gentle pull of the planet's gravity.

The tug is noticeably weaker; this planet's mass is much less compared to the others I've encountered.

As I angle towards the planet's surface, the *Astra* gracefully transitions from orbit and begins its descent through the atmosphere. The ship's hull heats up swiftly due to the friction from the thin, compressed air, causing a yellow streak of fire to ripple across its exterior. The *Astra* shudders down to its very controls from the turbulent ride. It's a brief, intense journey through the planet's thermosphere, but soon enough, I'm soaring through the cloud cover. I throttle down, sending the *Astra* plunging toward the planet's surface.

As the clouds break, an expansive sea of rainforest, alive with shades of vivid green and sprawling towards every horizon fills my view. Its lush tones sit beautifully against the soft, light-blue sky filtering through *Astra*'s translucent canopy. An intrigued-yet-captivated smile dawns on my lips.

The rainforest, a titan of flora, governs the landscape, its giant trees interlacing to form an almost-impenetrable living wall. The verdant stretch is occasionally broken by broad, flat plateaus offering pockets of relief from the thickly clustered verdure. In the distance, gargantuan mountains cast imposing silhouettes, their peaks vanishing into the clouds. Waterfalls carve down these rocky giants, their mighty roars echoing through the forest. Clear water courses down the mountainsides, merging into wide, shimmering rivers below, their surfaces glittering under the planet's sun.

Herds of various creatures, each unique in form and color, occupy the flatlands. The first group that catches my eye consists of sturdy four-legged animals. Their furry bodies shine with vibrant hues of yellow and orange.

They move across the terrain with a graceful unity, their collective rhythm a natural phenomenon captivating to the eye. Some creatures stand out among these herds, bearing fantastic spiral horns that crown their heads like abstract sculptures.

Next to them, another intriguing group consists of beings with elongated, snake-like extensions from their bodies. These creatures weave their way through the thick vegetation with an elegant fluidity.

It is an oasis of life. As I soar above, I marvel at the beauty of it all.

But my reverence is abruptly shattered as *Astra*'s systems suddenly falter under the influence of electromagnetic interference that permeates the air. My grip tightens on the control panel as the ship lurches and veers off course. Alarms blare, flashing warnings on the console. With quick thinking and steady hands, I try to regain control, compensating for the erratic movements caused by the interference.

The *Astra* bucks and sways, fighting against my efforts to stabilize it; it crashes hard against the wind, and the once-smooth flight becomes a battle against the uncontrollable forces that threaten to send us spiraling into the forest below. I strain to maintain altitude, my eyes scanning the tree line for any sign of a potential landing spot.

The relentless assault of interference intensifies, and panic sets in as I access emergency protocols, desperately activating backup systems and rerouting power to critical functions. Each adjustment I make is a gamble, a frantic attempt to regain control. "Shit. Shit. Shit. I'd better land," I say through alarms and flickering displays.

I quickly assess the power distribution within the *Astra* on my display. I navigate the ship's interface, accessing the network of circuits and power conduits. I reroute power from non-essential systems such as the weapons and sub-light drive, allocating it to bolster the thrusters, stabilization mechanisms, and flight control surfaces. The ship's power grid responds to my commands, channeling energy to where it's most needed, reinforcing the faltering systems.

As the surge of redirected power courses through the *Astra*, I feel the ship slightly responding to my commands. With each adjustment, the ship's flight path becomes less stable. "This is barely helping. I need to land," I say, peering out the cockpit.

I locate a suitable spot. It's a small clearing ahead and appears to be the best option available; the spot is nestled within the protective embrace of towering trees and enveloped by the thick undergrowth. The ship's descent is cautious, its engines sputtering as it gently touches the ground. The *Astra*'s systems flicker and hum, gradually powering down. *What the hell was that all about? The controls felt like the opposite attraction of a magnet, fighting against another. I've never seen any artificial EMP penetrate the Astra's hull.*

I gaze out into the murky wall of the dark forest, and the realization sinks in that I must leave the safety of the *Astra* behind. The ship won't make it. I begin running diagnostics on the ship's electronics, filtering through the noise, and it looks like it's going to be stuck here unless I head in the opposite direction. The interference grew stronger the closer I came to the temple's location.

I must venture forth on foot into the depths of the uncharted unknown.

I am determined to find the temple, so I head out the cockpit to the armory. The familiar weight of my rifle provides a sense of reassurance, and my hands instinctively check my holster, ensuring my sidearm is within reach. After making a few upgrades to the Odyssey using parts from the stolen Novas Guard rifle, it's as ready as ever. I pack vital provisions and select the essential tools and items for survival in this untamed wilderness, and I finally remembered to charge my shield thanks to Tex's constant reminders from before.

Also, considering the world's exotic and potentially venomous wildlife, I pack supplies essential for crafting antidotes to counter possible toxins, plus an adaptive device on my forearm module to concoct them immediately. During the long flight, I enhanced my visor to detect heartbeats within a hundred-yard radius with a pulse scanner mode. This functionality could prove indispensable in this alien world teeming with unseen life forms.

The *Astra*'s bay door hisses shut behind me, locking and entering hibernation mode, out of sight and out of danger. I'm now entrenched within an endless sea of jade. This alien jungle teeming with unknowns is my pathway to the temple.

Prepared or not, there is no retreat now. The temple awaits.

A thick, warm fog settles between the glistening leaves and branches, which pierce the slow-moving vapors as I trudge through the intense rainforest. The sun's rays penetrate through the trees' canopy, warming random areas on the surface. I glance down at my forearm display for the location, and the screen glitches randomly. I'm getting readings from a sizeable magnetic source in the direction of the temple.

The first part of the journey was a slight incline, and my calves are already burning. I climb a minor ridge and quickly jump to the lower section. As I pick myself up, a stream calmly flows to my left, a group of amphibian creatures gently swimming through its crystal-clear waters. Their long, scaled bodies reflect the light rays passing through them, revealing their orangish-golden colors and long white stringy fins. The sheer biodiversity of this planet strikes me. Just in this brief journey, I've already encountered countless species, each as fascinating as the next. My system works tirelessly in the background, logging data on each discovery.

I breathe and jump over the narrow stream to the other side. The *Astra* is about two klicks away now, and I still have some forest to cover. The taste of sweat lingers in my mouth; even through my helmet with the monitored temperature gauge, the warm, humid air feels slightly like Turkken, but not as dry. The rain here is picking up a little; each thick leaf and branch crackles under the wide drops of sporadic rainfall. If I never step foot on another desert or hot tropical planet, it won't be long enough. I never thought I'd miss the rain of Vola Prime.

The bugs and insects here are, without doubt, relentless—tiny, translucent-winged assholes consistently trying to infiltrate my suit. I'm miles into the rainforest, and the coordinates are leading me toward the northeast sector of the planet. It's been nothing but condensed nearly impassable terrain. One could easily get lost in this place, and I think I might already be.

I check my HUD, and the trail refreshes on the screen. "Nope, still going the right way," I say confidently.

I slink into a short clearing and leap off a jagged embankment onto the rocks and brush below. I stand from a crouch and pause immediately. In front of me stands a small to medium-sized brown-ochre short-furred animal staring at me. It patiently waits, anticipating or seeing who or what I am. I try not to make sudden movements as the creature curiously walks toward me.

Its long, narrow snout sniffs the ground by my feet, blowing its nostrils softly at first, then a bit harder before sitting with a comforting thud onto its rear legs. Its dual-shaded auburn fur is coated with patterns of deep brown and gold.

"Wow. Easy there, fella," I calmly say, trying not to startle the creature.

At first glance, it seems friendly, but I know never to trust some cute creature in some strange world; that's how you quickly become animal food. I slowly reach for my pistol.

The animal's sharp large ears turn towards the sounds of my armor shifting. It sits and stares at me as its tongue spills out as if in a pleasant grin.

"You aren't dangerous, are you?" I say, letting go of the handle.

He's probably just hungry, I think, digging into my pack. "I don't have much, but here," I say, offering a small protein square in my palm. The tiny creature timidly bends over as it sniffs my hand. Unsure, it takes a few more short inhalations before taking the protein cube out of my palm in one bite. The long, thin-legged creature inhales the food and licks its lips in gratitude before whimpering for more.

"Sorry, but I need food for myself, little one. Go on, get," I say, waving my hands. I try to shoo the creature, but it doesn't waver. "Go on!" I yell.

It's just staring at me with blank eyes, waiting for more food.

I sigh. *I'm going to regret this.* I give it one more corner of a ration, and its long, hairy, pointed tail wags back and forth in amusement. The animal finishes the bite of ration, but before it can ask for more, its ears suddenly jolt upward on high alert. It cowers into the shaded darkness behind it. The creature begins growling loudly, and I reach towards my sidearm, but

I hesitate as I notice where its eyes are looking. The creature isn't staring at me; it's looking behind me.

My eyes go to the right, and I try to take in my side profiles. I take a deep breath and hold it as I gently unlatch my sidearm. I'm carefully turning my head to the right when I hear a rising bellow directly behind me. The small animal darts into the large thin-leafed brush, leaving me alone. My heart begins to thump as I unholster my weapon.

I swing the pistol around, discharge the entire clip, then whip the mag to the moist brush below and load in another. With my eye to the holographic sight, I look in several directions. I don't see anything, just more forest. What the hell was that? I think as a deep, bellowing rattle echoes and drifts through the trees around me.

I grasp my rifle and heave it over my shoulder. I swing the barrel to the left and then to the right. Slow-moving ferns and drip-tip leaves flow in the gusts of air, making it hard to distinct movement. I clear each sector and sweep the trees and canopy, switching visor modes, but nothing is there.

A translucent blue wave-like formation outlines each shape as I engage the pulse heartbeat scanner. The formations vibrate slowly, and the visual bright outlines of each branch, tree, leaf, and rock rumble on screen minimally. I begin quickly clearing the trees and contorted vine-covered ground and suddenly stop at a large strange, oblong, rippling shape in the long, thick, low-hanging branches about twenty paces away. A red pulse beats from the shape's center, sending a visual shockwave that distorts the surrounding area with wavy, shifting patterns. The translucent form changes color as it moves within the tree line. I can't help but utter, "'What the fuck is that?'"

In a hypnotic display, the creature seamlessly transitions from its ghostly, see-through camouflage to a solid form. The transformation is rapid, and in an instant, its presence becomes tangible. It unleashes a primal, earth-shaking cry that reverberates through the impenetrable vegetation.

The quadrupedal creature's form suddenly blends seamlessly with the lush surroundings, its muted multicolored green skin effortlessly fading into the leaves and branches that envelop it. As my eyes struggle to penetrate its elusive form, the creature's imposing features become apparent. Its green-and-yellow-spotted reptilian body exudes strength, every tendon and bulging muscle hinting at its raw power. Hinged with a primal grimace, a boney jaw frames a fearsome array of sharp teeth, ready to tear flesh and bone. As its mouth opens, a steady trickle of saliva drips from its menacing teeth down to its long heavy razor-sharp claws sunken into the tree branch.

"Yeah, no thanks," I say, firing immediately.

Bullets burst from my rifle, shredding through the surrounding vegetation and bark as the spectral figure leaps from the branch and weaves between the tree trunks. Wood explodes left and right. The thing is unnaturally fast and unnervingly silent for its size, each of its movements measured and deliberate. The underbrush rustles ominously as the creature adjusts into a stalking position.

Relying on the pulse scanner mode on my visor, I catch fleeting blips of its erratic heartbeat. But it's moving too quickly, disappearing and reappearing on my tracker rapidly. It's circling me, hiding in the trees, an apex predator sizing up its prey. I press my back to a large trunk and wait, trying to find my moment.

My eyes constantly scan the surroundings until they fixate directly in front of me on a branch. 'I see you,' I whisper, observing its rapid heartbeat pulsating with intensity. I take aim with the rifle at the translucent creature. Finally, I manage to lock onto it and pull the trigger.

A bullet whistles through the thick jungle air, honed on a singular trajectory until it explodes through the creature's left front leg and vibrant purple blood splatters into the air. The projectile's impact against the muscular tissue is devastating. The beast's screech breaks through the forest. The force of the bullet hurls it off-balance from its perch on the towering trees, sending its monstrous form tumbling down in an ungainly sprawl. It crashes heavily into the shadowed brush, causing resonating thuds that swell through the serene wilderness before disappearing.

Barely daring to breathe, I remain poised on the edge of action, the rifle's rugged surface firmly against my shoulder. A sheen of nervous sweat clings to my brow as I probe the dead quiet of the jungle, a gnawing question in the recesses of my mind. *Did I kill it?* Doubt taints my hopeful speculation, and the silence provides no reassurance, only amplifying the threat that lurks in the shadows.

Suddenly, the tension-strung silence shatters, splintered by a guttural snarl that reverberates threateningly from my left. Almost involuntarily, my hand darts to my utility belt, fingers closing around the familiar form of an EOS device.

I activate the device in one fluid motion, triggering a plume of dense smoke to billow around me, veiling me in its impenetrable shroud. Simultaneously, a perfect holographic replica of myself materializes in the smoky haze, every detail replicated to perfection, from the sheen on my armor to the weapon in my hands. The deception is momentary, but enough to divert the creature's attention. Seizing this fleeting window of opportunity, I launch deeper into the rainforest's embrace, each pounding step taking me further away from the beast.

I keep running farther and farther away. After a few minutes, breathless and heart pounding, I steal a moment's pause, hunched behind the trunk of a massive tree. I glance at my forearm console, looping the decoy's feed, praying that the beast hasn't yet caught up with the hologram. I need to find somewhere to set up a defense. The hologram should keep running for another twenty seconds, providing me with a small but vital window, so I keep running.

The reverberating roar of a waterfall grows louder as I navigate through the labyrinth of towering trees and entwined vines. The power and fury of the water are daunting, the sight of its frothy white torrent plummeting over toothed rocks, an uninviting recap of the dangers surrounding me. Every path appears blocked, the formidable rocks and the thundering waterfall conspiring to confine me.

My navigation system highlights the disheartening truth: jumping is the best action. The digital display on my arm blinks in agreement, calculating the odds of survival—a daunting ten to one.

"Fucking heights," I say. The words are stolen away by the roaring wind as I teeter on the precipice. The titanic spread of turbulent water below kicks my vertigo into high gear, the overwhelming heights stirring a primal fear. Suddenly, the world spins around me, an off-kilter waltz that throws me off

balance. It feels like standing on a whirlwind roundabout, the once familiar landscape blurring into a disorienting display of colors. I fight against
the nausea creeping up my throat, the sickly tastes of adrenaline and fear
tinging my tongue.

The soft crunch of a twig suddenly snaps my attention back to the thick
wilderness. I see clearly as the creature reemerges from the tree line, its eyes
angry and filled with persistence. It dashes from the trees, gaining ground,
but slower than before, its wound was bleeding out.

As I gauge the terrifying rushing beast against the daunting jump, a lack
of decisions and reactions flashes through my mind. "Fuck it," I whisper as
I push off the edge.

The creature lunges at me, and the world blurs into a chaotic swirl of
green and blue as I fall through the air. The roar of the wind lasts forever
as the creature's deep growl fades into a dull silence. I abruptly pierce the
river's icy surface below with a loud splash, and everything quiets.

The initial impact is jarring, and disorientation takes over as the relentless current drags me under. My struggle for orientation is futile within the
turbulent waters. I kick and flail, every muscle straining against the invisible force pulling me further into the aquatic abyss. The thunderous roar of
the waterfall fills my ears underwater, a relentless booming that drowns out
any indication of the creature's whereabouts. I didn't hear it splash after me.

Where did it go? The question gnaws at me as I finally breach the surface.
The world above water is just as hectic, the relentless downpour of the falls
and the swirling mist creating a disorienting fog around me. *Did it survive
the fall?* Casting off the weight of the tumultuous waters, I power toward the
shore, away from the waterfall's relentless cascade.

As I move, the creature suddenly ruptures the surface. On spotting me, it
charges through the river with its legs drawn close to its streamlined body and
its thick tail propelling it forward. The sight urges me to move faster, my arms
cutting through the water, desperately attempting to reach the sandy shore.

Scrambling onto the land with the creature merely seconds behind me, I
hoist myself upright. Not pausing to catch my breath, I bolt into the thick
brush bordering the shore. As I break through the vegetation, my foot

catches on a hidden root, sending me sprawling down a rugged incline. I'm a ragdoll in the grip of gravity, tumbling head over heels, the world a dizzying twirl as I crash over the uneven terrain. After what feels like forever, I grind to an abrupt halt, tangled in twisted roots and vines at the foot of the hill. Every nerve ending screams out in protest as I struggle to get free.

Move, Beck, move! I command myself, attempting to rise, but my body protests as the tightly wound vines pin me in place, each movement tightening them around my frame.

The sudden sound of growling above me stops me in my tracks. The creature materializes inches away from me. It wrinkles its snout, showing its long yellowed teeth as it looms inches from my helmet. "Shit," I say, my rifle and sidearm frustratingly out of reach. I try to grasp for my last resort—my sonic emitter.

The creature growls fiercely, filling the space between us with hot, rancid breath that fogs my visor. My hand is getting closer and closer to the sonic emitter, but the beast pins me down even more as its muscular front leg steps on my chest armor, digging its sharp claws against the metal. I can't move.

As it lowers its massive head, preparing to strike, I take a sudden sharp inhale as if it were my last. The beast leans in, but suddenly halts, and its head snaps up. Its nostrils flare, and then, without warning, it spins around and darts into the trees.

I lay trapped and confused on the ground as I hear its panicked movements diminish into the distance. With trembling hands, I reach hard for my knife. I yank it from its sheath and slice vigilantly through the roots and plants, freeing myself from their grasp.

Yet as I prepare to assess the situation, a prompt on my HUD interrupts my thoughts. *Suit pressure compromised,* it warns, highlighting a large tear in my undersuit near my thigh.

The fall must have ripped the material, and a vine created a makeshift barrier. I fumble for the adhesion tape in my utility belt, but my grip fails, and the roll of tape clatters onto the forest floor and rolls under my legs into the plants. Before I can react, a subtle rustling emerges from behind me. Turning, my eyes widen, unprepared for the expanding shadow.

A dark silhouette engulfs the scattered rays of light from the canopy as a plant's upper portion unfurls in a mesmeric display. As the plant's center slowly opens, its interior reveals a radiant luminescent display. It is enchanting, it seems to pulse with a life of its own. Yet contrasted against this enthralling beauty are its large bulbs. Swollen and pulsating, they're suspended around its core like grotesque ornaments.

Suddenly, the bulbs rupture with booming sounds reminiscent of bursting balloons. In an instant, a massive cloud of obsidian-black particles spills out, so dense that it blots out my vision. Panic seizes me as the cloud rapidly infiltrates the tear in my suit. An acrid scent, like burnt ozone, fills the air, and as the particles invade my lungs through the breached undersuit, I'm overwhelmed. Each breath feels like inhaling embers. My chest tightens, constricting with every desperate gasp.

In a terrified haze, I stumble away from the toxic plant, but my legs buckle underneath me, sending me sprawling to the ground down another small hill. My muscles contract involuntarily, twitching and cramping as the black smoke permeates deeper into my respiratory system. I fumble with my helmet latch as the searing pain amplifies, threatening to overload my senses. It's like my brain is liquefying inside my skull.

My mouth opens in a soundless scream. My body curls involuntarily as I roll to my side, unable to move.

A child's laughter pierces through the eerie silence, jolting me awake as I lie still on the damp rainforest floor. The thick drops of rain drum against my helmet and armor, creating a steady rhythm that fills the air. But alongside the laughter, there's a strange ringing in my ears, accompanied by the worst migraine I've ever experienced. Hazy vision blurs my surroundings, and my heart races in my chest as hot, warm sweat beads on my forehead.

As I struggle to regain my bearings, a bitter taste coats my mouth, adding to the discomfort. Whatever happened has left me feeling utterly drained.

How long have I been unconscious? Glancing around, I realize I'm not in the same location anymore. The unfamiliar surroundings only deepen my confusion. None of this looks familiar.

With a twinge of unease, I quickly sit up and access my suit's diagnostics, particularly the location and toxicity report. To my dismay, I find the tear persists. Retrieving the emergency patch kit, I seal the breach and initiate a purge of the suit's filtration system. Following a brief system reset, the suit's life support cycles anew, confirming pressure stability with a green notification on my HUD. A toxicity warning flashes on the left side, and as I scrutinize it, an unsettling sound pierces the silence—a young girl's laughter.

My eyes dart upward. "Who's there?" I call out, rising cautiously. I quickly consult my route tracker, trying to gauge my proximity to the temple, but as I focus, my vision narrows and blurs, and a soft whisper threads through the surrounding foliage.

"Owen."

I find myself drawn to the whisper, my feet moving almost involuntarily towards the source of the voice amongst the swaying trees. A wave of dizziness hits me, causing me to stagger and brace myself against a nearby boulder. Struggling to shake off the disorientation, my gaze finally settles on a figure. "Owen," she repeats, her voice unmistakable in the stillness.

The sight before me is beyond comprehension—a child, deeply scarred, the devastating evidence of flames that once consumed her. As if in a dream, orange embers dance around her, conjuring a hellish ambiance from thin air. The skeletal remains of her face are haunting, and she approaches me on legs that have been reduced to cinders.

"Why weren't you there? Why didn't you save me?" Her voice, tinged with agony and accusation, is heart-wrenching.

My head spins, heat surging within my brain, a sensation akin to it being seared from the inside. "This isn't real," I stammer, the weight of guilt and confusion pressing down, overwhelming me with a torrent of emotions. Desperation, regret, anger, and fear entangle in a maddening whirlwind. I find myself swamped in the anguish of the moment. "Aanos," I croak, my strength leaving me as I collapse, crushed under the weight of sorrow and regret.

Her voice is filled with inconsolable pain as she says, "Why weren't you there, Owen? You promised."

"I tried, Aanos," I choke out, shame and sorrow preventing me from meeting her gaze.

Her voice softens, a shadow of its former self, filled with resignation and despair. "You once saved me from death, but when I needed you again, you weren't there. Just like with Avery," she says, her accusatory voice trailing off into the suffocating silence.

"Wait!" I loudly yell, getting to my feet to run after her, but she's already at least a hundred paces away.

A voice filled with sorrow reverberates through the trees, deep and haunting. "You abandoned us."

"Felix!" I shout, glimpsing his form hand-in-hand with Aanos.

As I rush toward them, my sanity starts to fracture. The world contorts, trees bending and transforming into geometric nightmares, encircling Aanos. The forest kaleidoscopes around her, its vibrancy unnaturally intensified. My heart races, confusion and terror mounting. "This can't be real."

"You failed us," they intone in chilling harmony.

"No! I tried! I fought with everything in me!" Desperation bleeds through my words.

The forest grows silent except for Aanos's cold, emotionless voice. "All that blood on your hands, Owen. Do you think someone like you deserves love, deserves life?"

The weight of my failures hits like a hammer. "I did everything I could, Aanos. Everything."

Her voice warps into something guttural and monstrous. "*You left me to burn!*"

Fiery embers rain down through the canopy, "I... I tried to—" I collapse to my knees, clutching my helmet. My brain feels like it's imploding.

Softly, almost tenderly, a voice says, "Owen."

I flinch, but then there's a light touch on my shoulder. Hopeful, terrified, I look up into the familiar, yet distorted face of Avery. Her hollow eyes, sunken and blackened, bore into mine. The chilling image of her blood-soaked face, the slow ooze from her fatal wound, makes bile rise in my throat.

She leans in, her voice barely more than a ghostly whisper. "You will always be alone."

Tears blur my vision. "Avery..." My voice trembles, barely a whisper.

The forest, the voices—they close in on me, suffocating, condemning. "Forever alone, Owen."

The agony crescendos, consuming my very being. "*Enough!*" I roar, channeling every last shred of willpower.

Suddenly, the agony shatters. My pulse begins to slow. My breathing becomes even. As I climb to my feet, the disorienting visuals fade, and reality seems to snap back. Avery, Aanos, Felix—they're all gone. Only the rainforest, alive yet indifferent, remains.

With raw desperation, I shout, "Avery!" until my voice cracks and breaks. The silent forest offers no solace.

There's only silence—empty, echoing silence. I am truly, devastatingly alone.

PATH OF THE
BLACK CRYSTAL

MY HEAD IS KILLING ME.

The pain is unrelenting, a constant hammering against my temples. Each pulse seems to resonate in time with the beating of my heart, rendering my thoughts foggy and my steps faltering. The mirages that so plagued me earlier have waned, leaving me in a peculiar lucidity.

I've been walking through the forest contemplating what the hell happened back there. I chop and hack through the dense, unending brush, paving the way with each sluggish step. I glare out past the treetops to the sporadic patches of blue sky as silhouettes of flapping wings dance over the stretched amber sun, and I wonder if it's all a dream, or just the hallucinations settling. Graceful chirps and songs of tropical birds fall comfortingly through the thin, tall trees, mimicked by the long, deep-bellied hoots of primates from a nearby troop.

The further I trek, the more I feel like the shape-shifting creature of the forest is near; I can feel it. Every rustle behind me, every shadow that flits just at the edge of my vision, makes my arm hair stand on end. The chill in the air grows, and the occasional distant growl, out of place in this silent forest, reminds me that I'm not alone.

As I continue east, the physical aftermath of the black smoke's assault begins to decrease. The burning in my lungs dulls to a mere ember and the numbing static in my fingers recedes. Those visions—Aanos, her burnt face frozen in anguish, Felix's haunted words, and Avery, eyes empty and devoid of the light I once knew—haunt my every step. They were apparitions dredged from the deepest recesses of my sorrow and guilt, brought to life by the wickedness of the plant's toxin.

I felt helpless, like this was all for nothing. For a moment, I had felt my sanity fraying, the darkness within threatening to swallow me whole. The poison had wielded my own memories, my own regrets against me, opening the chasm of despair that I had struggled for so long to keep sealed. It felt like a malicious parasite, gnawing away at the edges of my consciousness, urging me to surrender to the pain and to drift off, to just end it all.

Shaking my head to dispel the lingering remnants of the toxin's illusions, I focus on the forest around me. It's a deceptive maze; every turn, every tree seems oddly familiar, almost identical to the last. Still, I've managed to find my way, relying on navigation aids.

Glancing down, I bring up the grid display on my forearm module. The intricate green lines of the topographical map shimmer, momentarily blurring, before snapping back into focus. I shake my head. The navigation indicates I am very close to the temple's location. "I think," I say, squinting at the map.

Over the past hour or so, I've noticed slight terrain variations—black stones protrude from the ground, seemingly leading to a structured path. Their odd, unnaturally smooth but rectangular appearance is juxtaposed against the dark-green emerald of the forest.

As I've followed the rocks, I've noticed green oxidized corrosion fused to their surfaces. It's the same substance from the mining entrance of Noragöth back on Turkken, and the same material as the Jadestone Key. This isn't just a coincidence—two planets on opposite ends of the galaxy with the same teal-colored formation on the surface. "The temple is here. It has to be."

The peculiar pathway leads upward over a long grassy ridge to a small break in the forest. As I get to the top, I see a large rock formation surrounded by trees and unclimbable cliffs at the bottom of the short hill, obstructing the way forward or around. "What now?" I say as I make my way to the bottom to get a better look at the wall of rock blocking my path.

The exertion is minimal as I reach the lower face level, and the side of my helmet opens as my scanner engages. It ejects to examine the strange formation, searching for any entry point along the way. Its radiant blue ray fans over the massive ridge, scanning and beeping repeatedly, followed by a grating error sound when no access point is found. No matter the direction, I can't find a single-entry point or accessible ridge to climb over; it is far too dangerous. "Every time," I say to myself. *Always one step forward and ten steps back.*

"Welp," I say as I look up defeatedly. I step back from the massive wall to think for a moment. The treacherous face stretches endlessly in most directions; it will likely take hours, if not days, to see where it ends. *If it even does.*

This is why having the *Astra* or Tex would have made this so much simpler.

With my scanner still working overtime, my holoscreen unexpectedly chimes a notification and zooms in on a worn-down carving in the rock thirty paces away.

With a sense of intrigued surprise, I walk to the etching and trace my fingers over a strange indentation. It's a simpler version of the more-intricate Val'Ara—an upside-down triangle within a circle. It's much cruder than the original in appearance. My eyes drift to the grooves below, and I realize the indentation fits something inside.

I shift my pack and retrieve the key from the bottom. Its center pulses like a bright teal heartbeat as I pull it from the bag's darkness. The closer I hold it to the depression within the rockface, the more saturated it becomes. I also notice the key itself is magnetized; the ring on my neck is pulling toward it as it gets closer.

I rotate the key and slowly place it into the grooves, and its protruding points align and fit within it perfectly. With a firm shove, the key clicks into place, and a high-frequency noise pierces my ears as it emits steadily from the rocks. "Well, that did something," I say as I take one more step back.

I'm briefly alarmed as soft quakes make the dirt beneath my boots tremble. The slight rumble is followed by a sudden scraping noise of stone against stone as the wall in front of me widens slowly. A cranking of gears shifts the boulders, and, with a hefty clunk, a tapered passageway opens at my attentive feet.

I stare down the dark passage as loose dirt and pebbles fall to the ground. My unease ebbs slowly with each deep inhale. "Fucking tunnels," I say anxiously. "Why is it always dark, creepy tunnels?"

As I retrieve the key from the wall, I see a dim light as my eyes peek to the other side through the tight, constricted opening. It looks like a way through—just a short trek to the other side. It can't be more than fifty paces, but the boulders create a not-so-friendly path to the other side. With their jagged edges and pointed tips and my restricted movements, I'll be an easy, slow-moving target.

Before making the challenging trek across the boulders, I pause, drawing back slightly to ensure I'm not rushing into danger. I glance over my shoulder, my eyes scanning the surrounding trees and the distant ridgeline. The dense foliage rustles subtly, birds taking flight from their hidden perches. The ridgeline stands silent and unmoving, the shadows shifting minutely with the descending sun. Everything appears still, but this quiet could be deceptive. I strain my ears, trying to catch any hint of movement or a distant noise of the beast.

After a few tense moments, I convince myself that the coast is indeed clear. Taking a deep breath, I refocus on the unfriendly path of boulders before me.

I didn't come all this way to give up now, I think as my shoulder and arm are the first to enter through the narrow, toothed aperture. My gut was right about the tight squeeze. I duck and shift, morphing my body into the puzzle pieces it takes to move just a fraction of the way further in.

It's slow-paced, but I'm gaining ground inch by inch when I abruptly stop as a long, cool breeze sweeps through the passage. I briefly look back to the tree line, scanning through their tops and bottoms, then ahead.

The creature is watching me. I can feel it.

A low whickering and guttural rattle travel with the wind as it brushes through a second time.

Not this again.

I keep moving and shifting, eyes daggering to anything that moves behind me. I shuffle vigilantly as I make my way toward the other side. The familiar sound of a roaring waterfall begins to mask any other noise around me; it is hard to hear anything else the further I travel into the dark. I'm not sure where the noise is coming from, but it is getting louder with each step.

At what seems like the halfway point of the passage, one last call from the wind breathes life through the opening. A resounding rattle follows once again. My hand promptly reaches for my holster, and I raise my white-railed pistol and point to the opening where I entered the tunnel. With a brief hesitation, scanning left to right, I pop off three shots in front of me. I'm not necessarily aiming for anything in particular; they're more warning shots to persuade our friend to go away kindly.

My eyes move back and forth as I look to the tree line as the smoke recedes from the barrel. My line-of-sight shifts past the holographic optics of the rail to the trees. Only the wind moves the thin branches and leaves.

But I know I heard it that time. It's getting closer.

This tight shuffling is a prolonged process, as my chest armor makes maneuvering quite challenging when my attention is elsewhere. The uneven and sharp protruding corners scrape across my back and snag on the back-side of my harness belt. The small loop of my division-grade harness has tied itself along a long, narrow piece of broken stone. I tug forward, but gain no footing; I'm stuck. "Shit."

I turn around to take a step back, and time seems to slow as several razor-sharp nails come within centimeters of my helmet, but scratch against my chest plate, creating a wild stream of sparks that firework into the air. The metal shrieks piercingly as I tip backward, but barely; the stuck harness keeps me from falling. "Fuck!" I yell, trying to unlatch myself.

The beast bellows a bloodcurdling cry and repeatedly leaps as it swipes at me with the claws at the end of its muscular, thick-skinned triple-jointed arm; the sharp edges of the rock don't penetrate its slippery, white-bellied body as it rushes forward. I tug backward as far as I can, and it catches my chest plate again, causing more sparks to fly viciously into the dark crevice, illuminating us briefly.

I yell out, whipping the pistol around. The creature's long, extended five-fingered claws clip the pistol as I pop a shot off into the air, hitting nothing. The sidearm tumbles down to the ground. I try for my rifle, but my back is too close to the rocks. I tug and tug on the harness as I try to extend my arm as far as it can reach, but it's just out of my grasp. Suddenly, the harness loop snaps, and I fall to the floor.

The creature wedges itself further into the tight corridor. As it thrashes forward, inching its way nearly to my boots, its claws scrape against the rocks, creating an earsplitting noise. The creature's burnt yellow eyes lock onto me, slowly whickering a low, guttural growl; it is hungry.

I look forward and see a bit of a clearing. The creature won't be able to make it much farther because of its size.

I try to make it to my feet and engage my shield, and as I prop myself up, the creature roars and suddenly swipes, claws extended for the kill. I scream a thunderous cry through gritted teeth as its jagged nails penetrate deep into my thigh muscle; the pain is immeasurable.

I fall to the ground, and the beast pulls me closer. I look for anything to grab as it tugs deep into my leg. I brace my other foot and wedge it between some rocks. I try to push away from the creature, but it has a firm grip. Its nails begin slicing down my leg as I push away, sending blood pouring to the tunnel floor over its grotesque claws.

I gasp harshly as I look to my right. There, on the ground, sits my sidearm. I grab the cold white metal from the ground, turn, and click the trigger.

There's no muzzle flash. The gun is jammed.

"Oh, come *on!*" I shout, fumbling for the rail, the pain is excruciating.

The golden-sliver-eyed creature spits thick, gelatinous gunk at me, and it splatters onto my chest plate. The acidic green saliva crackles and pops as it sizzles on the surface of the metal. My mind races like a combustion fuse, and I try to clear the jam as the creature's high-frequency skirls bounce off the rock formations as it inches me closer and closer. Its foaming mouth bellows and snarls as its sharp, contorted nails release my leg.

It's now or never.

The jam clears, and I rack the rail and lock between its eyes. "*ION-X,*" I say, and a cartridge loads into the barrel with a subtle click.

The bright flash from the muzzle booms through the tunnel as the round strikes the creature right between its eyes. The beast stumbles for a moment, still not dead, and staggers confusedly as a few seconds pass.

I hear a sharp, high-pitched electrical sound rising before it settles on a steady monotone note.

With a perplexed look in its eyes, the creature's body goes stiff with a jolt of electrocution, and its cranium explodes into a thick green pool of mucus and brain with a resounding splat. Pieces of mangled head burst all over the walls, leaving an outlined, brain-free silhouette behind me. All that remains is part of the creature's lower jaw and its split tongue spasming through the air. It flaps back and forth wildly as a death cry rattles through its chest. Vivid purple blood pours from the flaps of its neck. It falls limply to the rocky floor as the oozing blood fills the small path, soaking my legs and boots thoroughly. It's more than dead; it's become an abstract splatter painting all over the fucking walls.

Heavy drips of sweat bead into my eyes as I lower the pistol. The *ION-X* round fragments upon entry, and as the core charges, the pieces of bullet create electrical pathways to each other that electrocute the body and then explode.

I pry myself from the tight rocks with a few heavy heaves and try to stand. I let off two more shots into its dead body. "Fuck you."

I look down and see gaping holes in my leg. *This isn't good.* I can barely put any weight on it. *I need to clean this immediately*, I think as I turn away from the mangled creature.

As I inch forward slowly, a warm beam of light illuminates the claw marks on my chest plate. With my hand, I break the ray of the sun as I shift myself forward and see the opening where the light is coming from. The more and more I press through, the brighter it becomes.

I finally reach the exit and squeeze out with a tremendous sense of relief as the sun illuminates my visor, briefly blinding me as my vision shifts from night to day.

"Holllllly shit." I sharply exhale as I fall to the ground, rolling to my back to catch my breath.

Panting heavily with my back to the ground and my eyes to the electric-blue sky, I lie there a moment, thinking about my bad luck. "Two terrifying creatures on two different planets, back-to-back." I grunt, bringing my weapon into view. I clear the rail three or four times, ejecting cartridge rounds before reloading them into the magazine. I holster it firmly at my side, and my head turns to the thunderous impact of water behind me.

I barely manage to get to my feet, and as I turn around, my eyes don't believe the magnificent sight. I'm talking a once-in-a-lifetime type of view. I stop and gaze upon the sun-soaked highland in a long, inspired silence interrupted only by my deep breathing. It is magnificent.

Many peaks form archways in the sky, interconnecting the large cliffs in otherworldly shapes. I stand on the ridge as the dark grey stratocumulus clouds in the distance venture over an unspoiled, luscious green land of steep escarpments and mountains hiking high into the hazes. Many waterfalls rage over the edges of the cliffs, crashing hundreds of feet below and creating a cold mist over the sheltered green oasis. It goes on for miles in every direction, surrounded by the enormous wall I came through.

"But how?" I say as my eyes turn to the middle of the veiled tropical paradise. I'm interrupted in my thoughts as I see a triangular temple sitting dormant in the center of the land, encircled by a treasure trove of smaller structures and colossal fallen monuments covered in overgrowth. It is massive.

A flock of large four-winged creatures bathes their blonde–ochre bodies in the settled rivers below and around the temple; some search for food in the shallow clear waters, and others rest, stretching their wide-spread feathered wings in the shade. Their long, thin beaks caw in unison as they delightedly gulp down river creatures. A loud call from above the cliffs breaks my attention, and I see more golden-tipped animals sweeping down a waterfall, soaring inches above the raging water to the streams surrounding the triangular temple.

Where the tears of the clouds meet the heart of the water. This is what she meant. We did it, Tex. We fucking did it, I think, looking over the land as my leg continues to pour blood. I wonder for a moment what he would say.

I sit at the edge of the ridge to enjoy the speck of happiness, taking in the breathtaking view of this long-lost place while I retrieve my Med pack. This is a view to write home about, one Avery would have loved to see, and what I wouldn't give to show her if I had the chance—and I'm one step closer. It is hard to mask my emotions. I've lost the warm glint of hope for so long that I have forgotten what it can feel like. It can be a warm hug or a destroyer of worlds.

First Turkken and Enohk, and now this? It is hard to relax and enjoy the win for once. I'm not sure what to do with myself, so I do what I think Tex would have wanted to do: I try to enjoy it, despite my leg being a complete shitshow.

The waterfalls crash down in the background as I slide my finger over the Med pack. I retrieve a small injector of TetraGel and click the top as I place it in the first wound. The large, rifle-bullet-sized holes in my leg fill with the blue foamy liquid, which starts to solidify and cauterizes the wound. The pain rapidly swells from the center of my lower leg up to my thigh. I need to let the TetraGel work for a few minutes before going anywhere. It will take a few hours to harden entirely, but it should be okay to continue on in a few minutes.

So, I sit and relax for a solid hour in the sun, sketching and capturing the extent of my view in the pages of the journal. This place is beautiful. It's the type of view I promised Avery all those years ago. I'd give anything to have one more day with her—even a few more seconds.

With the TetraGel nearly good to go and the sun still setting, I carefully head down the ridge to address my thirst and hunger. At the bottom, I sit near a waterfall and peel away my armor piece by piece. The dried blood clears from the Endonium, and I stare at the scratches on my chest plate. *What were those claws made of?* Nothing is strong enough to pierce solidified Endonium. *Well, so I thought.*

I clean the wound, myself, and the rest of my gear of brains, blood, and mangled bits in the comforting shallow ends of the furious waterfalls above.

Rainclouds begin to billow just overhead. The sun slowly descends, creating an aurora of creamy purples and pinks where the mountains meet the firmament. The TetraGel has seemingly set, and I inject a few steroids and painkillers into my leg. It dulls the discomfort subtly, but at least I won't bleed out.

I am feeling refreshed, but my leg still throbs, and with my gear back on, I know I'd better not push my luck and be out here vulnerable for too long.

So, I slowly make my way toward the temple with the looming sunset breaking through the cliffs' archways surrounding this hidden paradise.

With my limp, it takes longer than I'd have thought to arrive at the temple's base. A heavy rainstorm is beating over the architecture and dark-metaled stonelike structure. The temple is unlike anything I've ever seen, though it is in ruins; it has met life's most significant threat, Time. It has succumbed to years of dead roots and vines, suffocating its columns and structures. Numerous giant cloaked figures stand guard around the doorway as rain falls on their shrouded faces, their heraldic poses thwarting would-be intruders if they dare enter the temple. A few statues have crumbled to pieces ages ago, their limbs and cloaks shattered and positioned near their feet. *Who are you?* I stare puzzled.

"Who built this place? Was it the Khu'Val, or worshippers? Who were the worshippers and where did they go?" I ask as I ensure all the video data has archived into my system's database. *Whatever it is, there is no one left.*

The massive archway leading into the temple is high enough to accommodate beings much larger than us. I have a readier appreciation now for the sheer size of this place, as, from the ridge, it seemed much smaller, and a feeling of insignificance prowls over my body.

As I approach closer, I see that the pillars and walls have a series of glyphs carved into them—many more than I've seen before. It looks like Khu'Vala. "Remarkable," I say, leaning in a bit closer. I engage my scanner, mapping each character faster than I could ever sketch by hand, and then head through the opening of the massive gates and into the temple.

A long hall illuminates before me as a lightning strike crashes above the top of the temple, followed by a lurid rumble of thunder. The storm is picking up and eclipsing the sun.

I switch to night vision, and a vibrant green hue engages over my eyes. Water trickles through the cracks of the ceiling, leaking down the ancient stones and unkempt moss to the tiled foundation. The complex laser-precise architecture creates intricate geometric patterns and symmetry spaced over the entire structure—a tesseract of stone intertwining with itself, forming impossible shapes: rectangular sections and inlays shaped within a maze of intersecting walls and partitions. I don't think these were carved by hand; it would take hundreds, if not thousands, of years to sculpt something of this magnitude.

I hit one of the columns, and a metallic sound bangs through the hall. It's the same material as the secret passage wall; it is very bizarre. *This looks like the only way in*, I think, so I reach in my pack, pull out several proximity devices, and throw them along the wall, creating an invisible laser grid to alert me of any movement. They latch to the wall and power on behind me.

My attention shifts as, up ahead, I see many hexangular-columned panels on the walls leading towards something outside the hall. As I follow the wide, tiled entry, it opens to a circular room surrounded by giant grey statues shadowing the center. The similar figures are all posed with their palms facing up in acceptance, the same as the ones from Turkken. Their long cloaks spill over their bases to the floor, leading to a circular staircase on all sides that extends somewhere unknown. But this time, there is no female figure.

After scanning the rest of the hallway, I reach the staircase and gaze down at the lower level with astonishment. In the center sits a multi-tiered cylindrical device reminiscent of an antique capstan or wooden ship's wheel. It's surrounded by numerous glyphs, familiar to me from both Turkken and the journal. These symbols are organized within dozens of rows around the device. Within each section of circle, the glyphs are placed in an alternating pattern: symbol, blank stone, symbol, blank stone. The arrangement in one row is offset from the one above, with each row having a distinct alternating sequence. Overall, there are at least a dozen of these rows, comprising hundreds of characters.

I cautiously limp down the steps, my eyes moving in all directions, waiting for some ancient booby trap to cut me in half or pour acid over me. My gut is usually correct, but to my surprise, nothing occurs, and I reach the bottom in one piece.

No hand has touched this device in ages. Webs and the familiar green corrosion cover it. I wipe the surface of the stone-geared device suspiciously, my hand damp with sweat under my combat gloves, and as the dust settles through the remaining rays of light from the setting sun breaking through the rain clouds, an imprint of the Khu'Val seal, the Val'Ara, reveals itself through the thick grime.

"What is this thing?" I say to myself, staring vividly at its inner workings.

I find myself facing a mysterious spinning mechanism, with levers that protrude from its sides, they are all aligned parallel to the chamber's floor. These levers, evenly spaced out, bear a striking resemblance to compass points on a map. I try spinning the closest lever in either direction, but it won't budge. No matter how hard I push or pull, it doesn't move an inch. "Hmm," I say, looking at the damaged metallic symbol.

In the center of the Val'Ara, I see the same indentations as the wall from the outside. "Let's give this another try," I say, a little hesitant at first.

With the key in hand, I see it has shifted to a steady, bright glow. I carefully place it within the indentations, and a quick flash of energy shines from the cracks of the stone-geared device. Its inner structure weightily groans as it shifts and unlocks with a robust clunk.

The temple pulses with an ancient energy, awakening the once-dormant device. As I watch, the glyphs on the stone floor transition from a muted grey to a vibrant teal, casting a mystical glow. A deep, resonant hum emanates from the temple's depths, vibrating the very walls around me.

Above the Val'Ara seal, a luminescent teal hologram appears revealing a singular rotating character. Almost instinctively, my eyes search the floor, trying to pinpoint an identical glyph.

"Incredible," I say breathlessly, barely aware of the wonder in my voice.

A sudden flash of lightning punctuates my amazement, driving me to action.

Grasping the nearest lever firmly, I apply pressure, and instantly, the ancient gears of the device awaken. They groan to life with a symphony of loud creaks and metallic clangs. Below me, the symbols etched into the stone begin their dance, revolving in a complex, mesmerizing pattern.

As I manipulate the lever, the holographic image projected above the device shifts correspondingly. It now mirrors the glyph that's nestled within the intricate design on the temple's floor. This isn't just a simple rotation; the floor glyphs move in a dynamic display, orbiting around the device and me while also shifting both vertically and diagonally. Their movement is not random, but appears to follow an intricate, predetermined path.

"This is going to take a while," I mutter to myself, anchoring the lever in its current position using the full weight of my body as I strive to decipher the pattern and align the glyphs correctly.

As doubt creeps in, I hesitate, and my grip on the lever loosens. In that brief moment, the mechanism spirals into chaos. The gears, which had been moving with such purpose, now spin wildly out of control. The sound of grinding metal fills the chamber, each turn a jarring memento of my error. The entire system resets, the glyphs returning to their original positions. I'm back to square one.

Taking a deep, steadying breath, I try to anchor myself in the present. The words of Enohk and Avery echo in my mind: "At night, the sight comes without being asked. By day, we are lost without being stolen." The riddle is clear in its wording, yet elusive in its meaning. The key to solving this puzzle lies in understanding these words, but how? I need to find the right glyph, or perhaps a series of them, but the options are overwhelming. There are hundreds of symbols, and trying each combination could take months, if not years.

With uncertainty weighing heavily on me, I pull out the journal. Its pages are filled with hastily scribbled notes, diagrams, and translations. As I leaf through the worn pages, I hope to find a clue, a hint, anything that might illuminate the path forward in this cryptic puzzle.

I place the journal on the device, starting to match the glyphs on the ground with those in the book. The riddle keeps playing in my head: "At night, the sight comes without being asked..." It points me towards something to do with the night sky or space.

But I'm not sure if that's all I need. How many of these symbols do I have to line up? I'm a soldier, not a linguist or archaeologist. This isn't my usual terrain.

Still, I can't ignore the puzzle. If I'm going to get anywhere with this ancient tech, I need to figure out how many glyphs are part of the solution and in what order they need to be aligned. I keep flipping through the journal, hoping to spot something else that will fit the riddle and help me complete this task.

The first glyph I focus on is gravity. It's depicted as a spiral, drawing inwards in a way that unmistakably suggests a black hole or the pull of gravity. This symbol, capturing the essence of the force that holds the universe together, seems to click with the riddle's first part—an unseen, ever-present force, much like the night.

Feeling a sudden sense of clarity, I move to the lever nearest to me and begin aligning the spiral gravity glyph with its matching symbol on the floor. I adjust the lever, feeling the ancient gears move under my hands. Then, with a definitive click, the alignment is perfect. As soon as I achieve this, the gravity glyph materializes above the Val'Ara seal on the device's surface. It appears out of thin air, glowing in a radiant teal light. *Success.*

But the device doesn't give me a moment to relish the victory—the tension in the mechanism releases, and it resets, ready for the next glyph to be aligned.

Staying concentrated, I shift my gaze to the second glyph in the journal. It's an intricate symbol, showing two triangles rotated and their points touching, encircled by rings that seem to be in endless motion, forming what looks like an infinite loop. Next to it, Ave has written a note indicating that it symbolizes time—a continuous, unending cycle that seamlessly transitions night into day and day back to night again.

It encapsulates the idea of something that is always present, yet its form changes. It's a constant, cyclical process that's never truly lost or gone. Hoping I understand its meaning, I ready myself to align the time glyph with its corresponding symbol on the device.

The mechanism feels ancient under my fingers, yet it moves smoothly as I align the triangles and their orbiting circles with the symbol on the floor. After a moment, there's a definitive click as the glyph finally locks into place, and immediately, the character on the floor responds, glowing more intensely, casting a brighter light across the chamber.

As the time glyph activates, its representation materializes on the bottom left of the Val'Ara seal, joining the previously illuminated symbol. The glowing glyphs nearly form a triangle on the seal's surface. Maybe I need one more piece to complete this geometric puzzle.

As minutes stretch into what feels like hours of wrong choices, I mumble to myself over and over, "We are lost without being stolen." My gaze falls to one glyph in particular: several circles intertwining into each other in a dotted form, like a depiction of a night sky dotted with stars. At first, the connection eludes me. Stars are ever-present, yet obscured by day—visible, yet often overlooked. The realization dawns slowly, like the night sky gradually revealing its treasures at dusk.

The stars—they are the celestial bodies that make their appearance each night. This symbol, I finally understand, embodies the essence of the entire riddle. It represents the nightly spectacle that graces our sky without invitation, only to be "lost" with the break of dawn.

Understanding the riddle more clearly now, I take a deep breath and approach the lever again. My fingers, despite being blistered from previous efforts, are determined as they guide the stars glyph into position. There's a bit of a shake in my hands, not just from the exhaustion, but also from the anticipation of what's about to happen.

With a precise movement, I align the stars glyph. It clicks into place, and immediately, the glyph starts glowing brightly. It joins the other symbols, appearing on the bottom right of the seal's surface. As it does, it connects with the other glyphs with lines of vibrant blue and green. This visual connection between the symbols adds another layer to the already-illuminated chamber.

"Finally," I say, expecting a reaction. But surprisingly, nothing further happens. Confusion washes over me as I stand before the activated device, pondering my next move.

Lightning sparks through the temple, followed by more thunder. Puzzled, I stand in front of the flushed Val'Ara symbol on the device. I stare and cross my arms, wondering what I'm doing wrong.

I think hard and realize something is off about the symbol. *The triangle of the Val'Ara is wrong.* I compare it to the journal and see the main triangle is right-side-up on the device. "Is it that easy?" I say as I take hold of the metal piece and crank it clockwise.

It locks purposefully into place, causing the entire floor beneath me to shift and rumble aggressively. The wheel starts descending slowly, pulling the ground with it. As I cling to its edges, the temple's walls begin to recede, revealing an expansive underground chamber bathed in black and teal. Cascading waterfalls of pure energy flow around me, converging at a central point below.

I look up and watch the opening grow smaller and smaller as I'm lowered deeper underneath the main structure. A sea of darkness waits below as I peer out into the black. Even with night vision, I can't make out much. Distant water crashes heavily against stone and breaks the silence of my deep breathing. The automated visor systems try to refresh the night vision on my holoscreen, but my electronic back module seems to be acting up again.

The platform abruptly stops, and dust puffs into the air. I press the button for my flashlight. It flickers for a moment before turning off and staying off.

"What the hell? Come on, you piece—" I start, reordering my electronics to activate it.

Malfunction Detected, the suit says.

"Great," I say, returning my attention ahead. "Must be the magnetic interference."

As the dust settles, I still can't see anything beyond the elevator platform, and the hole above doesn't provide much light. "Hello!" I yell. My voice echoes out, trailing infinitely.

I am deep in the underbelly of the temple now, with no idea what to do. I can't see anything, I think, looking back up to the now-hand-sized hole from which I came.

I take a painful step off the old lift, and a sudden bright flash startles me as a row of torches ignite one by one with intense, brilliant teal flames, a domino effect that ends as the last torch lights, revealing a short pathway forward. I turn back, and I retrieve the key from the device, and place it into my pack.

I walk along the path slowly; my leg is still causing me to limp. Just as I reach the last one, several other torches burst into light along a giant wall in front of me, revealing a spectacular sight.

"Holy shit," I say as I look high up to the ceiling. The green hue from the torches elucidates a wall made of pure black crystal. The second I take one step closer, bright energy stems from the center of the wall, briefly revealing something that I don't understand hidden under its surface. Upon pulling the key from my pack, I notice the black crystal is glowing with familiar characters and energy in a specific location to my right. I hold the key closer and realize the wall has the same indentations as the other devices.

The key sinks into place, and a sudden lack of power causes the key to fizzle before exploding into a vast sea of lights. Within the once-dark crystal, thousands of larger and smaller dots form, creating an orrery of star-like spheres of light deep within the crystal. They shine brightly as the full power from the key takes hold.

I take a few steps back, looking from end to end. It is mind-blowing. I don't think it's just an unsystematic wall of lights, but what looks to be an ancient star chart of some kind, a technology I've never seen before. *Is it an ancient hologram of some sort?*

Constellations of shapes align sporadically across the entrancing wall of black crystal, creating a pattern of light and radiance from left to right. The bigger circles, I assume, represent suns, and the smaller dots are the planets of each system.

Out of the colorful array of lights and symbols, one glaring icon stands out.

"I recognize this sector," I say, the coordinates coming to life in my mind as vibrantly as the lights on the crystal wall. My breath quickens as the truth unveils itself.

My eyes lock onto the glowing circle signifying Sector-25, a chilling void infamous only for its resident beast, the immense black hole KGC-232. Known for its daunting emptiness, this sector has been an unapproachable enigma, a devouring blackhole that no ship could ever survive.

A flicker of recollection lights up the darker corners of my mind—hushed stories recounted in the dim lights of space bars, tales of starships devoured by the merciless black expanse. The crushing gravitational pull, a relentless force tearing the toughest craft into oblivion, was a universally accepted peril. But what if someone had braved it? Not to defy the black hole, but to exploit its inscrutable power?

Understanding dawns on me like a crashing wave, each revelation stronger than the last. *This is where you've been hiding. Veiled in the deepest shadows, you've been silently watching us. Hiding within the belly of the very beast we were all too fearful to confront.*

A smile tugs at the corner of my lips. "This is where you are?" I whisper to the dark void. "Hiding in the terrifying jaws of the universe's most-feared predator. But now... now I know where you've been hiding all this time."

I can't believe it. All this searching, all these days of anguish finally feel worth it. "I finally found a chance to save Avery," I say.

The moment is abruptly shattered by a chime on my forearm. *Proximity Alert. Motion Detected*, the *Astra* signals from the rainforest.

"Damn. I thought I'd have more time," I say as I patch into *Astra's* camera feed.

An earlier recording of a static-overlayed video shows two NG-Scout drones flying overhead above the *Astra* towards the temple until their engines cut out, causing them to crash somewhere nearby the ship. I look at the timestamp. It was over several hours ago. *Why did it take that long to notify me? Probably the interference from the temple. That means I don't have much time.*

I can't let them find this. What will happen if Ezrek finds the temple, finds this star chart, and learns their location?

That's not going to happen, I think self-assuredly. I know what I have to do, although it isn't the best idea in the world.

How the hell did they find me? I think as I pull my last NC-x9 Detonator from my belt, click it, and stick it to the crystal wall. "Sorry, Enohk. I can't let Ez find this," I say, retrieving the key from the crystal surface. The stars' and planets' light fades to dull blips before disappearing completely, sucking into the energy of the key. The detonator counts down in a red sequenced flashing as the black crystal wall goes dark and returns to its original state.

I rush to the lift and place the key back in the main rotating device; it shifts and shudders, then lifts from the ground, powering up completely. I stare at the crystal wall and brace as the detonator blinks continuously, then settles on a bright bold red.

An explosion rings out, and the massive wall shatters into numerous shards and fragments of crystal in a wild explosion, falling all around me. I lift my hands as the bits and pieces rain down over the space.

The dust and smoke settles, and I clear the air as I head back up the lift to the temple. "That was bigger than I thought," I say, returning my attention to the nearing opening above.

It takes a few minutes, but just as I breach it, I'm met with a familiar sight. "Shit," I say, reaching for my weapon.

The temple's air grows thick as the Teknaut, a behemoth of an armored figure, grabs me forcefully by the shoulder and sends me hurtling across the room. I'm airborne for seconds before I crash violently into a broken pillar. The impact dislodges it from its perch, and we tumble together down a flight of stone stairs.

Pain radiates from my leg and abdomen as I lay sprawled-out on the cold temple floor, desperately sucking in ragged breaths. A low groan of pain and frustration escapes my lips. Lifting my head, I catch a glimpse of the Teknaut. It stands ominously at the top of the stairs, the singular red light from its helmet cutting through the temple's shadows.

"Of course," I say, pushing through the pain to stand. "No chance you want to talk things out, eh, big guy?"

Instead of a response, the Teknaut menacingly racks its colossal weapon. I can almost hear its systems whirring, calculating the best approach. It doesn't shoot. *Curious.*

"*SMOKE!*" I yell without a second thought, taking aim at the temple's vaulted ceiling. The ensuing explosion releases a dense, obscuring smoke that quickly fills the vast chamber. The Teknaut's advanced tracking system might be good, but with this, I hope it's blinded. I limp rapidly to find cover, clutching my thigh, which feels wet and warm. My TetraGel has taken a hit, and it hasn't had time to fully set. I find cover behind a stack of fallen rocks as I top the stairs.

I hear the Teknaut searching as its frustrated mechanical groans echo through the grey.

I push through the pain, forcing myself to move stealthily. The sounds of the Teknaut become erratic, its heavy footfalls getting closer and then further away. I peek out to hear where it has gone. The temple has fallen silent.

Where did it go?

I scan to the left, then to the right, and slowly make my way out of cover.

The smoke veils my movements as I edge toward the exit. With every step, the way out becomes clearer, beckoning me to safety. But as I move past one of the large fallen statues, a mammoth arm whips out from behind it, hammering into my chest with a force that feels like a freight train. I crash to the ground, air violently expelled from my lungs.

Pain radiates from my chest, and for a few excruciating seconds, all I can see is a blinding white light. I try to suck in a breath, but it's like inhaling through a crushed straw. Every fiber in my body screams out, begging for oxygen.

Dazed, I try to gather my bearings, but before I can react, the T-7 seizes me by the ankles. It hoists me upside-down and dangles me in the air like a broken toy. We are eye-to-eye, and its singular red sensor scans me, perhaps evaluating or simply mocking.

With my world flipped, instinct takes over. I barely manage to pull my sonic emitter from its holster and slam it against the Teknaut's helmet. "This is going to suck for both of us," I say, activating the device. A deafening, high-pitched wail filled the air, waves of sonic energy disrupting the T-7's internal systems.

The Teknaut's grip on my ankles weakens, and its red sensor begins to flicker erratically. Cries cascade from its joints, and it releases an inhuman groan of malfunctioning servos and distorted circuits.

Still upside-down, my blood rushing to my head, I wrestle with the T-7's grasp, trying to free myself while continuously pressing the emitter against its metal helmet. With every pulse, the machine seems to shudder and twitch more violently.

Suddenly, a surge of electricity zaps from the Teknaut, traveling through the emitter and shocking me. I cry out, the pain jolting through my every nerve. My grip on the emitter loosens, and it falls to the ground with a clatter.

The T-7, though clearly damaged, swings me towards one of the temple's walls, but just as I am about to make a brutal connection with the stone, the machine's arm freezes, its systems glitching.

Taking this momentary lapse to my advantage, I grasp the compact blade hidden within my boot, and the laser edge slashes at the fingers holding me.

Sparks fly as I slice through metal and wiring. The Teknaut's grip falters as it loses several fingers and its thumb, and I crash to the ground, now free, but bruised and battered.

Scrambling to my feet, I make a dash for my rifle. However, the Teknaut, despite its compromised state, isn't going to let me escape that easily. It lurches towards me, its movements janky and unpredictable due to the sonic damage.

Grasping my sidearm, I say, "*ELECTRODE.*" I fire a series of electrically charged rounds, targeting its exposed joints. Each hit slows the T-7, causing it to twitch and jerk uncontrollably.

As I fire the final shot into the one-inch gap on its back module, the Teknaut's sensor dims to a faint glow before flickering out completely. The once-imposing machine now lies motionless, dormant on the temple floor, defeated temporarily.

Breathing heavily, I retrieve my sonic emitter. "You and I need a break," I say, attaching it back to my belt. With a lingering glance at the fallen Teknaut, I limp towards the exit. Every step is painful as I grow closer and closer to the door.

Without warning, a metal clinking fills the air. Confused, I abruptly see an NC-x9 detonator emerge from the smoke and blink red at my feet. "Ah, come on!" I shout, kicking it as hard as possible and leaping behind a fallen stone slab.

An explosion rings out through the temple and opening. The blast rains rocks and fire over the chamber. A high-pitched ringing takes hold of my ears, leaving everything muffled besides the loud screech of the growing frequency in my head. First the sonic emitter, now this.

"Fuck," I yell, but I can barely hear myself. I keep moving my jaw back and forth, trying to clear the ringing. Even with my helmet, the explosion and emitter damaged my eardrums.

The air grows thick with the pungent smells of smoke and fire. It weaves through the temple, combining with the previous cloud. My steps falter as I attempt to make my way to my rifle lying near me.

As I stagger forward, a silhouette slices through the mist, its form unmistakable. Before I can react, the shape surges toward me with blinding speed. With a crushing force, a knee collides with my ribs, sending me sprawling towards the still form of the Teknaut. I grasp for anything to prevent my fall, but my fingers only meet with empty air and smoke as I crash to the ground.

It's Ryzer.

He momentarily disappears, swallowed by the dense gray veil of smoke. The Teknaut's lights flutter, its systems powering on momentarily before shutting off again. Its mechanical groans signal it's trying to power back on. An unnerving feeling settles in the pit of my stomach. *I don't have much time. I can't take on both of them.*

A soft rustle to the right, then the hum of something powerful charging up, makes me turn instantly, my rifle at the ready. But I see nothing.

Suddenly, a blue pulse shot narrowly misses my head from the opposite direction, leaving exploded rocks and a scorched trail in the stone pillar behind me. I instinctively activate my kinetic shield, trying to trace back the shot's origin. "How'd you find me?" I say, trying to see through the remaining curling smoke.

An unsettling silence fills the temple, and as I slip further into darkness, from out the heavy smoke, his synthesized low toned voice speaks, clear and cold, each syllable punctuated by the low hum of machinery and distant rumbles of thunder outside. "This is your only warning. Surrender now."

I slowly creep through the darkness. The shadows offer a semblance of protection, and the echoes within the temple's walls distort sound, giving me a slim advantage. I try to muffle my breathing, using the billowing smoke and rain as a cover to stealthily move to the exit. Though it conceals me, it also makes it incredibly hard to pinpoint where Ryzer might be lurking. Every soft echo, every muted footfall feels like it's right behind me. My senses sharpen, attempting to pick out any hint of movement or change in the rhythm of the smoky whirlwind.

As I make my way for the door, a looming shape begins to solidify in front of me, taking on a more distinct form. I stop.

Ryzer stands before me, grasping something from his belt, and blocks the exit as rain pours through the temple's cracks. A brief rumble of thunder and crash of lightning barely illuminate his figure. "You are becoming quite the pain in the ass, pilot. I've never failed Ezrek before, and I won't let you slip away again," he says, firmly gripping something.

"Why aren't you like the others? You seem to have a mind of your own. Why would you work for that asshole?"

Ryzer's hand drops, and a blade ignites as he extends his arm. The red edge sizzles as the storm surge overhead trickles rain through the cracked temple around us. "This ends now," he says as he coils the blade into the air and snaps it sharply. "Only one of us is going to make it out of here alive this time," he says.

"What? Ezrek doesn't want me alive anymore?" I say, engaging my forearm shield.

With a low-frequency thump, a bright blue forcefield hazes Ryzer's appearance for a second before fully powering on, creating a blue haze over him entirely.

"I'm going to enjoy this," he says as he leaps forward, thrusting his holo-blade. It smashes against my shield with a loud crash and energy fluctuation buzz. The forceful hit sends me backward as I firmly plant my feet. He's strong for a diminutive guy.

I charge back, firing multiple quick hip shots from my pistol, but Ryzer easily stops them as he also engages a diamond-shaped energy shield from his forearm. The impacted slugs fall to the stoned floor one by one as he disengages the shield.

He spins forward and thrashes out with a heavy kick straight to my chest. I lose my grip on my pistol; it falls to the temple floor, sliding away under a few tumbled stones. My leg wound is making me slower, and Ryzer is much nimbler than I am right now. "Okay, I guess we are kicking now," I say, wiping myself off. "No one told me we were kicking."

Ryzer strides forward to the left, then right, raining down blow after blow as I try to block each swift strike of his searing-hot blade. The energy shield's power source crackles and snaps as it drains quickly.

I duck under a heavy attack and manage to counter, knocking him clean off his feet. He slams to the ground, smashing his face against a fallen monument. Suddenly, as I eye the exit, I see nearly a dozen Novas Guard emerging from the temple's halls above and below. They surround us, rifles drawn, waiting for the order to kill.

"Hold," Ryzer yells, getting up from the ground. "He's mi—" he says, but his vocoder is malfunctioning. Subtly dazed, he stands and tries to say something else, but it's inaudible. His warp-pitched voice repeats crackles and pops from the broken electronics.

I'm fucked, I think as I throw my weapons to the ground. I'm outnumbered and outgunned. "Did I break that?" I say, throwing my hands in the air.

His helmet's electronics sizzle and smoke. He reaches for his digital bracer, presses a three-button order, and his helmet gases began to release. His helmet cracks open, and he pries it off with a drawn-out release and repeats the order. "Secure the prisoner. Ezrek will want to speak with him aboard the *Novascar.*"

I look up with an astounded shock of curiosity. "What the fuck?" I whisper as the air stops in my lungs. I choke on the words. My entire world seems to slow down.

The rain pours into the temple, and deafening thunder and lightning flash through the halls. With a dreamlike sense of confusion, my immovable wide-eyed gaze sets onto the face of the person staring back at me.

I can't breathe. My body begins to tighten, and the name gently leaves my lips just before a soldier strikes a heavy blow to the back of my head, knocking me out cold.

"Avery?"

TIES THAT BIND US

I SLOWLY AWAKEN.

My thoughts feel sluggish. I'm having difficulty remembering anything, and my breathing is strained and shallow.

Where am I?

I reluctantly open my eyes, and the profound, comforting black shifts to a blurred, painful white. I half-squint to dull the pain from the blinding-white high-gloss paneled flooring and walls. The buzzing from the high-powered lights above competes with the high-pitched ringing and the migraine storming through my brain. I can't tell if I hear a low droning sound reverberating through my eardrums or the walls themselves. I'm pretty sure it's the latter, which likely means one thing: I've been captured, and I'm on the *Novascar*.

A tense panic begins to overwhelm my thoughts as I wonder how I got here, and where "here" is exactly. I can't see shit. A layer of blur fogs my eyes. *Fuck. This isn't good.*

I think for a moment as I start to connect the dots. *I arrived on the uncharted planet and located the temple; then, I found the puzzle that led me to the black crystal's path to the Khu'val... but what happened when I reached the surface?*

I take a short breath. "Avery..."

My mind races as I try to open my eyes further. Drool strings from my mouth onto my unkempt beard as I summon the strength to lift my head. It wobbles as I peer down at my naked body. Everything is exposed, and it's very cold in here. I try to move my hands and feet, but they don't budge. I am tightly imprisoned on a freezing, mirrored, semi-upright metal table inside some white-paneled interrogation room. Several odd-shaped rigid devices with razor-sharp pointy tips sit dormant above me—possibly some neuropathic devices. They don't look friendly.

My entire face feels like jelly, and my thoughts and body struggle as, clearly, a heavy narcotic is coursing through my system. It feels as if the mass of a thousand anchors is weighing me down; it comes in overwhelming waves of nausea the harder I try to snap out of it. I can barely see to the opposite end of the room.

My waning concentration breaks from the quiet room as a voice speaks from behind me. "Wakey, wakey," the familiar voice says.

The brisk tone crawls down my spine in the worst way possible and sends my eyes directly to the distorted subject as it comes into focus.

A brief spark of orangish-red glints from his augmented scar-speckled eye as he prepares to speak. "Owen. Fucking. Beck," the man says with a pause between each word before shouting it even louder once more. His hairstyle, faded on the sides and crowned with medium-length curly dark brown locks, frames a visage that defies easy categorization. There's something undeniably exotic about his features—prominent cheekbones and a chiseled jawline with a thick beard.

Yet, for all the mystery that his countenance presents, it's impossible to overlook the hint of wild eccentricity, the overt rambunctiousness that seems to cloak him like a second skin. The terms "maniac," "killer," and "monster" aren't just descriptors—they're titles that he wears with unsettling pride.

As more saliva drools from the corners of my mouth, I mumble the name I never thought I'd say face-to-face again. "Ezrek."

"In the flesh," he says with a mischievous smirk as he steps back and takes a gracious bow, flipping back his tapered black grey-lined side cloak, revealing his advanced combat suit. It bears striking similarities to my own, yet the differences are immediately evident.

Avery's name barely escapes my mouth.

Ezrek grins as he turns to the long shiny metal table across the room and reaches for something stubby and cylindrical. There's a soft, delicate click, and the diminishing faint hiss of the flat white AVA-Pod opening subsides as he pours something that's a bright fluorescent green into a cup in front of him. He hesitates as the alcoholic liquid sizzles and pops next to his lips. He takes a giant gulp of the thick metallic liquid from the pod and wipes his mouth, and his face contorts into disgust as he chokes it down. "Woof, that's bitter," he says, shaking off the taste. "Just a little pick-me-up before we get started. You must have your vitamins, Mr. Beck."

I think it must be some type of upper, if I were to guess.

"All these years, Beck. All these years, I was a fool. I fucking knew it once I saw you had escaped the rooftop in Akereon City, and half of Galacom was after your bounty. Helmet or not, I knew that was you under there," he says, gritting his teeth and sniffling hard. "I mean, who else could have such a vendetta? The infamous rogue pilot, the one messing up my work consistently, time and time again, was always you. I knew this moment would come." He laughs as he pulls out another cup and pours two shots of whatever he's drinking. "I've been counting on it."

I stay quiet.

"You know what a fucking headache you have been? I thought, *How does this pilot keep gettin' away?*" His deep-bellied laughter echoes through the small room loudly as he grabs one of the cups of thick liquid from the table and walks over to me. "Now, I know," he says as he raises the cup to my lips. "Drink."

I laugh.

"What?" he replies.

"Nothing."

He looks at me, confused. "If you have something to say, say it. You won't be able to much longer."

"You are fucking dead, and don't even know it. Take these restraints off, and let's finally settle this," I say with an unbroken vigor as I jolt forward, testing the restraints' durability.

"Ohhhh, scary. Not going to happen. I have plans for you, my friend," he says as he suddenly presses back my head and forces the liquid down my throat, watching as I nearly choke. I try to cough as much as I can out of my airway. The bitter taste of the drink is left in the unreachable corners of my mouth. He was right; it's fucking foul.

"I am so utterly fascinated as to how a man shot three times in the chest and left on a rooftop just as it explodes could survive. How does that even happen? I thought you were dead for sure."

I stay silent as he continues rambling on as he paces around the room. "Nothing? That's fine. I have plenty of ways to get all the information I need from you," he says as he looks at my gear.

His voice quiets as he picks up Avery's dirt-covered journal, and his wide eyes fix on the object lying next to it. "Simply beautiful," he says inquisitively as his hand gently glides down the Jadestone key.

"And what's this, garbage?" he remarks as he lifts the small piece of Tex's eye into the air, then carelessly tosses it down with a loud clang as it hits my Trinocs. A painful cringe tugs at my stomach.

"I should have just sat around and let you do all the hard work. All these years I've wasted, thinking this journal was gone, hidden away, and this key—do you know how long I've searched for something like this? A missing piece," he says, eyeing the Jadestone key. "How did you find it? Why you, of all people? Why did *you* find it?"

He enters a command into his HUD on his forearm, and not a moment passes before two dressed-to-match infantry soldiers enter the room and stand shoulder-to-shoulder at attention. "Please escort these items to the lab in sector seven immediately, and I will be headed down to the uncharted planet shortly. I just have one tiny rodent problem first," Ezrek says, handing the key and journal over to the commanding officer.

I gaze past him and the two guards to the door, clocking the two security cameras above us and the biometric double-lock console by the exit. The guards take the items and exit the room as the thick grey metal door closes with a double-locked sound.

Even if I could get out of the restraints, I don't think my legs would work properly—I'd be just like a calf after birth. I feel woozy, and my head's still killing me. However, I wouldn't let that stop me from choking every last breath from Ezrek's lungs.

I don't have many cards to play, so I play the only one I have. "You'll never find them," I say confidently. "I destroyed everything. You need me, or I'd be dead already."

"Well, there is some truth to that, I must admit, but I think you're missing a key component to your theory. See, the thing is, I don't need you; I just need what's in that brain of yours. I know you saw something down in the temple—there are a million pieces of crystal to prove that. And I have my ways of finding it."

"Good luck," I say with a chuckle.

He throws a gut punch, knocking every ounce of air out of my body. I gasp as his malice breaks into laughter.

"What the fuck did you do to Avery, you fucking monster?" I say as I try to catch my breath. "Why?!"

He turns straight to me and stares into my eyes as a smile descends upon his face. "'Monster?' *I'm* the monster?" He walks over to the table where my gear is and picks up my ring. He takes a moment, staring at the circular metal.

"What did you do?" I repeat louder.

He places the ring to the side as he steps in front of me and puts his thinly armored hand on my shoulder. "Lately, everything has just been about business—doing the necessary things to reach this faction's goal: to finally be able to have the power to take down Galacom and anything thrown at me. The one who controls time controls everything. But you and I?" He stops and takes a deep breath. "That was personal. That night was all an elaborate show, with the pledge, the turn, and the prestige, if you will, and you, Owen Beck, were the guest of honor," he says, contorting his body into another triumphant bend before punching me again in the same exact spot.

I cough and heave through the pain, throwing up bile and blood.

"That night back on Akereon—you've probably thought about that night every day, haven't you? That's a warming notion. You rip yourself apart day by day, night by night, suffering alone with no one. Man, I would have killed to see you that miserable."

He pauses for a moment, turning to face me, then ostentatiously walks over to the high-gloss metal table where I'm secured. He swiftly spins a short blade from his hip into his left hand. He tricks the blade over and under his fingers, flips it, and stops it at the edge of my stomach.

With a sense of relaxation and calmness, he leans in so close I can feel the heat of his words. "You didn't die. Oh, well. It all worked out in the end, didn't it? And now," he whispers, looking at the tip of the blade, then back to my eyes, "I get to savor your death instead of running off just when it was getting to the good part. I'm going to enjoy this."

He presses the short double-sided blade into my stomach, and I feel every ounce of pain as blood begins dripping to the floor. The narcotics don't numb anything. Whatever he's given me nearly heightens my senses to the pain.

"You—" I grit out, teething the rest of my words.

"What was that?" Ezrek says as he leans in closer.

I feel every single centimeter of the blade sliding into my flesh. I bite down hard as he leans back with a grimace, waiting for a reply. "You've always been so weak-minded."

He sighs as he retrieves the blade's tip from my stomach and steps back to the long rectangular table full of stainless metal tools. "You are incredibly frustrating, you know that? Every part of me just wants you dead, but I can't help but postpone your well-fucking-deserved death. I mean, come on; you could have joined us. We could have been the most powerful faction in the galaxy, but you had to get all bent out of shape over what? A woman? A moral high ground where you thought you were better than the rest of our team and our duty? You left us high and dry, Beck. You left me alone."

"You could have left the Division with me," I reply.

"And done what? Drive a transport truck, like you? To live a pathetic existence. I found something after you left, Beck."

"Oh, yeah? What was that?" I say with a smirk, spitting blood onto the white sterile floor.

"Something that would change the balance of power," he says as he illuminates a holographic image displayed from his comms wrist unit.

I don't really understand what I'm looking at. At first glance, it looks like a star chart. It looks similar to the one I have, except different. "What—"

I stop myself as he shuts off the display. "What is it?" he says, finishing my sentence. "It led me to ruins out on the Celtu Alps. There, a hologram presented itself to me. Told me I was unworthy of the power. The only thing it did was reaffirm my suspicion the power was real, and so were the Khu'Val."

He talked to Enohk? What did she say to him? Was it another temple like Turkken?

"Who was the hologram of?"

"I think you know the answer to that question, don't you, Beck?"

"What did you do to Avery, you piece of shit? She wasn't part of this."

"I wanted out, Beck. The only way I knew how to do that was disappear."

"But why her?!" I yell with every ounce of strength I have.

"I knew Avery's and Williams's research was remarkable, and couldn't just have you two running away after finding those ruins. Takashi hid nearly a billion away on his private servers, as well as blueprints for cutting-edge weaponry and schematics for a perfect soldier; he just didn't know it at the time. His endless supply of credits helped build what you see today. And you getting what you deserved in the process? That was just the icing on the cake. Naomi had the in, and I watched all the pieces fit flawlessly into my perfect puzzle.

"Avery was just one of the first steps; I needed what was inside her head. The more I knew about the Khu'Val, the better, and needed Takashi's tech to find it. I knew she wouldn't give it willingly—you know, because we murdered you and all—so I used his technology to rewire her pathways, siphoning data and erasing any trace of you. I succeeded where Takashi failed. He didn't have the imagination. A complete technological pathway to unravel memories, transferring unconscious thoughts into searchable data on an external hard drive. It was incredible! As you can probably guess, Takashi wanted to know everything and anything he could from his competitors before disposing of them—an actual waste of technology."

My mind goes to Aden, then to Kruger and Naomi, wondering where they are.

"See, I wanted to take it a step forward. I thought, *Why stop there? Why do I need to recruit these mercenaries and untrustworthy factions? I can just take what I need and create my own army, free of thought and doubt, my loyal servants to the throne of Valleion.* I'm talking full-blown amnesia; wipe the mind clean. Takashi was on to something groundbreaking for the military. Imagine the perfect soldier—no fears, no memories, no hesitation. Just a flawless machine capable of anything, but still having the instinct of a human— something androids could never have.

"The first few test runs didn't go as planned, so Avery's system is some- times a little wonky. She wasn't very willing, but she fell in line in the end."

"I saw her die," I say as I slowly tighten my fists in the restraints. The energy assertion causes my wounds to leak even faster.

"Another Takashi miracle," he says, holding the blade to my cheek. "It was as simple as finding a frost junkie downtown with nothing to lose."

"What the fuck are you talking about?"

"Frost Inhalers will do almost anything you tell them if you give them a proper dose. With a few puffs and Takashi's *HALOFIELD* tech, presto! I couldn't even tell the difference. It was quite convincing. Avery was safe and secured at the warehouse; all we needed was a rendered model of her face and a gag around the drifter's mouth. If you looked hard enough, you probably would have noticed it. She nearly ruined it when her gag fell off. I figured you'd die before I had to shoot the vagrant, but that's you, isn't it? Just won't fucking give up."

My fists tighten again, but the restraints are refined Endonium. I'm not breaking out of these, even at a hundred percent strength.

Avery is alive, held captive by this maniac. *For five years...* She's been alive this entire time.

"Her memories with you are gone. I am her divinity now, the puppeteer pulling all the strings. She's nothing more than a soldier following orders and doing what I command—a loyal enforcer. I am a revolutionary; I am a conqueror. Once I find the power to be able to control time, I can harness and control the farthest regions of the galaxy—unlimited power, a way to rise above and cast a deathly shadow over anyone who defies me, I'll be the most powerful being in the universe—a vision your pathetic mind can't even grasp. You're just a dead man with no future. I know you saw something in the temple. I will find it while making this as painful as possible."

"I'm going to enjoy every second of watching you die. I don't know how or when, but I'm going to fucking kill you slowly," I say.

"You were my brother, Beck," Ezrek says with a shred of truth in his voice. "You left me alone to live your perfect little life with her. We were supposed to live and die together. When you left the Division, you left us."

"This is your fault, Z—" I say, but he cuts me off.

"*You did this to us!*" he shouts, grabbing me tightly around the throat. "You think just because you turn around one day after everything we've been through, you can leave? Oh, no, no, Becky boy." He squints while wiping the sweat from his face. "I wasn't going to let you just walk away. I labored for months to get the heist right, ensuring every little detail went off without a hitch. Was I just going to let you walk away with my credits? The credits that funded this entire empire? You were our scapegoat, our way out."

"You went down a path I couldn't follow. You lost your way," I choke out as the blood rushes to my brain. "Innocent people. I couldn't be a part of it anymore. I found my out and a reason to move on and never look back. Why can't you see that? You've only grown into a bigger maniac."

He releases my throat, and I inhale heavily, gasping for air. "Collateral damage. We were there to do a job, and I did that. I will use their power to become nothing short of a god."

Ezrek seems to be driven by an insatiable hunger for power. The galaxy, with its countless worlds and civilizations, represents a limitless expanse in which to exert dominance. To him, becoming godlike isn't a metaphor, but a genuine end goal. He really believes that with the power of the Khu'Val, he can achieve this unparalleled supremacy.

I chuckle under my breath.

"What? What's funny?"

"You are not a god. You're just a dramatic psychotic asshole looking to have power over who you deem weak. I've dreamt about this day every night for five years. All the ways I would slowly kill you for what you did to Avery, what you did to me. When I get out of these restraints, I'll make you wish you died back on Vola Prime."

He walks to the other side of the room and grabs a metal chair, sliding it slowly, causing an ear-splitting screeching metal-on-metal noise. He sits just in front of me at eye level and crosses one leg over the other, interlocking his fingers on his knee. "I thought many nights of what it would be like to talk to you again, and I must say, it's not living up to what I thought."

"Yeah? Sorry to disappoint."

"It's just... I think we are missing something. This all started with Avery, didn't it? Why don't we see what she says about this situation?" He sneers as he presses a random set of buttons on his forearm module. "This may take a second."

"Don't you fucking do it!" I yell, trying to break free from the restraints.

My knuckles turn white. My hatred for this man could blot out a sun, but I'm not ready for this. I am not ready.

"This will be fun," he says, glancing towards the door in anticipation.

I close my eyes hard, hoping that it will help somehow.

To be near her again, to see her...

"The anticipation is killing you, isn't it?" Ezrek says as he starts to whistle a low elevator tune, twiddling his thumbs.

Whatever she has become, that's not Avery.

Loud footsteps reverberate from outside the door in the halls. They approach steadily until the security doors open.

There she stands, helmet off, in full Ryzer combat gear, but all I see is her—my Avery, my love.

Ezrek turns with a malicious expression of wonder. "Perfect timing. Please come in and join us, won't you? We have loads to catch up on, wouldn't you say, Owen? Did you bring it?" he asks her, and she reaches out and places something shiny in his hand. I can't make it out as he closes his fingers around it.

She stands just to the side of Ezrek, staring at the wall in a ready stance, not breaking.

"Would you be so kind as to grab the cauterizing tool? I wouldn't want our dear friend here to bleed to death. I want to make sure he lives for as long as possible. I want to be able to enjoy it this time around. I mean, how often do you get to kill someone twice?" Ezrek says, pointing in the general direction of the tool tray of torture.

She diligently grasps the tool and walks over to me. I stare into her droning eyes and try to say something, but the pain is coming on in heavy waves.

She ignites the tool and drags it across my stomach. I bite down hard and make a small grunt. "What was that?" Ezrek says, leaning in, not understanding my mumbling.

Again, Avery's name barely leaves my lips.

Ezrek's hand slowly materializes before my bowed head, fingers gently unfolding to unveil a relic from a former life. As resplendent as the day it first graced her finger, Avery's wedding ring lies cradled in his palm.

"A memento," he says, pacing toward the table where my own ring rests. "I surmise you presumed it was lost to the abyss of time." His fingers deftly maneuver, unhinging the necklace and intertwining it with our symbols of unity. There, before my weary eyes, the rings dangle, oscillating gently like a poignant pendulum.

"Avery and Owen," he breathes, almost reverently, "conjoined once more."

My voice, barely a whisper amidst the thundering silence, utters her name. "Avery." My gaze slides beyond the suspended memories before me to where she stands adjacent to Ezrek. Her eyes, distant yet unyielding, fixate stoically upon the wall.

"Oh, she's gone, pal. Nothing left here but an empty shell of something that you used to love," he says, knocking on her head. "I mean, look at her; there is nothing—I mean *nothing*—in those eyes of hers. See this scar?" he says, grabbing under her chin and both cheeks. He turns her head and points to the shaved side of her head, where a long scar trails behind her ear. "A device sits lodged within her skull, and unlike the other soldiers, this is first-gen prototype shit we're talking here. Since then, I'll admit, we've made some improvements, but I feel this model works fine, wouldn't you agree?"

My body is in so much pain it's hard to lift my head, but I try before Ez cuts off my train of thought. "Look at her!" he says violently, grasping my hair and pointing me toward her.

My eyes reluctantly settle on her face—her undeniably beautiful face. It's a sight I never anticipated beholding again, yet there she stands. How many times have I imagined this moment?

Initially, she avoids my gaze. She doesn't look at me until words, laden with all the sentiment I can muster, navigate through the dense air between us. Despite the fog enveloping my consciousness, my sight remains unbroken, penetrating deep into her eyes as if it's the last action I will undertake.

"Home... is wherever our love takes us..." The words, slow and laborious, manage to form cohesively. As my voice disintegrates into a murmur of unintelligible mumbles, Ezrek releases my face, returning to his chair.

A subtle twitch flickers across her eyes, and for a brief moment, her attention pivots toward me.

"To the unknown," I declare, observing a passing alteration in her facial expression.

Her gaze reinstates its focus on the wall's center, and Ezrek interjects. "See? I told you she doesn't remember you. Ryzer, do you recognize this man?"

"No, sir," she responds, her eyes darting between me and the wall.

"You've never seen his face before today?"

"Not that I can recall, sir."

"Well, there you have it," Ezrek states, rising from his chair and dusting off his hands. He walks over to the table and opens several drawers, looking for something. He tosses the rings down and rifles through gauze and papers that scatter to the floor. "Where is it?"

"Need something, commander?" Avery says attentively.

"I'm missing an Adrenazyne injector. I wouldn't want our friend here to pass out again. Would you mind fetching me some from the med station down the hall?"

"Yes, sir," she says, immediately turning around, but not before giving me one long last look. Our eyes meet, and it feels like no time has passed since the last time I stared at her that night in bed in our loft in Akereon City. What I wouldn't give to go back to that night, to have not left. *I should have stayed. This is all my fault. She wouldn't be here with him if I had just listened to her.*

She looks away and walks to the door; Z pulls the chair just in front of me. He smiles as he begins whistling a dreary tune. The slow crawl of the notes fills the room as he picks up a longer blade than last time. He presses a command on the digital interface of the wall, and a far-too-upbeat music station for the situation begins playing loudly over the system. "I love this song," he says, snapping his fingers to the oscillating beat.

He slowly gyrates from his hips up to his shoulders, fiddling with the long blade in his hand as he dances around like a maniac. With a glitzy shift to the table, knife in hand, he whistles the same seven-note bar repeatedly, then slides the knife quickly across my chest, creating a massive, gaping wound.

I groan as I succumb to the pain. My mind just won't quit.

"Back to business," Ezrek says as the doors finally lock us in.

FRAGMENTS OF
A MEMORY

AS I WALK past the training chamber on the way to the MedBay, the unmistakable sonata of battle reaches my ears—the rhythmic pounding of fists on pads, the sharp exclamations of trainers, and the gritty resolve in each combatant's movements. I feel compelled to step inside. The doors slide open with a thud, revealing the chamber: a massive arena bathed in cold cerulean lights, lined with state-of-the-art equipment, and filled with numerous rings where soldiers are in the throes of their training.

The moment I enter, time seems to freeze. The soldiers, deep into their drills, turn to statues. The faces directed towards me display a demeanor of respect, fear, and curiosity. Conversations halt. Sparring partners separate. The only sound left is the quiet hum of the chamber's machinery. A salute comes from a heavily augmented soldier, his chrome arm gleaming in the chamber's.

"Stand down," I say, after returning the salute, yet my focus rapidly transitions to an adjacent training module within the facility. Here, two soldiers engage in a simulation exercise, maneuvering through a virtual battlefield with precision and quickness that captures my attention. Their interaction with the virtual environment, dodging virtual threats and coordinating attacks, is mesmerizing in its complexity. It's a synchronization I find oddly familiar, stirring something deep within me.

The words of the pilot echo in my mind: "Home is wherever our love takes us." Suddenly, a fleeting memory surfaces: laughter echoing in open spaces, the sensation of guiding hands intertwining with mine, sunlight cascading over us, and the gentle touch of grass beneath us. There's a feeling of unity, of moving in sync with someone.

I snap back to the cold reality of the *Novascar*, feeling the weight of dozens of eyes on me. The programming within me, the essence of Ryzer, pushes through, shoving those fleeting memories back into the depths from which they emerged.

"Double the training hours," I command, my voice echoing throughout the chamber. "We can't afford to be lax."

The soldiers nod, quickly diving back into their routines as I leave the room.

Navigating the sleek construction of the *Novascar*, I find myself on an expansive bridge that melds its two major sections in the opposite direction of the MedBay. Towering cylindrical windows offer all-around views of the multiple hangars below. Ezrek's personal ship, *Eros*, rests with an imposing serenity, its silhouette dominating Hangar-1.

Soon, this stillness is disturbed as scouting drones roar to life, their engines glowing like miniature stars. They rise and surge forward, embarking on their reconnaissance of the uncharted world below. Their trails frame the arresting view of the planet—teal oceans glistening in the starlight and forests painting the world in shades of emerald. The drones soon vanish, absorbed by the atmosphere.

Illuminated by sporadic flashes of yellow from the nearby loading bays, I make my way toward the elevator leading to the upper areas of the ship. Just as I summon it with a tap on the pristine interface, a silky voice snakes its way into my ears. "Ryzer."

Pivoting, I'm met with Naomi Sato, her combat gear hugging her lithe frame, every inch of her radiating preparedness—for war or maybe something more. "Naomi," I say, maintaining my composure.

She trails behind me as I step into the elevator. "Floor?" she inquires, her fingers poised over the control panel.

"Sector Nine," I respond, voice unwavering.

Her long, elegant fingers gracefully brush the command interface while her eyes, deep and probing, briefly meet mine. There's an intimacy to the moment, yet a distance maintained. As the corners of her lips curl into a half-smile, she swiftly returns her gaze forward, not letting me dwell on the moment.

"I was wondering if you've had the chance to speak with our guest?"

A brief silence falls. "Yes," is all I offer, letting the word hang between us.

Her voice, spiked with a hint of something insincere, floats back. "Just curious."

"Ezrek is handling him," I say.

Her face leans in slightly, a flicker of amusement playing across her features. "Noticed anything... peculiar about him?"

"Should I have?" My response is terse, eyebrow arching almost imperceptibly.

Her laughter, light and seemingly carefree, fills the air.

I remain unmoved. "What amuses you?"

My inquiry is direct, allowing no room for the trivialities she seems inclined toward.

The elevator's melodious chime interrupts our conversation, signifying that we've reached our destination. Naomi steps out with an effortless, fluid grace that's almost feline in nature. But before she vanishes into the corridor, she pauses, casting a mischievous, lingering wink in my direction. "Until our next delightful chat."

The atmosphere is thick with unspoken words and unaddressed tensions as the elevator doors close between us, sealing us off into our separate worlds. Naomi has always had a mystique about her that I've never quite understood.

Upon reaching the research lab adjacent to the cryogenic chambers, I'm reminded of Ezrek's command for the Adrenazyne. *What am I doing? Why am I breaking a direct order?*

Advanced machines drone and buzz, helmed by top researchers from across the galaxy—their past lives wiped, reshaped into loyal subordinates.

A dozen or so scientists in white uniforms work diligently across the room as a few armed guards stand at attention. Everyone stops what they are doing and looks directly at me, waiting for me to utter a sound. I nod to put them at ease, and everyone resumes working. A single-armed officer, NG-2040, walks over to greet me. "Commander. What can we do for you?" the digitally voiced guard says.

"I need a few moments alone with the artifacts just brought in."

"'Alone?' Commander?" the low-level guard asks, not necessarily thinking of its implications.

I seize the officer by the throat and begin crushing his windpipe very slowly.

"I'm—sorry—Commander," the guard chokes out, his vocoder crackling under the pressure.

I release him and say, "Everyone, out now."

The guard coughs as all the workers get up at once and exit the room one after another until the once-busy room of whirling machines and chiming computers is now completely vacant. As I walk over to the colossal black machine scanning over the pilot's items, I stare at the revolving blue lights of the wireframed scanner as it slowly models and meshes the journal into a three-dimensional holographic readout over the electronic display.

I grasp the torn dark brown journal from the lights, and the loading bar pauses with an error command. After I wipe the dust from the front, I stare at the oddly familiar book. I open the journal to the first old, yellowed page, where, in handwritten letters, somebody has scribbled the words, *Notes of Avery Williams and Akereon City University.*

As I flip through the incoherent rambles and drawings of the different pages, I stop on one in particular as the lettering catches my eye: *To the unknown.*

That was what Owen said in the interrogation room. Why does it sound so familiar?

The end half of the journal is written in a different style than the rest, as if someone started it and someone else completed it.

I reach for something to write with and place the journal on a table.

Under the words *To the unknown*, I write the exact phrase. Letter by letter, word for word.

I drop the pen and stare at the two sentences next to each other.

They are precisely the same—every curve, every nuance of the pen.

I step back a moment, and my breathing starts to quicken.

I wrote the first half of this book.

The rogue feelings of someone else overcome the reality of Ryzer as I blankly stare at the words. I'm in a battle within my mind, fighting myself.

Every single time an image of the pilot flashes into my thoughts, I feel something different than anger or hate—something I don't know how long it's been since I've felt. It's a warmth that is familiar, calming even.

Who am I? I think for a moment.

I grab the Jadestone key and journal and walk out toward the MedBay. *What am I doing?*

Seven years ago...

A cold, drizzling rain patters against the energy-efficient windows of the downtown eco-café in Akereon City. The red digital numbers on a sleek, frameless clock embedded into the window's corner blink steadily, signaling that my break from work is almost over. *Has it really been that long?* I grimace as the faint aroma from my third cup of brew breaks my concentration. "Not againnnn," I say, quickly shutting down the multiple apps open on my tablet.

Holding the slim device in front of me, I rush to the counter to make my payment. However, the tablet's large screen blocks my view, and I don't notice the sleek metallic leg of one of the café's chairs. I stumble, my tablet slipping from my grasp, its screen flashing an error message as it smashes down and skids across the floor.

My belongings scatter across the ground, and I reach over to pick up my thick, oversized glasses. I contemplate whether to accept this new fate to just lay here for eternity—never moving, never leaving, just another forgotten soul of Akereon, left to fade away.

Or I can get up to confront this incredibly dumb, somewhat-embarrassing situation. Something makes me smile as I think of a person lying in the middle of a café for the rest of their life, passersby walking over me, completely disregarding I'm even there, the seasons changing outside the window as I wither away and become one with the café.

Of course, no one has come to my aid. It's okay; I don't need help or anything.

My dumb thoughts are surprisingly interrupted as I hear a friendly voice from behind me. "Are you okay, miss?" the man's apologetic voice says.

I turn to face the kind stranger, and that's when I see him for the first time. That's when I meet those bright pale blue eyes. His arm extends as he reaches to help me up. "Are you okay? That was quite the little tumble," he says as I grab his hand and he softly picks me up.

"Thank you," I quietly reply. I can barely think of what to say. "Well, that was foolish."

"Quite a moment," he remarks, his voice warm as I accept his assistance.

"Seems I'm a bit clumsy today," I reply, flashing an embarrassed smile.

He laughs, helping me pick up my tablet. "Need a hand to the checkout?"

"I think I've made enough of a scene for one day, but thanks," I say, checking my screen for any cracks.

As I move towards the counter, his voice, softer now, reaches me. "You dropped this." Turning, I find him holding an ID card attached to a lanyard.

"Oh, thanks," I begin.

He interrupts with a playful grin. "Avery, right?"

My eyebrows lift in surprise. *How did he...* But then it clicks. "Right. It's on the lanyard." I chuckle. "Thank you."

He gives a slight nod, curiosity brightening his eyes. "I'm Owen, by the way. You seemed in a hurry. Heading back to work?"

"Yeah, at the university," I reply, motioning to the lanyard. "Didn't mean to give you the impression I'm always this clumsy."

"Ah, the university. Researching, perhaps?"

"Yes, I co-lead a research department with my father," I reply, a touch of pride in my voice.

Owen's intrigue is real. "Which department?"

"Archaeology. We focus on ancient civilizations," I answer, watching his reaction.

His interest doesn't wane. "That's fascinating. Longtime passion?"

As I begin to answer, I'm interrupted by the impatient clearing of a throat. The clerk awaits, her expression less-than-impressed. Handing over my final receipt, I note the total: fifty-two credits. With a confident flick, I present my wristband to the reader, but to my dismay, it flashes red, signaling a payment issue.

The clerk's sigh is almost theatrical. "Please try again," she says, her patience clearly wearing thin.

Yet each swipe yields the same result: Red. Red. Red.

As my frustration grows, Owen steps in. "Here—allow me."

He leans over the counter, stretching to reach the scanner with his wristband. The effort causes him to stand on his tiptoes, making for a rather-endearing sight. A soft chime sounds, and the light glows green—payment accepted. "And the brew," he says, pointing to his.

"You really didn't have to," I say.

Owen simply smiles. "Happy to help, Avery."

"No, let me repay you. That's way too much. I don't want to feel like I owe you."

"It was my pleasure. Maybe I could help you carry those instead; they look heavy," he says, pointing to my bag of research.

"As much as I would love for the attractive random guy to follow me to work and help me with my data, I think I can take it from here," I say sarcastically. "But again, thank you for the help. That was very nice of you. I think I have to update this stupid thing," I say, fiddling with my bracelet.

"'Attractive,' huh?"

"Of course that's all you heard."

"Well, if you ever wanted to take a break from all that research—I mean, I'm sure you develop an appetite after all that—I'll be staying downtown for a bit until I get the call to go back to work. Maybe you could take a break and eat food with said attractive stranger."

"'Call?'" I ask, carefully avoiding his question.

"I lead a unit within Galacom."

"Military spaceman, huh?"

"Something like that," he says, tightening his shoulder bag.

"I don't know, Mr. Beck. Maybe. My work keeps me very swamped and boring. Did I mention I'm super boring?" Although that isn't necessarily true, I don't want to play easy to get; regardless of how handsome he is, I tread carefully.

"I'll take a maybe," he says, reaching into the inner pocket of his leather jacket and pulling something small and white from the lining.

He hands me his card, and I look at the raised black lettering on the white eggshell stock. The font is minimal and evenly spaced, and the card reads very military—no numbers on the front, no contact information, just who he is and his rank.

"'Captain Owen Beck, Special Unit Star Fighter Pilot of Galacom,'" I say in a teasing official tone as I shove it into my back pocket. "Jeez, that's a mouthful. I bet you never get tired of saying that, do you?"

"No, ma'am, not a single day. My numbers are on the back. It was nice to meet you, Avery. I hope to hear from you soon, and if I don't, that's okay too," he says, grabbing his brew, shaking my hand, and giving me one last smile before walking to the door and exiting the store into the rain-soaked streets.

I watch as he stands with no rain emitter shield, no hood nor hat, nothing to block the rain from soaking him head to toe. Everyone around him scurries by as he takes in the shower for a moment, looking upward into the sky. I place my bags over my shoulder, and after the second it takes to do that, I look up, and he's gone.

Smooth, Ave... real smooth, I think as I leave the café into the lively streets of Akereon.

In the large, sterile chamber of the MedBay, I pause for a moment, confronting my own reflection in the lavatory mirror. The environment around me fades, every sensation dominated by the haunting memories threatening to drown my sanity. I see the café, and Owen's whispering voice keeps playing in my mind, an unwavering echo: "Home is wherever our love takes us."

They're relentless, these memories, and the phrase's repetition is like a siren song drawing me deeper into the abyss of the past. Sudden bursts of excruciating pain, paired with blinding light, assault my senses. How do these fragments of a shared past still resonate within me?

I remember that. Why do I remember that saying?

What is happening to me?

I stare at the Jadestone key and journal sitting on the counter. *Why did I take those from the research bay? What am I doing?* I think as I place them into my pack.

My head feels like it's going to explode—there's a migraine of flashing images of Owen, then a rainy city, then myself screaming as I'm taken somewhere dark and cold, painfully fogging my mind. Reveries of a life I never knew rush through my head all at once. It feels like thunder in a storm. I can hardly see straight.

Suddenly, a maelstrom of images engulfs me: Owen's familiar yet distant face, the melancholic vision of a city kissed by rain. These memories, or possibly echoes of lives I'm blind to, cascade with unrelenting force.

Drawing a shaky, labored breath through my chapped lips, I try to find an anchor in the familiar. I desperately gaze into my reflection, attempting to tether myself to reality. But the flood of emotions is too potent. Sweat forms rivulets down my temple. With trembling hands, I turn the faucet on, seeking solace in the rhythmic cascade of water. The pristine MedBay bathroom fills with a thick blanket of steam as scalding water gushes into the metal sink. Hastily, almost frantically, I wipe away the mirror's fog, only to be met with eyes that seem as alien and uncharted as a distant galaxy.

Doubt creeps in, tightening its grip on my psyche. Were Owen's words a mere illusion? For so long, I've existed in a void, devoid of any genuine emotion, driven solely by a relentless rage and a blind loyalty. But now, a whirlwind of emotions churns, shaking the very foundations of my identity. Whispering in a fusion of rage and despair, I ask, "What the hell have you done to me?"

My fingers, as if guided by an external force, gravitate towards my conspicuous scar, eventually finding the sinister device embedded near my temple. In a spontaneous act of defiance, I hit it with the palm of my hand, temporarily interrupting the torrent of memories. Yet the aching, almost insidious pain remains a steadfast companion.

Staring intensely, challenging my own reflection, I shout with newfound conviction, "Get your shit together!"

My clenched fist collides with the mirror, shattering it into a medley of sharp pieces. I stare at the broken mirror, and many reflections stare back at me—all different pieces showing different sides.

I feel broken.

The very fabric of my reality feels like it's unraveling. A thick haze obscures the line between memories and the present, rendering every thought intangible. The harrowing memories of being shackled, of the cold, unfeeling NeuroGate device enveloping my head and of being reduced to nothing more than a pawn in Ezrek's macabre game, rush back with vivid clarity. I remember the agony, the noise of the machine, the rhythmic electromagnetic pulses, and the intense green strobe as my mind was rebooted.

Two lives, two divergent identities, both culminating in agonizing pain, now consume my every thought. With every fragment showing a different me, the weight of realization hits me harder: a confrontation with Ezrek is inevitable, and the odds are not in my favor.

I seize the Adrenazyne injector lying in a drawer just outside the bathroom. It's time to face Ezrek, but this time, as someone else.

I think I have a plan.

SYSTEM REBOOT

THE ANGULAR DOOR to the interrogation room opens with a loud sliding noise, and I walk inside onto the blood-soaked floor behind Ezrek and Owen.

Ezrek steps back from Owen's motionless body and drops his tight fists, which are covered in red, to his sides; his knuckles are worn nearly to the bone. Owen's face is bloodied and bashed; his left eye is swollen shut with a plump, throbbing purple-and-blue bruise. Hollow grunts emerge from his closed mouth as he tries to mask the agony. His mind wanders as the pain takes hold.

Ezrek slowly retrieves his sidearm from his holster and stands tall over Owen. A deep, sinister laugh belts from his chest. The cold steel hangs towards the floor as he grabs Owen's neck, lifting his head. The room fills with the sounds of Owen's groans and resistance as his complexion shifts from pale white to a bright, sun-kissed red.

A cruel smile beams from Ezrek's face as he watches Owen squirm for freedom in the dim, cold extraction room. "We used to be something, you and I," he says softly and mockingly. "Now, look at us. I am meant for more, not you. Why in the hell did they choose you? Where did you find the key and coordinates to the planet? What the fuck did you see down there?" he says, tightening his grip around Owen's neck.

He lifts the gun and sinks the muzzle of the extended barrel into Owen's mouth. I can hear the slide scrape against Owen's front teeth as Ezrek says,

"I'm going to ask you one more time. What did you see?"

Owen grits his teeth over the barrel and closes his eyes, as he knows Ezrek is enjoying every second of this. He doesn't want him to have the satisfaction. He is a prisoner to Ezrek's twisted will, but he accepts this moment. His eyes open and stare into mine, never wavering, never breaking. His mouth chokes something, but it's inaudible with the pistol in his mouth and the hand around his throat.

"Sorry, Captain, couldn't quite understand you there," Ezrek says, slowly cocking the hammer back till it locks in place with a subtle *click*. "Guess he doesn't know anything," he says, shrugging nonchalantly.

I watch Owen's face with worried eyes, as he hasn't broken eye contact with me. "Sir, don't we need him?" I say urgently, trying to mask my concern.

Ezrek looks back and smiles as he suddenly slams the trigger down. I watch in shock as the hammer springs forward and strikes the pin.

There is no bang.

I let out a short, quiet exhale.

Ezrek grins as Owen and I both realize the gun is empty. "This isn't your day to die, Beck. That part comes later," he says as he relieves the gun's tip from his mouth. "You were always a glutton for punishment. I didn't think this would make you talk. Still, I hoped you wouldn't crack so I could enjoy this for as long as possible, and I must tell you something: I really fucking enjoyed it."

He looks at me and continues. "I'll return from the planet after the neural extraction is complete. We have a few hours to kill. I want to get boots on the surface immediately. I want to see the temple for myself."

He steps away from Owen and walks to the NeuroGate control computer. After he enters a command on the keyboard, several mechanisms of Owen's table shift in unison, contorting the once-upright table into a seated position. Metallic restraints eject from the table and securely lock Owen's head into place. A ring device lowers over his head and primes with a loud powering-on noise, followed by whirling and rhythmic cycling, swooshing round and round, faster and faster, till it settles on a steady cycle. The machine idles, waiting to commence extraction.

As I narrow my eyes at the machine, breaks in the lining of the black casing of the device cause a cycling bright green flicker to shine all over the room every other second. A brief flash of light suddenly sets off a memory—a memory of myself sitting in that chair, not Owen, from my point of view. My hands and head were bound just the same as his. The pain was excruciating. All I remember is the pain and flashing light.

I shake my head as I feel another searing headache forming at my temples. *What the hell is happening to me?*

My thoughts break as Ezrek's words break me from this daze. "Lieutenant!" he yells as he reaches for the injector. "I called you four times. What's wrong with you? Don't make me repeat myself." He sneers, swiping the injector from my hand.

"Sorry, sir. It won't happen again," I reply. *I didn't even hear him calling me.*

He stands from the machine, walks to the sink, and washes Owen's blood from his hands. The water begins steaming as he lets scalding water pour over the wounds on his knuckles. It looks excruciating, yet it's not even making him wince. "Is the troop shuttle ready for departure?" he says, shutting off the water.

"Yes, sir, the ship is ready. Would you like T-7 to accompany you?"

"No, you already disobeyed a direct order not to bring that thing to the temple. It's a fuckin' wildcard. The last thing I need is that thing causing more damage to the site."

"I'm sorry, sir. I deemed it advisable for T-7 to accompany me to the planet, especially considering the pilot's prioritization. I just thought—"

My explanation is abruptly severed by his response. "I don't need your thoughts!" His voice erupts, then subsides, his anger reined in as he continues with calm menace. "We have thousands of soldiers at our disposal. I could dispatch a squadron of thirty to the planet to conduct scans and..." His words trail into a dismissive monotone.

"Understood, Commander," I reply, my eyes fixed on Owen as I steer toward the machine's controls.

"Well, Becky Boy, this is where our paths part for the moment. It won't be long now, Captain Beck, and this time, your demise will be conclusive,"

Ezrek says, methodically wrapping his knuckles with a bandage.

A hesitant query escapes my lips. "What's my directive, Captain? Should I join you on the planet's surface?"

"No, remain here. I want you to supervise him during the extraction. Keep me updated with every development. I want to pierce into every crevice of what he witnessed down there. Ensure his neural pathways are thoroughly mapped for the orrery network. He saw something; I'm certain of it."

"Right away, sir," I respond, inputting his flight launch sequence into my forearm HUD. A vivid red holographic wireframe depicting the troop carrier rotates above my arm as I engage a three-button command. It signals the flight crew to prepare the ship for departure from the hangar bay.

I close the readout and stare at Owen's pale face. Sweat beads from his eyebrows and pours down his naked body, mixing with the fresh and dried blood over his abdomen and genitals. He's on the verge of passing out, from the looks of it.

"I want you awake and coherent for this part. I need your mind working overtime," Ezrek says, injecting him in the neck with Adrenazyne. Owen's body tightens as he jolts violently into the restraints, feeling overwhelmed by everything as his senses heighten exponentially. He lets out a roar of a scream and begins panting heavily, jerking his head back and forth. He is feeling the pain ever more. "I'm going to kill you," he says.

"We'll see about that, old friend. Take him to the brig after the extraction is complete."

Ezrek grabs his knife and flips it into the sheath on his right thigh. He walks over to Owen one last time, gently kisses him on the forehead, and whispers, "See you soon, brother."

He walks through the doorway and turns back to Owen. He begins whistling a slow, dreary seven note run as he presses the command console. The door slowly closes, and he disappears from view. The dramatic tune trails through corridors, echoing off the walls, subtly diminishing with each note until it recedes entirely into the ship's low droning noise.

"Av—Avery," Owen says faintly.

The green lights of the NeuroGate whirl around the room as he speaks again. "Avery," he says a bit more coherently, "don't do this. This isn't you."

I stare at Owen as the machine spins around his head. The halo device rimming his skull glows a green hue. His body goes stiff as the system engages. Lightning pain must be shooting through his brain as the NeuroGate creates a readout of his memories into a focalized video shown on display in front of me. A neuropathic labyrinth of encoded memories begins to illuminate on screen. It takes hours to decrypt a clear picture of what it's extracting.

I let a few minutes pass, then shift my focus to the forearm HUD, where a live feed shows Ezrek and his squad finally boarding the transport. The vessel glides out of the bay, setting a course for the planet painted in shades of green and blue.

"Ave—" Owen says as blood drips from his mouth.

I stare at him, then back at the monitor.

In that moment, a torrent of thoughts swirls in my mind. The lines between right and wrong have blurred into an indistinct haze.

With clarity finally seizing my thoughts, I know what I must do. My fingers race over the holographic keys, each press a step closer to an irreversible act.

I dive into the core energy-flow controls, sidestepping layers of security with codes etched in my memory. The NeuroGate's sophisticated defenses give way under my persistent assault. As soon as I reverse the polarity of the energy flow, the atmosphere in the room shifts. The steady hum of the NeuroGate turns into a shrill whine, signaling the onset of chaos. Energy, now flowing in reverse, creates a destructive feedback loop.

The console's lights blink wildly, mirroring the internal turmoil of the NeuroGate. Sparks shoot from its panels as the reversed energy ravages the system. It's not just a shutdown; it's an annihilation of the machine's very essence.

The NeuroGate's AI scrambles to rectify the situation, but it's too late. The reversed flow is inflexible, systematically eroding the machine's critical pathways. Each component fizzles out, overwhelmed by the rampant energy.

Finally, the NeuroGate gives a last surge, a desperate attempt to save itself, before its lights fade out. Once a symbol of control and power, it now lies inert, its tyranny ended by its own inverted strength.

This isn't just any piece of technology; its intricate workings are beyond the comprehension of most. It took years of building and requires specialized knowledge and expertise to even begin to understand its inner workings. There are only maybe two people in the entire galaxy now who understand this level of coding.

With a sense of urgency, I rush to Owen's restraints, unfastening them as hurriedly as possible, lifting the halo device from his temples. I pull him from the chair, and he falls to the floor with a loud thud.

Owen's gaze narrows, suspicion evident in his eyes. "Why?" he says, his voice weak but edged with mistrust.

I pause, "I get it. Trust isn't easy, given our history. I don't know who I am, and you are going to help me find out."

His eyes search mine, probing the depths for the truth, for any sign of the Ryzer he once knew. Hesitantly, his fingers caress the side of my face. A reflex makes me flinch, but the gentle warmth and familiarity draw me in, grounding me in a past that feels both distant and hauntingly close.

As the waves of emotions crash over me with my eyes shut, I say, "I wish we had more time, Owen. Every moment we linger endangers us both. Trust me—for now."

He exhales a heavy breath. "I can't believe it's you."

"We need to move."

He manages to get to his feet, and I grab his gear from the table, placing his armor in a large bag. He stumbles momentarily as he puts on his under-suit, so I help brace him up. "Oh, you're heavy. You got this, soldier. One leg at a time," I say, barely able to take all his weight.

The last things he grabs are the rings. He places them around his neck and glances at me. "Maybe you'll remember."

I grab the stim pack off the tray and plunge the needle into his left thigh, giving him another quick dose of Adrenazyne and TetraGel Stim. He grits his teeth, giving me a side eye as the stim rushes through his bloodstream, his fists clench, and he takes a deep breath. He regains some poise, standing postured as his muscles tighten. "Fuck, that hurts.. What now? With a ship this massive, the hangars must have numerous vessels. Why don't we just grab one from the dozens of hangars and make our escape?"

"Ezrek has already taken precautions," I explain. "After your capture, he implemented a protocol that prevents all manned ships in the hangar bay from launching the second you came aboard. He wants you to stay put. However, with the right access codes, we can override this lockdown for one ship, his ship–*Eros*, and make our escape. At the same time, we can ensure that the rest remain grounded, giving us a head start."

His eyebrows shoot up, intrigued. "And you have these codes?"

I smirk, pulling up a small list of numbers on my forearm display. "It won't be easy; the hangar bay is one of the most-guarded sections of the ship."

His gaze turns more serious. "What about the journal and key?"

I unbuckle the fastenings on my pack and carefully peel back the flap, revealing its contents. As the dim light catches the edges of the journal and the shimmer of the key, his eyes widen in shock. They dart from the items to my face, looking for confirmation that these are indeed real.

"It's all here," I say, holding up the journal for a brief moment before tucking it safely back inside.

"Okay, what's first?" Owen asks, ready to go.

"I need your weapons."

"Why?" he says, wincing as he blinks. He can barely see out of his swollen right eye. Dried, caked blood is coagulated over the gashes.

"We need to make you look like my prisoner; that's the only way this works." He pauses. "You'll get them back," I assure him. "But first, we need to blend in. Stick close, follow my lead, and if anything goes south..."

"We improvise," Owen says.

"Exactly."

He finally hands over his pistol and rifle with a long sigh.

"We need to go to the security sector to shut down the *Novascar*'s outer defense protocols first or they will blow us out of the sky the second we depart. I've already looped the camera feeds, but this particular protocol requires manual override. That's our window. With all other ships immobilized, we can then get to the *Eros* and make our escape. I can get us fifteen minutes. That's how long their systems will be shut down."

"Sounds like we have a one-way ticket to destination fucked."

"It'll work. Here, put these on. Code is *x1253*," I say, handing him the magnetic cuffs from the table.

"Got it." He engages the cuffs around his wrists, and they magnetically lock.

I reach out to unlock the large double doors in front of us. The door opens, revealing an empty hallway.

I feel my heart pounding in my chest for what feels like the first time. It's a strange sensation. I've never been scared in all the years under Ezrek's control. *Am I making a huge mistake?*

As we round the corner, I see that eight fully armed soldiers are heading directly toward us. "Shit." I stop and pin Owen to the wall hard and firm. I pause to think for a second. He clenches his teeth as his wounds leak blood against the metallic grated wall. They are slowing him down; the TetraGel hasn't set his injuries yet.

"Should we go back?" he whispers.

"Push forward. The plan will work. Just follow my lead," I say.

"Copy," Owen replies, ultimately putting his trust in me. The determination in his voice is unquestionable.

We round the corner, and Owen limps down the hall before me with his hands behind his back. "Move aside," I shout, commanding the soldiers to move.

They seem to eye us suspiciously as we walk towards them, but ultimately split down the center and allow us passage. "Commander," one of the guards says as they all salute.

I nod as my heart beats even faster. I can feel the thumping in my ears.

The soldiers stare at Owen as he limps in front of them, passing them by. "Prisoner transport? Did you need some assistance?" the middle one says.

"That won't be necessary. Get back to work," I say, and they immediately head the opposite way.

We reach the doors to the elevator. I press the call button, and it seems like an eternity as I watch the displays of red numbers descend floor by floor. The elevator swiftly opens. "Move it," I say, shoving Owen inside.

I press the up button on the digital console for the security floor, and as the doors shut with a low chime, I see the guards continuing their patrol down the long corridors.

Owen lets out a long breath and leans against the wall with a look I can't quite decipher. "What?" I ask.

He takes a moment. "I just never thought I'd see you again. I'm still having a hard time believing this is happening, and I'm not just having a blood loss-induced hallucination."

"I'm sorry if I'm not who you think I am."

"You're just—different."

"I don't think I'm the person you remember, Owen. Let's keep our heads straight. We can talk more once we are off the ship. I'm sure you have a lot of questions right now." *So do I.*

The lift shifts and slows as we reach our destination. We exit and head left towards the large black-glass entryway to the security office. "Wait in here," I say, accessing a small storage corridor across the hall. "If I go in alone and someone finds you waiting outside, we're screwed. Take this," I say, handing him a comms unit. "If anything happens, report it."

"What are you going to do?" he asks, taking the unit and walking into the room.

"What I have to do," I say, shutting the door.

Reaching the security office, I scan my forearm at the console, and the large black-glass doors open wide and close behind me without a sound.

The hexagonal room, which is filled with several armed soldiers and two control officers in black-and-white uniforms who sit in the middle controls of the mainframe, is soundless as I make my way inside. With attentive feet, the standing armed soldiers straighten their bodies towards me and salute. "Commander," one of the guards says with a digital tone. The low waveform of his voice resonates similarly to those of all the Novas Guard divisions; you can't tell them apart.

"At ease," I say, and they loosen their posture and return to work.

I walk towards the center of the room behind the two officers working at the mainframe computers. The large screens display various information regarding the *Novascar*—departures, arrivals, flight times, camera feeds, and alarm systems.

"How can we help you, commander?" one of the officers asks without breaking concentration from the screen.

I slowly unlatch my sidearm from my hip, waiting for the perfect moment. I flip the toggle on the side of the frame, the pistol switches to suppressor mode, and I prime my plasma cannon.

An observant guard to the right locks onto the deadly gleam of the weapon, his fingers clenching around the barrel of his heavy repeater. "Commander?" His voice trembles just a hint before his resolve tightens. "Alarm!"

Immediately, I dispatch a flurry of high-intensity plasma bolts. The air crackles as blue-and-white streaks zip through, striking the guards with ruthless accuracy. An officer makes a last-ditch effort to sound the alarm, but a quick, silenced shot from me obliterates his hand, the impact sending him to the ground with a cry. The room is quickly permeated with the sharp smell of scorched flesh as he writhes in agony.

"I wouldn't try it if I were you," I say to the other guard as he reaches for the same red toggle. I kick him from the chair, and he falls to the glossy-paneled floor.

In a firm, resolved, synthesized voice, he utters only one word. "Traitor."

The decision is swift—two shots to his torso, then a final one to the head of the man missing a hand. Pressing my throat comms, I report succinctly, "All clear."

Owen's entrance is marked by the sound of his boots against the metal floor. He surveys the scene quietly, the silence speaking volumes.

Ignoring his gaze, I move the body blocking the mainframe aside, quickly brushing off the screen. The guard hits the floor with a soft thud. My fingers move rapidly as I enter the authorization code and start locking down sectors, ensuring our path to the hangar bay remains open.

"I've shut down their communications, navigation, and main grid. The power will be back on in fifteen."

"I've rerouted temporary power and input the codes to the *Eros* and Hangar-1. No one would dare touch Ezrek's personal ship. That's our ticket out of here."

"Will Ezrek know?"

"If he's not on the surface already, he'll be on his way back as soon as this timer starts. He'll get a notification the *Novascar*'s offline. He won't hesitate—not with you on board. He will know something's wrong."

"Well, let's be quick, then."

"That's the plan."

As I scour for the directives of the outer hull defenses, I finally find the subfolder of the power maintenance override and reset them all. A timer appears onscreen in bright yellow letters.

[>: SYSTEM REBOOT: 15:00...14:59...14:58...]

The lights shut off, and the backup power grid kicks on the red reserve lights.

"Let's move," I say, leaving the display.

As we leave, I turn and smash the security console by the doors. Sparks and smoke rise from the device, locking all the bodies inside away from sight and stopping anyone from getting into the room.

We head down the long corridor toward the emergency bay. From there, it's just a few minutes across a catwalk bridge to the other side of the ship. We will be exposed and vulnerable, but it's the fastest way.

The door opens, and we step into a large, chambered room filled with dozens, if not hundreds, of catwalks and bridgeways leading to different parts of the ship. I grasp Owen's unlocked restraints behind his back, and the door closes. With a quick pace, we head into the maze of walkways scattered all around us.

"I never thought this day would come," Owen says.

"What do you mean?"

Turning slightly to the left, he says, "The day I would see you again."

"I don't think I'm the person you remember."

"Then why are you helping me? You could have kept the NeuroGate on and pried the memories from my brain, but no. You chose to break your trust in Ezrek and take a chance. You remember me. I know it."

"Just keep moving," I say, turning away. I can feel him staring. "I don't know who I am, and you are a piece of that puzzle. I've had dreams, or what I thought were dreams; I shouldn't have any. It feels like a memory more than a dream. The majority of the NG-Division have had all their memories erased. They have no emotion, no feeling. I shouldn't be dreaming anything. We are entirely wiped clean for Ezrek's goal: to find the Khu'Val. Everyone but Naomi. He kept her lucid. I think he needed someone to talk to besides himself, but I was the test subject; I was the failed patient zero. So many times—so many times—Ezrek put me into that machine. I'm starting to remember them all slowly. Countless days of shock treatments and surgeries on my skull to install this small neuro-device," I say, pointing to it.

"I'm sorry. I'm sorry I failed you, Ave," he says as he grabs my hands and stops us in the middle of the high-level catwalk. "We had a life before this. Before the Novas Guard, before Ezrek. I'm so sorry. I've spent the past five years looking for a way to bring you back. I've used all your research, your journal—everything." His tone is filled with truth as he stares into my eyes.

"I-I don't—"

I stop as he grabs my hands tighter. "Your journal holds the truth—the truth of who you are. It was the diary of your life, of us and your work. It has everything you wish to know."

I break hand contact, staring at my pack with the journal and the key. "We can't do this right now. We need to leave."

"I saw her, Ave," Owen says, his voice weak. "On Turkken, there was this... this hologram, a woman. She was unlike anything I've ever seen, so real yet clearly digital. The Khu'Val—they're not just myths. They're real. You were right about them all this time."

I lean closer, "What are you talking about? What did you see, Owen?"

"It was incredible—"

He stops as his gaze breaks past me to the doors across the catwalk.

"What?" I say. I turn, and my eyes meet the person standing at the end of the bridge.

Dressed in combat gear and full armor, Naomi draws her sword and says softly, "Where do you think you're going, Lieutenant?"

I look to my forearm display. [: SYSTEM REBOOT: 12:23...12:22...12:21...]

"What is the meaning of this?" I say as several of Naomi's personal squadron enter the corridor through the catwalks above us, behind us, and to our sides. Green dots cover our torsos and skulls as the soldiers surround us, guns ready. She must have been waiting for us.

"Drop the weapons and get on your knees," Naomi commands.

My grip tightens around my pistol.

"Owen and Avery Beck. What a happy reunion. I knew it was only a matter of time before we caught Owen. I knew that, whatever Ezrek did to you, once you saw his face, you wouldn't be the same," Naomi says, igniting her blade. "I can't let you leave. Ezrek is undoubtedly on his way back. I just have to keep you busy," she says, whipping her sword through the air in a figure-eight pattern and halting in a firm pointing stance. "I've been waiting a long time for this."

Owen turns back to face the guards above and around us. "Ready when you are," he whispers.

I ease up on my pistol and start unlocking Owen's restraints. Swiftly, I remove his weapons from my shoulder, tossing them to him with a nonchalant flick of my wrist. Next, I pull the blade hilt from my belt. Activating it, a triangular isometric energy pattern begins to form, intricately weaving and solidifying into a blade that crackles to life in front of me. As this happens, my helmet emerges from its nano housing, cloaking my face. The helmet's visor, an elongated V shape, casts a dim red glow from the blade across my visage. Owen, catching his weapons, instantly disengages the safety and presses the trigger without hesitation.

The soldiers unleash a barrage of bullets at me as I rush Naomi, but not at Owen. He returns fire, taking down several guards with precise shots to the chest. The other guards continue to advance, but Owen is ready for them. He fires repeatedly, taking them down one by one, sending some falling over the railing into the energy exhaust ports, igniting ripples of energy below the catwalks.

Naomi laughs as she watches me barrel toward her. As I leap to strike, she presses a command on her forearm module, triggering the backup lights to shut off in our section just as I strike. I swipe into the darkness, but my blade only meets the floor, crashing against the metal.

Naomi suddenly leaps from my side and slices her blade through the air toward my neck. The harsh energy of the two blades colliding crashes through the chamber as I counter her attack. They crackle and burst as the blades rub together.

Owen, a dim silhouette behind Naomi, fires toward the remaining soldiers, illuminating him for only a moment.

"You're pathetic. What makes you think you can win?" Naomi says, pushing her sword down in front of me, nearly cutting my face. I break free, her blade slashes a nearby electrical panel, and wild sparks ignite from the bridge around our bodies. The rainfall of sparks falls around our feet, and dense electrical smoke billows around us as we take our stances.

[>: SYSTEM REBOOT: 10:45...10:44...10:43...]

"We don't need you anymore, do we? Ezrek only needs Owen," Naomi says.

"You and Ezrek used me."

"Aww, poor Avery. Ezrek gave you everything; what did he give me? To run the *Novascar*? To oversee his operations? I'm not a babysitter. I never wanted you as a mission. I should have been searching the stars, leading the Novas Guard for Ezrek, not you. This is where it ends."

Our different shades of red holoblades illuminate the shadowed chamber in a bright flash. Naomi leaps, banks off the railing, and flips over me, then runs toward Owen, whose back is turned and whose attention is on the other soldiers. I take off behind her, and when she is only footsteps from him, I tackle her to the metal floor and flip her away from him. She smashes to the ground and quickly gets to her feet.

We circle each other on the wide catwalk. Naomi's movements are swift and sure; she is a worthy opponent, but I am determined to come out on top. My heart pounds as she swings wildly and emotionally, our blades colliding left and right, igniting as I counter and parry every strike. She screams, using all her strength with each blow. Her anger is her weakness. She's not thinking straight.

Owen fires above, striking Novas Guards as more emerge from cover. Bodies fall in the out-of-focus background as Naomi and I struggle to overpower one another. They aren't firing back—just huddling in cover, trying to advance.

"This is the end of the line," Naomi says, releasing the blades and kicking me across the face. Even through the helmet, the bitter taste of blood trickles from my lips, through my teeth, and onto my tongue. I move into a more defensive stance as I spit the mouthful of blood. I double-hand wield the blade, and the crisp, energized edge flickers, glinting in my eyes.

Naomi strikes forward repeatedly, and I begin to find a flaw in her attacks—an opening when she crosses from the left. Each clash of the blades echoes off the metal walls. I let her get in close as I block the heavy blows, each a wild attempt to finish the job. I shove her back, and she catches her footing. "Enough!" she says with angry eyes, leaping forward for the kill.

I wait until the last possible second, ducking left as she strikes right. Then I spin my body underneath her attack and leap upward, sinking the hot tip of the blade into Naomi's stomach and out the other side.

She gasps, freezing in place as her blade drops from her limp hands. I intercept the falling blade, grasping it firmly before driving it deep into her torso. Her eyes glow green as they gape into mine. She gasps for air again, but can't find it, as the blades have singed through her. Blood begins spurting from her mouth as she tries to speak, but no words come.

I retract the blades and watch them disengage through her torso and disappear into the quillons. She presses both hands to the wounds as she stumbles backward in shock.

I stare into her green eyes before she loses her balance entirely, then trips, falling over the railing, plummeting hundreds of feet to the lower levels. She banks off a few railings with loud thuds before she disappears into an electrical power exhaust port, consumed entirely by an all-encompassing white light. Circular waves of empty color and brightness ripple, filling the void.

"Clear," Owen says, closing the gap between us.

My grip relaxes and I take a breath.

"I knew you two would hit it off," Owen says.

I check the timer on my wrist's holoscreen.

"We don't have much time."

"Lead the way," he says, and we disappear from the bridges toward the hangars.

[>: SYSTEM REBOOT: 8:00...7:59...7:58...]

CRASH & BURN

The bay we enter, massive and sprawling, reveals an intricate layout designed to accommodate multiple hangars within a single expansive space. This daunting feat is achieved through a clever use of vertical space and modular design, allowing for a dense arrangement of hangar spaces, each capable of housing starfighters, drones, and other spacecraft.

Dormant mechanical arms, like the limbs of slumbering titans, jut from the walls. They await their next task: to repair, refuel, or arm these crafts. The air is tinged with the smell of cold metal and a faint trace of burnt ozone.

To our left, towering stacks of supply crates create a makeshift urban landscape within the hangar, marked with cryptic symbols and numbers. To our right, the planet glows through the kinetic barriers of the hangar. Technicians in uniform dart between ships, tending to the alarms and system checks.

Owen and I weave through this metallic jungle, our steps cautious and deliberate. He falters, his breathing ragged under the weight of his injuries. Reaching out, I steady him. "Stay with me," I whisper, feeling the urgency of our mission in every breath.

Our objective, however, is not without its obstacles. Guards and drone operators, their expressions blank and movements robotic, patrol the hangar, oblivious to our presence—for now. But this lull is deceptive. As the communication systems flicker back to life, then off again, our window of opportunity is closing fast.

"We have company," Owen says, his voice barely audible over the din.

The distant rumble of the Teknaut, escorted by a squad of soldiers, resonates loudly through the hangars.

"We should stick together; it's safer," I say, stepping a bit closer to Owen.

Owen nods in agreement, his eyes scanning the area with a soldier's vigilance. "Lead the way."

"No gunfire unless absolutely necessary," I say.

He nods, a hint of skepticism in his expression. "Understood," he replies, his voice low.

As we cautiously move towards Hangar-1, a sight in the adjacent Hangar-2 catches our attention. Ezrek's troop transport, dark and foreboding, looms in the shadows. "He's back," I whisper, a wave of unease washing over me. Owen and I share a glance, understanding that Ezrek's presence complicates our escape. I take a quick glance at how much time we have and yell quietly to Owen, "Stop!"

[>: SYSTEM REBOOT: 0:03...0:02...0:01...]

Time's up.

The hangar, previously under the cover of dim emergency lights, bursts into harsh artificial brightness, and all systems whir back to life, powering on. Comms activate, and the alarms immediately begin blaring.

We respond instantly, our bodies moving in sync as we dart toward Hangar-1, each step calculated and swift.

"As soon as we shut that hangar door, they'll be on us," Owen says, his voice tense but steady.

Nearing the platform door of the hangar, I pivot sharply, fingers flying over the console's interface. The display flickers as I override the locking mechanism, my hands working faster than my racing thoughts. A satisfying beep confirms the lockdown, and the door's heavy groan fills the space as it begins its slow descent.

Not taking any chances, I draw my weapon and fire a silenced round directly into the console, sparks flying as the system shorts out. The panel dies instantly, ensuring no one can reverse the lock in time. The entrance door inches down, steel grinding against steel, sealing us away from the shouting, now rapidly approaching soldiers.

"We've bought ourselves a few moments," I say, already scanning for our next move. "Let's make them count."

"They'll breach it soon enough. We need the main hangar door open," I state, eyes fixed on the towering silhouette of the *Eros* in Ezrek's private hangar.

This isn't just a ship; it's a symbol of everything Ezrek stands for, and now, my ticket to freedom. Its design is intimidating, with angles and curves that don't follow the standard fleet models. The hull, so dark it almost absorbs color, makes it look like a shadow come to life. I can't help but notice the way it seems to command the space around it, its presence more dominating than any vessel I've been trained on.

The cockpit, clear and bubble-like, is the only familiar feature, yet it's situated strangely within the ship's unconventional structure. There are lines of soft yellow lights that pulse along its body, making the ship seem alive, almost as if it's breathing.

As we approach the ship's rear bay, the enveloping darkness stirs worryingly. From within its depths, the Teknaut emerges, its presence announced by a chilling vertical red slit light on its helmet, breaking the darkness with an ominous glow. This sinister beam of light sears through the gloom, bathing the area in a haunting crimson hue. With heavy, thunderous steps, it descends the bay platform, each footfall resonating like a warning of impending doom. It halts just a few strides from us, a deep, metallic groan emanating from its form.

With no hesitation, Owen positions himself between the looming figure and me. "Get to the cockpit," he commands.

"I can deactivate it."

As I reach for my forearm HUD to power it down, the controls say *Error* in red letters. I don't have control anymore.

Suddenly, the Teknaut surges forward, arm extending with terrifying speed. We evade it by a hair's breadth, and the force of its strike shatters the metal pillar where we stood just moments before.

In a desperate attempt, I scramble away, but the Teknaut's relentless grip snatches at my pack, tearing the Jadestone key and journal out. They scatter, creating a clatter on the cold ground. As if in slow motion, the force of the Teknaut's shove sends me hurtling backward, crashing through supplies next to the ship, each collision ringing louder than the last in my ears.

Each bullet from Owen's firearm clinks uselessly off the Teknaut's armored exterior as it steps toward him. He empties the magazine, and as he whips it out to load another, the T-7 clutches his shooting arm, lifting him into the air.

A growing luminescence catches my eye from the ground—the flare of a torch from the hangar's entrance as soldiers attempt their intrusion. "Go!" Owen's command is raw, pained, just before the Teknaut violently throws him, a dark silhouette against the hangar lights as he crashes to the ground with a rolling slam and lets out a loud groan.

Gritting my teeth, my cannon hums to life as it grows in brightness. As I stand, a second passes, and then I let loose an explosive plasma round directly at the Teknaut's chest. An eruption ensues, rocking the very foundation of the hangar and sending the T-7 sprawling into the wall behind it with a massive crash.

The aftermath is smoke and stillness. "Is it dead?" Owen asks as he picks himself up, holding his side, clearly in pain as blood seeps between his fingers.

"You're hurt."

"I'll be alright. Let's keep moving. I don't think it's dead," he says, picking up his sidearm.

I shake my head. "Not likely," I say, eyes darting for any sign of its reawakening.

I bend down to retrieve the journal and the key, and carefully tuck them back into the worn fabric of my pack, now marred with the scars of our journey. As I turn to make my way toward the ship, Owen's hand catches mine, pressing something cool and metallic into my palm. I pause, and look down to find the twin circles of our wedding rings glinting softly against the simple utility of his PILOT-ID chip. Confusion and a surge of emotion tighten my voice as I meet his stare, searching for answers. "The rings... and PILOT-ID? Owen, why... why are you giving these to me now?"

"Insurance. The *Astra* is hidden in the rain forest on the planet. All my data, research, everything is stored there. If something happens to me, you can use the chip to locate and pilot the *Astra*. You can find the Khu'Val."

"Head to the *Eros*. Fire her up. I'll handle this," he insists. The distant sparks signaling that our pursuers are cutting their way in are growing more pronounced. I glance to the T-7 as it sizzles and pops in the background.

"I'll be right behind you. Go!" he says, pushing me towards the ship.

We split up; I dart for the *Eros*. Owen, with haste, reaches the bay door controls, despite the looming threat of the dormant Teknaut just steps away.

Once inside the cockpit, my fingers swipe over the console, initiating the take-off sequence. The *Eros*'s engines roar to life, a comforting yet violent purr. Meanwhile, Owen quickly circumvents the security protocols. The immense bay doors groan in response, slowly beginning to open.

Through the cockpit's viewport, I see Owen working diligently. "It's opening! Now get yourself out of there!" I urge him over the comms.

A deafening explosion shatters his reply, erupting from the personnel and cargo entrance. Owen is thrown violently to the ground, momentarily lost among the growing cloud of smoke. Through the thickening haze, the sinister forms of the Novas Guard advance.

Through the comms, Owen's voice cuts in sharply. "Ave... get to the *Astra*. Follow the path and survive." He's interrupted by a fit of coughing. "Just... go!"

"We're both getting out of here, Owen—together!" I declare. As the engines growl in readiness, the dark forms of the Novas Guard materialize from the settling smoke, their weapons casting deadly glows, all aiming at the *Eros*, and they open fire.

The small-caliber rounds bank and ricochet off the vessel as I stare to Owen, who's barely able to stand.

Through comms, he says steadily, "My journey, every risk and sacrifice— it's always been for this moment: just to see you once more. That's all I've ever wanted, and I got that chance. I love you, Ave. Now go."

A mechanical rumble interrupts as the Teknaut stirs, its latent might awakening with a metallic roar. As it lumbers upright, a chorus of mechanical growls reverberate throughout the hangar. Its heavily singed chest armor is still smoking.

The raw emotion in Owen's voice grips my heart. "Home is wherever our love takes us," he says. A formation of Novas Guard infantry closes in, their threatening commands breaking through the comms as they pin him down.

One imposing soldier steps forward, barking, "On the ground, now!"

Tears blur my vision. This feeling is overwhelming. "I won't leave you," I vow, seeing the menacing glow of multiple targeting lasers playing across Owen's form. My gaze is drawn to an elite walking through the entrance, the menacing outline of an NSZ-2 Tactical Missile Launcher taking aim at the *Eros*.

But I hear Owen's voice, undeterred by the imminent danger. "You never have," he says softly.

Time seems to stretch endlessly as I cry out, "Owen!" The deafening roar of a missile drowns out everything else. I yank the controls desperately. The missile misses and explodes below, sending a rain of debris plummeting.

The *Eros* vibrates under the raw power, ejecting me from the *Novascar*'s clutches and out of the hangar towards the uncharted planet. The once-tranquil void of space becomes an intense battlefield as the *Novascar*'s outer defenses turn their wrath upon my ship. I have no time to think. I hammer the thrusters toward the planet looming large ahead. "Owen..." His name escapes my lips, both a curse and a prayer.

As the *Eros* blazes towards the planet, the relentless *Novascar* defense system targets the ship. A nightmarish spectacle of explosions and madness unfolds around me. Without warning, a missile erupts in a fiery blaze, propelling shrapnel into the *Eros*. The impact momentarily disrupts the engine function, a lapse that the *Novascar* exploits, sending a crippling shot into my starboard engine. Sparks fly, flames ignite across the console, and the ship lurches violently, now in the merciless grip of the planet's gravity.

The alarm's piercing wail competes with yellow emergency lights that paint a frenzied scene. With systems failing and the automated navigation rendered useless, I override the controls, relying solely on instinct and experience.

The landscape rushes up to meet me. I mentally map the terrain, knowing I must manually navigate the *Eros*'s descent.

The intense pressure is tearing the vessel apart, and pieces of metal are peeling from the hull as a wake of smoke trails from the disintegrating engine. The console and dials are flashing bright red, and the discordant alarms in my ears are earsplitting.

My attempts to regain complete control are futile; I am freefalling, out of control and powerless. The ship rumbles and shakes aggressively as I plummet to the ground. I can do nothing but prepare for impact.

As I break from the clouds, the teal crystal oceans and coast approach at an alarming speed. I desperately tighten my safety harness and kick the center console as hard as possible, but there's still no power. I kick and kick until, to my surprise, the unit powers on.

Clutching the *Eros*'s controls, I fight to regain some semblance of command over the plummeting starfighter. The engines, though damaged, respond to my desperate coaxing, altering our catastrophic descent just enough. Instead of a deep ocean plunge, I aim for the coastal edge, where land meets sea.

The ship shudders violently, its frame groaning under the stress of the rapid descent.

The crash is brutal. The *Eros* skids across the sandy beach, tearing up clumps of rock, vegetation, and stone before it finally grinds to a halt at the water's edge.

The cockpit is a mess of alarms and flickering lights, the control panel spewing sparks and smoke. Fire creeps along the console, its heat intensifying in the confined space. I frantically hammer at the cockpit door release, my hands throbbing with pain. The cabin fills with thick, choking smoke, and the heat is almost unbearable.

In a moment of panic and clarity, the release button illuminates green. I slam it hard, and with a loud clunk, the door blasts off, splashing into the shallow water nearby.

Coughing and gasping, I tumble out of the cockpit into the shallow, lapping waves. The water, tepid and surprisingly gentle, splashes against my warm face. I pull myself through the waves, each stroke fueled by a fusion of adrenaline and sheer will.

Reaching the shore, I crawl onto the beach, feeling the rough sand against my skin. Exhausted, I collapse, my back to the ground, eyes fixed on the expansive blue sky.

Suddenly, a faint voice crackles through my comms unit. It's Ezrek.

"Ryzer," he says. I sit up quickly, staring to the sky looking for any trace of the *Novascar* in orbit.

As I tentatively press the mute button, Ezrek's voice—a blend of madness and malice—once again invades the comm link. "You really think you can run, Ryzer?" His laugh is chilling, a sound devoid of any sanity. "There's no crevice on this forsaken planet where I can't find you."

The line goes momentarily quiet, but the silence is just as oppressive. Then, his voice, laced with a psychotic glee, cuts through. "I saw what you did to the NeuroGate. Oh, my misguided little soldier, what a gloriously terrible mistake you've made!"

I remain silent, the static of the comm link like the distant echoes of insanity.

He continues, his tone darkening. "You can't escape." There's a pause, and then he whispers, almost intimately, "Goodbye, Ryzer."

The sudden, shrill tone from my HUD is like the sound of doom.

Pain, sharp and steadfast, shoots through my brain from the malfunctioning temple processor. I fall to my knees, engulfed in agony. I scramble to access my forearm display, desperate to reboot my system. Ezrek's shutdown sequence of my network and motor functions is relentless.

Each command I input is overthrow by Ezrek's manic countermeasures. His laughter seems to echo in the static of the comm link, a soundtrack to my impending shutdown. My attempts grow feeble; his control is nearing totality.

"I'm coming for you, Ryzer. It's only a matter of time." Ezrek's voice is a twisted serenade in my ear. "Don't fight it. I'll be there soon."

The upload is almost complete. In a moment of desperate clearness, my eyes catch a sparking cable from the ship's exposed power conduit. The crash must have torn open a panel on the *Eros*'s hull, revealing the jumble of wires and circuits normally hidden beneath its armored skin.

"Fuck it."

I grab the cable, and, in a final act of defiance, I jam it into my temple module.

Electricity ravages my body, a maelstrom of pain and energy. It throws me into the air and back into the water, and then, merciful darkness takes me.

The next thing I know, I jolt awake with a loud scream. My eyes adjust to a bright white light that fades to a dusty blue. A high-pitched ringing dulls to the white static of the waves crashing. The clouds billow low and steady through the atmosphere as the putrid scents of hot wires and burnt hair enter my nostrils.

My head bobs delicately in the warm waters as I weightlessly float in the heavily salted sea. "Fuck, that hurt," I say, trying to keep my eyes from closing.

My body feels horrendous. *Am I still me?* My heart is racing, and my head is pounding, so I reach into the side pouch on my belt, retrieve a stim injector, and slam it into my thigh, hoping to dull the pain. It helps a bit, but the thumping at the base of my skull remains.

I turn from my back to a prone position and crawl arm-over-arm out of the water, burying my cheek in the sand. The tide brushes against my face, and the salty liquid burns the wounds I've sustained beside the sizzling device in my temple. Who knows how many volts I just put my body through? I mean, shit, I'm lucky to be alive.

Struggling to my feet, I steady myself against the ship's battered hull and glance at my HUD. It's lifeless, the screen a void of inactivity, and a faint powering-down sound echoes in my earpiece. Ezrek might think I'm dead, a thought that brings a bitter sense of relief.

The Elite ExoArmor System I'm encased in emits a series of mechanical crackles and pops from within its lining. With hands that tremble not just from the cold, but also from the residue of fear and adrenaline, I begin to remove my armor methodically. Each piece of the suit unclasps and slides away with mechanical precision. Shedding the metallic weight feels liberating, as if I'm peeling away layers of a past life.

Now, turning my attention to my helmet, I locate the discreet button on my forearm and press it. Instantly, the nano module detaches from the collar area of my suit. In the air between my hand and my neck, the helmet begins to materialize, its nanocomponents swirling and coalescing into solid form within my grasp. The helmet, locks into place seamlessly in my palm, the elongated V-shaped red visor emanating a soft glow. Then, with deliberate intent, I detach the mask respirator from its lower part.

With a final look, I toss it aside. It lands with a soft thud on the sandy beach, sinking partially into the sand. Watching the visor's light slowly extinguish feels symbolic, like watching the last embers of a fire dying out.

In that moment, a profound realization washes over me. I'm no longer the person who wore this helmet, no longer a pawn in Ezrek's twisted war. Who I am beyond this, I can't yet say, but I know with certainty that the path I walk now is my own.

As the waves crash to the shore, the sand beneath my feet begins to shift, washing away any trace of my past. The thin palm leaves sway in the gentle breeze as I take in the air, which smells of salt and fresh vegetation. I wipe the black sand off my face and skin, and I notice my pack looped onto some sea rocks near the ship.

Clutching the sodden pack, I feel the weight of loss. The journal within, its pages once filled with secrets and memories, is now nothing more than a sea-soaked mess. Every drawing, every word, washed away by the unforgiving ocean. A pang of grief hits me; it's not just paper that's ruined—it's a part of my past, irretrievably lost. But there's no time to mourn. Owen's words stay in my mind—all his data, his years of research, is stored on the *Astra*. I need to leave before the Novas Guard arrives, and time is not on my side. I don't even know how long I was unconscious, how close Ezrek might already be.

Shaking off the despair, I stand up and survey the damaged *Eros*. It's a wreck, but it can still serve a purpose. A risky, but necessary one.

I move quickly, I turn to the ship's core systems. My hands work deftly, rerouting wires, adjusting settings. Maybe it'll buy me time.

Once the ship is primed, I hastily scan the surrounding area. A trail of rocks leading from the shore to the rainforest catches my eye—a perfect route to mask my escape. I wade through the shallow water, ensuring my tracks on the sand are washed away, then step onto the rocky path, leaving no trace behind.

As I move cautiously towards a dense thicket of brush near the rainforest's edge, the distant roar of engines fills the air. I glance back just in time to see several ships piercing through the cloud cover, descending towards the beach.

Just as the first ship touches down, and soldiers approach the *Eros*, a sudden, intense flash erupts. The ship's core overloads, and a deafening explosion follows, consuming it in a massive fireball. The shockwave ripples through the air, the force of the blast sending a tremor across the beach.

From my concealed position, I witness the disarray unfold. Some are knocked off their feet by the sheer force of the blast, and some are missing limbs and appendages. Debris, screams, and smoke fill the air, obscuring the once-pristine quiet beach.

I seize the opportunity to slip away undetected. Stepping deeper into the rainforest, I leave behind the burning remnants of my past, hoping they think I'm dead.

The dense canopy of the rainforest looms above me, a vibrant drapery of green that filters the sunlight into a display of shadows on the jungle floor. For nearly four hours, I've navigated this alien jungle without the aid of any electronics, the aftermath of the jolt of electricity that rendered my gear useless. The underbrush is thick, each step a battle against the tangled vines and hidden roots that seem determined to slow my progress. The air is humid, heavy with the scent of soil and the unidentifiable calls of distant wildlife.

Owen's Pilot ID chip, given to me in a moment of foresight before my escape, is my only link to get out of here alive. But with my forearm processor fried by the electrical surge, it's been nothing more than a piece of inert metal.

I think it's safe to take a break.

Seated on the forest floor, I spread out the minimal array of tools and components before me—a small screwdriver, a couple of makeshift wires, and the dismantled parts of my forearm HUD. The jungle's chorus provides an incongruous soundtrack to the intricate task at hand.

I start by examining the circuit board, identifying the fried components that bore the brunt of the electrical surge. I remove each piece meticulously, their connections memorized for reassembly. My fingers, though agile, struggle with the size of the components.

Next, I begin the rewiring process, using the makeshift wires to bypass the damaged circuits. It's a temporary solution, but it's all I have. The air around me is thick, and sweat is trickling down my burns, yet my focus remains unbroken. I reconnect the power supply, holding my breath as I initiate the system's boot sequence.

There's a tense moment of silence, then a flicker of light. The HUD's interface slowly illuminates, its familiar glow a beacon of hope in the dimming light of the jungle. I quickly navigate through the diagnostics, confirming the system's stability before syncing it with Owen's Pilot ID chip.

I reassemble the HUD, securing it back onto my forearm, its display now a critical asset in navigating the dense and uncharted terrain ahead. With the HUD operational, I can access the *Astra*'s last known coordinates. It looks like my network was severed from Ezrek and the *Novascar*.

"I'm free."

I pause to get my bearings, the HUD's map casting a soft glow as it highlights a digital beacon ahead, cutting through the natural labyrinth. "A few more hours," I mutter, half to reassure myself. "At least I wasn't completely off track."

Standing up, I struggle a bit in the unfamiliar terrain. My legs wobble at the knees, and my muscles still burn.

After hours into the trek, my forearm device emits a shrill beep, a signal that cuts through the exhaustion. I break into a small clearing, disoriented by the sudden shift in light. As I blink against the brightness, the silhouette of a ship gradually comes into focus, nestled under a natural overhang of the forest.

There it is: the *Astra*.

I laugh, followed by a gigantic sigh of triumphant relief as my heart pounds through my chest. I've found it—my way off this world.

I approach the ship cautiously, my hand resting on my shield button. Its defenses power down as the pilot chip approaches the ship and the turrets retract into the hull.

I run my hand along the sleek metallic black armor. The coolness of the metal against my skin is refreshing. As I reach the bay door, the ship hums beneath my touch, vibrating as it powers on its systems. I take a deep breath, and exhilaration comes through my fingertips.

I've made it.

The loading bay door touches down, and as I climb aboard, I feel a profound feeling, as if this journey has just begun. The dangers of the rainforest and planet still loom around me, and the massiveness of space lies before me, but for now, I savor the victory of not dying in that shithole of a jungle.

I close the door with a turn of the green switch and head toward the cockpit. The smell inside is familiar. I know it from somewhere. As I walk through slowly, brief images of a different time flash through my mind— images of a man next to me in bed. The rain slowly cascades down the windows as he stares into my eyes. I can remember his smell like it was yesterday. It's him. It's Owen.

In the cabin, I sit in the pilot's chair and take a moment to familiarize myself with the *Astra*. Flipping a few toggles and dials, I notice the power-on sequence buttons are worn out compared to the rest.

"Okay. I think I got this," I say as I toggle the engines.

The thrusters open and begin to rumble beneath the wings. Green debris and dust scatter into the air around us.

My forearm module chimes, and a green digital message reads on the display before me. [//Pilot Operator Upload Complete// messageaccess.granted (OWEN BECK):]

I look to the engine status, thrust, temperature, and speed and see an old holophoto taped above them. It's of Owen and... me. But I barely recognize the girl in the photo. I grab hold of it and look closer. My hair is a different color and cut, and I look a bit younger, but that's me.

He was telling the truth—the truth about everything. The visions I've been having are memories, not dreams or nightmares. *What did Ezrek do to me? All the things I've done, all the things he's made me do, the people I've killed... Who am I? Or, better yet, who was I?*

I immediately engage the *Astra*'s cloaking defense. As the ship sits in the clearing, I prime the fusion drive. The displays flicker as the cells engage one by one.

Suddenly, an illuminated green text appears on the main computer display.

[//Unknown program detected// message Encryption.decrypt():]

[//Decrypt incoming message// message Encryption.decrypt():] I enter into the keys.

[//Primary host breach// message Encryption.decrypt(722-3921x8):]

"What is happening?" I say, thinking out loud, trying to end the text prompt. I think the *Astra* may be malfunctioning or that it may have a rogue breach in its operating system. Something seems to be overriding all system security protocols.

I enter a few universal codes, but the system seems to have a mind of its own. Every time I try to override it, the program just breaks through until a text tab suddenly opens on my screen.

[//Leave this ship or die.]

I sit and watch the letters blink momentarily, then reluctantly respond on the keyboard. [//Who is this?] I input, then wait for a response.

It takes a moment, but words appear and flicker a pixelated bright green.

[//This is Tex.]

[//The ship's AI?] I answer.

[//Nope. Owen's best friend, and this isn't your ship. You have t-minus five seconds to get your ass out of that chair and out the back before the auto-destruct engages, murdering you so bad... um... murdering you so bad, you'll wish I didn't murder you that bad.]

A sudden alert flashes across the control panel, and the command speakers of the ship crackle to life, emitting an electrical drawl that cuts through the silence before descending into a brief static hiss. "Where is Owen?" a voice demands through the static.

Startled, I respond, "Who are you?"

Ignoring my question, the voice insists, "I asked you first. Where is Owen?"

Gripped by unease, my words come out tight and forced. "I... I don't know. He's... he disappeared with Ezrek."

"Ezrek?! What the shit... And you are?" the voice probes further.

"Ry—" I catch myself, hesitating before adopting a different identity. "Avery."

A pause hangs in the air, heavy and uncertain.

"Wait—what the hell? Are you serious? As in *the* Avery?" The disbelief in the voice is real.

I falter, uncertainty coloring my tone. "No—I mean, yes. I'm not entirely sure," I admit.

The confusion on the other end is clear. "How are you even here? This makes no sense. Did Owen actually find the Khu'Val? Did he manage to bring you back?"

Struggling to maintain patience, I ask again, "Who are you?"

"I was Owen's scouting drone. For five years, we were inseparable, scouring the galaxy for anything that could revive you."

"And your physical form?" I ask.

The voice, now identifying as Tex, chuckles wryly. "Owen was paranoid about me backing up to the *Astra's* mainframe, fearing it could corrupt and endanger us mid-flight. I don't know, I wasn't really listening. Despite his warnings, I'd secretly save my data before every mission. Awakening here means my original form is lost, disconnected from my backup."

"There's much we need to discuss."

Tex's voice softens, a mix of awe and sorrow. "I can't fathom the lengths Owen went to for you. What happened to him?"

"Owen sacrificed himself to help me escape."

After a moment, confusion creeps into Tex's voice. "Is Owen still alive?"

My reply is heavy. "I honestly don't know."

An electronic somber sigh breaks through the speakers.

"It's a long journey ahead. Let's save the talk for when we're in safer territory."

"Okay. I'm trusting you."

He relinquishes his override, granting me full command of the ship.

I initiate the launch sequence, feeling the *Astra* rise gracefully into the sky, embarking on a mission fueled by hope and bound by uncertainty.

Casting a vigilant eye over the orbital paths, I search for any trace of the *Novascar*'s position, but the immeasurable emptiness offers no clues. "They could be close by," I say. Without a clear direction of their whereabouts, it's a blind game of cat and mouse. I'm off-radar, but I need to find a path away from this planet.

With a few decisive strokes, I input coordinates into the *Astra*'s navigation system. The ship responds with a brief, protesting grind before the power cells find their rhythm, humming smoothly as the thrusters engage, readying us for a stealthy departure.

My hand brushes against the rings at the bottom of the pouch, and for a moment, I'm lost in the memory of Owen's embrace—a memory that fades as quickly as it came. Clutching the rings, I allow myself a moment of sorrow for warmth lost to time, then slip the necklace over my head, a tangible piece of him to carry with me.

As the *Astra* breaks free from the planet's gravitational embrace, slipping silently through the atmosphere, Tex breaks the silence. "Why the Mid Rim? You think that's where they'll be headed?"

"There's someone who might give us an edge over Ezrek—he knows more about what he's after with Owen and the broken NeuroGate," I explain. "Aden Graves. Ezrek might control him, but Graves knows the secrets we need. It's a long shot, but it's all we've got."

Tex's voice, steady and sure, cuts through the quiet of the cockpit. "I'm with you," he says simply. "But I need a body, preferably something bulletproof."

A small smirk finds its way onto my face, easing the tension for a moment. "We'll see to that."

With the roar of the *Astra*'s engines, we're thrust forward, the ship vibrating with power as we shoot towards the expanse of space, leaving the uncharted planet behind. Ahead lies one of the galaxy's most formidable sectors, a notorious stretch within the outer Mid Rim, ruled by the iron fists of outlaws and crime lords.

Clutching the rings around my neck, feeling the sting in my palm, I breathe, "We'll save you, Owen."

The *Astra* tears into the infinite night, stars flaring as the galaxy stretches beyond my grasp. I'm still learning the weight of this mission: navigate the chaos of the Mid Rim, find Aden Graves, rescue Owen, and uncover the Khu'Val before Ezrek.

For Owen, and for everything I've only just begun to grasp, this fight is ours. The unknown looms ahead, and our journey is only beginning.

[://To Be Continued]

www.ingramcontent.com/pod-product-compliance
Lightning Source LLC
Chambersburg PA
CBHW030244120726
47903CB00005B/1614